The
Innocent

The Innocent

A Novel

POSIE GRAEME-EVANS

ATRIA BOOKS

NEW YORK LONDON TORONTO SYDNEY

ATRIA BOOKS

1230 Avenue of the Americas
New York, NY 10020

Originally published in Australia in 2002 by
Simon & Schuster (Australia) Pty Limited

ISBN: 0-7434-4372-1
    0-7432-7222-6 (pbk.)

First Atria Books trade paperback edition June 2005

10 9 8 7 6 5 4 3 2

ATRIA BOOKS is a trademark of Simon & Schuster, Inc.

Manufactured in the United States of America

For information regarding special discounts for bulk purchases,
please contact Simon & Schuster Special Sales
at 1-800-456-6798 or business@simonandschuster.com

To Eleanor Graeme-Evans, with all my love.
It's a privilege to be the daughter of a writer.

ALSO BY POSIE GRAEME-EVANS

The Exiled

Acknowledgments

I'd particularly like to thank Judith Curr, executive vice president and publisher of Atria Books, for her faith in this, my first book. What an experience to walk into her office one cold December day three years ago and come out with a three-book deal!

To Kym Swivel, my Australian editor. What a formidable, forensic eye you have—and aren't I grateful!

To Suzanne O'Neill, my New York editor. We got there! (tyranny of distance and the vagaries of couriers notwithstanding). Thanks for your patience and determination to get this book over the line. The next one will be easier.

To Susan Vass, and her husband Phaedon, friends and colleagues. Susan, you read the manuscript—much to my surprise! I didn't know you'd seen it—but then you kindly sent it on to Judith Curr, and the rest is, literally, history. This book is in print because of you.

To Jon Attenborough, Julia Collingwood, Camilla Dorsch, Clare Wallace, and Jody Lee, Simon & Schuster Australia. Thank you for your patience and kindness to this first-time author. I've had a lot of fun stepping from my mad industry into yours, and your help and support has made it so much easier than it might have been.

To Debbie McInnes, publicist extraordinaire. What a lot of fun I had talking to the press in Australia with your help and guidance. If *The Innocent* was a success in Oz, so much had to do with your canny placement and peerless contacts.

Acknowledgments

To Emeritus Professor Ralph Elliott, A.M. Scholar, teacher, friend. You opened a door into the medieval world for me when I was a callow nineteen-year-old. It's never closed. I am so grateful to have met you.

To Rick Raftos—colleague and friend. Thanks for allowing Rachel to take me by the hand and lead me into the maze of the literary world. You don't know what you've both started!

To my dear agent and mate, Rachel Skinner. We slaughtered many bottles of champagne in the service of this book. How on earth have you had the patience to stick with me, and it, this long? Bless you.

To all my kids—thank you for bearing with my obsession with history. At least it makes you laugh!

To my mother—Eleanor Graeme-Evans. You gave me the genes. Would love to know who passed them on to you!

And, finally, to my husband Andrew Blaxland. Thank you. And all my love.

Prelude

That winter had bitten down hard and early, the ground almost ringing as the horses stumbled against frozen clods on the track leading to the forest.

It was late afternoon and great clouds, bellies heavy with snow, were building into the west, crowding out the last light of the day. The wind was rising, too, and the man on the big roan horse was anxious. His exhausted animal stumbled again, and as he jerked its head up with a curse his eyes scanned the face of the darkening forest. This was not a good place to stop, too exposed, but he had no choice; he would have to wait for the messenger.

Behind him the small party of mounted men came to a ragged halt around the curtained wagon; military discipline still held them, but each face, and the state of their animals, told the same story. This had been a long, cold journey.

As the wagon lurched to a stop, a woman's white face appeared cautiously between the worn leather curtains: a strongly defined nose, prominent cheekbones, not beautiful but handsome, somewhere in her thirties. Clambering down onto the frozen ground, she quickly covered nose and mouth with a red gauze veil—one note of color in a white and black world. Dark was falling fast and the wind had turned to the east. Trying not to run, she hurried toward the man scanning the forest in front of them, shivering convulsively as the cold cut to her skin even through her fur-lined cloak.

The horse and rider loomed above but the captain ignored her. "Sir!" She spoke sharply, half panting from . . . what was it? Fear. Wearily the man looked down and the woman's words dried in her mouth as the hard eyes stared into hers. His insolence gave her courage. "Sir . . . the baby. My mistress needs a proper bed to give the child—"

"What, madam? Give it life? Better it dies now—her too."

As he spoke there was a shout from the soldiers around the wagon, and they both heard, rather than saw, the horse and rider coming at a gallop out of the forest. The captain called strongly, "Here, Peter, to me! Here! What did they say to you?"

Even angry as she was, Jehanne muttered, "Thanks be, Our Lady," as she hurried back through the gloom to the wagon. Now perhaps they might move on and make the hunting lodge while there was still time.

Her lips thinned as she clambered back into the wagon. That great oaf needn't think she was going to forget any of this. No, indeed—she was going to remember *everything,* from the cushions that had long since lost their stuffing, to the bearskin rugs that were old, foul with dust, and nearly hairless. And not even a proper escort! Just let them get this child safely born and then she would see that look wiped off his sneering face!

"Where are you, sweeting? We'll be on our way again soon . . . don't you fear." Jehanne reached out in the darkness for her mistress, keeping up a steady stream of bright chatter as the heavy vehicle lurched on again. "There now, where's that head of yours, just let me feel it. Has the headache left you?"

Poor child. All her adult life Jehanne had helped birth babies, but this one had felt wrong from the first pains brought on by the dreadful journey. Of course, she knew that very young first-time mothers often suffered greatly, but given the circumstances, and the danger, panic began to clamp her throat. The girl's flesh felt cold but her pulse had a fluttering speed that scared Jehanne profoundly. Suddenly the swollen shape in the dark, Alyce's body, convulsed and she screamed sharply.

"Ah come, mistress, lean on me," Jehanne soothed. If only they would give her a lantern, if only the journey would end, but the wagon swayed and bucked on down the forest road, behind its four stoic bullocks.

The captain heard the girl scream again as he led his party deeper and deeper into the forest on their thankless errand. He hardened his heart. His business and that of his men was to bring the girl and her woman to their destination safely—and to do that he had to find speed or they would all be caught in the forest this night; fine work for a man of his background and experience.

And that was his last thought as the arrow cut through his chest and into his heart, which exploded. Carried by the force, his body dropped off the stallion and the horse, spooked by the sudden smell of blood, plunged riderless into the darkness between the trees. The five soldiers in the party scattered, trying to find shelter from the arrows raining down from the men in the branches above.

There was no time for thought. Jehanne heard the screams of men and horses, felt the wagon pitch to a stop. Acting by instinct, she bundled the large fur rug around her barely conscious mistress and found the strength to pull Alyce out of the back of the wagon and push them both at a stumbling run into the forest.

Behind her, the soldiers had rallied, giving Jehanne precious seconds to drag the semidelirious girl away from the carnage and into the cold dark between the trees.

As she half carried Alyce deeper and deeper into the forest, away from the noise and terror, Jehanne forced herself to think, *think* hard. If they were to survive, never mind the child, they had to hide, very fast. The soldiers might be able to hold off the attackers for a while, and in the confusion, maybe they had made their escape undetected, but at the back of her mind Jehanne heard a voice saying, very clearly: *It's the baby they want. They'll not care who dies.*

Sudden shouting began again: the attackers had discovered the wagon was empty. She'd have to make Alyce run now, really run, and Lady Mary help them.

It was then she felt the hand of God, for at the moment she uttered her prayer, Jehanne heard the jingle of a bit, and turned to see the captain's horse nervously cropping forage two paces away. Sobbing with relief, she eased Alyce to the ground as gently as she could and, heart in throat, stretched her hand to the dangling reins of the destrier. The horse balked and threw his head up, but Jehanne had found the leather and hung on desperately, whispering all the while, "Gentle, gentle."

Frantic with terror, she heard men blundering closer through the trees, calling out to each other, as she dragged the horse to the girl and forced Alyce up into the saddle. She scrambled up behind and, with one foot in a stirrup and her kirtle up around her thighs, kicked the stallion on with a great jolting thump in the ribs. Startled, the horse leaped forward, nearly unseating them both as it ran blindly into the trees.

It was a wild ride—branches ripped past their faces, nearly sweeping both women off the animal's back—but somehow Jehanne held on to the horse and the girl as she tried to guide the animal. The stallion plunged on and then, under the animal's labored breathing, the thudding hooves, the men's voices disappeared. They were alone, careering through the darkness of the wild wood.

Jehanne let the horse run for a time to be sure they'd lost their pursuers, and then with all her strength, she hauled on the stallion's mouth to slow him. This was a destrier, however, a knight's horse, seventeen hands high with great solid legs, hooves like buckets, and a back built for carrying an armored man. He hardly felt the hands tugging so desperately at the bit as he settled into a lumbering gallop on an overgrown trail through the trees.

In front of Jehanne, Alyce groaned deeply as she felt the gush and splash of liquid flood out of her body—her waters had broken. The horse smelled the blood and panicked: putting his head down, he flew faster and faster over the broken ground. Jehanne knew the only way she could stop the horse was to turn him in a tight circle— a mad thing to try, racing between such massive trunks. With no time for conscious thought, she yanked down hard on the left rein with all her strength as the girl screamed and screamed again.

Unnerved by the noise, the horse broke his stride and stumbled. It was enough. Once more Jehanne wrenched the rein, savagely cutting the horse's mouth with the bit, and the stallion faltered around to the left, just missing a huge down-hanging branch. Now Jehanne dragged at both reins together and, arms screaming with the effort, forced the frightened animal to halt.

Before Jehanne could prevent it, Alyce slid to the ground and lay groaning, too close to the horse's dancing hooves. Jehanne forced the animal back and away by main force and, leaping down, quickly wound the reins around a branch and ran to the girl.

Alyce keened like a snared animal as every second breath became a scream. "I'm here, my precious, shush now, shush now, little Alyce," Jehanne murmured. But the birth was not going well. Strain as she might, the girl's frail body, caught up in the bloodied folds of her velvet kirtle, could not expel the child from her belly.

What light there was showed the staring, white face contorted in an agonized rictus, and Jehanne knew that if either mother or child were to be saved, she would have to help the baby out. Praying fervently to Saint Anne, the mother of the Virgin and patron saint of women in labor, Jehanne wiped her hands on her surcoat and then, as gently as she could, slid her fingers into the girl, trying to feel for the head of the child, just as she had seen her father's chief shepherd do on cold nights when the ewes would not bear.

Alyce was fading further into delirium but Jehanne persisted, trying to will life into the girl: "Push now for me, Alyce. Come, one more hearty push—*help* me, child." But Alyce did not respond. Fiercely wiping tears away, Jehanne slapped the girl, hard, her hand leaving a red mark on the white skin. "Alyce! Push for me, for your baby. Push!" And as the poor girl's body made a convulsive response, Jehanne felt the crown of the baby's head nudge her hands. "The babe's here—push, push down now. God's blood—*push!*"

With a wrenching wail, the girl half sat up and pushed the child into Jehanne's hands—white and covered in wax, mucus, and blood, but alive, crying loudly. It was a girl of good size and weight, the principal reason for her mother's long labor. Pulling her surcoat over her head, oblivious to the cold, Jehanne wrapped the baby in the sleeveless fur-lined garment and placed her on Alyce's belly. The cord was still pulsing and the afterbirth had not yet come away: time enough later to sever the baby's last physical link to her mother. Jehanne turned her attention back to Alyce. In despair, she saw there was nothing to be done. The girl was hemorrhaging into the earth—and the flood would only increase when the afterbirth came down. She would die.

The baby whimpered, and with great sadness, Jehanne unlaced the top of her mistress's dress, propped the girl against her in a sitting position, and placed the infant to Alyce's breast, smiling slightly as she saw the snuffling urgency with which the baby sucked.

Slowly, Alyce opened her eyes and Jehanne's heart turned over as she saw the girl fasten her gaze on the baby's nestled head: the look of passionate love transformed her face with a glimmer of some inner light. With infinite gentleness, Alyce arranged the folds of the surcoat around the child so that she was better covered, and tried to speak: "Jehanne, in my pocket . . . scissors . . ." It was barely a whisper.

Jehanne fumbled in the little drawstring bag that was slung from Alyce's slender, plaited belt and found a tiny pair of scissors, gold handled with chased silver blades designed for fine needlework, and very rare and valuable. Quickly undoing the belt, Jehanne used it to tie off the baby's cord, which in the uncertain light seemed to have stopped pulsing, and taking a deep breath, she snipped it through.

At that moment the girl gave a gentle sigh, and as if something had broken inside her, the afterbirth slid out in a great rush of blood. Jehanne knew then, even as she called out her name, that Alyce had died, the baby still tugging at her breast.

Sitting there in a daze of tears with the dead girl propped in her arms, Jehanne felt rather than saw someone standing in front of her; she flinched as the figure held up a lantern and flicked the horn light shield aside so that light poured onto her face.

"My name is Deborah; I am here to help. Do not be afraid."

Perhaps it was the unexpected light, perhaps the kidness in the stranger's eyes, but Jehanne did not hesitate. Gently she detached the baby from her mother's breast, closed Alyce's eyes and kissed her still-warm brow.

"Bless you and keep you," she whispered. "I'll pray for you, Alyce."

There was nothing else to be done. The cries of the child grew fainter and fainter as the two women stole away in the dark, night-hung forest, leaving the dead girl behind, alone among the trees.

Chapter One

The gluttony of Shrovetide was forgotten in the privations of Lent as the ice on the river broke up. The Thames swelled with meltwater from the deep west as London stretched awake from the long cold sleep of winter; snowdrops were budding in the fields outside the walls and the people of the city were impatient for spring and Holy Week, for after that came May Day—and warmth!

Anne was too cold and too excited to be tired from her long journey. It was hard to remember the silent winter forest she had left—was it only six nights ago?—among the clamor and press of people contained within this gigantic mess of buildings.

At dawn on the seventh day she and Deborah walked over London Bridge, part of a noisy crowd eager to enter the city and transact their business. It was slow going as the two women tried to hold a place for themselves on the broken stone pavement of the bridge, hugging the walls beneath the overhanging houses and shops that jetted out above them; it was the only way to avoid being splashed by riders and carts from the roadway's sloppy combination of mud, animal urine, and dung.

Anne's senses were assaulted by the smell and the noise. She had never seen so many beggars before, with their pathetic ragbound feet, their open sores and mutilated bodies—or been close enough to a strange man's mouth to smell rotting teeth as he called out to friends among the crowd. Anne was not frightened by disability for very few people escaped childhood without scars and injuries of some sort, but here every third person seemed malformed in some way. Deborah told her that many were veterans from the late wars at home and in France.

That puzzled Anne. "Does no one look after them? What about the king?" she asked.

Deborah's reply was swept away as yet another party of armed and mounted men cursed their way through the crush, forcing the people in the roadway to jump from the hooves or be trampled. Anne was astonished by their rudeness, the callous way the riders laid about the people with whips to clear space for their horses. Were ordinary people to be treated like animals, just because they looked poor?

Before today she never thought of herself as poor, yet when she looked at the Londoners, she saw that their own clothes, the city clothes that Deborah had made with so much careful love, were simple and drab compared to the rich jeweled velvets, the sumptuous furs and silks on the backs of so many men and women riding proudly into the city.

Where they lived in the forest coin money was rare. That didn't much matter because there was little to buy. You grew your own food, made your own cloth, sewed your own clothes, so there was nothing to be envious about in other people's lives. All had much the same. But London was a new world and Anne found herself covetous, for the first time in her life, of the pretty things others had.

Even worse than the way people behaved toward one another, however, was the reek of this place; the city smelled like a dung heap. The stench of animal excreta was compounded by the unseen fog of acrid human sweat trapped in winter's unwashed wool on the bodies all around them.

She, who was used to the clean smell of the forest, and the purity of untrampled snow, had to force herself to breathe—there was no escape. Breathe in and get used to it. And try not to notice that men she did not know looked at her boldly, their eyes roaming her body to see its shape under her mantle. One man even snatched back her hood to see her face. He laughed at her confusion—and her spirit—when she slapped his hand away.

After that Anne became terrified she would lose sight of Deborah, so like a child she held fast to a piece of her foster mother's cloak as the older woman patiently led her toward the farther end of the bridge up ahead.

On the bridge itself, the buildings were huddled so close together that the girl could not see the river below, but she heard it roaring around the great piers beneath her feet; heard the groaning of the ice as it was broken by the raging water. In that moment she was overwhelmed with fear.

What if the bridge, mighty as it was, should break under the weight of all the people and all the buildings and they were cast down into the roiling water below? As if in answer to her unspoken question, Deborah turned and looked at her, smiling confidently.

"It will take more than melt water to tear this old bridge down. Don't fear, small one. Another hour will see us there. Just walk as close to me as you can."

But the noise of the city was overwhelming too. It flowed around Anne with such intensity, she could feel it on her body like a physical buffet. She'd first heard it on the previous day, even before they'd reached the walls of the city and the Convent of the Poor Clares where they had spent the night in the strangers' dorter. Then it was something muttering on the wind that came and went as they'd walked the muddy roads toward the city—a resonant buzzing hum unlike any sound the girl had heard before. Fancifully, as she had lain awake on the scratchy straw palliasse among the other women in the strangers' dorter, she'd thought it was the voice of some great beast that was never quite stilled, even in the darkest hours of the night. Then she had felt happy and excited to be going to the city.

Now as she followed Deborah across the bridge, and looked up to check the clouds to see what the day would bring, she saw only a small patch of sky above her head between the buildings, and was engulfed by a choking sadness.

For all of her nearly fifteen years Anne had lived among the trees of their forest, hers and Deborah's, but there'd always been the sky and the clouds above their little mud-and-wattle house.

In the warm weather when she sat on the thatch of the highest part of the roof, Anne could see the weather coming and she could see where the forest ended and the straggling village at the edge of their domain began. It had always been quiet in their clearing except for the wind and the calls of birds, or the cough of deer in the depths of the trees. But now the enormous voice of this foreign place was all around, in her head, hardly allowing her to think.

Now, very soon, she and Deborah would part, and she would be left alone here in this buzzing, booming, reeking people-hive.

And all because of last Samhain, the feast to celebrate the time when the gates between the worlds were open and winter began. As usual they had joined the villagers on the common land outside their little cluster of wattle-and-clay houses, and contributed to the feast with good black puddings from the pig they had raised through the last year and just slaughtered. It was blood month, the time when animals that would not be fed through the winter were killed, like their pig. And as the last of the summer beer had flowed, Deborah had pleased the villagers, though not their priest, by future-telling for all those who'd wanted her to. He was a good man, their priest, and tried hard to win his people from their dark, old ways, but he'd given up with Samhain. It had an ancient force, this long day of gluttony and drunkenness, a force stronger than any sermon he could preach to them. So, like a sensible pastor who had the long-term good of his people at heart, he joined them at the feast hoping, by his presence, to curb the wildest excesses.

It was common at Samhain, however, for prophecy to be given and heard with respect, and this time Anne had asked Deborah for a future-telling as well.

"You're too young. This is not a game, Anne. The priest will not like it, you know that." Deborah had taken the girl to one side, away from the long trestle board crowded with shouting, well-fed, happy people. The older woman's expression was severe, and that puzzled the girl.

"Why do you want the scrying?"

"Only to see if I may have a husband too. You seemed happy to tell the others . . ."

Deborah had turned away when she caught the priest's eye, his shake of the head. Now she looked back toward their home in the forest. It was as if she were listening for something, searching for something among the silent trees, something that was far, far away. Then she sighed deeply and nodded, being careful the priest did not see. "That is fair. Sit here."

Anne settled herself against the trunk of an oak, burrowing into the dry brown leaves of last autumn, while Deborah went to fetch her scrying bowl from the trestle board. There was a little warmth left in the fast-westering sun, and filled with good meat and good beer, the girl had begun to doze.

Deborah's voice had brought her back. "Here, child. Look into the water, tell me what you see . . ."

That startled the girl awake. "Me? Will you not do the scrying, Deborah?"

Her foster mother's voice was pitched low now, soothing, almost humming. "Look into the bowl, Anne. . . . Concentrate. Just look into the water. . . . What do you see? What is there for you . . ."

Perhaps it was the last of a dream still clogging her mind, perhaps it was the tone of Deborah's voice, but the girl felt warm and secure—a child about to drift away to dreams in a warm bed as storms raged outside on a winter's night . . .

"There is a face . . ."

"Describe what you see." Again Deborah's voice had that strange humming tone.

Anne hesitated then her face cleared in relief. "Look. There he is. I see him. I can't see his eyes, though . . . that's because of the battle helm. Oh!" The girl then sat up so quickly she knocked the salt-glazed pottery bowl out of her own hands and the water spilled all over her dress. "Blood! Blood everywhere!"

Her scream had cut through the buzz of the feast; the villagers fell silent, staring at the two women under the great oak. Deborah waved cheerfully. "Too much good ale! And a young head!" she had called, and laughter washed away the moment—uneasy though it was. Everyone knew Samhain was an uncanny time.

Defiantly Deborah had locked glances with the priest as she'd helped Anne to her feet.

"Do not worry, Father, she's only tired. It's been a long feast."

From that moment things had changed.

Later, Deborah told the girl that with the spring it would be time for her to go to London and into service with a pious household. There she could complete the education that had been begun in the forest, for Deborah had no more to teach Anne in their small, safe world. The girl had cried herself to sleep for many nights, but Deborah was implacable, though it broke both their hearts. And so now, miserably, weighted with a sense of the abandonment to come, the girl followed her foster mother deeper and deeper into the city until they stood before the closed door of a great, dark house.

Chapter Two

"You say you can both read and write Latin?"

The man in the thronelike chair looked suspiciously at Anne as he smoothed the surface of the fine silk carpet covering his worktable with a capable, broad hand.

"Yes, master, I can—and a little French and some English—and calculate also. And besides this, I have a knowledge of simples and dying, I have been taught to dress and tan leather, to cook, and embroider, to make tapestry, to prepare and weave flax and—"

"Enough." A wave from the large hand and a hard look silenced the girl. Her throat tight with nerves, she dropped her eyes from his to disguise the fear.

Mathew Cuttifer frowned at her. These were remarkable claims for any woman, and this girl was a peasant. He turned to the girl's foster mother, a handsome woman with the permanently suntanned skin of the poor, who was also respectfully looking down at the floor.

"Mistress . . . Deborah, is it?"

Without raising her eyes, the woman nodded.

"Are these claims true?"

"They are, sir."

"And who has taught her?"

"I have, sir—the domestic skills she speaks of. And the good priest of our nearby village. He believed my foster daughter warranted teaching. He gave her letters, and the numbers. And the Latin. He also spoke French and she picked it up. She learns quickly and he is an educated man."

Mathew raised his eyebrows at that. An educated man giving his time to teach a peasant girl? He looked the girl up and down. Plain, neat dress of homespun cloth—finely woven though it was—and abundant dark, tawny hair pulled back tightly from a high forehead.

The girl's eyes were unusual too; they had the surprising jeweled flash of kingfisher feathers, or topaz, the whites so clear they shone. True, she did not have the smooth egg-shaped face considered beautiful, for hers had well-defined features and a mouth too wide for current taste, but it was pleasing, the skin burnished like ivory, and when she smiled, striking. But there was something else. Something disturbing. Did she look too . . . refined, or clever, perhaps to make a servant?

"How did you know of the place I have in my household?" Again, Mathew addressed the woman, Deborah.

"Sir, I am acquainted with Helvega, the sister of your priest, Father Bartolph. She's married to our squire's reeve and lives close by in the village next to our home. She visited her brother in your house, I believe, and when she returned she told me of the need. A hardworking and trustworthy girl to be a body servant for your wife?"

Mathew was puzzled. "But that was some time ago. You have come a long way on a chance, it seems to me . . ."

Deborah smiled calmly. "I trusted to Our Lord for guidance on the matter. He told me that all would be well if I brought my foster daughter to your house."

Again Mathew frowned. The woman sounded very sure, dangerously presumptuous. How could she know what the Lord's will in this matter might be?

A gentle cough shifted his glance to another woman standing in the shadows of his dark, richly appointed room.

"Speak."

Phillipa Jassy, Mathew's housekeeper, had also been looking at the girl. She too was uncertain about the gentility, even delicacy, of her appearance. Generally, Jassy looked for solid girls, girls with strong arms and broad backs who were capable of hard physical work. But she was also a shrewd judge of character—you had to be if you ran a large household for such an exacting master. A plain beast of burden would not suffice for her mistress, Lady Margaret Cuttifer, that she knew.

"Have you ever been part of a large household before, girl?"

Anne was nervous since Mathew had rebuked her, so she shook her head. That met with Jassy's approval. She had no liking for pert, bold girls with opinions freely offered.

Unaccountably, though, Mathew was faintly displeased. He had liked the sound of her voice, he realized; it was low and pleasing.

"Have you ever served a lady before?"

Again the girl shook her head, saying nothing.

The girl's response was to be expected, but the housekeeper was disappointed. In their current sad situation, it seemed unlikely that Mathew would want a girl waiting on his wife who had no real training.

"Master Mathew, in the circumstances, perhaps it would be good if we could speak together for a moment . . ." Jassy was already holding the door of Mathew Cuttifer's workroom open, as if to usher Deborah and her foster daughter out of Blessing House, out of their lives . . .

Then something strange happened. Something uncanny. The girl smiled, a radiant smile, and it so transformed her face that the man and his housekeeper were astonished—for a moment it seemed as if she were bathed in light from another source. Mathew even looked around to see where that light might be coming from.

Then the girl said simply, "Sir, my name is Anne and I am here to work. I will serve your wife well, you will see, and with all my heart." Her voice had a quality, a certain bell-like clarity, that sang through the air between them like music, and the sincerity in her eyes was guileless.

Deborah looked at Anne quickly. Was she surprised by the confident little speech? It was hard to tell.

Mathew was—but he didn't find himself offended. There

had been no presumption from the girl: she'd spoken truthfully. Rocking for a moment on his heels, Mathew threw a look at the housekeeper. She shrugged slightly before dropping her eyes respectfully—Anne did not see the gesture, having fixed her gaze on Mathew Cuttifer's face—but it was enough. He grunted and found himself saying, "Very well. You may stay under this roof for a period to be agreed between your foster mother and myself. Should you prove a useful addition to this house, your position with us will be confirmed by next quarter day."

Formal, dry words, but they were rewarded with a look of such passionate gratitude from Anne that Mathew felt a wave of heat in his head and neck. Of course, well versed by his religion against the snares of the flesh, he should have been proof against the gratitude of women and girls these twenty years, but life was sometimes surprising, even at his age. Hastily, he recalled the need for pious instruction if this girl was to be useful. There was much she needed to learn, and quickly. "Jassy will instruct you in all that is necessary. You are to obey her and Aveline, my wife's maid, as if they were me. This is a godly house; see you keep the Lord in your heart and not Satan." Then he waved toward the door of his workroom. The interview was ended.

Thus began Anne's time in Blessing House, and when Deborah kissed her one last time before she walked away into the London streets, the two clung to each other.

"Pray for me, as I shall for you, child. I shall miss you."

That was all there was time for; Jassy did not believe in sentiment: "Make your farewells, girl. There is much to acquaint you with if you are to be useful to your mistress."

Anne's last sight of Deborah was the swirl of her dull red cloak as she strode away down the dark London streets. Then she was alone with strangers.

Blessing House, Mathew Cuttifer's city base and place of business, was a very ancient structure, as Anne now saw, running to keep up with the housekeeper as she led the girl to her private room. Massive stone walls and dark passages with many turns spoke of the fort or small castle this great house had engulfed as it grew.

Indeed, many of the public spaces in Blessing House were gloomy because the high, narrow windows were barely enlarged arrow slits. Mathew Cuttifer saw no need to adopt the expensive new fashion for large, leaded, many-paned glass lights in the business parts of his house—he confined them to his private quarters. And there was a coldness breathing out of the massive walls that all the fires and braziers they passed did little to lift. Perhaps the built-over stream that wound past and under the footings on one side of the building was the source of the dank cold. The house must once have stood by itself with its back to the river in a good defensive position. Now a warren of narrow streets had locked themselves around the walls with buildings great and small lapping right to the very gate.

As Anne hurried after the housekeeper, she tried to fix as much as she could in her mind, observing first that her new home was a very busy place. Deborah had told her that Mathew Cuttifer was a self-made man and an increasingly important mercer; now she saw that for herself as tides of humanity flowed through Blessing House on numberless errands for the master himself, or for members of the nearby Court of Westminster with whom she knew he had close commercial links.

"Girl!" Jassy briskly cut into Anne's thoughts, no longer the meek and deferential servant of a few minutes past. "Through here. Lively now!"

Anne found herself in a low, small room at the back of the building that looked down on the river, the room from where Phillipa Jassy ran the household. Another girl of about her own age was spreading new rushes onto the floor as the housekeeper entered.

"Melly, fetch Aveline here to me now." The girl dropped her bundle of rushes as if they were burning, and scuttled from the room. Then the housekeeper began to describe what was expected of Anne. "You will find that much personal service needs to be done for Lady Margaret, Master Cuttifer's wife: everything from washing to dressing and even feeding her. Sadly for us all, her illness means your work here may not last long. Pray God spares her to us."

There was a knock at the door and as the housekeeper called out, "Yes!" a pretty young woman slipped into the room. She was dressed modestly in a plain, dark blue housedress with a sideless surcoat of dark red, but her elegance confused Anne. Was she Master Cuttifer's daughter?

"Aveline, this is Anne. The master has hired her to assist you with Lady Margaret. She will answer through you to me. She has skills you will find useful."

The girl who turned and looked at Anne with cool detachment was Lady Margaret's personal maid—that explained the fineness of her clothing and the smooth whiteness of her hands. After a moment's inspection, Aveline turned back to the housekeeper and said, "My mistress has no need of another attendant."

Jassy frowned. She was a very busy woman and this was just one of many problems to deal with this morning. "It is the master's wish and there's an end. Now take Anne and make her familiar with what must be done. I shall speak to you about this after prayers this evening."

Aveline curtsied rigidly and beckoned Anne to follow her out of the room, a set expression on her face.

The pair set off down another dark passage and Anne's heart sank as she followed the stiff back ahead of her. This was not a good beginning and she felt alone and afraid. Aveline moved on in the gloom as the corridor turned this way and that past closed doors and flights of stairs that disappeared to the upper parts of the building. Her felt house slippers were soundless on the flags and she did not acknowledge Anne's presence in any way.

Several minutes' brisk walking brought them to an iron-bound door, big enough for giants, which stood between two mighty pillars carved in the shape of naked men, each supporting the heavy burden of the lintel above. The lintel stone was shaped like a reclining woman, abundant breasts spilling out of her dress as she suckled a large boy child, an expression of pleasure on her broad face.

Aveline saw Anne's startled look and laughed briefly, a surprising, harsh sound, as she pushed the door open. "This, girl, is the most ancient part of the house. A lewd way to go into a kitchen.

Lower your eyes when you pass this way or you will be misjudged by the men."

As the door opened, the stone silence of the passage outside the kitchen was swamped by a resonant booming babble, and Aveline chivvied the girl ahead of her into a great space.

At first, Anne thought she had entered a vision of Hell, but after a moment she saw she was in a vast kitchen. It was vaulted like a church, with light pouring down from a central stone lantern set high above their heads in the apex of the groined roof.

Serving three gaping fire-filled caves—the cooking fires ranged around the walls—was a mass of hardly human beings, sweating and cursing as they rushed to and fro in apparent chaos.

In days to come Anne would understand she had arrived just before the morning dinner; and Blessing House had many souls to be fed—members of the family and their personal attendants, Mathew's clerks, his apprentices, the upper servants, including Jassy, and her underlings, the general servants, the men in the stables, the girls in the cow byre, the gardeners—but for now Anne had the urge to cross herself and whisper a prayer to Saint Christopher, patron saint of the beleaguered traveler, as she felt herself to be. The noise and the heat were terrifying to someone unused to the ways of a large house.

Aveline ignored the din and waved testily for the girl to follow as she plunged into the surging mass of men and women. Anne was so intent on not losing her guide, she barely sidestepped a wizened child, staggering under the weight of a huge pot brimming with fish heads and slopping guts. A high piping voice screamed out, "Way, way there, lumphead!"

Close up, Anne saw that the child was in fact a very old man the size of a boy, and the malice in the rheumy eyes was ancient and very real. Anne jumped aside, unreasonably frightened, and nearly caused another accident by backing into someone else. "I am so sorry . . . I'm new and—"

"I know that. Just get out of the road, can't you!" Melly, the thin girl she'd seen earlier in Jassy's room, rushed past her carrying a bright metal cleaver toward a man dismembering a side of beef and bellowing for assistance.

"Anne!" Aveline's high, clear voice cut through the racket and Anne hurried over to where the maid had beckoned her. "This is Maître Gilles. He cooks for this house." Anne, her wits regained, dropped a slight curtsy, taking care that her one respectable dress was lifted clear of the slick of fat on the flags near the cooking fire. "Maître, this girl will assist me as Lady Margaret's body servant and as such she may relay requests from the mistress direct to you."

Surprised, Anne found her hand being lifted and kissed by the chef. "Mademoiselle Aveline, this young person may be assured that my kitchen exists to serve Lady Margaret and her so charming new young companion."

"Body servant, Maître Gilles, that is all," said Aveline frigidly. "Come, Anne."

But, distracted by the courtly gesture of the cook, Anne had not heard Aveline, and when she looked back to find her, the girl had vanished.

Maître Gilles laughed out loud at her astonishment, blackened teeth a shock in that unremarkable but pleasant face. "Here—look! Sorcery!" With a flourish he pressed his hand hard against a particular stone near the fireplace and a stone door swung open into the thickness of the wall. "You'll have to hurry to catch her. This stair leads directly to Lady Margaret's solar. Up you go."

And go Anne did, fairly running because she could only just hear the sussuruss of Aveline's skirts on the stairs ahead of her. Narrow and almost completely without light except for guttering pitch-dipped torches in iron sconces, they wound upward toward the top of the house. And it was so cold that although Anne climbed as quickly as her long skirts would allow, she found herself shivering in the close darkness. It was a relief to round the last curve, panting, and find Aveline framed in a square of light that dazzled her eyes after the darkness.

The room that Anne entered was a world away from the sweating chaos of the kitchen below. The solar was high up in the tower at the center of Blessing House; here the stone walls had been softened by bright tapestries and there was a ceiling of blue-painted wood powdered with silver-gilt stars like the night sky. There were proper windows too, not just wooden-shuttered arrow slits in the wall. The casements were made with small-paned, thick leaded glass through which spring light shone, and the bright fire burning in a chimney breast was of applewood that filled the room with a fragrant smell. It was the loveliest room that Anne had ever seen. And there was her mistress, the woman she had come to serve.

Lady Margaret Cuttifer was pale and still in the vast carved bed that lay in the center of the solar; her body was so wasted with illness that the shape of collarbone and ribs could be clearly seen beneath her sleeping shift. Her face was pale as the fine sheets she lay between, but as the girl entered with Aveline, she turned her head and smiled slightly, beckoning with one long-fingered hand for Anne to approach, though this tiny movement plainly cost much effort.

The woman coughed and her hand dropped onto the bed as the cough became a spasm. Aveline hurried over, snatching up a small horn beaker filled with a thick fluid that she held to Lady Margaret's lips. Her mistress sipped at the liquid, grimacing at the taste. Lying back she waved Aveline away, closing her eyes. As Aveline smoothed the bedding, Margaret raised her hand again. Aveline beckoned Anne closer and both girls leaned down to hear Lady Margaret speak. "Who is this?" she asked softly.

"Anne, Lady Margaret. It has pleased Master Mathew to give her a place for the moment. She is to assist me with your care, as body servant."

Lady Margaret nodded slightly and spoke again in a reedy whisper. "My husband has too much care of me. Aveline, go down and walk in the pleasaunce; the air will be good. Leave this child with me."

Aveline was not pleased, though she nodded dutifully. She curtsied to the woman in the bed and issued her instructions quietly to Anne as she crossed to the main door of the solar. "See that Lady Margaret has everything she needs. She has eaten nothing today. It is your first duty to give her food even though she will not want it. You will see a posset of curds and honey on the small coffer. Keep the fire bright, and if she sleeps, use the time. The cypresswood chest contains her most-used things—and the oak press by the window has personal linen. There is always mending: you will find needles and thread there also."

Anne held the door open to a gallery high above the receiving hall below and curtsied as Aveline glided through, closing it behind her quietly. There was silence in the bright room now except for the cheerful crackle of the applewood in the fireplace and the gentle nudging of a spring breeze around the casements. It was a day for life, not death.

Anne looked around her with real interest: she'd never seen so many fine and beautiful things in one room before. There was even a brass washing bowl on an iron stand placed ready beside the bed—and a ewer before the fire with a blackened firepot for the water, standing next to it. Anne smiled: she'd had an idea!

"Lady Margaret, may I speak?" The woman nodded faintly. "I have the makings of a soothing wash here, in my pocket." The girl brought out three little packages from the small bag dangling from her girdle. "Just a few simple herbs that are sweet to smell. I could make it for you very quickly."

The woman in the bed said nothing. Taking silence for assent, Anne moved to the chimney breast—a modern innovation, she'd never seen one before—and half filling the firepot with water from the ewer, she hooked it on to the chain that dangled over the fire itself. Then she carefully measured small quantities of the dried herbs and flowers from her pocket into the brass bowl while waiting for the water to boil.

Anne moved as quietly as she could. She needed to establish a harmonious relationship with Lady Margaret very quickly to secure her place in this house, but her mistress had the look of death and plainly no one, including her husband and Aveline, expected she would live much longer. Perhaps the knowledge that Deborah had given Anne could prove them wrong.

The water boiled and the girl poured it on to the leaves and petals in the bottom of the bowl. Then taking a small stick of alderwood from her pocket, she carefully stirred the gently steaming liquid seven times sunwise and seven times countersunwise. The lady in the bed watched with a little curiosity—and a faint smile at the earnest expression on Anne's face. As the wash infused, the girl searched for something she could use to apply it to Lady Margaret's face. Not wishing to disturb her mistress with questions, she lifted the heavy lid of one of the coffers and was pleased to find a square piece of linen inside, perhaps a small drying towel, lying neatly folded on the piles of shifts and petticoats beneath.

Anne dipped one edge of the linen into the now warm water and squeezed most of the liquid from it—the cloth was so fine that she was able to fold it into as small a pad as she wished. Gently she applied the cloth to her lady's face, pressing it to her forehead and over each closed eye, then to each cheek and finally to her chin and neck. Lady Margaret did not resist the gentle pressure of the pad against her face. The astringent scent of the herbs added to the fragrance of the applewood from the fire, and as Anne worked on, the silence between the woman on the bed and the girl became dream-like and profoundly peaceful.

A slow tentative smile formed around Lady Margaret's tired mouth, and after a time the girl heard her mistress say quite clearly, "Thank you, Anne. I shall sleep now." Soon, deepened breathing told the girl that her mistress was indeed asleep, and she could see that some of the pain had gone from her face. Anne smiled delightedly. Now, if she could just persuade Aveline that she posed no threat for Lady Margaret's favor all might yet be well.

Chapter Three

It was Sunday, the Feast of the Birth of the Blessed Virgin, in the fourth regnal year of Edward IV, fourteen hundred and sixty-five years since the Virgin's son had himself been born, and church bells were ringing over the city in the still cold air of winter.

Blessing House had been in an uproar since before dawn as the household readied for today's double celebration—the Feast of the Virgin's Birth was also the name day of Mathew Cuttifer. This year there was an extra reason for joy. Mathew Cuttifer wished to give thanks for his wife's recovery from the wasting disease that had so lately threatened her life. The entire household would be present at a High Mass of thanksgiving in Westminster Abbey, paid for by Master Cuttifer, in which Abbot Anselm himself would lead the congregation. And then there was to be an almsgiving in the outer sanctuary, followed by a feast for specially invited guests at Blessing House in the presence of the king.

Anne had found it hard to sleep and had risen in the dark from her truckle bed in the solar. By the luxurious light of a wax taper— her mistress could not bear the smell of tallow candles—she was sewing a few last pearls to the gown that Lady Margaret would wear in the abbey today. Aveline was still asleep on her own bed, so Anne shielded her light and made no sound as she treasured these few moments to herself.

The dress was made from ink-blue Flanders velvet, the color of the night sky; the sleeves were lined in lustrous white figured damask folded back over the outside, and were tipped with rare white fox fur traded from Russia by Mathew Cuttifer's factor in Brugge. The low neck was filled with the finest sheer cambric—also snowy white—sewn with pearls the size of hawthorn berries. It was the most beautiful thing that Anne had ever made, but she'd had to argue hard to convince Phillipa Jassy to let her cut and sew the precious material all by herself. Normally seamstresses came to the house to sew for all the household, but Anne had been determined. This dress was the culmination of all the work she'd done for Lady Margaret over these last eight months. It was a tribute to her mistress's returned beauty, which Anne felt she knew best how to glorify. On this quiet morning she worked on, conscious of the gentle breathing of the woman in the bed, and smiled happily. She thanked God, and Deborah, for having been able to help restore her mistress's health.

Very soon after joining the Cuttifers' household, Anne had come to believe that Margaret's very expensive doctors were bleeding their patient to the point of exhaustion; collectively, they'd told the terrified Mathew that it was the only way the evil humors causing the wasting sickness could be extracted from his wife's body. They'd also instructed that spirits of mercury were to be taken in old wine boiled with rue as frequently as possible, since quicksilver was thought to replace lost vitality. But Anne had clearly seen Margaret sink deeper and deeper into the strange world between life and death each time she drank the dark, sticky liquid.

Somehow Anne had found the courage to speak to Jassy. In her opinion, the opinion of a humble peasant serving girl, the doctors were killing her mistress with their treatment. All life and death was in God's hands, but her mistress needed more blood, not less, if she was to fight the illness in her body. And would it not be better to remove all the "medicines" while trying to get Margaret to absorb some nourishment? Anne knew what starvation looked like, and her mistress resembled nothing so much as the emaciated villagers she'd seen in the one famine year of her childhood.

Mathew had grown increasingly desperate, even though the whole household prayed day and night for Margaret's recovery, and he'd had his chaplain Father Bartolph say countless Masses of intercession for his wife. When Jassy had dared to raise Anne's thoughts with him, it was as if a veil had lifted. Almost too late he had seen that he'd let excessive faith in modern medicine eclipse his native common sense.

He had sent for Anne and Aveline and questioned them closely. Because she was jealous of Anne, Aveline had been reluctant at first to agree that her mistress was worse each time she took the foul medicine prescribed by the physicians, but in the end, self-interest, and the possible preservation of her place in this household, had made her tell the truth. The question then became, how to proceed if Margaret's life was to be saved?

As a child, Deborah had fed Anne a tonic made from dried marigold petals, the juice of crushed parsley and rosehips, garlic, sage, honey, and fennel seeds. It worked to stimulate the appetite and strengthen the body during the time of winter ills. Cautiously, Anne had suggested she could make some of the strengthening tonic for her mistress—it could do no harm and might help. She also asked to make puddings from the yolks of new eggs and fresh bull's blood taken from a living animal, and thrice-boiled broth made from the flesh and bones of chickens.

Whether it was the removal of the "medicine," the suspension of the bleedings, or the tonics and puddings she'd been permitted to make, Anne had found, with great joy, that her mistress slowly, very slowly, regained her strength over these last months. And now, this day had finally dawned.

With the last pearl in place, Anne bit off the thread and carefully rubbed the precious needle in white chalk, to ward off the rust, before she put it away in a little oiled-skin bag in the linen coffer. Soon, it would be time to wake Aveline and her mistress, but first she should bring water up from the kitchen for bathing. She sighed. All the kitchen staff would be busy preparing for this great day, so Corpus would have to help her whether he wanted to or not. She shook Aveline to wake her, and before the sleepy maid could question her, she slipped out of the solar.

Anne felt her way down the stairwell, hurrying as fast as she could from step to step; she'd tried to convince Jassy that lanterns should be hung on these stairs at intervals—lanterns that would keep burning, rather than the unreliable pitch-dipped bundles of firwood that were jammed into the sconces—but the housekeeper had said it was needless expense, and Aveline had mocked her fears of the dark.

The housekeeper, of course, had more pressing concerns than the night terrors of a fifteen-year-old body servant, but Aveline took pleasure in Anne's fear, as usual. Now, in her haste to get down to the kitchen as quickly as possible, Anne stubbed her toes against the stone door as she wrenched it open, allowing blessed light and warmth and noise to flow into the darkness around her. There was the smell of food as well, great gusts of roasting meat and fat and butter and new bread. Anne felt the fear ebb as hunger lunged through her gut. Too bad she would have to wait until after the Mass.

"Anne!" Looming over her was Piers Cuttifer, Mathew's only son, a tall, thick-muscled man of about twenty-five with hard, gray eyes whom some of the women in the household considered good-looking. From the foxlike smell of him, and the sour wine on his breath, she could tell he'd been out carousing all night. He stood there swaying slightly, grinning at her.

Melly had long ago warned Anne about Piers. He liked to play "games" with the girls in the servants' hall; moving silently about the dark house in his felt slippers, he was often able to creep up behind the maids as they did their work, and slip his greedy fingers down their bodices or even up their skirts. Anne had very quickly learned to stay out of his way as much as she could. Now, gathering herself with dignity, she sketched a small frigid curtsy to the reeking, unshaven man in front of her. "Master Piers. Good morning, sir, on your father's name day."

"So formal, Anne. Come now, let us be friends. Kiss me or I swear I shall die from longing."

Anne saw that the kitchen staff were watching with interest, particularly Corpus who was skulking near the cooking fires, trying to avoid work while warming his backside. From under decently lowered lids, Anne darted a sharp glance around the kitchen; she needed Maître Gilles's help for more reasons than one now if she was to get back to the solar before her mistress woke, and avoid another excuse for Aveline to torment her.

"Sir, I have work to do for your mother—"

"My stepmother, Anne. She was eight when I was born to my mother, so an odd parent she would have made then—not so?" He smiled at her winningly, taking a step closer so that she found herself backing up against the wall. Her eyes flicked around the kitchen again—where was Maître Gilles!

"Here I am, little Anne. May I serve you?"

Anne jumped with shock as Maître Gilles touched her on the shoulder. Had he read her mind? Gratitude made her gabble her request: "Oh, sir, I would be so grateful if you could spare someone to help me bring water for my lady. She's still asleep but Aveline must wake her soon if she is to be ready for the service."

"Why did you not say you required assistance, sweet Anne? Here now I stand ready to help my dearest belle-mère. It shall be a small act of penance for me on this holy day." Piers swept her a deep but somehow mocking bow as if to say, avoid this if you can!

Anne shivered at the image of Piers following her up the dark stair. Without thought she responded, "No, sir, for then I should keep you from *your* bath." There was a real lash in the last words, for his smell truly did offend her.

He smiled at her then like a dog or a wolf, lifting his lips over his canine teeth. Then he moved closer, almost pressing her up against the wall, one thick arm blocking her exit. Fearlessly, she looked straight into his eyes, until he dropped his own. She'd been brought up with animals in the forest, and she knew she could show no fear with Piers.

Maître Gilles broke the moment: "Corpus! Shift yourself here and bring hot water!" The wizened little man grimaced as he moved away from the fire, and the cook turned smoothly to Piers. "Ah, sir, how kind you are to consider the welfare of even the lesser servants in this house: truly God is good. There is no need, however. It is the job of this worthless wreckage"—he waved a hand in the direction of the old man who stood mumbling beside him—"to haul water up to your lady mother's solar. Do not prevent him, sir, I beg, from performing one of the last services he is still able to render to this house."

Without waiting to hear Piers's reply Anne escaped back into the darkness of the stairwell, snatching a torch from a sconce to light the way up to the solar—feeling, with a shiver, Piers's hot glance as she went. She heard the old man follow her, spitting venom as he hauled up a heavy can.

"Spawn of the Devil you are, bitch. To wash the stinking body invites lewd and impure thoughts—which you know, slut that you are. I saw you, I saw you—out to get Mathew Cuttifer's son, don't think I don't watch you, pit of iniquity. Fiends from Hell, you and that Aveline; hot and shameless, the pair of you. You'll both get what you deserve . . ."

Anne hardly heard the insults the old man mumbled at her; ever since that first day in the kitchen she'd seen he treated all women in just this way. He hated women—especially girls—and, it was whispered, loved boys. It was best to let him talk, because he ran out of breath eventually, especially climbing the stairs. Not for the first time Anne wondered why he hadn't been turned out onto the street years ago.

The first faint light of dawn was filtering through the solar casements as Anne moved across the room and quietly pulled the heavily woven French bed curtains back. The old man, silent for once, poured the water into the washing bowl, while Aveline gently roused their mistress. As Corpus withdrew into the darkness of the stairwell, the woman in the bed stirred, waking with a light heart as she saw the girl standing by the fire warming a dressing robe. "So, Anne, here is another dawn."

Anne smiled happily and walked toward the bed, holding the dressing robe, while Aveline assisted her mistress out of the sheets, automatically chiding Anne as she did so: "Hurry, girl—your mistress will take cold!"

But Anne was determined nothing would upset her today, not even Aveline. The contrast between the healthy woman standing smiling beside the bed and the near-corpse of that spring morning nearly eight months ago was its own reward and no one could take that from her.

"Are you strong enough to walk to the fire, mistress?" asked Aveline.

"Strong enough, and determined to, Aveline—delighted to!" The happiness in Lady Margaret's voice made Anne smile again as she helped her mistress to the chair waiting by the fireside.

"Anne, I shall brush Lady Margaret's hair. You may begin washing. None of your clumsiness, now."

Anne suppressed a sigh. Young as she was, the girl understood that Aveline belittled her from fear of being supplanted, so with a determined effort she remained impassive. Aveline would only taunt her more if she thought the barb had hit home. Margaret was smiling sympathetically at her youngest maid, and heartened by the sweet expression on her lady's face, Anne patted the warm damp cloth over her delicate skin until her mistress laughed. "I'll not break, girl—use some vigor!" Anne rubbed the fine white flesh harder as Margaret talked on to Aveline.

"The robe is completed?"

"I believe it is, mistress," said Aveline, trying to sound as neutral as possible. "Anne, display the dress for Lady Margaret."

"Not yet, not yet. Dry me first and then I shall be ready for my surprise. We must hurry if we are to be down to the hall before my husband: he deserves a surprise, too!"

Aveline was warm for once. "Ah, yes, lady, he truly does after all the anxiety of this last time; you are sure that . . . ?"

"I am strong enough? Yes, with God's will and your help I shall be."

After personally applying scented cream—gillyflower essence in precious almond oil unguent—to preserve the whiteness of Lady Margaret's skin, Aveline allowed Anne to fetch the dress from where it had been hanging on a wall peg in the garderobe.

When she had first come to Blessing House, Anne had balked at hanging her mistress's most beautiful clothes in the cloaca as Aveline had told her to do, but then she had found that moths and fleas were much less likely to attach to the figured velvets and damasks because of the smell. And now, as she fetched her work from the anteroom to the latrine, it was a reward to hear Margaret's sigh of pleasure as she held out her creation for inspection.

"Oh, Anne, it really is very lovely. Come here quickly, I must have it on!"

For a moment, Aveline turned away, blinking tears from her eyes, a complex wave of emotions threatening her usual iron control. Margaret's joy and Anne's shining serenity at this moment of accomplishment made her feel unwanted. How had she let this girl wheedle herself so close to their mistress? Something else disturbed her too—an unwilling acknowledgment, deep in her soul, that Anne meant her no harm and, indeed, tried often to offer friendship. Why could she just not accept what was offered, open her heart and trust? Shaking her head to banish these unwelcome thoughts, Aveline deliberately raised her voice.

"First, we must have the underdress, madam. Anne! Hold the gown up off the floor properly! Really, where are your wits today?" Aveline was sharp as she slipped the fine silk underdress over her mistress's head. "Please, Lady Margaret, do stand still," she said in exasperation as her mistress jigged up and down, eyeing the lustrous velvet of the gown, impatient to get it over her head.

Margaret laughed. "Aren't you done yet, Aveline? I swear you're all thumbs." Finally, Anne was allowed to drop the deep blue dress over the delicate underdress and help lace the back as tightly as she and Aveline could.

"There, mistress—let me show you." Aveline brought Lady Margaret the convex mirror that hung on the wall beside the largest window. Though it distorted the reflection it still showed a beautiful picture—a tall woman with a white throat and an oval face that glimmered like a pearl above the night-colored velvet.

Margaret stood silent before the mirror. This was a precious moment. She turned away from her reflection and looked out of the window toward the rising sun. "I thank God that I have been given back life and health, and that I have seen this day dawn. All flesh is grass, I know, but for this day I am deeply grateful."

Then her mood changed again and she clapped her hands. "And now, I want to thank you for all that you both have done for me over these last months; for your devoted care and the healing power in your tisanes, Anne . . ." Aveline turned away scowling; the subject of the tisanes was a sore point between the girls. "I have presents for you both!"

The wooden coffer beneath the casement windows contained many of Lady Margaret's clothes and she quickly rummaged through it, unconsciously inhaling the smell from the little bags of last summer's lavender strewn among the garments to discourage insects. She lifted out a carefully folded gown of deep blue-green damask and another of fine copper-colored wool with a rich band of marten fur around the neck. "Please me by wearing these!"

After looking at each of the dresses for a moment, Lady Margaret handed the woolen gown to Aveline—a good choice, as the warm ocher would flatter her white skin and thick, almost black hair—and then she gave the green dress to Anne. Lovingly, the girl took the beautiful thing from her mistress's hand and with Aveline's willing help, for once, was dressed in less than a minute. The high bodice was loose in places, especially under her breasts, but a broad sash of red ribbon tied tight around the raised waist solved that problem.

"There, that looks fine." Margaret smiled. "Aveline, this veil and circlet are for you. Anne, you may wear your hair loose. Becoming—and appropriate."

"Anne, stop dreaming, girl! Fetch Lady Margaret's best cloak." Anne hurried to do Aveline's bidding, while the older girl quickly bound up her mistress's hair with a great skein of pearls and secured an airy veil of finest silk tissue to the crown of her head with a silver comb. It floated down like smoke around her shoulders.

Anne admired Aveline's handiwork; she was an artist and understood instinctively just how to enhance her mistress's beauty by this careful attention to detail. The younger girl sighed; maybe later today she would have the opportunity to talk properly to Aveline. It would be so much simpler if they could be friends and allies. Somehow she would find a way to make Aveline understand.

Lady Margaret was now finally dressed to Aveline's satisfaction and she stepped quietly toward the door, taking a deep breath as she passed under the lintel. This was the first time she had been out of the solar in many, many months.

Margaret's husband was on his knees at his prie-dieu in his work-room. Today he had great cause to pray, for he wished to give thanks for the recovery of his wife. She was twenty years younger than he but in the seven years she'd been in his house, he'd come to love her more and with a greater depth and meaning than he had loved either of his previous wives—God rest their souls.

Unusually, the hubbub in the hall found its way into his prayers and for once he abandoned the task he had set himself. The Lord would understand this was a great day: an important one for his household and its standing. After all, how often could a subject entertain his king on his own name day, and in his own house—and on the Virgin's day too, of course—and with God's good grace that is what he would do. He took a deep breath to steady himself and stood, almost unconscious of the pain in his knees. Now was the time for action.

As he strode into the receiving hall, it seemed that his entire household was one heaving mêlée of bodies and hysterical dogs; but no one saw him enter because at that moment Margaret walked down the broad stone stairs supported by her maids, and a ragged cheer started up as, one by one, the people of Blessing House saw her there.

Phillipa Jassy hurried toward her mistress, beaming. "We thank the Blessed Virgin to see you here, my lady."

"Amen to that. And I shall thank God and His Mother on my knees in their house for all their help and blessings; but now I should like to see my husband. Is your master in the work-room . . . ? "

"No, wife, I am here beside you."

At the sound of his voice, Margaret, Aveline, and Anne turned and dropped silent curtsies. The household grew quiet. It was as if three angels had flown down from the walls of the Abbey, such was the grace of the tableau in front of them. With tears in his eyes, Mathew raised the three women, first his wife and then the girls, and delighted the household by pulling Margaret to him in a hearty embrace before kissing her gently on the brow.

A loud voice cut through the rising hubbub of the happy crowd: "I say, let us cheer my father and the Lady Margaret!" On occasion Piers found grace and this was one of them.

The hall shook with cheering as Master Mathew draped the fur-lined cloak around his dignified wife and escorted her with ceremony across the hall and out to the portico to await their town litter. Unnoticed by the crowd, however, he was holding her tightly under the forearm to give as much support as he could.

But as Anne bent down to gather Lady Margaret's train she was suddenly conscious that Piers was beside her and, under the pretense of helping her up, had slipped a hand around her waist and quickly cupped one of her breasts, fumbling to find the nipple.

In her shock, Anne stood so abruptly that she knocked into Aveline before Piers could snatch his hand away—and then everything became very confusing. For a moment Aveline stood there, looking from one to the other, and suddenly her face was very pale. Then a wave of warm blood flowed up from Aveline's breasts into her cheeks as she turned away, snatching the train from Anne's hands, and mouthing "slut" at the discomforted girl.

Piers laughed and smilingly bowed low to them both. "Mistress Aveline, you look most charming in that pretty dress. And the high color you have, how brilliantly it makes your eyes shine. I salute you! And Mistress Anne. You should always wear green—it reflects in your eyes."

Unhurriedly, Piers sauntered away to stand beside his father as Anne tried to make sense of what had just happened. Why was Aveline so upset? Surely she didn't truly believe she'd encouraged Piers?

"Aveline . . . I'm sorry, but please believe me, I didn't—"

"Enough! Setting out to trap your master's son is the oldest game there is. I can see what you're doing!"

Aveline stalked away behind their mistress, loftily ignoring the impertinent, laughing looks Piers tossed in her direction. Then Anne's confusion cleared a little. Aveline and Piers? Was there something between them—something Aveline took seriously, seriously enough to defend? Anne felt submerged in a cold, miserable fog of sadness as she was swept forward by the crowd from Blessing House. Never had she felt more alone and friendless—trapped into playing this game with such truly unfathomable rules.

Chapter Four

The Abbey was barely four hundred yards from Mathew Cuttifer's front door but this was an occasion for maximum state and in any case he would not have his wife strained by unnecessary walking until he was sure she was entirely recovered. Impatiently he waited for the litter to arrive; it was a cold day and though Margaret was well swaddled up he was desperate that she should not catch cold from the treacherous winter air.

In the crowd of household people behind Mathew and his wife, Piers watched Anne as she waited beside Lady Margaret, her long hair fluttering in the cold wind. He smiled to himself but then realized Aveline had seen him ogle the younger girl. With a gallant gesture he swept off his velvet cap with its brave feather, but Aveline turned her head away disdainfully. Piers snorted—no more games from Aveline, she had seen he had new interests now, so let her take care not to offend him!

Mathew Cuttifer's great town litter finally made its appearance at the portico of Blessing House. The groomsman leading the horses had found it nearly impossible to bring the vehicle to the door from the courtyard behind the house because of the great press of people jamming the roadway, and he apologized profusely for the delay until a sharp look from his master made him shut his mouth with a snap. The master never liked excuses.

The few hundred yards to the abbey took nearly an hour to accomplish through throngs of people filling the narrow road that led toward King Street and the abbey buildings beyond. Aveline and Anne were some way back now behind the litter, surrounded by most of the kitchen staff and other household maids, all in their very best holiday clothes—many with sprigs of holly pinned to their breasts in honor of the Virgin.

The Abbey Church of Saint Peter had been much decorated and rebuilt over the last one hundred years because the tomb of Saint Edward the Confessor King that lay therein was still, after Canterbury, the most important shrine for pilgrims in the kingdom of England, and successive Abbots had made sure that each king in nearby Westminster Palace was aware of his obligations to extend, beautify, and restore the work of previous devout generations. But while work was always going on, some said that to enter this holy building was to experience a foretaste of paradise. The great colored windows, the painted statues, the gold and silver altar plate, the jeweled vestments—these alone were enough to overwhelm the senses. But when this glittering surface was touched by the voices of the brothers singing praise to God in his house, the soul might sense the very stone walls of the building breathing grace to the air like perfume.

Or so it seemed to Anne as she tried to track her mistress and master through the crowd moving up the great nave toward the high altar. Candles bloomed in the darkness and everything she saw that had been made by man to praise God was so beautiful, wreathed in the aromatic smoke from the candles, that her head swam.

In a half-dream, she allowed herself to be carried forward by the mass of people all around her as if she were swimming in a friendly sea. She felt protected even as she was shoved and elbowed about by those looking for the best vantage point to view the Mass, and the king when he arrived.

Then voices began calling, louder and louder, "The king, the king . . ." Straining to see, Anne was climbing almost before she realized what she was doing. Like a child in an orchard, hand over hand she hoisted herself up a stone structure covered in small statues that made convenient handholds, and found herself a precarious roost. Only when she looked down from the top did she realize she had scaled the elaborate monument of some noble with more money than taste; below her, a number of women shook their heads in scandalized disapproval, though men who'd seen her climb were smiling.

For once, Anne was too excited to feel abashed. From high above the congregation she had a clear view back toward the north door from where the king was expected to enter. Ever since she had come to the city she'd heard about him, though never seen him, but now, below her, the nave was crammed with a slow-moving procession of people heralding his arrival.

The first company to enter the Abbey was comprised of young men, all dressed alike in the royal livery, with the leopards of Anjou and the lilies of France embroidered in gold upon their blue jackets. Their hose had one leg of blue, and one of white, and Anne giggled as she wondered if they were not cold, their jackets were so short. These were men of the royal household, though they did not bear arms since this was a church.

Next came as many officials of the court, at least two hundred of them, chains of office around their necks and long gowns of sober color sweeping the stone floor of the Abbey. Then came the magnates, in town for the coming Christmas Court; grim, weathered-looking men mostly, richly dressed; they were fighters, very few soft bodies among them. And then, finally, the king and his party.

King Edward IV was easy to see because he was so tall—he topped the nearest man to him by half a head at least—and because of the magnificence of his clothing. He wore a black velvet cote-hardie embroidered with silver leopards under a flowing black cloak lined with cloth of silver; his long, muscular legs, too, were clothed in black velvet hose, the ribbon of the Knights of the Garter clearly visible below his left knee; but there was only a plain gold circlet around that red-gold head.

He was a young man too, this king, just over twenty-three, and with an open, charming face and sharp white teeth. Candlelight glittered and winked on the jewels he wore as he made his slow progress up the aisle. Clearly he was delighted to be among his people—they pressed so close their breath was his breath. And they loved having him so near; they cheered and stamped and clapped again and again, to the scandal of the court and the priests.

Anne was awed by the wave upon wave of sound that came from the throats of the people; it pierced her body as the stone building rang like an old bell and she found herself calling out the king's name just as he passed below.

Her voice cut through the all-encompassing deep, male bass of the sound and the king looked up seeking the source and saw an angel above him, an angel dressed in shimmering green, the color of new love. The procession stopped for a moment as their eyes locked. The impact of that glance was palpable and Anne became completely still, her eyes fastened on his as all sound receded . . . then the moment broke as the king smiled, waved, and walked on among his people toward the high altar.

"Anne. Anne!" The girl was pulled from the dream of the king's face abruptly. "Look down—here!"

"Deborah!" Her foster mother was right beneath her, wearing her old red cloak and holding up her arms, laughing.

"No, stay there, sweeting. I shall climb up to you." And she did, the nimble grace of her movements and the strength in her arms belying her age, which could be seen plainly as she slipped back her hood.

"Deborah! I've been longing to see you but it's been hard for me to send messages to you—Aveline watches me all the time and we've been so busy."

"I know that, sweet love—and so here I am! And after the Mass you shall tell me all."

Below them a collective settling passed through the crowd like wind in a standing field of corn. Deborah and Anne were too far away from the high altar to hear much, but both women could see that the Abbot of Westminster was surrounded by his monks and acolytes ready to begin the Mass. He turned toward King Edward and held up his hand in blessing before looking back to the altar and the great rood that hung above it. The familiar words began: "In nomine Patris, et Filii, et Spiritus Sancti . . ."

Anne could see her master, and Lady Margaret, kneeling just behind the courtiers who surrounded the king and she was awed by the transfigured expression on her mistress's face; she looked like a newly born child.

Deborah touched the girl's hand and smiled as Anne turned back to her. "God be thanked for the help you have been able to give to this woman."

"Amen to that," whispered the girl, but then she shivered. Which God did Deborah mean—the Christ on the rood before them, or the older ones from their other life in the forest?

Chapter Five

The frenzy in the kitchen at Blessing House had reached storm proportions. Maître Gilles was red in the face and hoarse from shouting at the staff. Even Corpus had not escaped duty; he was chopping the heads off live squirming lampreys with vicious determination and at great speed. He'd already experienced a kick in the behind and did not wish for another one.

The great receiving hall was not much better than the kitchen—men and maidservants collided with one another as Jassy did her best to be heard through the din of people desperate to finish preparations for the king's visit. So many fresh rushes had been spread that the level of the floor had risen by a full foot, and still Melly worked like one possessed to spread more.

The housekeeper had a sinking feeling that she had forgotten something vital and bitterly regretted that she hadn't managed to tear her staff away from the Abbey as soon as the Mass had ended. Really! The way some of those kitchen girls had gawped at the court suite, one would have thought they'd never seen men's codpieces before. Still, the master and the king would shortly be upon them—and heaven help her staff if they had not finished what she'd set them to do: there would be a reckoning later!

Outside the Abbey, the day had turned bitterly cold as a good part of the crowd emerged, breath smoking in the freezing air, all bent on the same thing: the alms giving that would shortly take place outside the sanctuary.

Twelve shivering old men, beggars clad in rags, were lined up in the charge of a red-nosed monk, waiting for their benefactor, Master Mathew Cuttifer. They had been swept up off the streets at random the previous evening by some of the burlier lay brothers of the Abbey, given a meal and a bed for the night, and dragged out here this morning to receive this unexpected blessing. They were all quite prepared to be grateful, but to a man they wished someone would get on with it, for they'd been waiting this last hour in a rising wind from the river that cut to the bone.

A ragged cheer made its way around the throng and all heads turned to look back toward the doors of the Abbey. The king was on his way, and craning to see, the old men were gratified by the sight of their sovereign walking slowly toward them surrounded by members of his suite. Accompanying him was a man in the place of honor on his right hand: their benefactor, Mathew Cuttifer, mercer and an increasingly important unofficial banker at court.

Mathew's throat was painfully swollen with pride and his breath was short with nerves. If only his mother and father—God rest them—could have been here to see him on this day. How far he had brought them all from his grandparents' tannery, now to be walking on the right-hand side of his king, about to conduct that same sovereign to his own house!

Six paces behind him, Margaret walked beside Lady Daphne Rivers—a pretty, finely dressed woman, a distant cousin of the new queen. They had been acquaintances for years but until this day Margaret had always been snubbed by Lady Rivers in company, perhaps as punishment for marrying beneath her family's status. How things changed when the winds of fortune set fair in one's direction! Now Daphne walked too close beside her and addressed little whispered asides as if they had always been the closest of friends, pressing her to come to court during the coming Christ-Mass wassail and bring the members of her family with her . . .

Margaret said as little as possible but her heart was hammering. Privately, she was delighted by the dignified but transparent happiness of her husband and this very public change in his status. He deserved this favor and she blessed Edward for offering it to him, though a corner of her heart was troubled; this king was said to be crafty for all his golden splendor. It was rumored that he never did anything but for advantage, and that thought made her worry even while she, too, was swept up by the glory of this day.

This new king was so different from the last, the luckless Henry VI, whom he had usurped. Edward seemed so open, so pleased to be part of the lives of his people, so happy to be accessible, whereas Henry, by the end of his rule, was so dominated by his hated French wife that he was a virtual recluse, isolated from the people of his country.

Eventually, the frustrations many of the old noble families felt over the actions of their French queen, who had controlled access to her husband, and plundered the country to her advantage and that of her lover, Somerset, had boiled over into an alliance with the alternative royal house, headed by the Duke of York, Edward's father.

The Yorkists had prevailed—Somerset was dead, Henry VI in hiding, Margaret of Anjou fled—yet parts of England were still ravaged as if wolves had been unleashed onto the people. Now it was the nobles themselves who plundered the suffering poor and the minor gentry, while fighting among themselves for advantage, and it was too early to see how this young king, rumored to be addicted to pleasure rather than government, could or would set matters in his kingdom to right.

Margaret shivered—not from the cold. It had all been going on for such a long time. More than ten years ago, her family had been forced to choose which party they would align with in the coming political storm, and with great good fortune, her father had recommitted himself to the Yorkists. He'd even fought for them at Wakefield, where Edward's father and younger brother had been killed, and all had seemed lost in the bitter cold of the turning year.

Yet now it seemed this new king valued the loyalty that Margaret's family had given his in difficult times, and in courting Mathew today with such a public show of respect—dining at his house, allowing him to distribute the Virgin's pence to the poor—he also showed he needed the support of his wealthier subjects if he was to rule this nearly bankrupt kingdom. And that in itself was cause for concern: Margaret feared the favors of today would bring trouble in their train from the court party.

That Mathew Cuttifer was to be permitted to transform the lives of twelve poor men—twelve being the number of Our Lord's Apostles—with his sovereign's blessing on the birthday of the Lady Mary, Mother of all, was a worrying sign of what might come, in the eyes of the court; a king who favored merchants over his traditional allies, the landed nobles, was to be watched—for who knew who might be elevated next? Or who might be displaced?

Today, the representatives of Christ's apostles looked a truly louse-ridden bunch. Huddled together to avoid the freezing wind, rheumy eyes watering and toothless mouths clamped shut, they watched the court approach and, having all survived long lives through sheer rat cunning, sank to their knees as one, calling out blessings on the heads of the king and their benefactor, Mathew Cuttifer.

Master Mathew looked at them with distaste but then hastily crossed himself. He had nearly blasphemed, if only in thought. These pathetic remnants of men were in place of his Savior to whom he owed such great thanks. He would treat them like brothers in Christ and count that an honor and a privilege. He walked forward and gave a hearty kiss of peace to the first reeking old man, manfully suppressing the revulsion he felt for the smelly old flesh and ragged clothes because he felt the glance of God, and his king, directly on his back.

Anne stood with Deborah near the back of the throng on the steps of the cathedral as her master performed the blessing and almsgiving to the twelve old men.

"He's a fine man," Deborah said.

"Yes, he is," replied the girl dreamily.

"I meant your master, Anne."

The young woman started and said hastily, "So did I."

Deborah frowned. "You were looking at the king."

And Anne blushed. "They're both fine-looking men." She managed to say it dismissively but the truth of Deborah's words startled her—she *had* been watching Edward, letting her eyes roam over his face and body, and all the time she'd been thinking of the moment in the abbey when he'd looked up at her. Foolish thoughts. Impatiently, she shook her head to clear it and tried to concentrate on what Mathew was saying to each of the old men. That was hard, for the gusting wind from the river kept snatching the words away.

The older woman said nothing more. Anne was still very young, even though she'd handled the responsibility of the last few months well. There was a real difficulty to be overcome here, though; one that filled Deborah with anxiety. It was easy to forget, at nearly fifty, that young girls fell in and out of love so easily, but the king was a dangerous object for any girl's affections. His eye for female flesh was notorious, even though he was recently married; it would be a tragedy if Anne were to become just one more expendable leman; a fearful fate without a powerful family to protect her.

Consciously, Deborah closed her eyes for a moment and asked for guidance for the girl—perhaps she would be given a sign that all would be well; but today the cold made the bones of her hands ache and, unusually, she could not banish the distraction of the crowd around her. With a sigh she opened her eyes as Anne, getting restless, tugged at her sleeve.

"I must go to Lady Margaret—she'll be wondering where I am. Can you come to Blessing House tonight? There is so much to tell you—you were right about so many things! Mistress Jassy doesn't like us to have visitors at night, so perhaps it would be best to use the kitchen door from the stableyard—Maître Gilles won't mind so long as I let him know you're coming. He'll leave it unbolted."

Deborah nodded as the girl kissed her cheek, and Anne would have gone immediately except that the older woman held her arm for a moment and looked into her eyes before kissing her gently on the brow. "There. Away." Impulsively, Anne hugged Deborah again, then slipped into the crowd.

"Remember me?" A small, well cared for hand touched Piers on the shoulder and he whirled around to find Aveline smiling up at him. He laughed easily and his eyes flicked over her body out of habit. She preened, but her face tightened when she saw his attention slide away toward the knot of courtiers who surrounded the king, among whom were his father and stepmother and . . . there was Anne, who had managed to work her way back to Lady Margaret through the crowd. She was standing behind her mistress now, holding the train of that lovely dress up out of the mud. Aveline went white with rage and the fury in her eyes shocked Piers when he casually glanced back at her again. She dropped her eyes from his and in a colorless voice said, "I shall not detain you further, master," before she hurried away.

Piers laughed to himself. Well, suppose she had worked out which way the wind was setting—jealousy in a woman often had such stimulating results. She might try even harder to please him. Aveline was distressingly strong-minded at times, and even though he would like to go on enjoying her, if she became troublesome about Anne he could always speak to Jassy and have her dismissed. Their affair was becoming common knowledge belowstairs and Aveline was trying to lord it over the other servants as a result—or so his own body servant had told him—and she was not greatly liked. Anne, however, had any number of champions, including Jassy, especially since his stepmother's remarkable recovery, which was generally attributed to the herb teas and the blood puddings the girl had made for Lady Margaret. He'd have to watch that too—didn't want others getting there before him, especially not some randy stable lad or kitchen hand.

"Way there, way. Dolt! I said *way!*" Piers pushed toward the court party. Rejoining them, he watched with amusement as Aveline snatched her mistress's train away from Anne, before the party set off to walk the little distance to Blessing House.

Master Mathew was in a daze of anxious joy. He walked beside his king, Margaret's hand folded through his arm, as he pointed out to Edward the fact that he had had this section of the road, leading from his house to the Abbey, paved with river cobbles for the convenience of the general public.

The king laughed genially. "What, Master Cuttifer, just for the general public? Not at all for your convenience? Come now." The laughter of the court sycophants actually made Mathew blush, something he had not experienced since he'd been a stripling.

Margaret dared to speak up and turn the joke in defense of her husband. "Ah, sire, it was for the blessing of Blessing House, to be sure—but yet also for the blessed general!"

Edward looked down at her and smiled. "Well, Mathew, you are a lucky man to have such grace and wit about you. And such beauty." Then his glance slid away from Lady Margaret's face, just for a moment, and allowed itself to linger on the two girls following obediently behind.

Aveline blushed and curtsied, as did Anne, but as Anne raised her head she found that the king was again looking directly into her eyes. She felt that same still, electrified connection before his attention was distracted, this time by a pack of mummers spilling out of the stable courtyard behind Blessing House.

The gaudy, crudely painted band of men and boys was dragging a large flat wagon on which was mounted a small castlelike building made of plaster, very realistically painted to look like stone, complete with turrets and a fantastical dragon curled up before the wooden portcullis. The crowd cheered and clapped as the wagon halted at the front of Blessing house, blocking its entrance. One of the mummers, a big fellow dressed all in green and twined around with ivy and holly, leaped up onto the wagon and called loudly for quiet while banging on a great brass gong. The king turned toward his host with a charming smile, clearly determined to be pleased with all he saw. "What now, Master Mathew?"

"Sire, this knave asks leave to display a wonder to you," answered Mathew Cuttifer in a strong, clear voice. Excitedly, the crowd hushed, those at the back calling for the mummer to speak up.

The green man banged his gong vigorously again till their heads rang and then began: "Great King, you stand by the Keep of Despair, built by this beast, for this is his lair!" The architectural beast—a mummer dressed in a canvas suit with ingenious scales made of small gilded wooden plates—opened a cavernous red-painted mouth and put out a lolling great tongue that it shook at the courtiers accompanied by lusty roaring, to the huge delight of the crowd and the happy squeals of small children.

"We plead you bring your martial hand so you may save this maiden dear!" Then a remarkable and scandalous thing happened.

A rather fat young woman, with breasts bulging out of the bodice of her gown, appeared on the battlements of the plaster castle. The fragile canvas walls shivered as she waved her arms with lavish abandon, wailing loudly and beating her nearly exposed bosom with enthusiasm. That brought a fascinated "Ooooh" from the crowd, delighted with this disgraceful show of flesh. Normally, boys played the parts of women; this break from tradition would no doubt inform sermons all around the city next Sunday!

Just then, the green man snapped his fingers. There was a loud bang and a cloud of green smoke enveloped the wagon. The crowd yelled with delight as the smoke cleared to display a flight of red-covered stairs up which the king was being beckoned by the green man.

Edward turned to his host. "So, shall I venture here, Master Cuttifer?"

"Sire, your people long to see you slay the Dragon of Despair and rescue this fair maid." Mathew made the deepest bow he could muster.

The king looked up at the rocking plaster construction before him—the "maid" was outdoing herself and the whole thing was in real danger of crashing off the wagon—and he smiled. Airily waving at the delighted crowd, he entered into the spirit of the play, ceremoniously accepting a blunted stage sword from the green man and running lightly up the steps to confront the fearsome dragon.

Once on the wagon, the king made a speedy and professional job of dispatching the repellent beast with three pantomime thrusts to its throat, belly, and back, earning wild cheers and screams from the crowd, whereupon the dragon made a great business of rolling over and dying with the maximum noise and effect, fake blood spouting out of its mouth. The green man banged his gong with sweaty verve as the king, waving his sword in victory, heaved up the wooden portcullis and entered the plaster castle, emerging a moment later manfully carrying the "swooning" heroine, to the huge and vociferous delight of the crowd.

"So perish all who fight our king and Blessing's reign has now its spring!" yelled the green man as Edward restored the fainting maiden to her feet, whereupon she sank into the deepest curtsy she could manage in the limited space available, the tableau somewhat spoiled by the dragon also leaping to his feet to take a bow. The king acknowledged the roars and cheers of the crowd before sauntering down the steps to the slightly more restrained applause of his court.

"Ah, sire, that was Towton all over again!"

"So, Warwick, is that what you think?" The king's tone was cool as he turned toward the speaker, a tough dark man in his thirties who was standing beside the beaming Mathew and his delighted wife.

"Swords and er . . . hearts were ever Your Majesty's strong suits," Warwick replied, sardonic though oily smooth.

It was as if clouds had covered the sun. One moment Edward had been delighted with all he saw and heard and now his face was closed tight with anger. He said nothing for a moment and then very deliberately turned his back on the other man. "It seems, Master Mathew, that some members of my court do not understand when the entertainment has ended. For that lack of . . . understanding, I must ask your forgiveness."

Mathew Cuttifer swallowed hard as he heard the King's frigid tone. His heart sank; perhaps this day of triumph would end in disaster, after all. Plainly the king and the Earl of Warwick were at each other's throats again and his little tableau was today's cause.

Lady Margaret stepped into the breach once more. "Sire, you must be sharp-set—as I declare I am. Would it please you to enter this poor house and break your fast with us?"

Edward registered the dignified calm with which he was addressed—and being aware of the courage the remark would have taken at this moment, swept off his flat velvet cap to the lady and smiled at her most charmingly. "Lady, it would please me greatly, but first . . ." He turned toward the group of grinning, shuffling play actors who were waiting to be dismissed. "My thanks to you— and here . . . Almoner!"

A little man dressed in a rich old-fashioned brocaded houppelande hurried forward, offering the king a fine leather pouch into which Edward dipped one long-fingered hand. A shower of small coins arced through the air and hit the cobbles with a satisfying ring. The mummers scrambled for their reward, led by the "maid," who determinedly elbowed the green man *and* the dragon out of the way as she scrabbled in the dirt for the coins, blond wig askew. The courtiers and the crowd laughed at this display of greed as the wagon with its castle was pushed away from the front of Blessing House by Watt and some of Master Mathew's bigger menservants.

Miraculously, inside Blessing House everything was ready for the great company that thronged around the king. Outwardly Mathew was impassive but he was delighted to find the entire inside staff of his house kneeling, heads bowed, as he entered with his exalted guests. It made a pretty and well-ordered sight in his spacious hall. In a clear voice he gave the welcome: "My poor house is graced by your presence, Lord King, and in token we greet you thus." Then he and Margaret, and the girls behind her, sank to their knees in front of the household, and humbly bowed their heads. It was an inspired gesture.

The simplicity of the owner of this great house warmed the heart of the king and charmed him out of the black mood that had threatened a moment or so ago. Smiling, he went to his hosts and gracefully raised Lady Margaret, giving her the kiss of peace, and then her husband, saluting his cheek also. Next, to the delight of the assembled servants and the scandal of the court, he handed Aveline and then Anne to their feet as well.

Was it Anne's imagination, or did the king's fingers linger in her palm, lightly stroking the hollow for a moment? And when he raised her, and she stood close beside him for the space of three heartbeats, she felt such a fizzy breathlessness in her chest that her legs nearly buckled and a slow tingling warmth spread from the palm he had touched all through her body until it lodged deep in her belly—a sensation at once confusing and delicious. Fighting to control her breathing, she fixed her eyes on the rushes as the king bowed to Mathew with a graceful flourish.

"Enough of this formality, Master Mathew. I salute you on your name day. Come! Let us eat!" And the king swept into the banqueting hall with Lady Margaret on his arm, servants scrambling to their feet and scattering out of the way of the advancing courtiers.

Piers found himself so caught in the rush of eager guests as they surged toward the long boards set up in the banqueting hall, al-

ready weighed down with platters of steaming meats and great
bowls of sauces, that he nearly fell headlong into the rushes when he
snagged his foot on one of the long tippets trailing from the sleeves
of his cotehardie. Corpus saved him by grabbing a handful of the
elaborate fabric at the back of the jerkin, though with disastrous results, for in his haste he slopped some gravy onto the precious brocade from the dish he was carrying.

"Oaf! This garment is worth more than your hide!"

"Ah, master, sorry, sorry! Here, shall I . . . ? "

"No! take your greasy hand away!"

Piers was burning with embarrassment. Not only had he nearly
fallen headlong in the presence of his king, but now his new particolored cotehardie was ruined. Worse, he could hear the ladies who
had seen the exchange laughing at him. He turned on the hapless
Corpus and kicked him, sending him sprawling into the rushes.
There was much laughter at seeing the old man covered in scalding
gravy—and even more to see him leap to his feet and run, shriek-
ing, out of the hall.

Mathew frowned as he looked down the hall from the high
table to which he had ushered the king and the greatest of the magnates, including Warwick. His son looked back defiantly and
backed out of the king's presence to change his coat.

The king had seen the byplay also and was laughing heartily at
the little drama; Anne, standing behind Lady Margaret's chair, was
perplexed that the king would laugh at someone's pain, but then she
shook her head, impatient with her own squeamishness. Edward
was the king, and kings were beings appointed by God to rule and
look after all their people in body and soul, therefore he must know
very much more than she ever would, or could. He was also a man
and much of what men did made no sense to her at all—perhaps
Corpus had deserved that kick planted square in his twisted back
and would be more civil in future.

Suddenly, she felt a viciously sharp pinch on her upper arm and
turned to find herself almost nose to nose with Aveline who hissed
at her, "Stay here, girl, and see you look attentive. If our mistress
asks, I've gone to the garderobe." Aveline slid away from behind
the high table, weaving through the stream of servants bearing food

into the hall from the kitchen, and being heartily cursed for getting in the way. She ducked into a wall embrasure, watching for a break in the flow so that she could slip away through the crowd of servitors unnoticed by her mistress.

"Lady Margaret, I salute you!" The king's voice called Anne's eyes back to the table. "Wassail!" With a long heroic swallow the king drained the wine from the silver drinking vessel after first offering it to his hostess to touch her lips against. Anne watched the movement of Edward's throat as he drank, and as he slammed the delicately made cup down on to the board in front of him, belching robustly in appreciation, she shook herself alert, remembering that it was her awesome responsibility to offer the refill.

Hurriedly, she moved forward and, as carefully as she could, started to pour more of the rich, sweet hippocras out of the silver-gilt jug that had stood between the king and her mistress. The nearness of the king was intoxicating; her hand started to shake as she poured, unconsciously inhaling his smell. How she wanted to touch the long fingers that lay on the table so gracefully curled as he chatted easily to his hosts.

"Master Mathew, I seek your advice as a merchant of note in this city— Enough, girl!"

Anne blushed to see she had nearly let the beaker overflow.

The king laughed. "This fair child will have me under your festive board in a trice, Master Mathew, should she keep filling my cup like this!" But the warm look he cast up at her took any sting from the words, causing her more confusion still and a return of the breathlessness she had felt earlier. The king noticed her reaction with delight. "Come now, such a modest maid—and a true one, I'll vow, unlike the fair 'virgin' outside with your dragon, I think."

Amid the hearty laughter that followed—even Lady Margaret joined in—Anne managed to back away and return to her place behind her mistress's chair, lowering her flaming face and doing all she could to still the hammering in her chest. She would have to find a way to compose herself, but after this embarrassment, why did she yearn for more such delightful torture at the hands of her king?

. . .

Aveline was nearly out of the hall when she heard the king laugh at Anne. Turning, she saw the girl shrink back, head bowed, and she rejoiced at the silly fool's embarrassment. Then she saw the warm and speculative glance the king threw toward the child. Anne did not see, eyes desperately fastened to the floor—but again Aveline felt a shiver of rage as hot black thoughts burned her mind. How was it that every man seemed drawn to this whey-faced little slut? Had she herself become suddenly invisible? Torn, she hurried on to find Piers. Usually, she was very sure of her physical power over men, but now, even in this new and beautiful dress, the uncertainty she was beginning to feel ate into her confidence. She shook her head to clear the fog. No, she had set herself a course today and would not back away from the task.

It was good, then, that Piers had worked out most of his bad temper by beating John, his body servant, so that when the last button was fastened on his second-best red velvet cotehardie and the knock came at the door of his room, he was calmer. But even so, he frowned on seeing Aveline and spoke more harshly than he intended: "Well, what do you want?"

The girl flushed and glanced at John.

"Well, idiot, don't stand gawping. Go!" Piers yelled. John, a thin young man with a missing front tooth—courtesy of one of his master's earlier rages—scuttled gratefully out of the room, closing the door behind him with exaggerated care.

Piers turned back to admire himself in the polished silver surface of his washing jug, savoring the moment, as Aveline stood uncertainly just inside his doorway. He enjoyed being in control and plainly there was more sport to be had from this game or she would not be here, looking at him so imploringly.

Taking his time, he turned and boldly ran his eyes over her body. "You look very nice in that gown, Aveline. Russet suits your coloring."

Aveline looked puzzled and then hopeful.

"Close the door, girl." His voice was silky now and Aveline smiled—this was much more what she had in mind. Slowly and sinuously she moved toward him, letting him see the full effect of the pretty dress she was wearing—particularly the bodice she'd pulled down as far as she'd dared. She knew she looked like a lady, though wanton enough to be provocative.

"I have something for you, Aveline. A surprise." She'd reached him now and he slid an arm around her waist. "Come, I want to show it to you in the light." He walked her over to the open casement window, one hand moving down her back to find her buttocks, and the other easing around the bodice of her dress to cup one breast. Suddenly he pinched her hard and saw the flicker of pain in her eyes: it hardened him. Aveline forced herself to look lovingly up into Piers's face. She knew that a faint whiff of fear would excite him, and she felt him stiffen.

Now he forced his hand roughly down inside her bodice, while the other hitched up her voluminous skirts. She was wearing nothing but an underskirt.

At the window he pushed her in front of him, forcing her to bend forward over the sill as he thrust his fingers up between her naked thighs from behind. She was wet, slippery, and hot, and her breathing was coming as fast as his now.

Halfway out of the window, Aveline closed her eyes and allowed herself to become completely limp—she knew he liked that—as he nearly tore the material of her dress, so impatient was he to pull it up and away from her legs and belly, exposing as much of her smooth body to the pale winter light as he could. But she kept her thighs tightly closed around his questing, tearing fingers, whimpering slightly, because she knew he would want to force her legs apart. He held her down hard, as he made her lean ever farther out of the casement into the cold air, breasts completely exposed, and fumbled urgently with the lacing on his codpiece. Then, pulling her thighs savagely apart, he grunted as he rammed himself up into her body. She gasped and tried to brace herself as the cold stone sill ground into her belly.

"Spread your legs wider—wider. Do as I say! There! Right up to the roof—as you like it, don't you, Aveline. There, and there, and there. Tell me, tell me what it feels like." She knew his face would be brick-red by now and suddenly she wanted to laugh—what if they should be seen from below?

"Oh, master, be gentle. You are tearing me. Oh, so deep, so

hard . . . oh . . . but if people hear me scream, they might come running. They would see us. I am nearly naked, Piers." Aveline was calculating; she knew his lust would be inflamed by the risk.

"Scream, then girl. Let them come. I want them to see you." He bit her neck so that Aveline cried out.

"Ah, not so hard—oh, oh, oh, you are so huge, master, you'll break me. Have pity."

He growled, bit her again, and this time the shriek was genuine, for the bite was hard; that true note of pain sent an exquisite ripple through him. He loved that feeling, utter domination—but then he couldn't stop it, the explosive spasm and shiver. Always over too soon. He lay upon her panting, as she gently moved her hips back and forth, back and forth, against him as he gathered his breath.

"What did you want to show me, master?" the girl said demurely. He grunted and slipped out of her, wiping himself on the tail of her gown as he did so. That annoyed her and she turned around sharply, though hoping that the disarray of her clothing, her naked lower body and tumbled hair were still provocative to him.

"Cover yourself, girl." The testiness in his voice alarmed her. She'd have to be extra clever now.

"Ah, come back to me, Master Piers—we have a little time now, the feast will go on for hours yet." And she held out her arms to him winsomely, but noted with dismay that he had fully laced himself up and was smoothing his tight cotehardie down with an impatient look on his face.

"My father requires my presence—and yours, Aveline, as well you know. Come now, we will find time to *speak* later—tonight." He smiled at her slightly as he emphasized the word "speak."

"I am glad of that, Master Piers, because I have much to talk to you about also."

She was relieved by his smile and bared her teeth alluringly, running her red tongue over her lips to make them glisten, but it was hard to make her words sound graceful and pleasant. She was angry that the byplay between them meant her news would have to wait, but she knew there was no point in pushing him.

Perhaps there would be more time later—and they could spend

some part of the night together, in his bed, rather than another snatched moment such as this. She would have to be careful if she was to get what she wanted from him.

He strode to the door and turned to look back at her. She did make a winsome picture as she languorously laced her breasts back into her gown, a faint smile on her face. Yes, it would be entertaining to have them both for a time, Aveline and Anne. Anne, a virgin, would not know how to accommodate him initially—though it would please him to teach her—but meanwhile this one had real skill and could always provoke his lust, even if he forgot her almost completely between the times he had her. He could smell her on his fingers and that was exciting. Amazing—he could feel himself stir again.

He shook his head. "Mind you, look sharp now. Your mistress will wonder at your absence for so long."

The slight smile he directed at her as he pulled the door open made her smile even more widely back at him. Then he was gone, and she stopped smiling. Yes, she needed some real time with him—just a few hours—and she would find a way to get him to give her pleasure, too, this next time. And after that, well, then she would tell him.

Even though he had been gone less than fifteen minutes, Piers returned to find the banqueting hall becoming rowdier by the moment. Perhaps it was his father's excellent wine, but wherever he looked there were red faces around the hall, and even those sitting at the top table were joining in, taking their lead from Edward. His father frowned when he saw him and beckoned sharply. Piers put a suitably dutiful expression on his face and hurried up to the top table, gracefully sinking down on one knee before his father and Edward.

"Piers, my scapegrace son, Your Majesty."

"New coat, I see, young man."

Piers flushed but managed to hide his annoyance. "Sire, all is made new by the radiance of your presence in my father's house."

The king laughed warmly. "Well, Master Mathew, you are lucky in your household—and the grace of your son." Waving a chicken bone with practiced aplomb, he signaled that Piers might retire.

Piers backed away while bowing deeply, careful not to trip on this new set of trailing sleeves, until he found his place at the trestle-board immediately under the dais upon which the high table stood.

A moment later, Aveline slipped back into her place beside Anne behind Lady Margaret's chair. "You can go now," she hissed. "I'll attend Lady Margaret." Anne was about to protest but another vicious pinch from Aveline made her yelp before she could stop herself, causing her mistress to turn and look at them both.

"Aveline, there you are. Run and fetch my pomander, this close atmosphere is making my head swim."

"But, mistress, cannot Anne . . . ? "

Lady Margaret frowned at the older girl. "No, Aveline, I particularly desire that you fetch it for me. Anne is busy here."

Sitting below the high table, Piers watched the tension mount between the two girls; watched Aveline's quick curtsy before she sullenly hurried away; watched Anne working her way from guest to guest, filling the cups on a look from her mistress.

The king, too, appreciated the girl, charmingly flushed now as she tried to concentrate on her task. He was watching Anne covertly, enjoying her graceful movements and enchanted by the beauty of her skin and hair, as he made small talk with his host.

"Master Mathew, I hear that you credit Lady Margaret's late recovery, for which we all give thanks this day, to the taking of herbs. A mighty power they must have; perhaps you should be selling them to the doctors for the good of us all."

"Ah, sire, it is truly a miracle, and no one, not even the learned physicians who attended my wife, have been able to explain her cure, except in the terms we scarcely dare credit."

"And what does the Lady Margaret herself say?" Edward asked, still watching Anne. The girl had lovely hands, too, he noted, and she was very clean, unlike some of the ladies of his court.

"Sire, I believe it was the prayers of my husband and this house-hold, and also the strength in the herb teas and the special foods I have been taking, that have brought me to this board today," Lady

Margaret explained. "Anne, tell the king how you prepared the tisanes for me—and the puddings." Anne looked up from her work, startled as King Edward turned, surprised, to his hostess.

"This girl had a hand in your recovery?"

"Indeed, I believe she did, sire. Anne came to us not eight months ago when I was truly lying in the shadow of the dark angel, but within some days of her arrival here, and after drinking the teas she prepares from the herbs she gathers herself, I had enough strength to eat again. And she fed me special puddings made from fresh blood and eggs and then—well, as you see . . ."

"Come here, girl." The king beckoned Anne to him as the entire table of dignitaries looked on with interest. "Do you truly believe that you aided your mistress with your medicines?"

At first, Anne opened her mouth to reply to the king and no sound emerged. Then, seeing her struck dumb with his attention, and those of the magnates around him, he reached over for her hand, patting it gently, and smiled at her encouragingly. The girl let out her breath in a deep sigh and, gathering courage, said simply, though her voice shook, "Sire, my foster mother has a physic garden and taught me the making of medicines and simples from the time I was a child. I believe that if Lady Margaret profited from the poor help I was able to give it was because our good Lord wished it so." And she sank into a deep curtsy, dropping her eyes to the rushes.

This little speech was delivered with such modest and winning grace, and so clearly sincerely meant, that the king applauded, as did those around him. Then, reaching across to Anne, he tipped her face up with a finger under her chin, saying softly, "Bravo. An excellently fair and clever little doctor. We must see that your talents are properly used."

Now, with the king's dark blue eyes looking down into hers, the same delicious shivering rush Anne had felt earlier prickled its way up and down her spine and lodged in her nipples and groin with a buzzing warmth that made her squirm, though she tried to hide it. She smiled up at Edward tremulously, then once more dropped her glance as he handed her to her feet.

Lady Margaret, wishing to help the girl recover her composure, smiled warmly at her and issued a suitably diverting request:

"Anne, would you find more lampreys in saffron for my Lord of Warwick, please—and then I should like you to ask Jassy to come to me for a moment."

Below the dais, Piers found his attention caught by the charming Lady Rivers, kinswoman of the queen. She had a remarkably fine pair of breasts, so nearly exposed in the very low-cut, tight-laced bodice of her gown it was hard to look elsewhere, but he saw something of what was happening at the high table out of the corner of his eye.

Piers was enraged to see his stepmother's younger maid having her head so comprehensively turned by the king's attention. With Edward's reputation, today's small dalliance might not be the end of the matter. He might have to move fast. Perhaps very soon, indeed. And he smiled at that thought: the chase was sweet after all.

His smile delighted Lady Rivers. The new powdered carmine in her cleavage was clearly a success; this rather good-looking young man might also enjoy her newly gilded nipples a little later also!

A further hour passed and it became apparent that the king was restless to be gone. Margaret caught her husband's eye and, using Anne as an intermediary, gave him a message that she felt the feast should end soon, and would arrange it if her husband was willing.

He looked back at her and nodded discreetly, proud of the good show she and his household were making. In truth, Master Mathew had had just about enough of this rowdy crowd from the court. For all his desire to advance, he was not a court sycophant, and even though he was sure that entertaining this motley crew of aristocrats and magnates would advantage his business, he was heartily sick of their patronizing ways—especially toward his beautiful and cultured wife who, he reminded himself with a snort, was better bred than most of them. He watched with admiration as she signalled, unobtrusively, for Anne to once more fill the king's cup; clearly she felt this would give him the opportunity to gracefully take his leave.

"Your Majesty, would it please you to have more of these comfits—or a little of the sack?" Anne kept her eyes down and her head modestly lowered as she proffered the last of the sweetmeats to Edward.

"No, sweet child—I have eaten and drunk my fill at your master's board," Edward said, then raised his hand to the herald, who had stood behind him, unmoving, for the entire feast.

The herald, a good-looking boy with the first fluff of a beard on his bright pink cheeks, called out in a surprisingly deep and loud voice for one so young: "Pray silence. Silence there for His Majesty."

"My friends, it is time for us to depart and leave Master Mathew and Lady Margaret Cuttifer to the enjoyment of their day without this swarm of locusts to further waste their substance!" The ladies laughed gently behind their hands at this sally from their king—clearly he wanted them to laugh because he was smiling easily. "Sir, and you, lady, I have something for your name day and in celebration of Lady Margaret's miraculous restoration."

And with that, William Hastings, the king's Lord Chamberlain and greatest friend, moved forward and with the deepest of bows held out a blue velvet bag, embroidered with the leopards of Anjou, to the king. Edward rose from his chair and from the inside of this bag drew out a handsome heavy gold chain made of interlinked Ss studded with carnelians, crystals, and small, exquisite enamel medallions.

Carefully he dropped the chain over Master Mathew's head. It was a particularly fine piece of work—altogether a princely gift—but the largesse was not yet done. Stepping gravely to where Lady Margaret had sunk onto her knees beside her husband, the king placed in her hands a small object, an exquisite little Book of Hours richly illustrated in glowing colors and gold leaf, with an embossed cover of worked gilded leather, again studded with gems, in this case garnets and topaz bound with gold wire.

Lady Rivers was not the only member of the court who was interested to see the extravagance of the king's gesture to Master Mathew and his wife. Earl Warwick, too, was caught by surprise. This gift-giving was fascinating indeed and might signal a shift in the wind. Perhaps the king was about to have a need for money and plenty of it—else why so suddenly single out a jumped-up merchant—even if he did have a well-born and excellently connected third wife?

Master Mathew's cup was full to overflowing. The clear evidence of favor the king had bestowed, and his princely generosity, made it hard for him to gather his wits as he slowly rose—the king holding out a hand to him, another honor—and assisted his kneeling wife to her feet. "Sire, never shall this day be forgotten by me and mine. And may you ever know that my house, and all that is mine, is at your disposal while I have breath in my body."

The king laughed in warm amusement. "Now, Master Mathew, that is a remarkable and most generous offer, and before witnesses! But I shall not hold you to it, or not yet, at least. But I give you fair warning: should the queen present me with a babe each year, as she has loyally declared she will, and I am thus threatened with being eaten out of hearth and home, I may have need for you to remember your words to me today."

It was a jolt, yet why did Anne feel such disappointment when His Majesty mentioned the new queen? Was it not natural in a married man to want a family and to enjoy the lawful pleasures of the marriage bed? But then how could he have looked at her with such interest? Did she just imagine the warmth in his eyes because she wished it were there? It was mortal sin to think carnal thoughts about a married man, she knew that. When she confessed, Father Bartolph would give her penance and she would deserve it.

Her contemplation was broken as the chattering company began streaming out of the hall behind the king and her master and mistress, as they walked together to the great front door of Blessing House.

Once again, she and Aveline bore up Lady Margaret's train, though Anne saw with some anxiety that her mistress was exhausted now, standing stoically beside her husband to bid her goodbyes to each member of the court as they left her house.

Mathew, too, was worried—he could see how tired Margaret was—and some of his salutations became a little brusque as he tried to encourage late-stayers out of his door, while trying to preserve the mask of a good host.

With the last straggler gone and the front doors closed again, Mathew touched his wife's hand and gently said, "Come, wife. This day has taken its toll. Aveline! See that the bed is warmed as I walk your mistress to the solar."

Turning to Anne, Aveline snapped, "Fetch coals immediately and make sure you get enough for two pans. Hurry now, I want this done before Lady Margaret reaches her bed." Then she turned away to pick up the train of the blue dress once more, as Anne, walking as quickly as she could, set out for the kitchens.

Of course Anne knew her way around Blessing House now as if it were Deborah's garden in the forest, and once out of sight of the hall she hitched her skirts up and ran. But still it took her several minutes to reach the great doorway leading into Maître Gilles's domain.

Before today, she had been careful to avoid looking at the lolling stone woman on the lintel, conscious of Aveline's words about guarding her reputation with the menservants in the house, but now she paused a moment and looked up at the heroic face and body above her. The look on the woman's face was arresting: eyes half open, mouth slightly parted and smiling, she was enjoying the tug of the baby at her nipple and one of her hands was opening the top of her robe as if to free the other breast for the baby's, or the onlooker's, further delight.

Perhaps it had been the heady events of this day, but the smile on the woman's mouth and the clear pleasure she had in her own sensuality affected Anne in a way she'd not experienced before. It was clear that the sculptor had real skill, for the two very male bodies that supported the gigantic woman had also been lovingly shaped so that each knotted muscle appeared flexed. Tentatively, the girl reached out to touch the carving where there was a solid bulge under the loincloth of each giant.

"Well worked, is it not, Anne?"

Anne whipped around guiltily to find Piers just behind her, leaning on the passage wall with an amused look on his face. Her face glowing with embarrassment, Anne bobbed a panicked curtsy as she went to pull the door of the kitchen open, but she was not fast enough. Piers got there first and his fingers closed around her wrist, forcing her hand away from the iron latch as he made her turn and face him.

"Do you know that some of the men of the house touch this, here, just as you wanted to"—he pulled her over to the carving and forced her fingers to rub the straining loincloth of one of the giants—"before they bed their women?"

"Let me go, you're hurting me and I have to—"

But now he had her other hand and was forcing her farther away from the kitchen door, pressing her up against the wall, pinning her shoulders against the stone. "I could show you why they do it, Anne—would you like me to? Do you feel that—hard is it not?"

Holding her wrists tightly pinioned with one hand, his mouth was at her throat now and then his tongue was sliding down toward her breasts while he fumbled up under her skirt.

"Piers, let me go—now!"

He was very strong and had her crushed against the wall, dress up around her waist, as he forced his body against hers, legs straddled around her, rubbing himself, panting against her belly.

Anne made a supreme effort and wrenched her knee into his unprotected groin with all the desperate force she could muster. He grunted in pain, dropped her wrists, and she escaped.

Sobbing with anger and fear, she heaved the door of the kitchen open and slammed it again as she stumbled through, her mind a jumble, but conscious that she must compose herself—and fast. The kitchen was a mess, the servants still cleaning up after the feast. Many of them were drunk from having sampled the leftover wine on empty stomachs when they'd cleared the hall, so while happy shouts from here and there greeted her, they were all busy enough not to notice that she looked distressed. Covertly, she pulled the bodice of her gown together as best she could and tried to tuck the torn cloth back into the neckline from where it had been ripped away.

Maître Gilles was counting the nutmegs and putting them away when Anne found him. He saw at once that something was very wrong but did not attempt to interrupt the girl as she stumbled over her request for coals for the solar.

"Certainly, dear one. Now sit here while I have them brought," he said, pressing her gently down onto a settle beside his worktable. She flinched when he touched her. Then he called out, "Corpus, two buckets of coals for Lady Margaret. Yes, now!"

Gilles turned back to look pensively at the girl, she was visibly shivering though seated very close to the fire. He also noticed that she kept trying to rearrange the fichu of sheer material at the breast of her dress; it looked odd somehow, askew. Striding over to a black pot hanging over the flames, the chef ladled out a quantity of the hot liquid that was simmering there into a horn beaker. "Here—hot wine."

She smiled gratefully at Maître Gilles as she pressed her hands around the warm cup, but as she quickly looked down again, the cook was alarmed to see her eyes had filled with tears.

"So, will you tell me what has happened?"

Anne swallowed some of the scalding wine and shook her head. "Perhaps God wishes to punish me for my sins."

She looked so miserable that the chef was nonplussed for a moment. Putting two and two together, he worked out what must have happened—and who was likely to be responsible. "Would you like me to speak to Jassy for you?"

"No! Oh, no, please do not. I'm sure this was just some sort of . . . that he did not intend . . ." she stumbled on.

The cook was conscious of a flicker of prurient interest—quickly suppressed. He liked Anne but could not deny the lustful thoughts that her youth—and her body—brought into his head from time to time. Kindness fought with flesh and, sighing, he brought his mind back to the task at hand—to help, not make things worse for her.

"Corpus! Lazy dogsmeat! Take those coals up. Now," he bellowed.

As the old man stumbled over to the concealed door, complaining under his breath, two heavy iron canisters of coals swinging from the wooden yoke across his shoulders, Maître Gilles held out a hand to Anne to help her from the settle. "Now listen to me. I'm here and I'm your friend. If you change your mind, I'll speak for you to Mistress Jassy when you're ready. But for now, I think it would be wise if you avoided going about by yourself."

Holding her head high as she crossed the kitchen, Anne swallowed her tears as she followed Corpus up the stairs to the solar, hardly hearing the usual stream of invective. Everything had changed. How could men be so confusing? And so strange in their relations with women?

Piers and Aveline—and Piers and Anne: the initials were the same but the substance was so very different. She could not understand why Aveline would want anything to do with Mathew's son. Anne felt physically sick as she thought of Piers running his hands over her body—and yet, unwillingly, when she thought of the king, the hot rushing warmth made her head spin . . .

How could she have woken so childlike this morning, and now, at the end of the day, feel as if she had been swept away on a sea of her own darkly turbulent blood? With Deborah's help she would pray tonight—to the old gods of the forest and to the Mother of Christ. She would need all the help they could give her.

Chapter Six

Anne hurried into the solar behind Corpus, and found her mistress sitting, eyes closed, in her dressing chair by the fire. Aveline turned as Anne entered the room and the younger girl's heart sank at the look of venomous triumph that Aveline shot at her.

"See, mistress, here she is at last! So, girl, you thought you would take your own time with the men in the kitchen while Lady Margaret waited on your good pleasure!"

Saying anything was futile. Anne clenched her teeth and silently directed Corpus to fill the warming pans as she turned down the sheets on the bed.

But Aveline seized the chance she'd been waiting for. "Madam, it's not as if I haven't told her often enough to concentrate on her work and speak only as necessary to the men. But light girls like her never listen. There, you see—she has spoiled the fine gown you gave her. Ripped at the bodice no doubt while sporting with one of the pantrymen or maybe even the pig man."

Corpus, tipping the coals into the pans with his back to Lady Margaret and Aveline, leered at Anne and lewdly jigged one forefinger in and out of a circle he made with his other hand, while licking his toothless gums lustfully.

Anne stayed silent though she flushed bright red, a fact not missed by Aveline. "There, mistress, see—her face condemns her!"

Lady Margaret decided to put a stop to the persecution of her younger maid. "Enough, Aveline, quite enough. Bring me the dressing robe. And Corpus, that will do. You may go back to the kitchen."

As the old man scuttled out with a final flicker of his startlingly red tongue at Anne, Lady Margaret beckoned the younger girl over to her side, while Aveline flounced over to the garderobe.

The older woman could see that Anne was very unhappy about something and also that the girl had tried in vain to disguise the rip in the bodice of her gown. She tried to draw the child out. "Tell me what is wrong, Anne. I can see something is troubling you very much."

Anne shook her head, steadfastly looking down at the floor, hands locked together.

"Come now. This is not like you. If you do not tell me, it will be hard for me to protect you. Whatever has happened, well, I do not think it can be your fault. Being pretty can be a curse sometimes, you know, until you are a little older and understand how to deal with the face and body the good Lord has seen fit to give you."

The gentle tone in Margaret's voice found its way into the girl's heart and her eyes filled with tears that slid down her cheeks before she could stop them. "Madam, it is nothing. Just a foolish incident."

Aveline snorted bitterly as she returned.

"Aveline! You forget that Anne is young. Something has upset her very much," Margaret protested.

"With respect, madam, if something has caused her pain there is nothing more certain but that she has brought it on herself. As I said, she's a wanton."

Anne burst out: "I am not! Oh, madam, I am not and you must believe me. This was not of my seeking!"

"There now, child, there now. I believe you. Calm yourself. We shall deal with this sensibly, you and I, but first you must tell me what happened."

But Anne shook her head again, and Margaret, looking narrowly at the girl, came to a decision. There seemed to be no great harm done, apart from shock. Perhaps sleeping on the matter would give the girl courage to say more tomorrow. She would deal with it then. For now she was bone weary and desperate for sleep herself.

As the two girls undressed their mistress and put her into the warmed bed, some instinct warned Aveline, too late, that she had overstepped the mark in persecuting the girl. Anne was telling the truth and their mistress believed her. Sudden cold certainty came unbidden: Piers. The thought made her head spin with fear and anger. She'd seen him sniffing after the girl, even today. Desperate to know what had happened, she tried to get Anne to tell her without Margaret hearing their conversation. But as they carefully packed Margaret's beautiful velvet dress away together, cleaned the solar and rebanked the fire, Anne refused to be drawn out. The short winter day was darkening when Aveline released the girl in frustration, telling her to get some food and warning her to return as soon as she had eaten.

Wearily, Anne walked down to the receiving hall as trestle-boards were being set out for the evening meal. She knew that there would be plenty of food if she went directly to the kitchen, but she balked at the thought of going there. She touched the bodice of her gown where she'd managed to repair the rip during the after-noon—remembering Piers tearing the smooth material set her teeth on edge.

As she looked at the cheerful bustle around her, she smiled at one or two of the other servant girls she particularly liked. Melly, who was banking up the ashes in the great fireplace before the men brought in more wood, waved to Anne happily, for once. Melly had really enjoyed today's excitement and was looking forward to eat-ing some of the tasty leftovers from the feast.

Anne was so tired that she slumped down on a settle near the fire and closed her eyes. The events of this day played through her mind like an entertainment from the mummers and she wondered if it had all been some sort of dream. Had the king really looked at her so warmly or was that a delusion? And was Piers really in-volved with Aveline? She'd become used to dodging him as he pur-sued her half-jokingly from time to time, but never before had he tried to seriously molest her. She longed for tonight when she would see Deborah and could ask her advice.

Slowly, the sounds of the receiving hall slipped farther and far-ther away and she drifted toward sleep, until a hand shook her by the shoulder. It was John, Piers's body servant. "My master needs you. Now."

Anne looked at the boy in horror. "But John, I cannot. It would cause terrible trouble for me." She could not keep the fear out of her voice and the boy shifted uneasily from one foot to another, eyes on the floor.

"He said if you would not come I was to tell you he would be speaking to his father tonight about your unsatisfactory work in this house." The poor boy hated his message but his tone was clear.

Anne stumbled to her feet, forcing strength into her muscles, but her gut churned with terror. The stone staircase leading from the hall to the upper galleries stretched away into darkness. As slowly as she dared, she followed John as he hurried on, the skirts of her pretty green gown trailing over the rushes. Too few minutes later, John raised his hand to knock at Piers's door.

She grabbed his fist and whispered urgently, "John, after you have let me in here, go as fast as you can to Lady Margaret's solar and tell her . . . tell her that Master Piers has asked me to speak to him. And please say that it is not of my making and I would be grateful if Aveline could come to fetch me—immediately."

Nervously, the boy shook his head. "I cannot do that, Mistress Anne. He would beat me and turn me out into the street."

The girl looked at him in utter despair. He was right—she could not ask for his help because Piers would indeed turn him out of the house for disloyalty. She dropped her hand from John's arm as he looked at her, guilt and shame in his eyes, before his knuckles beat upon the door.

"Enter."

John pushed open the door, ushered her through with a hurried bow, and then backed out, closing it again.

Anne was alone in the room with Piers Cuttifer. Deep night had fallen outside. The room was warm and cheerful in the light from the fire and several expensive, fat wax candles. Piers sat beside his hearth in a thronelike chair, watching her silently. She stood just inside the door clenching her teeth against her shivering. "Come here."

She did not move.

"I said come here, Anne." Quiet menace this time.

Again she said nothing, but forced herself to walk toward him, stumbling slightly against a rich rug that lay in her path.

"There now, come and stand here: let me look at you properly."

She was standing about an arm's length from him now, the glow from the fire picking out the contours of her face and body.

"Do you know that I am disappointed in you?"

"And I you, sir," she said sharply.

"Oh, ho, this little thing has a tongue like a needle. Spirit is good, but too much spirit must learn obedience. Kneel. Now!" The silky voice became a bark as he fingered the stock of a whip lying across his knees.

The hammering in Anne's chest was so loud she thought he must hear it but she said nothing as she knelt. She knew he wanted her to plead with him and this she would not do—if she could stop herself.

Silence as he looked at her. He was waiting for her to speak and when she did not, he smiled slightly. Then, almost conversationally, he said, "Anne, you belong to this house, yes?"

She looked up at him, keeping her voice calm. "I am freeborn, Master Piers. Not a serf."

He laughed pleasantly. "You are a chattel. We give you meat and drink and a roof over your head. We expect loyalty in return." He was on his feet and walking around her now, round and around, his fingers playing with the shaft of the whip. "Is this how you repay kindness from this house, Anne? You offered me violence today."

Now Anne was on her feet. "Piers, that is a lie—you know it." Then she felt the short lash of the whip through the cloth of her dress as it fell across her back. She choked down a scream as he circled her again.

"Servants in this house do as they are told. If they do not, I must inform my father. Especially when that disobedient servant is guilty of lewd conduct. You have tried to entrap me and that is wicked . . . Unlace the bodice of your gown!" The whip cracked thunderously beside her ear.

Mutely, she looked up at him and could not stop the appeal in her eyes. He saw it and smiled down at her. "Do as I say, Anne." He said it softly, almost whispered it, but the threat was clear and she began to unlace with shaking fingers, working as slowly as she could and bending her head to keep her breasts in shadow.

He walked around her again, closer now. She felt the handle of the whip under her chin as he raised her head. "Open the bodice, Anne," he said almost patiently, as she stared at him, nearly mesmerized by fear. Slowly, she did as she was told, then, delicately, he eased the top of her gown off her shoulders so that her breasts were exposed in the light of the fire.

"Better." Now he trailed the whip over and around each of her breasts and then down toward her belly as she stood there almost naked to the waist, trying to prevent the gown from dropping farther toward the floor.

"What was I saying before you distracted me?" This time he trailed the thong of the whip around her bare shoulders and then down her spine. "You can imagine, can't you, Anne, what my father would do if a servant tried to corrupt his son? Such a girl would be thrown out of this house and whipped naked, at the tail of a cart, chased from this town as a slut and whore."

Anne gasped. The handle of his whip had plunged down inside her dress. She grabbed the whip to stop him, saying as strongly as she could, "Your father would not believe you."

Abruptly, Piers sat on his chair again, eyes bright with excitement, and laughed. "My father is much more likely to accept what I say than listen to a— What are you? Fifteen-year-old slut of a servant girl."

Anne straightened her back and looked him full in the eye. "Sir, I ask you, in the name of Our Lord, to be generous and compassionate. I am a virgin." She had said the wrong thing, she saw that immediately; he was enjoying forcing her to submit. Asking for mercy told him she was weakening.

"On your belly." The tone of his voice was thick as he flicked the whip back and forth, back and forth. Swallowing the acid in her throat, she stretched herself on the flags, shivering again as she felt the cold stone press against her breasts. "Crawl to me, Anne." She lay there feeling the tears start. "Crawl!" A deep breath gave her the strength to slither toward him, trying all the while to retain some modesty as the long skirts entangled themselves between her legs.

The man in the chair looked down at the girl now huddled at his feet. He allowed the handle of the whip to meander down her spine—he enjoyed seeing the little convulsion it caused.

"How can you treat me like this when Aveline loves you?" The words were muffled because she would not look at him, but there was defiance in them.

"Aveline? I doubt love is a part of it—Aveline, too, is a slut, just as you are."

Anne scrambled to her feet, burning with rage and misery. "You are a vile man. And I will not be called a slut—neither is Aveline one. I do not understand how she can love you, but she does."

"If you dare to couple her name with mine again, she will leave this house as well as you. Think carefully, for it will be your responsibility when your friend is cast out into the street. Perhaps silence is preferable; scandal must not touch the Cuttifers—that would be bad for business, would it not? You must think on what I have said, Anne, but it is now time for you to be in your bed." He smiled wolfishly.

She looked at him warily, and when he made no move toward her, she pulled the bodice of her dress up over her breasts. But before she could make a dart for the door, he grabbed both her wrists, forcing them behind her back, his mouth covering hers. She tore her head away to scream, but he brutally clamped his hand over her lips.

"Now that's a silly thing to do. Just let me tell you what I intend. Ah! Now listen, listen . . ." She was struggling with him but he held her clamped against the length of his body, his hard groin pressing into the base of her belly. "I will let you go for now, but be aware that you will come back to me, willingly, when I tell you to. If you do not, I will speak to my father and you will be disgraced—and thrown out of this house. As will Aveline. Virtue is not its own reward. Ever."

Anne looked at him with despair, though she tried to hide it. Clearly he enjoyed spinning out the moment when she would be forced to acquiesce on his terms.

"Next time, little Anne, next time I will teach you to enjoy this game." He took his hand away from her mouth, and rested a finger on her lips, pantomiming silence, whispering, "This game is delicious, I promise you. And soon, ah soon, you will beg me, yes, on your knees and on your belly, crawling as you did just now, beg me to play it with you." He forced a knee between her thighs and was rubbing against her as he bent her farther and farther back over the arm of his chair, pressing his mouth to hers, biting her lips, the weight of his body so great, she could not breathe.

"Go." He released her so suddenly that she almost fell as she fled, his amused laughter following her out of the room. He stretched lazily—very soon now, it would be Aveline's turn to please him. He'd never had two women under the same roof before—it was vastly stimulating and enjoyable, even in thought. Perhaps, in time, he could have both of them pleasure him at once? Yes, that was an aspiration, indeed . . .

Anne hauled up her gown as she ran, along the dark passages of Blessing House, ran and ran, and up the stairs to the solar, the gorge rising in her throat as she tried to wipe the remembrance of his hands on her body from her mind. She would *never* permit him to humble her like that ever again! Never!

At the door of the solar she halted and, taking a deep breath, tried in vain for calm as, with shaking hands, she relaced her dress as tightly as she could and raked her fingers through her hair. She entered very quietly to find Aveline stoking the fire.

"Where have you been?" Aveline's tone was neutral, but she was gimlet-eyed.

Bobbing a curtsy to her mistress drowsing against the bolster, Anne hurried to the big coffer and scooped up the pile of Lady Margaret's garments to be washed. "I'm sorry, Aveline. Shall I take these to the laundress?"

"No. Read to Lady Margaret while I see about something from the kitchen for her and the master. He will dine here tonight." She took the pile of laundry back, and for a moment the girls locked eyes; it seemed as if Aveline wanted to speak, but then, shaking her head, she went to the little door that led down to the kitchen, closing it quietly behind her.

Anne breathed a deep, shaking sigh as she hurried over to her mistress in the great bed. Lady Margaret smiled drowsily at her, but seeing the girl's stressed expression she tried a little ironic lightness. "Well, Anne, it's not often you're this quiet. The service this morning must have done you good."

"Oh, madam, I pray you are right. And that Lady Mary and all the saints guard and defend me, sinner that I am!"

Lady Margaret was surprised by the intensity, but thought Anne must still be dwelling on whatever had happened after the king's feast. "Come, child, make me one of your tisanes and then you can read to me from the prayers in the king's Book of Hours."

Master Mathew entered the solar a little time later, unobserved by his wife and her youngest maid. It was a charming picture he saw: his wife was in her bed, hair brushed and spread out over her shoulders like a child, and Anne was reading to her from the king's gift as the firelight winked in the precious stones on its cover.

Mathew felt the prick of tears behind his eyes. For a long time now he had suppressed the anguish Margaret's illness had brought him, striving hard to see it as God's will, but now, here, she was restored to him. He was a man of moderate appetites but he felt he had managed his restraint for long enough. He yearned for the closeness that flesh to flesh brought. He waited for Anne to finish reading her page and then applauded gently.

Margaret turned her head and saw him standing there. "Husband! Anne, pour your master some of the wine."

When the girl had brought Mathew the beaker, he saluted first his wife, and then Anne courteously, before taking a hearty swallow and walking over to the bed to kiss Margaret on the cheek.

Lady Margaret looked up into her husband's eyes and, seeing something of his intention, gently took his hand. Never taking her glance away from his, she said, "Anne, you may go down to the kitchen for a little time. I wish to speak with my husband alone. Please tell Aveline that the master and I will eat later."

Anne curtsied to her mistress and then her master, and backed away to the door. As she entered the stairwell she saw her master gently place his hand on Lady Margaret's breast, while she looked up at him, her face transformed with love and longing. The girl pulled the door closed, feeling desolate and alone. To see such tenderness, such trust, was to know what should be between a man and a woman. All she understood was fear and pain. And guilt. Quickly she fled down the stairs seeking a dark, warm corner of the kitchen to hide in until Deborah came.

Chapter Seven

 It was late, for Deborah and Anne could hear the midnight bell being rung from the Abbey.

True to her word, Deborah had come to the kitchen door after the household had bedded down for the night, and had found Anne waiting on a warm bench near the banked cooking fires. After her encounter with Piers, Anne was almost feverishly exhausted—his attacks on her seemed like a waking nightmare as they played and replayed in her mind. Earlier, she'd helped her mistress prepare for the night, after Mathew had left the solar. Changing from the damaged green dress—a dress she'd try never to wear again—into her house kirtle, she'd escaped to the kitchen to eat a very late supper and wait for her foster mother.

Anne wanted no prying eyes when Deborah at last arrived, even those of her friends, so she'd hurried her foster mother across the mud of the inner ward in biting sullen rain and together they'd disappeared down a flight of steps beside the washing house that led into the winter root cellar; it was one of the few private places in Blessing House where they could talk undisturbed. Once inside the door, Anne groped for the lantern she knew was stored on a stone shelf. She'd brought flint and, even though her fingers were stiff with cold, managed to strike a spark and then another that finally caught the flax wick of the tallow candle inside. That small wavering puddle of light pushed the darkness back from the barrels and racks of stored summer vegetables.

Deborah held out her arms, and Anne ran to her with a sob. Gently rocking, the older woman let the child cry as she murmured soothing words. After a time, the sobs subsided and she wiped Anne's hot cheeks with the hem of her own linen underkirtle. "I should like to help. Tell me."

Taking a deep, shuddering breath, the girl began her story, stumbling and tongue-tied as she searched for words to make sense of the conflicting emotions she'd felt—and was feeling still. Deborah's face became more and more severe, though she didn't interrupt Anne as she listened to the pain, the confusion, and the fear.

Finally, the girl was quiet and almost warm as the two of them cuddled together. Anne had trusted this woman all her life: and now there was the comfortable, familiar feeling that she was safe once more and close to sleep just like a comforted child.

The older woman looked down at the exhausted girl in her arms and sighed. "Come. It's late. We must be careful you are not missed."

Deborah helped the girl get to her feet. "Time for you to sleep—tomorrow is another day."

"But what can I do, Deborah?"

The older woman looked at Anne and smiled slightly. "Do? Many things. Pray to Christ's Mother, whose day this is. Avoid the king, should you meet him again." There was a momentary flash of resistance from Anne but Deborah held up one hand. "Girl, he is too powerful for you. As he is, and as you are. If you do not believe me, look into the flame with me . . . Perhaps Aine can help us—ask her to give you sight."

Anne shivered. She'd seen Deborah use candles often enough to concentrate her thoughts when she wanted to "see," or to seek guidance, but tonight, by invoking the name of Aine, the old goddess from over the sea in the west, whom the common people prayed to in matters of love and fertility, she was acknowledging that Anne's concerns were serious and needed more help than she herself could give.

As Deborah carefully slid back the horn shield to reveal the tallow candle inside the lantern, Anne took a deep shuddering breath. The goddess was not to be called on lightly, and Anne had never prayed to her before. "Look deep into the light, child. Give breath to the wavering flame . . . ask that Aine show you what you need to know." Her foster mother's voice was warm and low and comforting; since childhood, Anne had heard Deborah chanting to her plants under the waxing moon each night to make them grow in strength, and now the familiarity of the tone took her back to the security of the past, and she relaxed.

"Aine, Aine, Aine . . . come to me. Help me . . . help me see . . . help me know." It was an ancient, simple prayer and as Anne whispered the words three times, and then seven times more gazing deep into the candle flame, she began to float down deeper and deeper into shining darkness. And images formed—perfect small pictures as if from a Book of Hours—and she heard sounds . . .

First, there were the king's hands, holding hers, and she could see his face smiling down—but then he turned away and kissed the hand of a richly dressed blond woman, whose face she could not see, and slowly they both walked away from her. And then there was Piers, too, and Aveline, and the sound of a woman weeping. Heartbroken sobs, so deep and wrenching that they were wounds given sound . . .

Sadness and terror washed over her in a cold, lonely wave, so intense she found herself wailing with fear, and Deborah's arms were around her in the cold cellar again. She choked on the words as she tried to explain what she'd seen—her sense of loss and anguish so great it hurt her throat to speak of them.

Deborah held her and stroked her hair gently and rhythmically, and after a time, Anne relaxed and the fear and pain receded as Deborah spoke quietly about what should be done.

"Think carefully about what you saw. There is sadness and trouble here and Aine has given you a warning. The king has turned away from you and that may be a blessing. Do not try to see again until we are together once more, but you can ask help from the goddess when you need strength, and you can pray to the Lady Mary as well. The two of them will give wisdom when you need it. But Anne, always make sure you have someone with you as you work around the house . . ." She saw the look of panic on Anne's face, and said soothingly, "Sleep tonight. That is your greatest need.

In the morning, if you need me, I am at the Green Tabor, down in the East Chepe, and I shall stay there for two more nights. Perhaps I can speak to your mistress for you about Mathew Cuttifer's son, if you feel you cannot tell her about Piers—she is a good woman and clear-sighted."

Anne nodded gratefully, suddenly tired beyond speech.

Yet now, something had changed—she felt strengthened. The power of Aine, Mary's compassion, they would be both sword and breastplate in what was to come . . .

The rain had stopped when the pair doused the light of the lantern and pulled the door of the cellar closed behind them. After hugging Anne, Deborah hurried away into the darkness and Anne ran quickly back to the kitchen, knocking quietly to be let in. A very sleepy Melly pulled the door open just enough to let her friend slip through.

Aveline pretended to be asleep when she heard Anne burrow down under the coverings on her small pallet bed. She had been awake for the last two hours, waiting patiently for the dead heart of the night and the tolling of the midnight bell from the Abbey, when she would visit Piers as she had promised. But the bell had long since tolled, and it was her presumption that Anne had been with Mathew's son all this time—where else would she have been? And she'd lain there in the darkness becoming more and more furious.

Angry bile clogged her throat as she carefully rehearsed the speech she wanted to make to Piers, but she waited until Anne's breathing was even, before sliding from her bed. Quickly stepping into her linen underskirt and chemise, and draping a fur coverlet around her shoulders, she slipped out of the solar and down the quiet, dark passage that led to Piers's room. Surefooted and silent, she made her way to his quarters and saw a thread of light still slanting out from the gap under the door. Heart hammering with rage and anxiety, she paused for a moment as she forced herself to think. She must not alienate him now. If what she suspected was true—that he now preferred Anne—she would have to be very careful.

On the other side of the door, the fire in the room was burning low as Piers, on his father's orders, sat calculating the costs of the king's feast as penance for his clumsy behavior before the court. He was resentful, bored, and very tired. To his mind, he was treated worse than any of Mathew's clerks, for they, at least, were permitted to sleep! The door to his room squeaked—it was opening! The feathery hairs on the back of his neck rose when he saw a small white hand slide down the edge of the door as it was pushed inward.

"Who's there?" He was on his feet and in three long strides had flung the door open to reveal a kneeling woman, head bowed, hands clasped chastely in prayer before her chest. For a moment in the semidarkness, his eyes played tricks and he felt a flicker of disappointment: if Anne had come to him without compulsion, it took away some of the gloss. Then the woman raised her head. "Aveline!"

"Ah, my lord, do not be angry with me." The girl stretched out full length upon the flags, abasing herself like a penitent, modestly hiding her face with her hands.

"Well, girl, get up, get up." He pretended to be impatient, but then that was part of the game—a game they'd played many times before.

"Alas, lord, I fear that I cannot, for I am not decently dressed and merely wish to humbly confess my sins and beg for penance. Mortify my wicked sinful flesh, oh, my lord."

Piers looked down at her body stretched out under the fur covering and his groin stirred. The house was quiet and there were at least six hours of the night left; he'd forgotten that Aveline had said, earlier in the day, that she'd visit him after the feast.

Very well. Brutally, he grasped her wrists and pulled her into the room, kicking the door closed. She whimpered but said nothing as he dragged her over to his hearth, and then she lay still, on her belly, as he let her hands go. With the toe of one boot he flicked the fur bedcovering aside, revealing the girl in her bodice and undershift.

"Is this how you would confess? Half-naked? Speak!"

"Alas, lord, what would you have me do? I am a terrible sinner and deserve no pity. Do with me as you would, for admonition of my sins is yours to give."

How easily she twisted the words she'd learned in the confessional for his pleasure now. And how hard it had been to make her say them at first—he remembered that with a flicker of dark pleasure. How he'd enjoyed her fear of the Devil as he'd forced her to blaspheme while he raped her.

"Stand up!" His voice was harsh and thick with the memory of that first delicious time with Aveline. Quickly, she stood with hands crossed over her breasts and downcast eyes, the picture of the distressed innocent she'd once been.

For a moment all she could hear was his breathing, then he tore her chemise so violently the linen fell in two pieces to the floor. She was wearing nothing now but an underskirt, made transparent by the fire behind it. Roughly, he ran both hands over her breasts and torso, excited by her sharp intake of breath. Slipping one hand down her belly, his fingers slid between the fabric of the underskirt and her skin. She moaned slightly. "Silence! Penitents speak only when addressed."

He yanked hard and the waistband tore—the girl was naked, a pool of fabric around her feet on the floor.

He pulled her over to his great chair. "Kneel." His voice was hoarse. Obediently she sank to her knees as he tied her hands to the back of the chair with a strip of fabric he ripped from her skirt. "I am the Lord's instrument. Confess!"

"Oh, my lord, I confess to the mortal sin of lust." She whispered the words, so low he could hardly hear her.

He was standing behind her now, legs straddled, whip in hand. "Louder. Describe this sin to me." He swung the whip above his head and brought it down across her naked back.

She gasped. "Ah, lord, you hurt me, but no less than I deserve."

"Speak on for the good of your soul." His voice was a thick whisper now.

She swung her head forward modestly, using her hair as a cloak for her breasts. She was panting slightly and her words were sighs: "Lord, in my mind I have seen you enter me as beasts do in the field." Since she knew him so well, she lingered slightly on the word "enter," letting her little red tongue slip out between her lips to lick them. These were the times when she had power over Piers, no matter what he did to her, and she'd been able to use that power to advantage—a purse of money from time to time, even two pretty dresses that she took care to hide from Lady Margaret. Of course, she'd hated what he'd done to her at first, but had very quickly understood that, since there was no escape from him in this house, she could make him do what she wanted when she allowed him to degrade her. It was only her body he used—that was how she comforted herself—only her body, never her soul . . .

Now, saying nothing, he walked around her as she knelt naked on the floor. The thin stripes from the whip were deepening in color—she would be bruised tomorrow. He'd never gone so far as to mark her skin before; that thought was exciting for he'd tied her hands very securely and the chair was heavy; she'd not escape easily if he wished to experiment further. He smoothed out the tangled thongs of the whip as he paced.

"Woman, you know that you must mortify this corrupt and stinking flesh so that you sin no more. You will say the Paternoster on my command." He was standing behind her again now and could see the dark opening between her slightly parted thighs as she hung her head in apparent distress. Slowly and pleasurably he unlaced his codpiece. "Say the words."

"Our Father, which art in Heaven— Ah! Ah, sir, no!" He had allowed the thongs of the whip to flash up between her legs, finding her cleft.

"This is for your salvation. Now. Say it again." For a moment she could not speak because she was on fire with the intense pain, but then she stumbled on. "Our Father, which art in Heaven, hallowed be Thy name . . ."

As she repeated the words he forced her to stand, pushed her thighs apart, and rammed himself into her from behind, pulling her hips back and back until he ground her arse into his belly. The tearing pain of the cuts from the whip intensified her agony but he knew her well, for now she gasped with involuntary pleasure. Then both hands were on her breasts, massaging, tweaking her nipples, as he breathed hot into her ear: "You must be cleansed. Speak the words."

"Thy Kingdom come . . . Thy will be done . . ."

He was thrusting and grunting. "Yes, indeed, my will be done."
"In Heaven as it is on Earth."

Now he ripped her hands free and turned her around, pushing her backward into the huge chair. For a moment he looked at her naked body before he thrust back between her thighs with a groan. "Describe the pain of your penance."

"Ah, sir, you are tearing me apart in just retribution for my sinful thoughts." Against her will, she really was enjoying what he was doing now, and as he pushed her back and back with each thrust, she allowed herself to become limp, jerking back and forth as if he had speared her.

He growled with pleasure as he bucked and thrust into her unresisting body. "You are in need of more chastisement than I thought. I believe you are so far gone in sin that penance has become a pleasure to you." Again he pulled himself away; this time, grasping her by the hair, he wrenched her out of the chair and, forcing her back on her knees, picked up the whip. "Open your mouth. I must punish that which says such things."

Obediently, she knelt before him and opened her mouth, into which he plunged himself. "Unless you earn remission right well, I shall cut you harder. Suck!" He felt enormous, spearing down her throat, and even though she did what he demanded she felt the whip on her back again, and then again. Desperately, she slid her tongue and lips along the length of him, tasting herself, sliding back and forth and bobbing faster and faster as she felt the whip flick up and down her spine and buttocks.

The girl had a magnificent body, and the sight of her so busy with her lips and tongue as he lashed her was exquisite, but Piers could feel how close he was. "Enough. On your back."

Whimpering, she fell backward and obediently parted her thighs a little so that he could just see the dark pink opening between them. To make the moment last, he breathed deeply and took his time as she waited for him. "Wider so that I may view the entrance to the Devil's pit."

She did what he asked and as she saw him looking at her, fully exposed now to his gaze, an involuntary rippling shiver of deep pleasure ran through her.

"What are you here for, slut?"

"I am here for my penance, lord."

"And for my pleasure; is that not so?"

"Yes, lord," she whispered. She closed her eyes, moving her hips involuntarily

"Say it louder." He was stroking himself too as he looked down at her, writhing beneath him.

"I am here for your pleasure, lord." She began to whimper, as, with a roar he plunged into her with such force that she screamed and they both came; she helplessly clenching and unclenching around him and he shouting with a pleasure so intense it was close to pain.

After a time, Aveline became conscious that she was cold, or rather, the part of her facing the fire was hot but the rest of her felt the chill stone where she lay on the floor. Piers was sitting back at his worktable watching her—she could see his eyes glitter in the light of the flames. He got up and dropped the fur-lined coverlet over her body. She chanced a smile, which he did not answer as he walked over to the hearth; she sat up, aware the dice were in her hand and ready to be thrown.

"Piers?"

He was looking into the flames, not concentrating on what she was saying.

"We sort well together, you and I," she ventured.

"Well enough."

His tone was so cool it made her swallow the words she so wanted to say to him. Despairing, she forced herself to face the truth—pragmatism and survival had made her mold herself into what he'd wanted, but now there was Anne, and it was clear Piers was pursuing her in exactly the same way he had herself. They were both just bed sport and so he would never willingly couple his life with hers just because she carried his child—for that was the news she had for him.

With bitterness she understood, at last, that in failing to resist the corruption between them, it had tainted her soul. Her growing enjoyment of what he did to her told her that she'd made a bargain with the Devil, and now he wanted payment for the innocent life that was growing like a rose in the darkness between them. But the life of this child was also her one hope of salvation. Was she strong enough to protect it and, thus, herself?

"I will say good night, sir." It was an effort to keep her tone neutral. He remembered sufficient grace to brush her cheek with his lips as she slipped out of the door. Yawning mightily, he turned back to his fire and stretched with delicious exhaustion. Time to sleep. Damn the accounts; he would do them tomorrow, whatever his father said. And he would sleep well now. He laughed as he pulled off his clothes. Yes, he would sleep well this night.

Chapter Eight

Mathew Cuttifer was restless and worried. Cold gray sleet on the window underscored the loss of yesterday's pride in the king's favor, which had evaporated with the contents of the parchment just delivered to Blessing House and now lying unrolled and weighted down on his worktable.

Mathew was a prudent man and his prosperity owed much to his sources of information. He tried not to spend much time at court—unless it was to petition the king personally, or some of the greater magnates about the trading interests of his house—but he had taken care to plant one or two trusted men in the Palace of Westminster. And today Thomas Howe, a man he retained, attached to the Earl of Warwick as one of the earl's almoners, had written to him with tidings that made him nervous.

It seemed that Elizabeth Wydeville, Edward's queen, was making her move toward power by bringing members of her enormous family to court to build a political base, but she had grim opponents. Warwick would not forgive her for marrying the king in secret. As the king's most powerful vassal, the man who had put Edward on the throne, Warwick had negotiated a French marriage for Edward. In stealing the king from under his nose, Elizabeth had made Warwick the butt of jokes all over Europe. She, on the other hand, would not forgive Warwick for making his displeasure in her marriage so widely known at court. Mathew had important matters of trade patronage in play with both factions and the more he brooded on his situation the clearer it became. His burgeoning prosperity stood between two mighty and gathering forces and he would have to be very clever to steer a clear path for his household—and to see a return on the hefty parcel of money he'd outlaid in bribes to both sides to secure his trade interests. Perhaps the king himself would be his bulwark?

In times of real difficulty Mathew found comfort in prayer, even though the pain in his knees was close to unbearable if he knelt for any length of time. Gout, said the doctor, stop drinking. But Mathew had lived too long to give up wine. Pain or no pain, he would petition his God, and through long experience, he knew there would be an answer if he stilled himself to hear it.

The brazier in his chamber barely warmed the chill air and he was grateful for the marmot skins lining his good woolen robe as he carefully wrapped the skirts around his shanks and lowered himself onto the hard wood of the kneeling rail. A great concentrator, that piece of good oak—his confessor said lack of padding would help him to meditate on the sufferings of the Lord.

As he began to make his prayers to Mary the Mother of God, to whom he was especially devoted—and to whom his chapel was dedicated—another level of his mind considered the great cost of this prie-dieu. Made from oak cut on his own northern lands and fashioned and decorated by Maître Flamand, the Flemish master woodcarver, it had been inlaid with ivory and lignum vitae from Africa and had cost much more than he'd been quoted. But the piece itself was an investment; he could see that in the eyes of those who came to do business with him. His prie-dieu advertised his piety—and his substance as a man of business. Perhaps it lulled the unwary into thinking that he might be unworldly about money too. And that was a mistake.

He smiled faintly. Being thought unworldly gave him pleasure. Abruptly, he was aware that his thoughts had drifted. He composed himself with another Ave Maria and then one more. And then a fourth; but even with those ancient words he could not rid his teeming mind of the fear that lurked there. What he needed now was a sign of some sort, a sign that She was listening to him and would be prepared to intercede with her Son and bring him guidance.

There was a knock at his door. Straining to direct his prayers, to sink down into the familiar reverie, he ignored it. The knock was repeated and Mathew had become conscious of the hot pain in his knees; he allowed the agony to propel him to his feet—too fast, more pain. "Well!" he snapped, unreasonably angry.

Very cautiously the door opened and the housekeeper's anxious face could be seen. She was white and Mathew cooled a little. It must be important for Jassy to have knocked twice.

"Well, woman? What is so important that I must be driven from my prayers?"

Nervously, the housekeeper bobbed a curtsy. "Sir, Lady Margaret has asked if you may wait on her. There is a matter . . . that is, your wife, sir, feels that . . ." And here the poor woman stumbled to a halt.

Against his will Mathew was intrigued. Jassy was his most trusted servant. She had been brought up in his parents' household and had been his housekeeper through his entire adult life—and his three marriages. Some days, when there was no one to hear, she would call him Mathew and he would call her Phillipa or even Pip in memory of their shared childhood. It amused him sometimes that his household thought her so formidable, because he remembered the stick-thin little girl who used to steal apples with him and who as a young maiden so plainly loved him; sometimes he suspected she still did. But he'd never taken advantage of his position as son of the house where she was concerned, to his credit he believed. His tone softened.

"Now, Pip, what's this?"

"Sir, I feel that Lady Margaret really does need to speak to you." She refused to say more, folding her lips quite firmly, and would not look him in the eye.

Mathew grunted, waving her on as he followed her out of his study. He was not ungrateful for the interruption; perhaps his mind would clear for thinking of something else, some trivial household matter. And as he followed Jassy through the house, approving of the industry he saw all around him and the quiet order of the place, it gave him great pleasure to think of entering his wife's solar, especially since she no longer kept to her bed. Shortly, she would resume full control of his household and he would once more enjoy her company and astute advice—for which he did not cease to thank his special patron, the Holy Lady Mary.

But the atmosphere in his wife's room was very far from the peace he had been expecting. He found Margaret seated in her chair in front of the fire, dressed in a somber velvet gown with a plain but good linen coif on her head. Beside her was another chair, which was empty. His wife looked so severe that she might have been a statue of some saint, or an angel of God, sitting in judgment—he had rarely seen her look like this and was surprised to find himself intimidated for a moment. It did not do to forget her breeding; she was the lady of his house in more than one sense, and whatever her expression, it gave him great joy to see her so blooming again.

Rather to his own surprise, he found himself bowing to his wife and kissing her hand formally as if he were still a suitor in her father's house. That little gesture brought a slight smile from her as she stood to receive him.

"Jassy, you may go, but please be aware that I may require you shortly," Margaret said, and the housekeeper scuttled out of the room, a remarkable sight in one so dignified and stately.

"Husband, I have asked to speak to you because I am perplexed and concerned."

"Speak on, wife," Mathew replied as he seated himself beside his wife. Carefully, Margaret arranged the folds of her gown, composing her words. Mathew waited patiently.

"Mathew, I must speak to you about your son. I believe he has debauched Aveline and, if this proves true, we have the future of this unfortunate girl and her baby to consider. As well as the state of his immortal soul."

Mathew was not a man to allow his feelings to control him, but this was too much. All his unacknowledged envy of his son's youth, inflamed by corrosive disapproval of Piers's constant gambling and drinking, coupled with the nagging fear he still felt from this morning's message out of the palace, now had a focus and he allowed himself to become very angry indeed: "Where is Piers? What does he say?"

Soothingly, Margaret touched his arm, surprised by his ferocity. "I have only yet spoken to the girl. We do not have any but her word for it and I thought it best you should speak to Piers after you have heard her story."

Mathew searched for composure as Margaret walked over to the garderobe and opened the door. She beckoned and Aveline entered the solar, eyes downcast, hands clenched together. Margaret resumed her seat beside Mathew and left the girl standing in front of them.

"Now, Aveline, tell your master what you told me this morning."

Aveline cleared her throat and opened her mouth to speak. Twice she tried to force sound out of her throat but nothing would come. She burst into tears and slid down onto the floor at their feet—a pathetic sight if one were prepared to be moved.

Margaret let the girl cry herself out, conscious that Mathew was barely restraining his impatience. The sobs diminished, and Margaret said, "We are both quite ready to listen, Aveline."

"Oh, sir, madam, I hardly know how to begin."

"I suggest you find a way, girl." The dangerous edge to Mathew's voice worked wonders.

"He raped me, sir; and I was frightened. He made me do such things . . . and swore that if I told anyone, anyone at all, I should be whipped out of town, but now . . ."

Fresh tears slid down the pretty face. Mathew saw she was one of those lucky women who could cry without disfiguring herself— a useful asset.

"And now, Aveline?" Margaret's tone was gentle but firm.

"Madam, I am more than four months gone." It was said in an appalled whisper and the girl tried to make herself an even smaller bundle at their feet, desperate to swallow her sobs.

Mathew felt a stirring of pity. He'd never greatly liked this girl but she'd come into the household with his wife when she'd been eleven or twelve and Margaret had always valued her. He'd never had cause to chastise Aveline, but this was a different matter.

"Where is my son?"

Aveline looked up terrified and Margaret calmed her as if she were a frightened animal. "Hush, girl. He will not hurt you. Mathew, you must speak to him."

"Sir, and madam, I have not told him. He may refuse to own my child." It was said forlornly and for a moment Mathew felt relief. That was it, this girl was trying to trap his son—perhaps, indeed fairly likely, the child was not Piers's get.

Piers was in the stable yard of Blessing House having a long, boring, and frustrating conversation on his father's instructions, trying to extract information as to why the feed bills for their London operation were currently so enormous; Mathew suspected his London servants were skimming profits, hence Piers's attempts to interrogate Perkin Wye, the longtime stablemaster.

The stablehands were watching the conversation in the yard with covert interest. Not many of them liked Piers, but Perkin had a heavy hand and they'd be pleased to see him done down for once.

"Master Piers, your father has often and often said that I have the best-kept tally of all in this house. Plain as day, clear as water, set out for all the world to see!"

"Perkin, my father still has concerns and so do I. The price of the barley you bought this last week for instance."

"Ah, sir, this last wet summer rotted most of the standing grain. What's left to buy is poor quality and more expensive than it's ever been."

It was at this point that Anne hurried into the yard looking for Piers. She'd been sent by Jassy to find him and given no time to protest as she and several of the household staff were sent off in all directions over the house. He saw her and smiled charmingly, though his eyes were hard and bold. She looked at him straight back and, taking a deep breath to control the quiver in her voice, told him his mother and father wanted to speak to him in the solar.

"And will you light the way, sweet Anne?"

"No, sir, I am needed elsewhere; but Mistress Jassy did stress that your parents are waiting."

He frowned slightly, then gave an exaggerated bow to her—as if she were some great lady paying him the courtesy of a visit—and sauntered out of the yard, saying as he went, "Don't think I've forgotten we need to finish our conversation, Perkin. I shall return directly."

However, Piers wasn't thinking of barley or Anne as he pushed the solar door open. It was rare to receive a summons to see both his father and Margaret together in the middle of a working day, so that made him cautious. As well it might, for, entering the room, he saw a tableau that could well have come straight off the walls of the Abbey Church. His father, seated in a thronelike chair; his stepmother, composed, regal, the folds of her gown so carefully arranged they might have been carved out of Purbeck marble; and Aveline—standing beside his mother, eyes modestly downcast, but . . . what? What did she look like? Walking closer, he saw the tracks that tears had made down the pretty face, and the white clenched knuckles of the tightly clasped hands. And then it came to him: the penitent Magdalene.

His father spoke. "Aveline. Repeat what you have told me and your mistress." The girl did not look up and, in a voice that was so low Piers had to strain to hear, said, "I am with child. Your son is the father."

The silence in the room grew as they all waited for him to say something. He wanted to—glib words formed on his tongue, nearly got out of his mouth, but he stopped them. Time stretched as he tried to muster his wits. He shivered involuntarily. "Father . . . I—"

"Piers, I am ready to hear what you say, but consider very carefully. Your mother and I want only the truth." His father's voice was surprisingly restrained. The two women remained utterly silent.

"Father—and you, Mother—I cannot be the father of this girl's child for I have never slept with her."

"Liar." The word was quietly spoken but said with complete certainty and Aveline was no longer looking at the floor. She was staring directly into his face and daring him to meet her eyes.

Mathew Cuttifer made up his mind—there was a way to settle this. He turned to Margaret. "Please take Aveline and Piers to the chapel. I will join you shortly. And you, sir—and you, girl"—he looked directly at them both—"spend the time on your knees before your God." He rose grimacing at the pain from his knees—seized up by sitting so long—and left the solar.

Aveline looked unwaveringly across at Piers, her expression composed and distant. Now she'd said what she had to say, she felt detached, though there was a soft fluttering in her belly, a poignant reminder that her body, and its occupant, felt fear even if she refused to acknowledge it.

Piers ignored her. "Mother, whatever Aveline has said to you, I ask you to believe that I am not, cannot be, the father of her child."

"I am not your mother, Piers." Margaret's tone was neutral but the severity in her eyes warned him to be silent. "Come, Aveline, wipe your face before we go."

There was a hasty knock at the little door that led on to the stairs to the kitchen and as Anne hurried through she saw something she had never seen before: Aveline, vulnerable. The older girl cast one quick glance at Anne and ran toward the garderobe. A moment later they all heard the unmistakable sounds of vomiting.

"Piers," Margaret said, "you will accompany me to the chapel. Anne, please bring Aveline to me there when she has composed herself." Piers did not acknowledge Anne as he stalked past her, furious, followed by Margaret, the new Book of Hours held gracefully between her hands.

In the silence of the empty room Anne heard Aveline vomit again. Collecting her wits, she dipped a cloth in water from the brass washing bowl and silently joined the older girl as she knelt over the stinking hole in the garderobe.

Aveline raised her pale face and smiled bitterly at Anne. "Well, Anne, you'll know soon enough. I am quick with Piers's child." Her stomach heaved again and she threw up thin green mucus—there was nothing left in her belly. Anne hurried forward and, before Aveline could protest, wiped her forehead with the cool, damp cloth.

Anne shuddered. This could have been her—how close both of them stood to the edge of ruin, all because of Piers. Truly this city was a savage place, much more frightening than the untracked forest and wild beasts who dwelt among the trees. They killed because they were hungry—they did not destroy for sport, as Piers did. Aveline was in a desperate state and the future for her and her child was frightening. Perhaps she would be cast out, as Piers had said, and then who would help her?

Heart clenched with pity, Anne gently kissed Aveline on the brow. "I shall pray for you and the baby, Aveline. There is always help, if you know where to look for it."

Poor Aveline. It was such a long time since anyone had been truly kind to her. The fierce pride that had always been her guardian and friend began to crack, so that Anne saw, for the first time, that Aveline was not much older than she was and a lot less sure—of anything.

Chapter Nine

Even midsummer did not take the cold edge out of the air in the chapel of Blessing House and now, deep into winter, the place felt like a cave. The space for the chapel had been made by removing the floor between a disused storage loft, partly built into the thickness of the walls that faced the river, and a large belowground undercroft. It was opulent but dark though there was a fine, small choir gallery above the expensively tiled floor and, in the main body of the chapel, a number of carved oak stalls for Mathew and his family placed as near to the altar table as was decent. Rows of plain wooden benches stood behind for his household: men on one side, women on the other.

Mathew had taken great pleasure in having this family chapel dedicated to Our Lady and he'd spared no expense creating a space filled with beauty and richly glowing color in her honor. He was particularly proud of the fashionable, very costly Flemish-style frescoes he'd had painted at the altar end of the chapel. His favorite was Adam's expulsion from the garden with the penitent Eve pursued by Satan in the form of a wily snake. The other fresco he'd always been less certain about—it was so lifelike it made him uncomfortable when he looked at it. Its theme was the separation of the Saved from the Damned at the Last Judgment, and the expression on the Lord's face was utterly pitiless as he thrust the screaming, naked men, women, and children down into the arms of waiting black devils, while His Holy Mother, painted to look a little like Margaret, tried to intercede with her Son out of pity.

Since it was the current custom in both Flanders and Italy, Mathew had also included himself and his family in the judgment painting. It always gave him a guilty frisson of pleasure to see his painted likeness, and that of all three of his wives plus Piers and Alicia his daughter—now married and living in the north—kneeling below Our Lady, eyes fixed on Christ Pantocrator in all his fearful glory. He'd wondered whether it was blasphemy to place himself and his family so close to Christ, but Father Bartolph, his confessor and private family chaplain, reassured him.

The subject matter of the paintings was surely designed to bring the penitent to God through the intercession of his Holy Mother. She would understand that his humble desire to be painted kneeling close to her son was the expression of a grateful heart dedicated to her service. And besides, it set a good example to the household to see their master and his family so close to members of the Holy Family: it gave them something to aspire to. Father Bartolph also said that the colors on the frescoes remaining so bright, among the smoke from the candles, the oil lamps, and the incense, was a clear indication of her favor toward this place and its owner.

Now Piers and Aveline knelt before the altar on each side of Lady Margaret, who occupied the time waiting for her husband by counting off prayers on her fine onyx rosary.

Aveline shivered with cold and tension, but silently continued to implore the Mother of God to hear her prayers. She would understand what it was like to be alone and fighting for yourself in a heartless world. Life was so unfair. Why could she not have been a lady with fine clothes and a complacent husband, rather than the illegitimate daughter of a minor squire in the West Country? Her father, trying to do what he could for her, had placed her as a child in Lady Margaret's family home where she'd done well—and she'd been overjoyed to go with Margaret to London when her mistress married Master Mathew. As she grew into late girlhood she'd taken care to learn the ways of the polite world so as to please her mistress, and she'd realized early that men wanted her, not for her manners but for her body. Using her wits and sometimes her strength, she'd fought them off—not always easily—until Piers had forced her into his bed. Those first few desperate contests had left her with bite marks on her breasts and torn thighs, but then the fight she put up became something else, and in submitting to him, she'd begun to feel physical pleasure among the pain and fear. Yet, in her heart there was dark confusion and shame—but shame, even now, she had to suppress, both for survival and because she could not bear to leave London; she would not be sent back to the country to bear this child in disgrace, branded a slut, with no future but to prostitute herself in some stew in a provincial town.

Her resolve strengthened. Yes, with Our Lady's help she would find a way to have Piers as her husband, dowerless and pregnant as she was, for she had nothing to lose. She would become a lady and she would protect this child and, with the help of Christ's Mother, eventually atone for all the mortal sin Piers had forced on her, and that she had learned to enjoy, to the peril of her soul.

She squeezed her eyes shut and repeated the Ave Maria faster, doing all that she could to push away the certainty that she'd embarked on a terrifying course. Today Piers truly hated her—could that be turned? Could hate be turned, if not to love, then tolerance? Would she have the strength? Unconsciously her hands strayed to her belly and stayed there. Mary would understand.

Silently, Father Bartolph arrived and lit the two tall candles on either side of the altar table. As the priest opened the ornate little casket in which dwelt the body of the Lord, Mathew arrived in the chapel and knelt before his own stall, crossing himself with an unconscious sigh.

Piers noticed with a start that the priest was dressed in his full regalia as if about to say Mass, and he felt Father Bartolph's eyes bent severely upon him as he turned to face the little congregation of four people kneeling before the altar.

"In nomine Patris, et Filii, et Spiritus Sancti. Amen."

Automatically, Piers muttered "Amen" as his stomach clenched with confusion and fear. His initial response in Margaret's solar had been to deny what Aveline had said, but now he was feeling uncertain. He knew that his father, above all things, despised him when he lied and was caught out in it; perhaps he should have confessed to the sexual relationship—got it over—but there was no way he was going to own to a child in Aveline's belly. The girl was a slut, her behavior with him proved that; she loved what he did to her. No doubt there were others in the house who had also enjoyed what she had to offer.

The priest spoke, interrupting Piers's uneasy thoughts. "Aveline, and Piers, would you come here to the altar, please."

The girl got to her feet gracefully and with modestly downcast eyes stepped daintily up the three shallow steps to where Father Bartolph stood holding the Host.

Piers had no choice, and he felt his father's eyes bore into his back as he went to the altar to stand beside the girl. Even then in the midst of his rage he found himself noticing the smooth white swell of her breasts at the top of her gown, and a brief image of her naked, lying with legs splayed wide at their last encounter, distracted him momentarily from what the priest was saying.

"I am going to ask you both to swear an oath before God and on the body of His most precious Son. If you lie you will imperil your immortal soul and when Christ comes in his judgment you will surely join the host of the damned who writhe eternally in hellfire."

Involuntarily, both Aveline and Piers looked up to the fresco above them and just as quickly dropped their eyes—the images were too graphic.

"Aveline, you stand before your God and His Mother, just as you, Piers, stand here before your earthly parents who are God's own deputies on earth."

The girl shivered, and though she had had nothing to eat since breaking her fast after Mass at dawn, another wave of nausea spread throughout her body, making its way inexorably toward her throat. She could almost smell the roasting flesh and hear the screams of the sinners cast into the fiery pit. Sheer will alone kept her on her feet, mouth clenched shut, when she felt like howling with despair; she knew that she had to win this contest with Piers or she was doomed here on this earth too.

Father Bartolph held out the box containing the Host to Aveline and signaled that she should place her right hand upon it. "Aveline, you have accused your master's son of rape and now say that you are carrying his child. In the name of God and the Holy Virgin, and in fear for your immortal soul, do you still say that this accusation is true?"

Sweat ran down her sides, but Aveline looked directly into the severe brown eyes of the priest and spoke without hesitation. "I swear by Our Lady, her precious Son, and by God himself that Piers is the father of my child and that he forced me against my will."

Now the priest held out the box to Piers. Reluctantly, he placed his right hand on the cold metal. "Piers, you have heard Aveline swear before God. Do you still say now, before your father on earth and your Father in Heaven, that she is lying?"

Piers was not religious but he was superstitious, and now, standing before the altar beneath the images of naked men and women tumbling down into Hell and the waiting pitchforks of demons, he was stunned to find that he could not say the words of denial.

"Piers, I ask you once more. In the name of the Father of us all, and his Son, and his Holy Mother, are you the father of Aveline's child?"

In agony, Piers burst out, "If she is with child, perhaps it could be mine since I have known her; but she is a slut who came willingly to me after many other poor fools had been there before. She begged me on her knees to—"

"Enough! This is God's house." Mathew's disgusted roar cut across his son's words as he strode forward. Before the priest could stop him, Mathew hit Piers around the head with his clenched fists. And with that, Aveline fainted, striking her forehead hard on one of the stone steps as she fell, leaving blood on the pale marble.

The priest was paralyzed by the drama being played out in front of him, but not Lady Margaret. "Husband!" The word was said quite sharply and it was enough to turn all three men's faces toward her. Lady Margaret knelt down beside the unconscious girl on the floor and then spoke quietly once she had their attention.

"Piers, please go to Anne in the solar; ask her to come to me here. She must bring linen and water." As the young man started on his way, almost flinching as he went past his father, she added "And then stay in your room until you are called. Father Bartolph, I ask you now to pray for us all."

Silently, the priest nodded and then saw with relief that the girl was stirring.

"Husband, we have much to discuss. May I come to you a little later in your workroom?" Margaret asked.

Not for the first time Mathew was filled with admiration for his wife's breeding. Her training as a child had taught her the art of managing difficult situations with restraint and tact. She gave him the confidence to act correctly, and with dignity, when he needed it most. "Wife, I shall expect you there," he replied as he straightened his gown and stalked out of the chapel without so much as a glance back at the green-faced girl, now being held up by his wife.

Some moments later, Anne, hurrying down the passage, curtsied and pressed herself back against the stone wall outside the chapel to let Mathew pass, trying not to spill the water in her basin. Mathew did not even see her as he strode away to his workroom, deep in thought.

Balancing the brass basin in the crook of an arm, Anne knocked at the chapel door. It opened silently and Father Bartolph pointed toward the two women on the steps of the altar. Anne was truly shocked to see Aveline, lying like a corpse with blood covering half of her face. She hurried to her mistress as the priest retreated in silence to his robing room.

Anne knelt down beside Lady Margaret on the cold stone floor and, without waiting to be told, dampened the cloth she had brought, gently starting to sponge away the blood on Aveline's face. For Lady Margaret it was a profound relief not to have to talk, or answer questions, and she was grateful for Anne's silent competence.

Aveline was beyond tears as well as speech now. She half lay across Lady Margaret's lap and her still, pallid face did not change as Anne wiped the blood away and then held the linen firmly against the gash on her forehead.

"Lady Margaret, shall I take Aveline back to the solar? I can change this linen and bind a pad of it to her head. The bleeding will stop very soon."

Wearily, the older woman nodded assent, and between them, Anne and Margaret lifted Aveline to her feet where she stood swaying slightly, as if her legs were no real support. Anne put an arm around her waist to brace her and Aveline leaned gratefully into her shoulder as the two walked slowly out of the chapel.

In the solar, Aveline lay on her pallet, eyes open but saying nothing. She'd managed to make it back with Anne's support, but once there she'd collapsed. She was not a stupid girl, but after this morning she realized she had been very naïve. While she knew that Mathew Cuttifer was a just man, he would be most unlikely to accept her as a daughter-in-law: she'd seen that in his face. She and this child were a problem to solve, to square with his conscience and honor, but there'd been no pity for her, only anger at the action of his son. Her best hope for marriage, and a name for this baby, lay with Lady Margaret. She closed her eyes and felt lonelier than at any other time in her life. Determined not to let Anne see her weakness, she turned her face toward the wall and tried to stifle her sobs. Soon exhaustion overcame her and she slept.

Gently, so as not to wake Aveline, Anne spread an extra coverlet over the sleeping girl. In the clear light of late morning she looked very young and vulnerable, the usual guardedness gone, and it was possible to see the little girl she had once been. And Anne was touched when Aveline turned her face and, for a moment, smiled in her sleep, the tension melting away as her brow smoothed out.

For Piers, there was no such blessed relief. Up and down he paced, crossing and recrossing his room, trying to think his way through the situation. What would his father do? Mathew Cuttifer, above all else, feared offending his God, and his father's morbidly active sense of sin had been a powerful presence as Piers grew up; illicit carnality—possibly because Mathew denied it to himself—filled his father with special horror.

For many years now Piers had managed to avoid marriage and find sexual pleasure secretly on his own terms. It was the only rebellion he had managed against the path his father had so rigidly allotted him as eldest, and only, son of his house.

There'd been two other girls before Aveline, both of them former maids in the household, and he'd congratulated himself on how neatly he'd been able to remove them from his life when the inevitable happened. It was one of the reasons he liked very young virgins: they'd never been a match for him in will or cunning and they always fell in love with him—something he'd encouraged, as it lessened the chances of their sleeping with other men and thereby helped ensure they caught no diseases that could be passed on to him.

Aveline was something else. If he wasn't so angry and frightened now, he could almost admire the cool way she'd played the only hand she had. He was almost certain that she hadn't been with anyone else from the time he'd first raped her.

A tentative knock brought him back to the reality of the present. "What?" he spat. After a moment's hesitation the door eased open and John, his gap-toothed servant, scuttled into the room.

"Sir, your father asks that you join him in his closet."

A pewter mug, accurately thrown, caught John on the side of the head and the young man gasped and fell to his knees, one hand cupping his ear. He could feel the blood welling up but he said nothing: these moods brought out the worst in his master.

"Oaf! Get out of my sight and tell my father . . . tell him . . ."

Perversely, the kneeling boy enraged Piers further. Changing his mind, he strode out of the room, aiming a solid kick at the boy as he passed. "I want this place spotless on my return. Spotless! Hear me, or it will be worse for you." And then he was gone, the door slamming after him.

John breathed deeply and got up rubbing his back, looking for a rag to stanch the blood from his ear. He'd clean the chamber—scour it—but not for one moment would he stop thinking of ways to leave the cursed employment of the son of Blessing House.

In his closet, Mathew Cuttifer had been pacing, too, as he listened to what his wife had to say. Lady Margaret sat on a prettily carved backless chair, Roman style, shaped in the form of a graceful X, as she calmly dissected the situation between Piers and Aveline.

"We have looked for a bride for Piers these eight years or more,

Mathew, and yet none of the contracts has come to completion. I know that the first girl died and the second took the veil in the end, yet it seems to me a number of quite respectable families have been unwilling to commit their daughters to your son. In another man's case I would call this bad luck or ill fame—but I wonder now if it is not God's will?"

Mathew frowned. He could hear the way his wife's thoughts were trending and he was reluctant to face the implications of what she was saying. Marriage contracts, marriage contracts. They always caused so much grief but, of course, in uncertain times, family alliances were vital weapons in the battle to survive. He'd always planned for his son making a grand match: one that would bring honor and increased substance to his house. But now . . .

"Mathew?"

He turned to look at Margaret and for a moment was distracted by her beauty, forgetting to answer.

She smiled faintly. "Ah, my dear. I am a lucky woman."

He sighed deeply. "You believe the child is his?"

"I do, husband. And now you must decide what God would wish us to do."

Mathew sighed again. Margaret was right, he would have to ask his God. Unwillingly, he knelt at the prie-dieu—could he face what God might have to say to him?

Piers arrived at the door of his father's closet and stood for a moment before knocking, composing what he wanted to say. He knew his father needed him to help run the business of Blessing House but he was under no illusion that he would not be punished if Mathew decided to accept Aveline's story. The question was, what kind of punishment would he have to bear?

The door stood before him, blank, black with age. How many times had he waited, a knot in his stomach, for his father to summon him to the other side? Fear, with an undertone of anger, this was what the door called out of him. He hesitated another moment and struck the door sharply. He was a man, not a child.

Margaret opened the door to her stepson and signaled that he should enter quietly, making him aware that his father was praying. Sullenly, Piers walked over to the brazier and held up his hands to the meager heat, while he waited for his father to finish his prayers.

Spine held straight, Margaret sat and took out the little Book of Hours the king had given her, leafing through carefully to find the prayers suitable for times of trouble. This was most unpleasant for them all and she needed to settle her mind before dealing with what must surely come.

The silence deepened. There was nowhere for Piers to sit and he became increasingly impatient and agitated—how long would his father's prayers last?

Mathew's impassive profile was outlined against the winter light of the small-paned window. It had been fully fifteen minutes since his son arrived and, though he was still deep in meditation, the bells from the Abbey were calling him, making him aware that the dialogue with his Savior had ended and he was back in the closet after being . . . where? Somewhere else, somewhere infused with the Presence . . . And now, he knew what had to be done. As briskly as he could, allowing for the burning ache in his knees, he got up, nodded to his son in an almost friendly fashion, and walked to his worktable, aware he was feeling strangely calm.

"Piers, I have prayed for guidance in the matter of . . . Aveline"—strange how she had changed from a servant to a girl worthy of consideration—"and the baby; and I feel that God has guided me toward what must be done."

Piers felt the sweat gather and slide down his sides, for all that the room was cold.

"It is God's will that you and this girl should be married. No—" He held up his hand as Piers tried to speak. "I do not pretend that this girl is the bride I would have chosen for you, portionless and a serving maid, but did not Ruth—and Hagar even—prove their worth in the eyes of God, humble women though they were? Our Lord has told me that this child is yours. It is time you faced your responsibilities as its father, and my son."

Margaret looked from her implacable husband to Piers, his face a fierce red, and even though she approved of the outcome, she felt fearful. Piers was not a boy—even if Mathew treated him like one. It was the fury of a man she saw; a vengeful man.

But Mathew did not see the expression on his son's face, so intent was he on conveying God's will. "This . . . Aveline and you will sort well together. God has told me that. You are of a kind; she is clever, I believe." He looked at his wife for affirmation. Margaret nodded. "And she will be a good helpmeet to you; better able to tolerate the hard work of a merchant's house and its interests than some of the fine young ladies of the court we have dangled for. And besides, I will not have bastards of my house thrown out into the streets as a reproach to me and mine." Again Piers attempted to speak. "No! You will hear me out!" Mathew continued.

"This is your sin and you must work your penance through. I shall ask your stepmother to convey my wishes to Aveline: you must prepare for your wedding. Tonight, before the household, I shall announce it and we will seek leave to have the mass performed under special license by Father Bartolph."

Now at last Piers managed to break in, the words forced out through clenched teeth. "Father, I will not wed this slut. How can I be sure the child is mine?"

"Silence! You sacrifice your immortal soul in opposing God's will! This is my house, I am your earthly father but your greater lies in Heaven. If you attempt to defy me in this, it will be to your eternal shame and damnation. I shall cast you out and raise this child in your place."

The two men stared at each other and, as usual, Piers was the first to look down. But Margaret was unsettled to see that the expression on the young man's face was hate, not fear. And suddenly, her vigorous husband looked old—and helpless. Quickly, she stepped into the breach.

"Piers, I suggest that you go about the affairs of this house in your normal manner. After all, there is much to do. We shall speak of this again later, after evening prayers when we are all a little cooler."

Without a further word, Piers left the room, banging the closet door behind him with a mighty clap, as Mathew slumped into his work chair, exhausted and distressed. Margaret went to him and touched him gently on the arm.

"Now, husband, the worst is over. There will be malicious tongues, but they will soon find something else to rattle over. We must be proud and silent. No explanations."

Speechless, he nodded without opening his eyes until he felt her soft kiss on his mouth. And then he wrapped his arms around her and was not ashamed to let her see the dismay and uncertainty on his face.

News travels very fast around a great house. Perhaps it was what the priest had hinted at when he had his small beer after Mass in the kitchen; or maybe it was the look on Piers's face, and the viciousness he visited on the youngest stable boy, that told its own story, but by the time the household was assembled for evening prayers in the chapel at the end of a tumultuous day, each one of them was avid for confirmation of the rumors.

It had been a difficult day for Anne as her friends in the household pleaded for information—even Jassy had unbent sufficiently to question her about what had happened in the chapel. But pity for Aveline and fear of Piers had kept her silent.

For Aveline, the afternoon had been a light-headed blur. And now, when she heard her name called out by Mathew after the evening blessing delivered by Father Bartolph, she rose unsteadily from her seat beside Anne and had trouble putting each foot in front of the other as she walked toward Piers, aware of the greedy glances of the household all around her.

Piers, too, had risen, and was standing beside his father, next to Lady Margaret in front of the altar, his back to the congregation, face remote as stone. As the girl took her place beside Piers and his family, Father Bartolph cleared his throat nervously and would have begun his prayers to mark the betrothal, except that Mathew held up his hand for silence.

"My people, this is a night of celebration in Blessing House. Tonight you see before you my son Piers, and Aveline, chief servitor of your mistress, my wife Lady Margaret. We have decided that this pair shall marry and shortly Father Bartolph will pronounce the necessary prayers to mark this time, and read the banns. And indeed, very soon there will be a marriage here when these two will be joined, man and wife. We ask God's blessing on their union."

A buzz ran around the people gathered in the chapel but the stern expression on Mathew's face quelled it quickly. He looked around for a moment, seeking out evidence of unseemly emotions among his household, then nodded to the priest. Father Bartolph hastily signaled that Aveline and Piers should kneel, and gabbled out a stream of Latin, finding it hard to control his shaking voice.

At the back of the chapel Anne breathed deeply and clenched her hands tightly together in prayer so that the knuckles showed under the skin. This was the moment that should have released her from fear of Piers, so why did she feel such terror, so many dark thoughts? She ducked her head, afraid that those next to her would sense her agitation, and tried to concentrate on what the priest was saying.

The prayers were quickly over and the congregation rose as the newly betrothed couple linked hands and followed Mathew and his wife out of the chapel. Then came the household, which left in order of precedence, none daring to say a word until they had hurried safely away from the family part of the house.

Aveline's hand was cold, Piers's was warm, but he dropped hers as soon as they walked out of the chapel, and the look he gave her made Aveline's stomach lurch. He stalked off to his room, leaving her standing alone in the great receiving hall, the household streaming past casting sly looks in her direction.

Coming out of the chapel at the tail of the crowd, Anne saw the distress beneath the pride. The frozen look on Aveline's face spoke clearly of the humiliation she felt, and yet there was a certain forlorn magnificence in her refusal to turn and walk away from all the mocking glances. She held her head up and returned each glance, her face flushed, back rigid with defiance.

Anne hurried over and, sketching a slight but definite curtsy, carefully picked up part of the skirt at the back of Aveline's dress, managing to hold it out in such a way as to suggest a train. Lady Margaret observed Anne's kindness and approved it.

"Aveline, Master Mathew and I would like you to join us in the solar. There is much to discuss. Anne will attend you." Margaret's voice was a rope thrown to the drowning. But Aveline had enough instinctive dignity to bow gracefully to her future mother-in-law, before her erstwhile employers led her toward the stairs to the solar, Anne holding out the "train" of her dress as if it were a coronation gown. Distant thunder rumbled as they walked. It would be a cold, wild night.

Chapter Ten

A month had passed and Blessing House was again in an early stir. Aveline and Piers's marriage would take place this morning, and after the ceremony, held by custom at the door of the chapel, Father Bartolph would sing a Mass, then there would be feasting for the household and guests.

After the betrothal, Anne and Aveline had been given a tiny chamber all to themselves in the thickness of the tower wall—Anne now slept on a palliasse at the foot of Aveline's new wooden bedstead—and each night for twenty-nine nights, Aveline had lain, half waking, half sleeping, on the first feather mattress of her life under a fine woolen rug lined with catskins. The unaccustomed luxury had made little difference to Aveline's dreams, though. Often Anne was woken by Aveline crying in her sleep, the older girl always refusing to talk about her fears in the morning.

In the last few days, Aveline's retching had finally stopped but she'd lost so much weight her hipbones stood out painfully and her knees and elbows were sharp though, as yet, only the slightest roundness to her belly hinted at the pregnancy. Anne had, unbidden, prepared against the inevitable by letting out the seams of Aveline's few house dresses, and the one good dress of copper-colored wool that Aveline now wore every day to the chapel services.

Anne knew, too, of the humiliations the last few weeks had brought to Aveline—the source of the many bitter tears shed by the older girl in the privacy of their tiny room, though she did her best to hide them from Anne.

Mathew Cuttifer had sought out Aveline's father to speak about a marriage settlement; he'd been willing to attend the wedding but, being a poor man, knight or not, he was truly unable to do anything financially for his illegitimate daughter. After only token negotiations between the men, a settlement of sorts, which Mathew largely financed, had been drawn up. In real terms, Aveline brought nothing to this marriage, not even an honorable name, and so it was a poor, one-sided agreement. However, in the event of Piers's death she would be given a modest living, just as if she had brought a dowry to the family table. Lady Margaret had even provided the gown in which Aveline would be married today—heavy, scarlet velvet trimmed with miniver around the neck—and with Anne's capable help, it had been cleverly altered to fit her now spare body; another humiliation.

It was time to face this day.

Anne set the brass ewer full of hot water down on Aveline's small wooden coffer—another donation from the Cuttifers—as she gently woke the bride-to-be.

Aveline saw that she was hiding something nervously behind her back. "What is it, girl? What do you conceal?" Aveline could hear the false note in her voice. It would take some practice to sound as if she were truly the mistress.

"Mistress . . . Aveline—I've brought you these. For joy today." Tentatively, Anne held out a bunch of snowdrops, their fresh green smell spreading through the small space around them.

Aveline sighed, and closed her eyes, tears burning behind the lids; it was time for peace between them—soon she would need friends. "I thank you. A kindly thought."

It sounded gruff but she was sincere and that was enough for Anne.

Shyly, they smiled at each other, almost for the first time, and Anne dropped a brief, graceful curtsy as she held out the red dress that had been hanging all night on the peg beside the door. The dress that meant that as of today, everything would change.

Anne watched the girl who was about to become Piers's wife get out of the bed. Though stick-thin, she was still beautiful, and there was something else: a proud grace that was touching. Her arms were frail enough for a strong man to snap but her head sat high and strong on a long neck, and the blood-colored velvet flattered the white skin and the brilliant dark eyes. She looked magnificent and as finely aristocratic as any court lady.

As all brides did, Aveline wore her hair loose, down to her waist. Anne brushed and brushed it—Margaret had lent her her precious horse-bristle brush. And then, because Aveline's face was so pale, Anne crushed geranium flowers and rubbed them into her cheekbones and her mouth. Color in the blank whiteness.

Passively, Aveline allowed Anne to finish preparing her for her marriage, and she hardly registered the image the girl showed her in the burnished silver mirror that was Margaret's valuable wedding gift. Blurred oval face, dark eyes, stark red mouth—the lustrous velvet showing off the tops of her white breasts with their tracing of blue veins, nursing veins.

Aveline shivered violently. Nausea hit her and she sat down, head between her knees, as saliva dripped from her mouth into a linen cloth Anne pressed into her hand. The moment passed. Aveline's breathing quieted. Gently, Anne offered a hand to help her up. Time to go down and face Piers—face all of them.

Downstairs, the household and its chief guests were crammed into the chapel, waiting for the bride to appear. Expectancy and envy were dominant emotions, but there was a bit of excitement too, almost as good as the Christmas revels.

Margaret waited in her stall near the altar. She could see her stepson standing at the chapel doorway, and when he caught her eye, he smiled—or rather sneered—and made her a great bow, sweeping the velvet cap off his head just as his father, leading Aveline by the hand, came up behind him followed by Anne bearing the train of the bride's red gown.

Piers swiveled and managed to convert the bow into another obeisance—this time apparently to his bride—and as he rose, a brilliant smile transformed his face; for all the world, he looked the lovestruck groom.

Mathew took Aveline's hand and placed it in that of his son as Father Bartolph approached to speak the words of the service at the door of the chapel. Despite the intrigue surrounding this marriage—or perhaps because of it—the congregation sighed with pleasure. Jassy was even inclined to sniffle—after all, everyone loved weddings, no matter how ill-advised this one seemed.

It was a brief service and Piers spoke the responses clearly on behalf of himself and his bride, accepting Aveline as his wife, swearing lifelong fidelity, and even managing to sound sincere.

Anne shivered as she looked at the graceful couple, the bride with her head modestly bent, beside her the handsome groom arrayed like some great noble.

She found herself praying to Saint Anne, the mother of the Virgin, asking her to protect Aveline and bless the child to be, when suddenly she heard a voice, barely a breath, chanting, "Aine, Aine, Aine . . ."

Quickly, she looked around for the source of the sound but there was only the priest's voice, pronouncing the final blessing. She shook her head, but again she heard it. "Aine, Aine, Aine . . ." Many voices now, and flames, and screams of joy; red drunken faces, wild eyes, and sharp white teeth in the darkness. She was back at the Beltane fires . . . that was when she'd last heard them, heard them chanting Aine's name.

Anne closed her eyes, squeezed them shut, but she could not escape the sound, and when she forced them open again, she saw the figure of a tall, strong woman behind Aveline, staring fixedly at Piers. She was wrapped in a homespun cloak, pinned back on one shoulder with a dragon brooch, the animal biting its tail in a circle, rubies for eyes. Her naked arms were covered in thick gold bands, while around her neck was a torque, again of solid gold. And she was holding an ancient sword. Anne blinked in shock, and when she looked again, the woman was gone. Fearfully, she looked around her, but the other members of the congregation were concentrating on the priest, or greedily whispering to each other about the bride being so pale, the groom so handsome . . .

Could she have seen the mother goddess—and, if she had, why was she afraid? Was it not a good omen? And then she remembered. Aine had two forms—the mother was one, but the other was the destroyer. Why had she come here now, to this Christian marriage?

Chapter Eleven

 The wedding feast had begun well. Mathew used the celebration, once again, to impress court connections with his success, though Westminster was daily becoming a more and more frightening place, as the young king played with mighty forces he could barely control.

As the Christmas Court grew closer, Warwick's affinity was growing, his retainers massing in the capital purposefully intimidating the citizens, stealing their goods and assaulting their daughters, unchecked by their master. However, in the last week, Edward, supported by his youngest brother, the Duke of Gloucester, and many of the Wydevilles, had begun to exert his strength by summarily arresting three of Warwick's more troublesome lieutenants, beheading the one who could be called a gentleman and hanging the other two at Tyburn. This was a stark message to the man who had placed Edward on the throne: be warned—the king would no longer tolerate lawlessness in his own capital and no one was immune to punishment. Warwick was said to be incandescent with rage and had withdrawn temporarily from court to his own lands in the north—by kind permission of the king, reluctantly sought and freely given.

Clearly, the time was close when sides would be chosen, but for now the wedding of the son of Mathew Cuttifer was an important moment in the life of the city. There was no shortage of friends, rivals, and courtiers happy to celebrate the event; they were all curious to meet the baseborn bride and covertly sneer at the extraordinary choice Master Mathew had seemingly allowed his son to make. To be seen at Blessing House, to wish the couple happy, was a diversion from the fear gathering outside—and a feast such as this was the best place to swap recent news and gossip.

As the daylong celebration began, the young couple greeted their guests at the entrance to the hall; there was the usual harvest of crude jokes, bountiful food, and pitchers of good, strong sweet wine—all that was expected of a marriage feast. Margaret and Mathew had talked long on this matter and she had advised him that this wedding should be feted as if Piers were marrying one of the greatest heiresses in the kingdom—it would be their signal to the world that they accepted Aveline as a valued addition to their house. Plainly it was God's pleasure that it should be so, for the winter day had dawned brilliant, though cold.

However, even though Blessing House was thronged with courtiers, Mathew, Margaret, and Piers were all aware that many of their principal invited guests had not appeared. Court hangers-on there were in plenty, but many of the greatest lords, Edward's closest companions, were missing. At a time like this, they clustered around the king or withdrew to their own lands to await events, and to sweat on the most advantageous time to show their hands.

The king, too, had graciously, but very recently, declined the invitation, though he had sent handsome gifts to the new couple. For the bride, four English ells of sky-blue figured damask embroidered with gold thread. The groom had been sent a handsome Spanish leather saddle and bridle, worked with silver and bronze ornaments. There was also a set of gossamer-fine linen sheets from the Levant for their bed.

More than kingly, thought Mathew, but he'd have been happier with the presence of their giver. With all the uncertainty of the hostility between Warwick and Edward, the courtiers were buying less of Mathew's most expensive goods and that was bad for the overall balance of his very costly trade with the Mediterranean seaports. Perhaps he would be able to tell the way the wind was shifting when he went, personally, to thank the king for his generosity to the new couple. He looked across at his new daughter-in-law, a handsome girl; perhaps she should accompany him—and Piers, too, if he could be persuaded to practice the manners so expensively acquired from the numberless tutors he'd been provided with as a boy. Thanks in person to the king always meant more, and might get him more as well.

Among all the noise and heat, the shouted congratulations, the hearty kisses, Anne saw that Aveline was feeling very alone. Her father had said he would attend the wedding to give his daughter away but in the end hadn't come. From gossip, Anne had heard he was too poor to buy the fine clothes that such a feast demanded, and his legitimate children were too proud to honor the bastard half sister who'd somehow managed to make a better marriage than any of them.

Anne ached for Aveline. There was no one here to wish her happiness who really meant it, and she saw that Aveline's hands had strayed to cover her belly, as if to protect her unborn child from all the unkindness of the brittle world surrounding her now. Yet Aveline never allowed the calm joyful expression on her face to waver and Anne found that touchingly courageous. For she, too, could see the many sideways looks cast at Aveline's waist and hear the sly comments on how blooming the bride was looking on her wedding day. She felt offended on Aveline's behalf and longed to stand behind her in support, but now that the feast had begun Anne was rapidly too busy to think about much other than not spilling the wine she was pouring for the bride and bridegroom's guests.

Aveline and Piers, seated under a rich tapestry canopy of honor in the center of the high board in the hall, had little to say to each other. Piers stared sullenly into his silver beaker when he was not openly ogling the breasts of women at the tables below the high board, a fact that did not go unnoticed among Mathew's guests. Aveline, to her credit, kept up a bright stream of conversation with John Lambert, an important mercer and business partner of Mathew Cuttifer, seated beside her. He was one of the aldermen of London and also had the ear of the king, hence his position of honor at the feast.

Lambert's daughter Jane was one of the celebrated beauties of London and she, too, had been invited to the marriage with her merchant husband, Master Shore. Anne saw that Mistress Shore's husband looked none too pleased with the glances his wife's beauty drew, even though she sat with eyes modestly downcast, gracefully attending the tricky task of keeping her veil out of the sauce on the dish of larks in front of her.

Master Shore was a plain, careworn man, at least ten years older than his young wife, while Jane Shore herself was the model of current fashionable beauty. Anne could not judge Jane's height, since Jane was seated, but there was more than a suggestion of sinuous curves beneath the tight-fitting, low-necked gown of expensive embroidered satin.

Delicate, pale eyebrows hinted Jane was blond, though it was hard to tell since her high forehead was capped with one of the lower-crowned hennins that completely hid her hair. Radiant skin, a pure oval face, and a mouth that was sweetly soft and pink, rather than red, gave an impression of gentle grace but then, when she looked up, very large, very dark blue eyes brought her face to life.

Anne had never seen a more beautiful woman yet, oddly, she felt not the least twinge of jealousy. Perhaps it was the way Jane laughed that made her so likable?

"Anne, please take some wine to Master Shore and his wife. My husband particularly wishes to salute Master Lambert's charming daughter."

Anne jumped. It was odd, uncanny, to have inner thoughts expressed by someone else. She hurried to obey Lady Margaret, and as she poured the sweet hippocras for their honored guests, Jane's husband bowed low to his hosts at the high table, calling out, "Such excellent wine—and such a happy day. We drink to the bride and groom!"

"The bride and groom!" The cheers echoed around the hall.

But as Anne turned to hurry back to the high table, Jane spoke to her. "I should like some candied violets when you next return." Jane Shore's sea-blue eyes were fixed unwaveringly on Anne's face. Anne found herself smiling warmly, and when Jane Shore smiled in return there was a moment's deep connection between them, just as there had been between Anne and the king that day in the abbey. The suddenness of it was startling—Anne believed she had successfully forgotten the king since the night of Deborah's visit. Now, three faces, her own, Jane's, and the king's, seemed to melt into one. They were all bound together, the three of them, she was certain of that; bound by fear made from treachery, and made from love. It was forming, this thing, getting closer, gathering power, though she did not yet have the strength to see it clearly.

For a moment Anne forgot what she was doing until she heard her name called. Melly was beside her, discreetly trying to attract her attention. "Anne, Lady Margaret says please make sure the musicians are given no more wine." Anne bobbed a quick curtsy to Jane Shore as she hurried off to do Margaret's bidding.

Musicians had been hired to entertain the gathering during the meal, and at first they had played and sung tuneful but sedate airs of courtly love and undying devotion. But as the day wore on, and course followed course—over thirty separate sets of dishes were laid before the guests—the music had become much faster and earthier.

The tone of the feast was changing, everyone eagerly anticipating the moment of the official bedding of Aveline and Piers as the short winter day drew to its close. Restraint would be abandoned when darkness fell, as everyone knew. Margaret had other plans, however, though she wasn't quick enough to stop one of the minstrels kneeling down beside the bride and striking up a well-known round about chastity and the need for a husband to control his wife's lust, lest it wear him out.

Delighted, the crowd joined in as each chorus became broader and broader, while Aveline sat, frozen with embarrassment, as her new husband joined in the words—to roars of approbation. Only Aveline could hear the harshness of the emphasis as Piers sang about the sluttishness of women and how they represented the power of the Devil to lure pious men everywhere into a life of debauchery.

Finally, the culmination of this long day of celebration could not be delayed any longer: the bride and groom were to be put to bed. As Aveline stood up, Anne ran forward to arrange the folds of her train becomingly, and Lady Margaret rose to conduct the bride to her husband's chamber and into a bed adorned with fine new sheets given by the king.

Passively, still as carved stone, Aveline let Anne fuss around her, but as Lady Margaret advanced with a chaplet of fresh flowers with which to crown the bride, her iron composure broke for a moment and Anne saw that she was very close to crying. Margaret, sensitive as ever, managed to cover the moment. "Bend forward, Aveline—you know how very short I am. I'll never reach up far enough." It was a delicate little joke—they were almost the same height—but it was a token from the older woman that she understood and paid honor to the troubled girl standing before them all.

It was enough. In dropping her face forward, Aveline took several deep breaths that stopped the tears, and once the flowers were in place, her new mother-in-law took her gently by the hand. The grasp of her fingers was strong, steady—comforting—and with Anne gathering up the train behind, Margaret escorted Piers's bride toward the great staircase from the hall that led into the upper part of the house.

A trailing crowd of ladies streamed behind them, making much noise, speculating that the bride was about to have a very long night indeed because of her beauty and the virility of her handsome husband. But Aveline said not a word. The staircase loomed before her like a great stone mountain, the shallow slate treads disappearing upward into darkness despite the profusion of torches flaring in the gloom.

They were followed by the musicians, trying not to stagger as they played and sang their way up the stairs, and immediately behind them came a crowd of boisterous young court and city gallants surrounding Piers. As their blunt comments about the charms of the crowd of women ahead of them on the stairs floated up into the darkness through the smoke of the flaring torches, there was an uneasy undertone to it all. Drunk though they were, many could still sense something out of kilter at the heart of all the noise. Others, afterward, would say it had never felt like a real wedding for all the money spent.

There was a dangerous glitter in the eyes of the groom—Anne saw that when she chanced to glance down. He'd been drinking steadily through the whole day, though no one thought he was drunk. Now he kept his eyes fixed upward on the small party of women surrounding Aveline as they reached the top and turned down the corridor toward his chamber.

In Piers's chamber John had lit a host of candles with a fat-soaked rush spill from the fire and stood back to admire the room, which he'd decorated with evergreen branches and holly, as the crowd of women entered to put the bride to bed. He'd never really liked Aveline because she could be so haughty, but he wasn't like the rest of the household servants. They'd been alternately outraged about her good luck in marrying Piers Cuttifer and scornful of her ability to keep him in her bed once the knot was tied. Aveline gave John hope—if her life could change, perhaps his could too. The women shooed him out the door, but not before Margaret made a point of giving him a half angel for all his hard work in preparing the bridegroom and his chamber.

Now the time had come to bed the bride. With much giggling, Margaret and several other ladies helped Aveline out of her scarlet dress and gave her water to rinse her mouth and to wash her hands, face, throat, and feet as she stood shivering in her fine silk shift, though the fire was bright and warm.

"First night nerves" was the general opinion of the bride's gooseflesh. Aveline said nothing but her eyes were drawn to the bed in the shadows. Unwilling images formed—sinful images—and she knew she had much to atone for now that it had pleased God to allow her to marry the source of her sin. She clenched her jaw to stop her teeth from chattering.

With much laughter, the women drew her over to the bed, pulling back the curtains as Anne warmed the sheets with a brightly polished copper bedpan, a luxury that had come from Paris with the last consignment of French fabric that Mathew had imported. Then, at last, they settled her under the coverlet and called the groom to view his bride.

There was hullabaloo in the corridor outside the room. The door was thrown open wide and the room filled with the smell of wine and male sweat as on a tide of oaths and with a tremendous rattle of cymbals and drums Piers was jostled toward the bed. He had been dressed in a long gown of fine woolen cloth tied around the waist with a tasseled cord; underneath, it was clear that he was naked. There was much comment on the size of the bed and how useful that would be in the night to come as the groom was pushed onto the bed beside his wife.

"Not on top, not on top! Underneath!" They meant, get underneath the covers, but the words provoked more drunken laughter, and in the shadows away from the light of the fire and the candles, a number of the girls attending the bride felt groping hands and hot breath on their necks. Margaret signaled to Mathew: time to finish or order would rapidly depart. Mathew agreed, and waving for the musicians to be silent, he strove to raise his voice above the hubbub.

"My friends, we thank you all for the honor of your company on this happy day, but now the time has come for us to leave my son and his new wife as they contemplate the joining of their lives today."

He drew the curtains on the bed as a definite statement that the wassail was finished and the crowd should leave the chamber— which they did, though some lingered for a moment to address the closed curtains, wishing the new couple joy in one another.

The last to leave was Anne. As she quickly tidied Aveline's clothes, she looked at the great shrouded bed in the corner and had the urge to say something to Aveline, something comforting, but at the last moment, her courage failed and she left quietly. But as she turned to close the door something moved in the shadows beyond the light of the fire. Was it her imagination or did she glimpse the figure she'd seen this morning in the chapel? For a moment there was a flash of gold glimmering in the darkness, and a hint of cold light catching the edge of a sword blade.

Then the door closed suddenly, as if in a gust of wind—when there was no wind—and Anne was left on the other side with the feeling she was standing right up to her neck in ice-cold water.

Chapter Twelve

Winter had lingered this year but now it was May Day and all the city was awake. Whatever the sky said, the people of London would have their celebration to welcome in the longed-for warmer days. Everywhere shutters had been thrown open at the tops of crooked houses and the sky anxiously scanned. This year God had been good, however. As they woke, neighbor called out to neighbor, "Look, the sky is clear," and it was—even the air felt balmy, the last of the chill gone. The sound of hurrying feet was everywhere as the people, dressed in fine new holiday clothes, thronged the narrow streets on their way out into the fields around London to join the May Day revels.

There were even those who said the fine day was an omen. Today was the anniversary of King Edward's marriage to Elizabeth Wydeville, so surely it was the Lord's way of signifying approval of this match—even if Lord Warwick opposed the marriage still. Perhaps the times were finally changing, perhaps the future *really* would be as golden as this dawn. England had a beautiful, newly crowned queen who was pregnant and very close to term, a handsome young warrior-king bent on restoring order to his shattered kingdom. So yes, there was cause for celebration. The babies born from these May Day revels would enter a much safer world, one ruled by youth and beauty.

That was what the people thought, but Mathew Cuttifer was less optimistic. In the months since Aveline and Piers's wedding much had changed at court and none of it seemed good to him. The continuing trouble between the king and Warwick was foremost in his mind today as he heard early Mass surrounded by his household. Shortly, he would allow his people to join the throngs heading out toward the green fields of Chelsea, though not before Father Bartolph preached a determined sermon about the heedless, reckless lure of the flesh. But after the privations of Lent, which had followed a long, cold winter, the people of Blessing House were in no mood to listen, and sat in resentful silence as the priest thundered that Satan crouched among the wine butts, in the pagan bonfires, and, most of all, roosted at the top of the foul Maypole with all its filthy rituals. Earnestly, Father Bartolph entreated the women in the house, especially the girls, to remain with him today, on their knees, and pray for help from Mary Mother of God, their master's patron, for all the wanton souls who would sell themselves into damnation through the snares of lust and gluttony.

The priest did his best, but even Mathew became conscious after a time that perhaps, today, enough was enough. Besides, very soon another generation would begin—he'd been wakened during the night by Margaret and told that Aveline had begun her labor—and he would need all the prayers of his priest for the new child and its parents.

In his heart, Mathew could acknowledge that the birth of this child meant a great deal to him. Somehow, with Mary's help, the baby might prove the bridge he so desperately wanted between himself and Piers. That is what he prayed for because, God knew, the last five months had been the most emotionally tumultuous of his entire life. At times he had despaired; while he believed in the guidance he had received from the Lord, he had forced Piers into this marriage and it seemed that only evil had been the result. But that could not be right, surely? God had spoken to him, he had obeyed, and had expected that obedience, in return, from his own son.

Of all the members of the household he'd had most cause to be fearful of what Piers was doing to his wife in the privacy of their chamber, but he'd not known how to intercede. Since this marriage had been of his making, he knew Piers was punishing him through the suffering he imposed on Aveline. Mathew felt powerless. Often he'd been tempted to intervene, but when he'd asked the advice of Father Bartolph, he had always been cautioned against it.

The priest had reminded him that the husband was his wife's keeper in the eyes of God—he was the head of this new family in a literal sense and her body had been given to him on the day of their marriage. She must learn obedience to his will, like the patient Griselda, and if God had seen fit to allow Piers to chastise Aveline, possibly for her own good, it was not Mathew's place to interfere between them. To do so would be to call into question the whole established order on which society was based, and surely this would displease God very much indeed.

But as the months had worn on and the girl had become thinner and thinner and more and more silent, it was hard for Mathew to ignore what was happening. When her pregnancy had begun to show, he and Margaret had both tried, in small ways, to offer support and encouragement to Aveline. Yet each kind word to the girl was paid in extra, even more imaginative brutality by Piers at night, when the door of their room was closed, and that was terrible knowledge.

Mathew's contemplation was broken by the increasing sound of restless shuffling from the benches behind him. Though he knew this was as close as his people would go to open rebellion, he decided enough was enough. Catching Bartolph's eye, he shook his head slowly and deliberately. Bartolph paused and then sighed, giving them up as a bad lot. Grumpily, he intoned the words of a blessing and had hardly finished when the congregation fairly bolted out of the door of the chapel, leaving his master and himself alone in what seemed like the blink of an eye.

"I thank you, Father, for a fine sermon. They're not bad people, you know. They mostly have the knowledge of God in their hearts and it is you who keeps that there. My household is grateful for your presence."

For Mathew it was a long speech and the priest was startled—and grateful. Sometimes he felt as if he toiled in the German salt mines of the soul for no result and that public revels such as May Day stripped away a thin veneer of goodliness to show the evil pits of paganism lurking under the skin of everyday life. He shuddered when he thought of the Beltane fires; the old ways were a long time dying.

"Come, Father, will you pray with me? If Blessed Lady Mary will intercede with her mother Saint Anne, we will see another member of our household before the bonfires are fully burnt this day. We should pray for the mother, the babe . . . and the father."

While the priest and his master intoned the rosary together, upstairs in the bed in which it had been conceived, the child was struggling to be born. So far it had not been a long labor—only a matter of hours from just after midnight—but now Aveline was finding it hard and her painfully thin body was already close to exhausted.

For what seemed a long time now, she had been able to avoid screaming. Margaret and the women with her thought she was very brave. Little did they know she refused to give Piers the satisfaction of hearing her cry out. But with each contraction it was harder, soon she would have to howl, if just to scream the pain out.

The room was very hot, the fire had been built to a huge blaze and the windows stopped up so that no draft of putrid city air should find the laboring woman and harm her or the child. Aveline lay on a mattress filled with fresh straw covered by three layers of thick, coarse canvas with moss between to help soak up the blood and birth waters, and she was slick with sweat though she insisted on wearing her long-sleeved shift. All the women in the chamber—even Anne—had either birthed children or helped others in confinement and, while they were all inherently modest, they were surprised at Aveline's extreme reticence. What a woman most needed in the laboring bed, or on the birth stool, was freedom of movement, and they were all sisters under the skin—Aveline had no need to cover herself. But then, when she finally let out a mighty scream and tore at her shift in anguish, they suddenly understood.

There was not much light in the room but what there was showed them a dreadful sight. Aveline's entire body, belly and all, was covered in bruises and welts, some of which were old, the color around them faded to dirty yellow. She had been repeatedly beaten on the trunk, back, and legs but not around her neck or chest or anywhere where clothes might reveal what had happened.

Margaret set her mouth in a very grim line indeed as she caught Jassy's eye. She had known things were bad between Aveline and Piers but this was too much: he had deliberately risked his child's life, not to mention his wife's, and for that she would not forgive him. Let this child be born and she would reckon with Piers—and force Mathew to as well—before he was allowed to do any more harm.

Aveline, far gone in pain now, was unconscious of the effect her pitiful body had on the women around her. All she needed, prayed for, was relief from this universe of agony. This birth was fitting payment for all her scheming; Satan was punishing her, she could smell him, there was sulfur in the room, surely he was coming for her now, for her and for her child! Now her screams were terrible indeed, the screams of a lost and drowning soul.

Margaret was perplexed and so was the housekeeper. Of course, pain was normal in childbed but Aveline was beginning to sound as if madness had her by the throat. She was biting her lips so hard that blood trickled down her chin, while her eyes rolled back into her head. Margaret forced an ebony wand between her teeth; if Aveline went into fits, the task would become even harder.

Anne could not bear what was happening. Like all the women in the room she was stunned by the ferocity that had been visited on Aveline, and so, summoning up courage she did not feel, she whispered urgently to Margaret. "I know how to help her—please let me try, mistress." Margaret looked at Anne questioningly for a moment, but seeing the girl's intensity, the conviction in her eyes, she nodded. That was all Anne needed. One last look at Aveline and she was gone from the room, running as if indeed pursued by Satan himself down to the great kitchen. What she needed now was a pestle, a mortar, hot water, and some honey.

The cavernous room was empty; Maître Gilles, like all the kitchen staff, had left after the Mass and for once the great hearths were black and empty. Not even a pot with stock bones left to simmer. Feverishly, Anne went about building a fire as quickly as she could. Seizing twigs and straw from the piles neatly left beside the flags in front of the fire mouths, she laid them down as carefully as she could and then, after finding flint, tried to strike a light. It took several attempts but at last a spark leaped into the straw and caught. Breathing gently, praying for help, she nursed the little flame and then the draft from the cavelike shaft of the chimney came to her aid. The dry twigs blazed up suddenly and the fire was away. Now all that was needed was more fuel, and water for the huge blackened kettle she swung over on its trivet to sit above the blaze.

Once the fire looked secure, Anne hurried over to one of the slate-topped benches that lined the walls between the fire mouths. The one nearest to her had an oak barrel on top of it with a spigot. It would either be water or small beer. God was good, for when she turned the tap, sweet water gushed out into the earthenware bowl she had found.

Conscious now that every moment in the kitchen might be critical to Aveline's survival, she ran back and forth several times between the bench and the fire pot, slopping as much water as she could into it, willing the liquid to boil. Now she needed a pestle and mortar.

Maître Gilles ran a well-ordered kitchen. The cooking equipment was neatly ranged on rough but serviceable shelves attached to the stone walls by sturdy elm pegs. In the light flooding down from the great stone lantern overhead, Anne could see a line of carved stone mortars, ranging in size from tiny—for spices—to huge, for grinding up large quantities of meat, or almonds for marchpane. She would need something to stand on to reach up so high . . .

She hauled over a joint stool and was reaching out for one of the smaller pestles when something cold dived under her skirts and up her legs. Startled, she swung around and nearly dropped the vessel she was holding. There grinning up at her was the face of a devil indeed—leering, red open mouth, stumps of blackened teeth, foul breath. And the cold hands went on trying to explore. Corpus.

Enraged, Anne acted without thinking. Picking up the biggest of the pestles, she used it like a club on the old man's skull. The sneering lust on his face changed to an expression of utter bewilderment, and he dropped like a stone to the flags.

Shaking, the girl dropped the mortar as if it burned her hand, but she had a job to do. She jumped down and, with great distaste, made sure Corpus was still breathing, then ran over to the bench beside the fire and feverishly began to grind a handful of shriveled, blackened seed pods that she pulled out of the skin bag in her pocket. It went slower than she'd hoped but she knew she had to grind the material to dust or it would not act swiftly enough. At last the grinding was done and all she needed now was honey. She remembered Deborah telling her that the powder needed to be well mixed into the honey before it was added to the boiling water, for the honey would help the patient take the bitter-tasting drug. But honey was valuable stuff—anything sweet was—and it was sure to be locked away safely somewhere. The still room? The buttery?

The old man was starting to groan as he lay on the floor. Anne steeled herself; there was no time for delicacy. Picking up a shovel used for sliding bread into the new brick oven—built into one of the ranges—she approached Corpus warily. Standing over him as he opened first one and then the other evil old eye, she carefully placed the blade of the shovel at his scrawny throat.

"If you do not tell me what I need to know, I shall kill you. Do you understand?" It was said so calmly, so matter-of-factly, that the old man didn't doubt her. He tried to nod, as much as the shovel would let him. "Where does Maître Gilles keep the honey? Quickly now."

The old man's eyes bulged. Honey? Now? What did this little slut want with stealing honey? The grim look on Anne's face told him not to argue. She might look young but she was strong, bigger than him. If she wanted honey, well, he'd make sure she paid for it . . . in time. "Buttery. He keeps it in the buttery."

"It'll be locked. How do I get in there?"

The old man snorted. He knew where a spare key was kept, but right now, as he felt the pain in his head, maybe he wasn't going to tell her, after all.

Anne clenched her teeth. So be it. She leaned on the shovel and it pressed into the old man's throat just under his Adam's apple; she was calculating he didn't have enough strength to force himself up against her weight and indeed he didn't. He flapped his arms ineffectually: she took that to mean he'd show her. She eased off the pressure, conscious that the water in the kettle would boil away very soon. "Corpus, there isn't time. If I let you up you have to help me—or it will be worse for all of us in this house."

He had no conscience at all—a long lifetime living close to the bottom of society had taught him to be pitiless—but something, a note in her voice, caught him off guard. Reluctantly, he nodded and, as she let him up, shambled over to Maître Gilles's spice cupboard, rubbing his throat grumpily.

"Turn your back." His voice was a rasp but the command was clear. He didn't want the slut to see how he'd perfected springing the lock on the cupboard without a key. He'd done well over the years, stealing from this cupboard—nutmeg and saffron, along with pepper, fetched the best prices—and no matter how many investigations Maître Gilles had conducted, he'd never pinned the thefts on him.

Anne did as she was told, but, grasping the shovel, she warned, "Be careful, Corpus—I'm quicker than you." He knew she was, and anyway, he was curious. He grunted with satisfaction as the door swung clear and there, hanging on a small peg inside, was the key to the buttery. Should he use it as a bargaining chip to find out what was going on? Then he felt the tip of the shovel nudge his back, just near his kidneys. He sighed. No, he'd find out later.

Anne snatched the key from the wizened, filthy old hand, nails black and broken, and for a moment, pity flickered through her. An evil old wretch he might be, but his tiny body told a long story of starvation and bad times. There was no time for compassion now though. Pushing the old man in front of her, she feverishly unlocked the buttery door, and there, sure enough, lay a huge, deep salt-glazed dish with a blanched wooden rack sitting in it. On top of the rack there was a slab of honeycomb dripping its precious contents through the slats.

Quicker than thought she scooped up the honey with another smaller bowl and whirled out again, leaving the old man inside as she locked the door. She'd have to explain to Maître Gilles later; right now she needed to ignore Corpus as he cursed her for a whore and devil spawn, and finish the task at hand.

• • •

In the birthing room, Margaret was fast running out of ways to help Aveline, and Jassy had tried everything she knew as well. Hot cloths and cold cloths had been applied to the heaving belly alternately to help ease the contractions. They'd dripped good mutton broth into her mouth to give her some strength but she had vomited it up. Red flannel had been hung all around the bed in an extra effort to ward off infection and defeat any cold air from the outside, and one by one, the women had each tried gentle massage of the back and the belly. But nothing seemed to help. With Father Bartolph's permission, they'd even cast beads of incense onto the fire to help bring God, the Virgin, and Saint Anne, her mother, to the aid of the laboring girl on the bed.

The contractions were coming very fast now but Jassy and Margaret both saw that the child had not shifted down—the birth canal had not opened as it should. Jassy looked at Margaret hopelessly. Perhaps this ill-begotten but now much-wanted child would not be born.

Margaret despaired at that moment. Perhaps this was God's will after all, perhaps he did not want this child to see his light. If the mother and the baby died, Piers would have had his wish granted—freedom from this marriage he so clearly did not want. One thing was certain; if mother and child did not survive, she would not permit Piers to go on living under the roof of Blessing House. What he had done to his wife had weakened her terribly. Her body did not have the strength it needed to give birth to this child and her agony was doubled by the broken ribs Margaret suspected Piers's last beating had given her.

As she pushed open the door, the smell of blood and incense hit Anne like a blow. Briefly, she felt nauseated, but she had to ignore it. "Mistress, I have it. Please let me give some to Aveline. It will help her, I promise you."

"Well," said Margaret grimly, "there's nothing else to be tried, short of cutting the babe out." Jassy and she looked at each other—would they truly think of such a thing? Perhaps they would, soon, though it would mean Aveline's death.

Aveline looked as close to a corpse as a living woman could.

Chalk white, she lay groaning, body convulsing with each contraction, eyes open in a dull stare. Anne sat by her head and wiped her brow then, talking as one would to a frightened young horse, gently asked Aveline to open her mouth. Aveline did as she was told, coming out of the dementia of her pain long enough to cooperate.

The women in the birthing chamber had no faith that Anne's remedy would make a difference, sure that Aveline was dying, breath by screaming breath. But then a strange thing happened.

As Aveline took tiny sips from the pot that Anne put to her lips, her anguished face and body changed. The rigid arms and legs relaxed and then it seemed the girl was sliding into sleep. Her eyelids sank down, veiling the staring eyes, and as she continued to swallow she sighed once and breathed deeply, then again. She was asleep, deeply, though her body continued to contract in shuddering spasms. This was miraculous—how could a woman sleep while her body still labored?

Anne spoke urgently. "Mistress, I need your help. There is no time to lose . . ."

Jassy and Margaret were to hold Aveline's legs open, while Anne pushed a pessary, made from the remains of the honey not used in the simple, into the girl. There was only a tiny amount and she prayed she would have enough to do the work. If Saint Anne was with them, the drug that had put Aveline to sleep would relax the muscles of the neck of the womb so that the child could be born.

Aveline moaned in her deep narcotic sleep as Anne slipped the honey-based paste up into her vagina, but she did not wake. Surreptitiously, one or two of the women crossed themselves. Was it not ordained in the Bible that women must bring forth in agony as a punishment for leading Adam astray in the garden? None of them had enjoyed watching Aveline's torment, but was it not God's will? If Anne succeeded in saving mother and child it would be a miracle surely, but perhaps the means was a blasphemy?

Miracle or blasphemy, something was working, for before the candles had burned down another finger-width Margaret, massaging Aveline's belly, felt the child shift down as a great wave of contractions seized the sleeping woman. Indeed, suddenly Jassy said she could feel the crown of the child's head between its mother's legs. And in another moment there was the little blue face—closed eyes, waxy skin—and with the gentlest of tugs, the shoulders slipped through and the boy was born. There were anxious moments as they rubbed him with oil and salt and he did not breathe, but then, suddenly, he opened his mouth and yelled. He was alive, rapidly flushing from white to red as he expressed his displeasure at being so rudely brought into the world.

When the afterbirth came down, they cut the cord with a sharp knife, and Jassy hurried the baby over to the fire tightly wrapped in linen and red flannel. His mother slept on, the stress melting from her face. Margaret hugged Anne and kissed her and then sent her to tell Piers and Mathew that the child had been born, safely, at last. She was also to find Father Bartolph. The child must be christened as soon as it could be arranged, for while he seemed robust, against all the odds, he must have the Devil driven out of him as quickly as possible. To die unchristened would send his new soul straight to Hell. Time after that to consider the future for them all.

May Day was over and the house was still partly empty. Some of the older members of the household had returned from the bonfires, but most of the younger people would straggle home some time after dawn. It was the same each year and the tongue-lashing from Father Bartolph was a small price to pay for the memories they had to last them until next May Day.

Anne found Mathew in his study, pretending to work, though in truth he'd given up trying to concentrate hours ago. He'd asked for reports and from time to time Margaret had slipped out to bring him news. The last conversation had made grim hearing. He fully expected that Aveline and the child would die.

So it was a very troubled man that Anne found in his workroom. The knock on the door called him back from a painful audit of all his faults as a man and a father—an unaccustomed task. "Enter."

"Master, the child is born. A boy."

"A boy . . ." He looked up, haggard, wanting to ask the question but frightened of what he would hear. Her confident, strong employer suddenly looked old and frightened, and Anne learned in that moment that men suffered too, something she had never understood. They, too, needed comfort when the world was too much—and today, she could give that comfort. Quickly, she went to him and laid a gentle hand on his arm. "Sir, the child lives. And so does Aveline."

He had tears in his eyes as he looked up at her and, for a moment, covered her hand with his. And it took him a moment to remember who he was—the master of Blessing House. "So, a live child, and a son for them both. This is good news indeed." Abruptly, he stood up and crossed over to the window that looked down into his chapel, his back to Anne. "Please convey my hearty best wishes to Mistress Aveline. When Lady Margaret can be spared, perhaps she could be asked to join me in a prayer of thanksgiving. I shall be in the chapel."

Anne curtsied to the back of the silent figure and left to find Father Bartolph.

Mathew heard the door close and then breathed deeply. Life had been given, death had been kept at bay.

It would be his task to preserve this child—he felt it was God's will.

Chapter Thirteen

It was high summer now—late June—and the city lay sweltering under a pall of filthy, stinking air that did not move. Even the winds of Heaven were exhausted by the heat.

Mathew Cuttifer and John Lambert were walking together in the pleasure garden that stretched down to the river's edge under the grim old walls of Blessing House. The pleasaunce had been another of Lady Margaret's innovations, an attempt to make the semi-fortified old building feel more modern.

With a French gardener—a monstrous expense that Mathew had grumbled about at the time—Margaret had designed gently sloping walks with gracious wide steps radiating out from a central bed where low hedges had been planted in the shape of a large heraldic rose. Inside the hedges, an actual rose garden had been planted, and there were espaliered fruit trees on the warm brick walls that divided their garden off from their neighbors'.

Everywhere, young trees had been planted, and as time passed, each had been shaped, cut, and bound into witty, even fantastic designs: griffins and a castle, even an eagle in flight. Each year the shapes had become clearer and the design of the garden an unfolding delight.

Of course, when Margaret had first planned the garden, Mathew had allowed her to follow her fancy, but later he had complained vigorously about good land being wasted and the extra expense the pleasaunce had put him to. Formerly, goods coming to Blessing House had been landed by his water gate at the bottom of his land and hauled up the incline from the water. Now the pleasure garden took up all the available space and thus barred access to the storerooms under the house. To remedy this he'd had to buy a strip of land running down his boundary to the river and make it into a separate way to and from the river.

Now, on this hot day, sweltering in his thick velvet houppelande and heavy flat hat, he was glad he'd given in to Margaret's determination. The arbors were shady as the trees were all in thick summer leaf, and there was a breeze lifting off the water. It pleased him to invite his guest to sit on one of the handsome marble benches he'd had brought from Venice to surprise his wife one year for her name day. Perhaps she was right; after all, he worked very hard, God would not disapprove of his taking some small amount of delight in the work of his wife's hands. Not when what she had created was so pleasing to the eye and gave such ease to the heart.

The two men were waiting for the moment they would be called to go with the members of the family and close friends, to Aveline's churching after the birth of her child. As a special mark of favor from the king, it would take place in the Lady Chapel of the Abbey, and since the child had been christened Edward, the churching had been planned to take place on June 20, the feast day of another Edward, a long-dead, sanctified Saxon king.

As they sat in the brooding heat their talk turned to the king and Warwick once more. As an alderman of the city of London, John Lambert had even closer connections to the court than Mathew, but lately all sorts of disturbing rumors had reached both men.

It was said that the king had taken up his old ways with women again. The queen was close to term with the first royal baby and surely, for some time, even she would not have allowed the king into her bed—it had been a great scandal at court that the king had lingered in his wife's bed long after the pregnancy was officially known. To John Lambert's mind, any right-thinking woman would not have tolerated sexual relations with her husband once she knew she was with child. But then, perhaps the queen was not like other women. It was said they lusted equally for each other, and that, knowing Edward, meant mightily indeed.

So the king had turned his attentions to other women—several of them, if the gossip were true—while he waited for his child to be born. The whole kingdom was praying for a male child to secure succession to the throne, and therefore, stability for the country. Mathew sent a brief wish to Heaven that their prayers might be granted.

Perhaps, after all, it was better for the country that the king occupied himself with women rather than fighting Warwick. Mathew felt a twinge of sympathy for his sovereign. If his wife was pious, a man remembered her pregnancies as a sexual desert. The church said sexual relations were only for the conception of children, and once that work was done, a faithful husband should bend his thoughts to serving God as a way to slake the rage of lust. Mathew had remained chaste for the entire time that Piers had been in the womb—much good that had done! Yes, he understood why Edward should want solace when he could no longer go to his wife, but he did not approve. He heaved a deep sigh. No discipline, this younger generation, no discipline at all.

Meanwhile, he listened to John Lambert recount his fears about what would be unleashed once this child was born. His chief concerns were the queen's relations.

"It's all of them, Mathew—the whole pack of the Wydeville family. Every day there are more and more of them at court: sisters, brothers, uncles. And rapacious! You have no idea. The mother is the worst of them all, milks the queen's grace for every favor she can wrench out of her. I tell you, it worries me. Do you know that Duchess Jacquetta even petitioned her daughter, the queen, to allow her to *acquire* the goods of Joshua-within-the-Walls after he died? Yes, he was a Jew, but did that give her the right to despoil his family before the poor man was cold? I'm told she marched right to their door with armed men at her back and broke it down. Arras, gold, plate, furniture—they took it all. Said the family'd be paid later and flourished a warrant from the queen! I tell you, Mathew, I'll not be able to keep order in the city if this goes on much more. And the king does nothing!"

Mathew frowned. If the king's child was a boy, Elizabeth's power base would be greatly strengthened. A male heir for the king and the kingdom would entrench her family in an unassailable position, something Warwick would not tolerate.

He was brought out of his reverie by Anne curtsying to them both. "Yes, child?"

"Master, the Lady Margaret and Mistress Aveline ask if you and your guest would join them, please?"

As usual, Anne made a pleasing picture. Today her hair was bound back under a low-crowned, neat cap from which trailed a fine veil. She was Lady Margaret's chief servitor now, and her status in the household had increased. After the birth of Aveline's child, Mathew had paid for a new set of good clothing for her as a thank-gift for the part she had played in saving the child and the mother.

Motioning for the girl to precede them, he took pleasure in watching her walk gracefully up to the house in front of them. Lady Margaret had given her new, fine velvet slippers and she held the skirts of her gown up carefully, so that the hem of the new dress should be preserved as long as possible.

Inside, the house felt gratefully cold after the hot sun as the two men strolled toward the main hall where a small party was waiting for them.

Anne hurried ahead to take her place beside her mistress. Outwardly, at least, all looked well with the three generations of Cuttifers assembled in Mathew's hall. But Anne could not banish the feeling of dread that was now her constant companion with the family she served.

Since the baby's birth she'd tried to show Aveline unobtrusive support, but Piers's wife had become more and more detached from everyday events, as passive and expressionless as a child's rag doll, and ever more silent. At least Piers had stopped beating her— gossip said there'd been a particularly painful interview between Mathew and his son the day after the baby was born in which Mathew had threatened Piers with a public penance if he continued to abuse Aveline—but Piers had now completely ceased to speak to his wife and showed no affection for little Edward at all.

Thus, as usual, Piers stood silently beside Aveline, while Lady

Margaret held the tightly swaddled baby who was sleeping peace-fully, a thick wad of dark hair sticking out from the top of his head like little black feathers. For one swift moment, Anne saw Mathew's face transform with tenderness at the sight of his grand-son—she'd heard him say to Margaret that there was a look of his own father in the baby's face, and she knew he'd loved his own fa-ther dearly—but he composed himself as his wife called out to him.

"There you are, Mathew. Master John." Margaret dipped a small curtsy to their guest. "Melly, you can take Edward now." And Melly, Anne's friend newly promoted to the honor of maid to the child, hurried forward, carefully taking the sleeping baby from his grandmother. "See that the nurse does not overfeed him if he wakes. And please make sure he is well swaddled again after he has eaten. We'll not be very long."

John Lambert thought it was odd that neither of the child's par-ents showed any concern for the baby. Aveline said nothing at all, she walked off after Margaret beside her husband, eyes down, hands clasped around her missal, pale and contained, followed by Anne.

Master Lambert could see that Aveline appeared to have recov-ered well from the birth of her son and clearly they'd stopped bind-ing her breasts to suppress the milk—having married Piers, she would, of course, not be expected to feed the child. But Mathew frowned when he saw that the bodice of Aveline's new, fashionably high-waisted gown had no lacing in the front; he thought this new fashion where women of quality did not feed their children was foolish and dangerous. Who could say whether a hired wet nurse would feed someone else's baby with the devotion she would give her own child? He'd given in, though, when Margaret explained it would not be seemly for his daughter-in-law to be judged by the court women to be a milch cow. But he'd insisted that he, with Mar-garet, should choose the woman who would feed his grandson, since Aveline and Piers showed no interest.

After the quiet of the house, the streets were a babel of sound as the party walked out from the main door. Preceded by servants dressed in new particolored livery of blue, the Holy Virgin's color, and rose to celebrate the birth, Mathew and John Lambert strolled along with the family behind them. Ahead, Piers's body servant took pleasure in scattering small handfuls of groats to the crowd from a fine leather purse stamped with the Cuttifer arms. Such generosity brought more and more people out onto the street and soon the party was finding it hard to push through the press of people, all shouting and scrambling in the dust for the tiny coins.

It was just as Mathew wanted it. London, for all its size—it was the greatest city in the kingdom with at least one hundred thousand souls within and without its walls—was a small place in some ways still. Let his competitors hear of this fine gesture; it would only add to his credit in their eyes. He smiled for a moment at the irony—sometimes throwing money away was good for business.

Finally, the money was exhausted and the crowd let them pass through the gatehouse and into the Abbey grounds, thronged, as they always were, with pilgrims visiting the shrine of Edward the Confessor.

It was close to noon and the light was dazzling, but Mathew's party had been well prepared for by the Abbot's people; not for them the tedious wait in the heat at the west door with the herd of common people. As a special mark of favor, they entered the Abbey through the great north door, the one used on state occasions and kept closed between such times.

Following her master into the gloom of the mighty building, Anne realized that she had not been into the Abbey since she had first glimpsed the king, and unwillingly she heard again Deborah's words: *"he is too strong for you . . ."* On Deborah's advice, she'd willed herself to almost forget Edward, yet now, among this huge man-made forest of stone, she looked up to see a vision of Edward's face, smiling down on her from the center of the great rose window that Henry of Reyns, the long-dead master mason of this place, had made.

Shocked by remembering again the almost blasphemous beauty of the king's face, she hurried after the party into the Lady Chapel, determined to concentrate on the service of thanksgiving for Aveline's survival of the birth, and banish all thought of the distant king.

Anne filled her mind with the sight of Aveline, kneeling at the front of the chapel next to Piers, waiting to receive the prayers of the Abbot, but as the old man began intoning the Latin words over the woman's bowed head, there was a slight commotion behind her, and the priest looked up, frowning at the interruption. In that moment, his expression changed as he saw who had entered the chapel. It was the king, surrounded by a small number of companions.

Quickly, Edward and his party made their way to the front as places were made for them. Mathew insisted on vacating the stall he had been given, but the king would not allow any of the courtiers to take Lady Margaret's place. The new party were accommodated after some ceremony and the king signed that the service should continue.

As the prayers droned on—the Abbot supplicating God that his servant, Aveline, blessed and supported through her agony by his almighty power, might always find faith to follow the path laid down for a good Christian wife and mother—Anne found it impossible to concentrate because of the king's presence. Her heart was pounding and she dropped her head so that none of the household women kneeling around her in the congregation would see her consternation. Would he remember her from six months ago? And if he did, what then? She was just a servant, just an anonymous girl, and he was a king who met hundreds of people every day of his life. Helplessly she muttered once more what Deborah had said: *"The king has turned away from you . . . the king is too strong for you . . ."* but she might as well have been reciting the names of the seasons or days of the week, for Deborah's warning could not touch her now. He was far too close—so close she could smell the ambergris sprinkled on his clothes . . .

The prayers stopped and everyone stood up, waiting for Aveline to present an offering to the Abbot as a mark of her gratitude for the safe delivery of her son. Anne stood just in time to see Aveline walk quietly forward and bow to the Abbot over a finely embroidered set of altar linen, the work of her own hands. For Anne, knowing the terror and the misery of Edward's birth, and what had gone before, it seemed as if the embroidery had been sewn with tears, tears given form by the pearls attached to the edges of the fine blue cloth. Piers stepped forward to stand beside his wife, bowing over his own offering, a fine silver salver for the altar of the Lady Chapel, his face a mask.

Anne suddenly felt very cold, for Piers was standing next to a gruesome effigy, a grinning death's head on the tomb of a former abbot, meant to remind all who saw it of the transience of life. When Piers turned his head, a trick of the light picked out the skull beneath his skin and he was transformed, in that instant, from a living man to a waxy, walking corpse. It was a vision from Hell moving toward her now, away from the altar, and before she could stop herself she half screamed and tried to hide behind Jassy.

The housekeeper was most surprised. She liked Anne, thought of her as a levelheaded, hardworking girl, and this was unlike her. "Anne! Are you well? What is the matter, child?"

Shaking her head, dismayed by the attention she had attracted, Anne tried to stumble out an excuse as the royal party prepared to leave the chapel, followed by the family.

"The heat, Mistress Jassy, I am sorry . . ." she whispered. "I don't know what happened . . . I just feel so strange." And dizziness rushed up from her stomach to her head as she swayed on her feet. Jassy tried to hold Anne up as she hurried her to one of the monks' stalls. To the scandal of the brothers serving the altar, Jassy made Anne sit down and pressed her head onto her knees.

Lady Margaret became aware that something was wrong, but custom meant it was not possible for her to turn away from the king, who, now that the service had concluded, was chatting with Mathew and John Lambert. The talk among the three men turned naturally to babies as Edward complimented Mathew on the successful birth of a new heir for his house. The queen, too, was close to term and was formally about to be confined to her suite of rooms. She would not be seen at court again until after the baby was born and she, too, had been churched in this same Abbey.

Now Edward's attention was caught as he stood in the chapel doorway with his host. A girl was walking toward him from inside the chapel, supported by an older woman, a girl he knew he had seen before, since he rarely forgot a face—a valuable talent for a king to possess. He had a flash of the banquet on Mathew Cuttifer's name day: this was the charming serving maid whose hand had trembled as she'd poured his wine . . . She'd done something remarkable, he seemed to remember. Yes, she'd cured Lady Margaret of the wasting sickness. Now she was wan herself, almost transparent in the light from the great rose window.

"Lady Margaret, it seems your little maid yonder—the doctor, is she not?—is not well. Perhaps she has need of your ministrations." It was said discreetly to his hostess but, being the words of the king, the entire party hung on what he said and, as one, they turned to watch Jassy who was supporting Anne as she walked unsteadily toward them.

"Your Majesty is very kind to notice," Margaret replied and saw that Anne was indeed alarmingly pale and only just able to stand.

"Lady Margaret, I shall detain you no longer." Edward signaled to his companions and after stooping to kiss Lady Margaret's hand and that of her daughter-in-law—very cold, Edward noted, and her eyes were quite dead—turned away as if to go. But then he stopped and in one quick step was beside Anne.

"Feeling wretched, sweeting?"

Poor Anne, if only the stone floor could open and swallow her, her head was swimming as she stood there. With Jassy's help she dropped into a curtsy but was terrified of vomiting all over the king's embroidered shoes.

"No, sire. The sun perhaps . . ."

"Ah, yes, the sun in splendor!" It was said lightly by Lord William Hastings, Edward's chamberlain and one of his favorites. Stifled laughter rippled around the king—it was a clever pun on the fact that the king's badge was a sun with rays of splendor flashing out all around. Here was one more maiden dazzled by the light, just one more to add to an ever-lengthening list. The king frowned, he was not pleased by the joke. The laughter died abruptly.

"I shall send my doctor, Master Moss, to your maid, Master Cuttifer." The king strode away, courtiers hurrying after him, leaving Mathew and Margaret and the Blessing House party startled.

"Was he serious, husband?"

Mathew shrugged, bemused. "He was just being gallant."

John Lambert was wrestling with the green worm of envy. The

relationship between the king and Mathew Cuttifer would bear watching. It might be wise to cultivate his own strong links with those in Blessing House if that was the way the wind blew now. Why would Edward bother with a servant? It was excessive. He looked measuringly at the girl—and then thought he understood. Lady Margaret was talking to her now, and as Anne raised her head into the light he saw what the king had seen—a face of surpassing delicacy now that the last of the childlike roundness had gone—and something else. Strength. And even more oddly, she reminded him of someone, someone he'd known well in the dim past . . . Suddenly startled, Lambert shook his head at the impossibility of the resemblance. Just some trick of the odd light in the Abbey, surely?

"What's that, Lambert, did you say something?"

"Nothing, Mathew. I said nothing . . ." But as he looked more searchingly at Anne, waiting quietly now in the shadows next to the nave, he was very greatly perplexed. Such likeness was uncanny—the two of them could have been twins . . . if they had not been separated by so many years. But such things did not happen. Could not happen. Perhaps he'd been struck by the power of the sun as well . . .

Detached, Aveline stood beside Piers as the fuss over Anne gradually quieted. She was at peace now, for God had spoken to her in the chapel. All her life, it had pleased the Lord to bring her suffering and now she knew why. On the night of her son's birth, Satan had stood beside her bed, ready to claim her soul, but the Lord had not allowed it—he had permitted her to live and Edward, her son, as well, and she was grateful for the mercy he had shown. She startled her husband by placing her hand in his, and as he turned to her in surprise, she smiled at him for the first time in many a long month. Her hand was very cold, and hoping he would not be observed, he dropped it as soon as he could, refusing to respond to the overture. But Aveline continued to smile, something that discomforted her husband very much and stirred his resentment. If Aveline thought Edward's birth was going to change their relationship she was much mistaken; as far as he was concerned, she was his wife in name only. While she lived she would pay for the humiliation their marriage had brought him, no matter what his father had to say on the matter. He was her husband, and he had the right, the church said he did.

Aveline, walking stoically by his side, still felt the impress of his fingers in her palm. Poor Piers, he did not understand. She smiled in pity; her husband couldn't know that God now had her in his keeping and there was nothing Piers could do about that. It was a beautiful day and for the first time in many months she found herself laughing. The sound of it gave Mathew and Margaret great joy, so that soon the whole company was laughing, too, as they strolled back toward Blessing House. Only Anne did not laugh, but Jassy put that down to the heat . . . just the heat.

Chapter Fourteen

Evening prayers had come and gone and the late twilight of high summer lingered over the city, lending grace to the squalor of the streets. As darkness fell, lights appeared in the windows of the rich and at the Palace of Westminster, but the rest of the town settled down into the night, the people going to bed with the dusk. Here and there noise and the flicker of torches spilled out from taverns and brothels, but mostly all was quiet in the still-warm, narrow streets.

Anne had spent the afternoon dozing on her palliasse in the solar on the instructions of her mistress. After they returned from the Abbey, Margaret had made her lie down because she was still feeling strange, and while she had not actually vomited, she had had restless dreams as she lay on the thin straw mattress in the heat of the afternoon.

It seemed that she was running, running from some dark shape that was pursuing her, and no matter how hard she ran there was nothing she could do—the loathsome thing came closer and closer. She could feel its hot breath on her neck, saw its teeth, smelled it, and it smelled like an open plague pit. And just as she could run no more . . .

A knock at the solar door woke her and she sat up, sweating and disheveled. A tall, saturnine man stood there in a long purple gown with a flustered Jassy beside him; the good-looking stranger carried a pierced, burnished silver pomander that gave off a sweet smell. Jassy, rather insulted that he plainly thought Blessing House might stink, nonetheless rushed over to the girl on the pallet and pushed the hair back from her eyes, grabbing the sheets and pulling them higher around Anne's throat. "Here she is, Doctor Moss, though I'm not sure Lady Margaret will want you to talk to the girl without her being present."

"Mistress Jassy, I have been sent by the king, and though I am happy to see this child, I have little time. The queen is the center of my thoughts now, as I'm sure you will understand."

"Oh, yes, of course, sir, the queen . . ." Jassy guttered to a halt as the doctor strode confidently into the room and over to the pallet. For a moment he stood over Anne and looked at her. Now he understood the king's odd request to attend a serving girl; she was beautiful. There was something striking about her too—Venus in Scorpio? And Mars also, he was certain of that—it was there in the wide-set eyes, the direct, jeweled glance, the proud, narrow-bridged nose; unusual to find Mars so strongly in a woman. It might not bode well for her future husband, for she would not be a complaisant wife. Perhaps, too, since Mars ruled the heart, there was a clue here to the fainting fit that had afflicted her. He would enjoy listening to her chest—if he could remove the housekeeper.

"Tilt your head, child. Good. Now, the other way. Excellent. Now, show me your tongue."

Doctor Moss was a skilled physician and a student of human nature; he put his success with the capricious ladies of the court down to equal parts of both. But he had a secret weapon that helped him with his female patients: the power of his voice. Early in his career he'd found his patients responded best when he spoke to them soothingly, quietly, warmly. He'd picked up the technique from watching a very good horsemaster in the royal stables. It was all in the way he spoke to the horses, that, and the gentleness of his touch.

Then, in becoming one of the royal physicians—and sometimes, drinking companion to Edward—he had seen that part of the king's success with women came from his ability to make each woman feel she had his whole attention. It was an unconscious part of his own practice now. Even here, with this serving girl, Moss focused on her as if she were the only being in his universe, the most important patient he had ever had.

"Now, Anne, is it?" The girl nodded, but she was wary of his steady gaze and the gentle pressure of his hands as he felt around the soft skin of her throat and up under her ears. Moss could feel her tense, and was slightly surprised: he'd found that most of his women patients enjoyed his touch and relaxed completely. Clearing his throat a little impatiently, he tried once more to soothe his patient. "Anne, I'm going to ask you to do something for me that may embarrass you a little; however, it is most important that you do as I say. I have the king to report to and he's most anxious to know how you're getting on. Will you help me to make you better?"

Anne looked searchingly into his eyes and found herself nodding, though reluctantly. He was powerfully persuasive, but still, she was embarrassed for a man to touch her so intimately.

Jassy, too, wasn't easily won over. Now that she saw him work, she thought the doctor just a little too smooth. "How can she help you, Doctor?" It was said with some asperity—she didn't hold with all this.

"Mistress, I shall need a large necessary pot. You could obtain it for me while I continue to check the patient."

Jassy stood her ground. "The mistress would want me to ask, sir, what you are checking for."

The doctor stood up abruptly and escorted the unwilling housekeeper to the door. "Buboes," he hissed, softly, so that the girl did not hear. "This child has been in contact with the sovereign. It is my duty to make sure she does not have the plague. Now, *fetch me a large pot*." He pushed the door open decisively and went back to the girl.

"Now, child, when Mistress Jassy returns you must go into the garderobe for me and make water. Your water will tell me much about your condition. But while we wait for her, please pull up your shift. I shall need to listen to your chest and feel under your arms."

"I have none of the symptoms of the plague, sir. There are no swellings."

He was curious. "What made you think of that, girl?"

"Since I was feeling ill and running with sweat, it is logical you would be concerned. But I am quite recovered now, the sleep has made me better. I must have eaten something putrid when I broke my fast this morning—that would have made me want to vomit."

It piqued him that this girl should tell him his business and he spoke quite sharply. "I am the judge of your state, young woman, and it is my duty as His Majesty's physician-in-ordinary to be sure that you have nothing that I should feel concerned about on his behalf. Come now, raise your shift."

Was it his tone or the mention of the king that made Anne do as she was told? Whatever the cause, she pulled up the soft, much-washed calico as modestly as she could, but only so that her side, one arm, and one shoulder were bared.

"Now, lift your arm, if you please." Beautiful matte, creamlike skin was under his fingers and fine, soft hair in the pit of her arm. She was gracefully made, he thought—his master would enjoy the description—and she was right, there was no swelling under the skin. He grunted. "The other, if you please." With elaborate courtesy he turned his back as she rearranged her clothing.

"You may turn around now," Anne said when she was ready, and he did as he was bid, repeating the search under the other arm. All was clear.

"Very well, when Mistress Jassy returns I shall leave instructions for you to take a tincture I shall make up—after I have checked your water."

He strolled over to the casement and opened it as the girl pulled her shift back into its proper place. Beneath him the river slipped by far below and he could make out a few lights on the farther shore. The last wherries were being rowed downstream with late passengers toward the curve of the river that led to the race beneath London Bridge, and close by he could see the dark bulk of the palace with its concentration of lights. He would need to finish here very soon, no matter how beguiling this little patient might be. He could not afford to be long away from the palace with the queen about to drop her royal brat at any time. Where was that damned old woman?

"I understand that Blessing House has a new inhabitant—a grandson for Master Mathew, I believe?" Little did this girl know the honor she was being done. More usual targets of his polite banter were duchesses or at least ladies no lower than the wives of barons.

"Yes, sir, that is so. Little Edward was born just a few weeks ago and today was his mother's churching."

"Ah, so it was there that the king noticed your condition."

Anne blushed. "He was indeed kind enough to see that I was not well."

"And here am I to make you better." Where had the old woman gone? He was running out of things to say. Civilized bantering did not come easily with this girl—she looked at him too directly. If the king did indeed fancy her, he might have heavy weather of it; she wasn't his most usual type of girl. Perhaps she was just too young and innocent to understand.

For a moment he felt a slight flicker of pity but it passed; the king was always generous. If he took up with this child he'd not be entirely unkind and his favor might make her fortune. Perhaps he'd arrange a useful marriage for her with someone complaisant, an upper servant at the court, for instance, someone with an eye to the main chance . . .

He shook his head, his thoughts running away with him. Drat the woman, where was she? He drummed his fingers on the sill, forgetting the girl behind him as his mind returned to what he would have to do to keep hold of the queen's favor. The key, of course, was a successful birth with minimum fuss—yes, minimum fuss and pain, if he could arrange that.

Anne could sense the doctor's impatience and she was daunted. What would he tell the king when he returned to Westminster? Then she chided herself heartily. The king was *married*. She had no business at all having personal thoughts about him in any way. He had been extraordinarily kind to her, sending his own personal physician, but that was all, and . . . That was odd, of course, when she thought about it. Why would he be so kind to her? She'd seen him at the feast, all those months ago, and he'd shocked her with his warmth, but also, when she remembered it, his cruelty to Corpus, yet now— Her thoughts were cut off as Jassy returned at speed, brandishing a large salt-glazed chamber pot.

"Here, child, do as the doctor says." And pressing the vessel into Anne's shrinking hands, the no-nonsense housekeeper pulled the girl out of the bed, draped one of the bedcoverings around her, and pushed her toward the garderobe. Poor Anne, in an agony of embarrassment, cast a piteous look in Jassy's direction but it did no good.

"Go on! For goodness sake, Anne, as if I didn't have enough to do!"

So the girl stumbled into the cloaca, pulling the door to behind her, leaving the housekeeper and the doctor eyeing each other uneasily. In the absence of her mistress, it fell to Jassy to maintain the honor of the house.

"So, Doctor, may I offer you a little refreshment when you have done here?"

"You are most kind. However, I shall need to return to the palace as quickly as can be arranged."

"Then I shall send someone with you, to light your way back to Westminster."

The doctor bowed in thanks. The words dried up between them as they waited for Anne to reappear. She seemed to be taking her time. Casting around desperately for another topic of conversation, the doctor thought of the new baby.

"You will be pleased to know that the girl has no symptoms of the plague or sweating sickness. It appears to me that she must have eaten something putrid, perhaps at breakfast." The housekeeper bridled at such a suggestion in the house she ran; the doctor saw it too late and hurried on. "So that is a relief in a house with a new child. Tell me, was it an easy birth, Mistress Jassy? I understand you played a major role in easing the mother's pains?"

It was a guess, but a good one. In a large house such as this, the housekeeper would more than likely have been present at the birth of a grandchild of the owner. But Jassy was not so easily patronized.

"No, sir, it was not an easy birth." It was said with a distinct snap. "And indeed, my mistress thought we would lose them both but for a draft that Anne prepared that seemed to bring deep sleep to our young mistress."

"A draft? What sort of draft?" Against his inclinations, the doctor's interest was provoked.

"I do not know, sir. From her upbringing, Anne has extensive knowledge of herbs and tisanes. Last year Lady Margaret had the wasting sickness and we thought she would die, but Anne cured her with tonics and teas that she brewed, and certain strengthening foods she prepared also."

The doctor's rather fixed smile only just covered his incredulity. Jassy saw the look and folded her lips stubbornly. "As real as I'm standing here, she did it. And what's more, she made a salve that helped little Edward into this world. Without it we were despairing that his mother's womb would ever open to let the child out."

They both heard the door from the cloaca scrape, and poor embarrassed Anne put her head around it. She had the pot covered by a cloth and, scarlet-faced, held it out to the doctor. Doctor Moss gave her a dazzling smile and like some magician at a market fair whipped the covering off and gave the contents of the pot a hearty deep sniff.

The women's faces were something to behold—the doctor laughed heartily at their disgust. "Come, ladies, there is nothing to offend you here. Rarely have I smelled waters of the body so clear and fresh. Young lady, I believe your diagnosis was correct." Anne looked at him startled.

"Yes, yes. I believe I am in the presence of another professional, a lady physician." He laughed even more heartily. "Still, it is the truth. You have correctly said that nothing ails you and indeed I agree. The king will be delighted when I tell him. And now"— with a long stride he crossed to the window and threw the contents of the pot out into the night—"I must be on my way. I hope our paths cross again." With a flourish he bowed, handed the pot to Jassy, and was gone.

"Well . . ." was all that Jassy could manage as the door closed decisively behind the doctor. "Doctor indeed. More like some sort of pander if you ask me."

"What is a pander, mistress?" asked Anne curiously.

"Nothing you need to know about. Come, girl, your mistress will return shortly, best clothe yourself and make the room straight again."

Anne found her dress on the peg in the garderobe and dropped it over her head, as Jassy, being especially kind, tidied the little trundle bed at the foot of the bedstead. It was unlike the housekeeper to unbend to this extent and it made Anne curious.

"Come down to the kitchen with me, child. I'm sure Maître Gilles is still out of his bed—he'll make you a posset with an egg perhaps—you must be famished."

She was; she had had nothing to eat since morning, and now that she had shaken off the effects of that strange moment in the Abbey, her stomach grumbled for food.

Jassy was wrong. The kitchen was quiet and seemed deserted, though a fire was banked in one of the fire mouths and all the other hearths were neatly laid out ready for next morning's cooking. Then, as their eyes adjusted to the low light, they saw Corpus asleep under one of the great benches in a heap of rags—snuffling in his sleep like a dog and scratching like one since he lay against one of the great alaunts—the war dogs much favored at court and prized by Mathew—for warmth.

Jassy looked at the old man with a certain sympathy. "There you see, age spares none of us. I remember Corpus when he was young. He was fair to look on then . . ."

Anne was startled.

"You needn't look so amazed. He was, when I was a maid like you. And he looked to do well in the service of this house, but then, well . . ."

"What, Mistress Jassy? What happened?" Anne was curious in spite of herself. Corpus filled her with crawling dread after that night six weeks ago, but she felt a small flicker of pity for him. He was old and deformed and only grudgingly tolerated by the other servants. Soon the day would come when he had no strength left and then . . . She shuddered.

"It's a long story, child, one that does credit to your master's compassion. Corpus has always been a fool, but once he was a skilled cook, as clever as Maître Gilles. But he drank, you see, and stole—well, of course they all do, though I try to keep it in check here—but Corpus overreached himself. He used the profits from skimming the household accounts to keep a doxy for himself outside the household. Trouble was, the doxy was a boy, a runaway novice from the Abbey."

Anne was perplexed and Jassy, who had drifted away in the telling of the story, came back to the present.

"It happens, you know, some men love other men . . ."

"I know that, but he . . . that is, when Edward was being born, Corpus tried—"

"Tried to jump you? Yes. Of course he does that, disgusting old fool. But he does it out of hate of women. Can't have what he wants anymore, you see, might as well get what he can."

Jassy unlocked the bread cupboard as she spoke and found a good part of a quartern loaf. "Get me a small pot, child, and I'll make us both a treat."

The housekeeper broke the coarse bread up into the little iron kettle Anne found and then poured on flat small beer plus a quantity of precious loaf sugar and some grated nutmeg, both obtained from Maître Gilles's special store with keys from the chatelaine swinging from her belt. She even added a little carefully preserved rind from lemons brought from Italy last year. Anne swung the pot over the fire on a trivet, and then, while the posset was heating, the housekeeper beckoned the girl to join her.

Anne was fascinated. Her relationship with the housekeeper had always been formal—she was just another servant the older woman governed with a sometimes heavy hand—and she had no idea why she was being treated so kindly now.

"Don't stand there gawping, girl." That tone was much more familiar and Anne hurried to sit down beside Jassy on the old well-used bench—one of the few pieces of furniture in the kitchen.

"There's much you don't know about this house, and this family. I've known them all my life and little goes on without my knowledge . . . even what happened to old dogsmeat over there." The housekeeper was silent for a moment, gathering her thoughts. Anne said nothing, allowing the moment to take its own time.

Then Jassy looked searchingly at the girl. "You're an unusual girl, Anne. Very unusual."

"Me?" Anne was astonished and her face showed it.

Jassy took pity on her confusion. "Yes, you are, but I think you are honest. Now, I believe that vanity is a curse, since all flesh is grass, but you've been given a pleasing face, and a pleasing body—to men, that is—yet you seem not to know that. Or perhaps you pretend well."

Anne was stung and unwillingly, remembering the shock of Piers's attacks, said hotly, "Men cause much sadness and terror with their lusts; I would be invisible if I could."

The housekeeper was startled and began to speak but saw the posset was boiling over. "Ah, now, quickly or it'll all go to waste!"

Anne rushed to find two wooden bowls and a spoon to share as the housekeeper jumped up to save the liquid from the flames. Soon they were companionably settled in front of the fire again and the housekeeper continued to muse aloud.

"Being young and pretty, well, now, that's a bit of a blessed bane in a way, though it gives you power, for a while. That's what I wanted to say to you ... after the visit of our *good* doctor, just gone ..." The "good" was said with just enough asperity to alert Anne.

"What do you mean, mistress?"

"I do not trust Doctor Moss and I shall tell Lady Margaret of my feelings. I believe that our young king has a light fancy where women are concerned and I do not think it was for your health that you were attended by his doctor. It's said he uses this man as a way into the homes of the girls he covets."

Anne felt warmth in her groin and a chill down her spine. Fear, uncertainty, pleasure, and guilt became one muddy lump. "You must be mistaken, Mistress Jassy. The king could have no special interest in me. He would care for each of his subjects, given to him by God, as he has cared for me today."

It was a dignified little speech that Jassy spoiled with a snort of laughter. "You aren't the first and, believe me, you won't be the last. Plainly, you're innocent in the ways of the court and men, and that is a very good thing. If what I suspect is right, Master Mathew should speak to your foster mother—Deborah, is it? She seems a good and decent woman who has cared for you well. She placed you here in this household for your advantage and she would be the first to agree that it's time you were safely married before there's any trouble. Someone here, in the household—a good steady man—would be best for you. Perkin Wye needs a wife; his goody's been dead more'n a year and he has five children to be seen to. You'd have status then—if he married you—and a secure place in life. I presume you're dowerless so such a thing should be welcome."

Married to Perkin Wye! He was an old man and his breath stank. Anne shivered violently. "Oh, please, mistress, please. I don't want that. Not now, or ever! I'd rather be pledged into a convent than marry a man I did not love."

Jassy suppressed another snort—no convent would take a girl without a dower. But Anne was so clearly distressed the housekeeper softened momentarily. This silly little thing must have been infected by the ideas of courtly love while reading to Lady Margaret in the solar from all those tales of courteous knights and their fair ladies. Jassy herself had not been unmoved by such stories, on the occasions she'd been invited to bring her mending and listen as well, but any fool could see that life couldn't work on that basis. If people chose for themselves, chaos would result quick as you could say "knife." She sighed. The professional side of her, the woman who ran the household and was concerned by the havoc this girl might unwittingly cause if she found favor from the king, fought with shreds of compassion, long buried. However, practicality would win here, in the end, for it was her duty to tell her master if anything questionable came from Doctor Moss's visit to Anne, anything at all.

"Look, child, since it makes you so upset I'll say nothing for this time. But if things should change, if I should hear—" Jassy was interrupted by the scrape of stone on stone behind them as the little concealed door to the solar stair opened.

Guiltily, Anne jumped to her feet, expecting to see her mistress looking for her, but instead a horrifying sight—truly shocking—paralyzed both women.

Aveline was standing there vacant-eyed. She was dressed in a long shift that left her arms bare—covered once more in new bruises—and the front of her garment was soaked in blood. Her face was chalk white and her hair was wild, eyes staring out above a dreadful wound that had laid open half of one side of her face from her cheek to her mouth.

Anne ran over to her, her first thought that all the blood must be coming from some other, unseen gash, while Jassy ripped a piece out of her undershift to staunch the wound on her face.

Aveline swayed when they reached her, as though she might fall. Jassy screamed at Corpus to wake up and find the master and mistress, *at once*. The old man did as he was told, stumbling to his feet in a daze, but one look at Aveline sent him at a run out of the kitchen door, while Anne lowered Aveline to the floor and ripped open the front of her shift, trying to find where all the blood was coming from.

However, the only damage to Aveline's poor thin body was the deep cut on her face, and while Anne rushed to get water to clean it, Jassy implored Aveline to speak to her, to tell her what had happened. But Aveline would not, or could not talk. The gash on her face was very deep and Jassy knew it must be hurting the girl as she did her best to clean it, but Aveline made no sound.

"Anne, bring me linen. Quickly!"

The girl did what she was told, scurrying up the solar stairs. She burst into the chamber and began riffling through the little coffer just as her mistress entered with Corpus hot on her heels. Margaret's voice was sharp with fear: "What is all this nonsense, Anne? Where is Aveline?"

Unwilling to waste time with talk, Anne led the way at a run down the perilous, shallow stairs where, in the kitchen, Jassy was supporting Aveline across her lap, still trying to get her to speak, to no avail.

"There now, Aveline, here's Lady Margaret. We'll just get you cleaned up and you can tell us what's happened." But the housekeeper looked at her mistress with a terrified expression as Margaret hurried over to her daughter-in-law. Beside Aveline on the floor there was a hunting knife with blood all over it.

Margaret's bowels filled with ice. "Anne—go to the baby, find out if he's all right. Now!"

Anne turned and fled back up the stairs, grabbing a torch from a wall sconce as she went, while her mistress tried, like Jassy, to get Aveline to talk.

For once, Corpus had used the few remaining brains he had. He hadn't raised the household, only gone to find the master and mistress, so the house was still asleep as Anne ran through the dark upper passages, as she had done all those months ago, to Piers's chamber, only this time she was running toward him, not running away.

She knew that the baby slept with Melly and the wet nurse in a small chamber that was separated from the main room—which contained Piers and Aveline's bed—by a sturdy plank door. However, the little space the three of them occupied could only be reached by passing through the greater room. When Anne arrived breathless outside the bedroom, relief flooded through her, for she could hear the baby screaming. He was alive! And she could hear Melly yelling as well.

The door to the main room was standing open and Anne hurried in. It was dark and as she rushed toward the door that led to the baby's room she stumbled over something and fell full length on the floor. Despite the rushes on the floor she hit her head quite hard—it took her a moment to realize she was lying with her face inches from someone else's. Piers. Open eyes stared into her own and everywhere there was the iron smell of blood.

Anne screamed as she scrambled to her feet, and then, when Piers did not move, she snatched up the torch, which had fallen dangerously among the dry rushes on the floor, and held it high above her head, ready to fend him off.

It was then she saw that the whole front of his body had been slashed and slashed again with a knife and there was blood wherever she looked—the bed, the floor, the rushes.

"Who is it? Who's there?" It was Melly's terrified voice she heard over the screams of the child and that snapped Anne out of the desire to howl with terror.

"It's me, Melly—Anne. It's all right now, shush . . ." Saying the words automatically, Anne brought herself to touch Piers's face, putting her fingers near his mouth. Was he breathing? No. And his face felt cold. Time to tend to the living.

She ran to the plank door and saw that a wooden bar had been dropped across the outside. Melly and the baby, and the wet nurse, had been locked in, but by whom?

Feverishly, she hauled at the bar and in her panic found it hard to pull it out of the catches. At last, she opened the door and found Melly and the wet nurse both trying to soothe the screaming child. He was frightened but unharmed.

Melly stumbled over to Anne, sobbing bitterly. "Oh, Anne, it was so dreadful. He was beating her again and she wouldn't beg for him to stop—that's what he always wanted—and then she started screaming. God's handmaid, she called herself, and then he must have really hit her because she howled like an animal, and then *he* started screaming . . . and then . . . it all went quiet . . . Aaaah, Jesu . . ."

Melly's shocked sob was swallowed in silence as the women looked down at Piers, dead in a spill of moonlight.

Anne gathered her wits. "Give me Edward."

With Anne clutching the child, the three women fled from the room, leaving Piers to stare sightlessly into the rushes of his floor, as his blood slowly dried and stiffened the hangings of his marriage bed.

Chapter Fifteen

It was June 24, the Feast of Saint John the Baptist, and the sluggish, iron dawn spoke of a storm before nightfall.

The market sellers, heading for the space outside the Convent Garden of the Poor Clares where they would set their stalls, walked quietly past Blessing House, not even calling out what they had to sell. No one inside would hear them; all the windows that faced the street were shuttered fast.

"Must be dark inside there," said John from Spittalfields to his mate as they trudged past, each with a barrow of green worts to sell. His friend agreed and crossed himself as he passed the brooding front door. They might be common, unimportant men in comparison to Mathew Cuttifer, but at least they didn't have daughters-in-law who went and murdered their sons.

Inside the house, the stink of decaying flesh made it a trial to be in the chapel. Piers lay in an open coffin set on trestles before the altar, and the last three days had been hot, so the body was rotting fast. Also, the heat from the fat, wax candles surrounding the bier—each the height of a man—was adding to the speed of decay.

Apart from finding the stink offensive, Father Bartolph was frightened. No matter what Lady Margaret and he said to Mathew Cuttifer, the master would not allow them to bury his son and he would not allow the coffin to be closed. For three long days and nights he had kept watch by his son's body, praying constantly, refusing all food and drink.

Father Bartolph had seen a lot during his rather long life—he was somewhere over fifty that he knew—and yet what had lately happened in this house seemed to eclipse even the rape, fire, and slaughter he'd seen during the civil wars between Margaret the Angevin she-wolf and the House of York. It was blasphemy to think it, he knew that, but he detected the hand of God working here. There was something biblical in the vengeance that Aveline had wreaked on the body of her husband for all he had done to her.

Aveline had not denied it when he'd asked her if she'd stabbed Piers, but perhaps this could not be taken as confession, because she'd not spoken since she had stumbled into the kitchen clutching one of Piers's hunting knives, slick with his blood.

There had been a terrible scene when Mathew Cuttifer found his son's body lying among the rushes in his own congealing blood. Oblivious to all else, Mathew had knelt beside the body and tenderly cradled it, as if the corpse had been a sleeping child. Rigor mortis had set in, however, and it was almost ludicrous, if it had not been so sad, to see the old man trying to cuddle the stiffening cadaver.

Privately, the priest thought Mathew was well rid of his son, especially now there was a grandson to take his place. Perhaps this new child could be better shaped for life by his grandmother's teaching. After all, when Lady Margaret and he had tried to prise Mathew away from the corpse, it had been the wife who had made her husband understand reason. Margaret had also convinced Mathew that the corpse had to be laid out and properly attended to while the household was organized, and made calm, now that everyone had been awakened by the tumult.

The problem had remained of what to do about Aveline. Margaret had again taken charge. She'd instructed Anne to take Aveline to the solar and then to burn the stained clothes she was wearing.

Passive, Aveline had allowed Anne to peel off her shift, stiff with dried blood, and had stood naked, in complete silence, as Anne washed her. The younger girl found herself choking back tears of pity, for it was clear that the gash on Aveline's face would close in a terrible scar that would distort and destroy her beauty forever, though Anne did what she could, binding a poultice of woundwort and honey over the wound.

Then Anne had covered Aveline with one of her own calico shifts and put her to bed in the same tiny, airless room in the tower they had briefly shared before the older girl's marriage. At Margaret's suggestion, Anne had slept across the doorway, but Aveline had not stirred for what remained of the short night.

The next day had begun in muted chaos. Mathew had insisted his son's body be dressed in the finest clothes that could be found and placed in the chapel on a bier covered with a new black velvet pall. He had personally ordered delivery of the candles that now burned day and night in all corners of that gloomy space. Personally, too, Mathew had led the mourners who arrived in a steady stream to pay their respects.

The lavish display around Piers's coffin caused comment. He'd not been an aristocrat or even a gentleman, but the candles, the roses from the heber, and the rich vestments that Mathew made the sweating Bartolph wear were marks of honor, as if Piers had died a great man after a long and magnificent life.

Those who chose to visit and keep the father company knew well the disappointment Piers had been to Mathew, but in death people are mostly kind and so, many decent lies were spoken over the dead man as he lay among the candles and the flowers and slowly turned a pale waxy green, filling the chapel with the cloying sweet smell of putrefying meat.

However, nothing could assuage Mathew's anguished grief for his son; this murder had created a burning, jagged stone in his gut, a stone he knew he had made for himself. The heat and the bile around his heart were feeding the fires of guilt, and they were his rightful and welcomed burden to carry; for he had never loved his son enough to face the evil that had been bred in Piers. For that dereliction, God required payment.

As dawn seeped into the chapel on the brooding fourth day after the murder, Bartolph, rocking on his feet with exhaustion, suddenly saw the mural of Mathew and his family at Mary's feet with new eyes. Somehow the painter had divined the truth that no one else had seen. He'd insinuated a curled whip into the picture beside Piers, a whip that looked like a snake. Yes, the painter had known. Piers's brutality was the work of the Devil—the serpent in the garden. Now it had killed him.

Finishing the prayers, Bartolph bowed to the Host concealed in the pyx and turned to face his patron. Mathew was gazing at the glistening face of his son as if to imprint each feature eternally on his mind. Twice the priest cleared his throat to speak but Mathew heard nothing; he was wrestling with God, asking him to take his soul in exchange for the life of his son—surely it was not too late for the God who had raised Lazarus to act, even now?

Bartolph found his voice. "Sir . . ." There was no response. "Master Mathew . . . Sir!" The strangled tone cut through and Mathew left off his feverish pleading with God.

"Yes, Father?"

"Master Mathew, today is the Feast of Saint John the Baptist. The cousin of Christ."

"Well?"

"In the spirit of the sacrifice made by the blessed John, I believe that God has spoken to me. About Piers."

"And what has he said, Father?" Mathew sounded calm but his tone was flat, remote.

It was daunting for the priest but he continued. "Sir, He has said that today should be the day that your son is laid to rest, for you have suffered enough—even as John did."

"No!"

Lady Margaret heard the anger in her husband's voice as she entered the chapel and saw the helpless look on the priest's face. Holding one finger to her lips, she beckoned for Bartolph to leave them alone. The priest took the hint and left, and Lady Margaret joined her husband, kneeling, in front of the coffin.

"Have you come to instruct me in God's will also, wife?" Mathew's tone was bleak, but Margaret, while compassionate, was practical. She had the whole household to consider and the presence of a three-day-old corpse in the warm weather was her chief concern.

"No, husband," she said briskly, "but I have come to remind you of your duty. It is time to be done with prayers beside your son—he must be buried. He stinks, Mathew."

Cold water thrown into his face could not have been more shocking. Before he could say anything she took his hand. "Ah, my dear, if I could spare you this I would, but we have no more time. Decisions must be taken and you are the head of this house."

Abruptly, Mathew began to cry, as if an invisible animal had him in its grip and was shaking his body to and fro. Margaret put her arms around him and held him as tightly as she could with all her strength, pressing him against her breasts, kissing his face, kissing his tears.

Eventually he leaned away from her, wiping his face with the cuff of his sleeve. He smelled very rank, for he had not changed his clothes—the heavy velvet houppelande, the thick hose—since the day of the churching.

The good wife in Margaret knew what was needed. Gently she helped him rise to his feet and walked beside him to the door of the chapel, saying nothing. Together they moved on toward the great receiving hall, and once there, Margaret found Jassy.

"Jassy, would you see that Master Mathew is bathed, please, and that he is supplied with clean, fresh clothes and a good breakfast in his workroom as soon as you can arrange that. And then I want you to send me Wynken and Alain from the stable—and also Dermot from the forge. I shall be in the chapel."

Consigning her husband to Jassy's care, Margaret went back to the chapel where she found the priest in his robing room. "Father, I have decided that you and I shall pick a resting place for Piers under the floor of the chapel that I shall then submit to my husband for his approval. The grave shall be dug this forenoon. Meanwhile, the coffin must be closed. We shall fumigate as best we can and tonight you will conduct the funeral Mass. Do I have your approval?"

The priest bowed speechlessly to the lady and followed her into the body of the chapel. Not for the first time he thought this house would be in a sad state without her wise counsel—she was as the Bible said, a wife whose price was above rubies, *and* she had the brain of a man. A rare combination, one to be prized.

Margaret stood very still as she looked around the space before her. In a real sense, this place was a monument to her husband's success, but now it would have another function too. It would be the resting place of a good part of his hopes. They must build a great tomb for those hopes.

Margaret sighed in deep sadness as the priest coughed gently, trying to attract her attention. "Yes, Father?"

"Lady Margaret, do you suppose the master would like his son to be buried before the altar?"

Margaret considered the proposal for a moment, thinking where the morning sun shone into this gloomy place. It was important that Piers be buried with his head toward the dawn, the east, so that he would be ready for Judgment Day, but for that to happen he would need to be buried away from the altar, which faced north.

"A noble thought, Father. And a comforting one. We should bury Piers there—do you see where the sun strikes the flags?" A pool of light had fallen to the right of the altar under the figures of the Cuttifer family group. It would give Mathew comfort when the sun shone onto his son's grave.

There was a discreet knock on the chapel door and Margaret turned to see two strongly made youths and a large redheaded man. Wynken and Alain worked under Perkin Wye in the stables and were ideal for the hard digging to come. But first they needed to seal the coffin to stop the stench and for that she had summoned Dermot, the wild-haired Irish smith.

Dermot had never liked Piers; once, he'd even told him so and it was only his great size and strength that saved him from a beating, plus the strange reputation he carried. Smiths and wizards were still interchangeable in many people's minds, and despite his nearly impenetrable accent and strange clothes, he inspired a lot of respect in the house because he said odd things—things that came true too often for comfort. And in his little lean-to behind the forge there were wooden carvings, black, primitive-looking things with small eyes and long heads. Dermot was known to pour wine and cocks' blood over these "friends" on a full moon—something Father Bartolph was well apprised of. He'd never confronted the smith with his knowledge, however. The deep black eyes of the man stopped him.

But Margaret liked Dermot for his honesty, her patronage kept him safe at Blessing House, and now she carefully explained what she wanted done. First, the lid of the coffin was to be nailed down as tightly as possible and then hot lead poured over the nail holes. Further, sheets of lead were to be wrapped around the coffin and their edges sealed to form an outer casing for the elm box inside. This was especially important since the body was to be buried under the chapel floor and she was anxious to avoid noxious humors seeping up through the flags.

As Margaret left the chapel, Mathew, newly shaved and bathed and wearing clean clothes, slowly walked over to the little window above the prie-dieu in his workroom, a window that he'd had installed into the thickness of the wall so that he could look down into the chapel below and contemplate God's Son on his cross above the altar table whenever he had need of guidance in his business. Below, he could see the lid was on the coffin; Dermot and his assistant were filling the last few nail holes with lead. Mathew was too late—too late to see his son's face for one last time on this earth.

Too late. He'd always been too late for Piers.

For Anne, it had been a morning fraught with worry. After the dreadful events of June 20, Lady Margaret had decreed that Anne was to be Aveline's constant companion and guardian. Margaret had dissuaded Mathew from locking his daughter-in-law in one of the cellars under the kitchen, but as an alternative, a bolt was attached to the outside of the tower room where Aveline had been confined these last three days.

Now the day was turning thunderous and Anne had been asked to take Aveline walking outside in the garden for an hour or so before the storm descended. Lady Margaret felt pity for Aveline—let her breathe fresh air while she still could, for it might be some of the last she ever tasted.

Aveline was in a shocking state. She had refused to eat since the night of the murder and her clothes hung on her as if made for a much larger woman. Despite Anne's treatment, the knife slash was proud and hot on her face and she was clearly running a high fever, but she'd refused to let Anne touch her face again or tend further to the gash. At least she was clean—Anne had seen to that—but something had snapped in the girl's mind. Aveline was talking again but not to anyone living. Her conversations were with God and the Devil—and Piers.

Anne knew time was running out for Aveline; those who didn't understand how Piers had come to die were howling for blood. A man might kill his wife and be acquitted by the courts since she was his property. A murdering wife, however, could be convicted of treason, for which the penalty was death. The last day or two, crowds of men had gathered outside the main portico of Blessing House calling for Aveline to be burned on Newgate Hill as an example to all wives.

The process of justice was moving slowly, however. Refusing to be hurried by the mob, John Lambert, who maintained the king's peace in London, along with his fellow aldermen in the city, had been to see Mathew and then had interviewed Aveline. He'd tried, quite gently, to get the girl to talk about the night Piers died, but the only response he'd had was silence or prayers to Jesus to have mercy on a poor sinner. Now his patience, officially, must be wearing out, and Anne knew he'd be back later today and this time he'd most likely take Aveline to face the king's bench and, probably, death.

The day became more and more oppressive, the sky a dead leaden gray. In the pleasaunce the trees drooped, unaccustomed to day after day of heat, but the river passed by jauntily as ever and the cries of the rivermen saluting the girls in the garden were a happy change to the tension indoors.

Anne encouraged Aveline to sit beside her on one of the marble benches so that she could inspect the wound on her face without seeming to do it deliberately. It was too late to do very much but Anne wanted one last try. She'd made another ointment of Deborah's, one that was used to bind wounds together in the forest where she'd lived as a child. It stank and was sticky—being made with borage, comfrey, fermented garlic, and salt—but it did clear infection. How to get Aveline to accept her help was the issue here. Anne picked up one of Aveline's hands. "Are you thirsty, Aveline?"

Aveline was staring at her feet as if something about the pointed toes of her velvet slippers displeased her, but she said nothing.

"Can you hear me, Aveline?" No response. Anne leaned closer. She could see pus in the proud flesh on each side of Aveline's wound. If the ointment was to work effectively, she'd have to clean it somehow. "Do . . . you . . . want . . . some . . . water?"

Aveline turned and looked her directly in the eyes. "You don't have to shout. I can hear you."

Anne jumped. Aveline's tone was normal.

"Thank you, sweet Jesu . . ." murmured Anne. "I've been so afraid for you . . . so afraid that—"

"Afraid I'd gone mad?" Harsh laughter from the other girl. "No. I'm not mad." She frowned. "I've been thinking and . . . asking for help, though I don't deserve it."

"Of course you do—we all want to help you . . ."

Aveline gently patted Anne's hand and then linked her own fingers together, twisting them in her lap. "Sweet child. I've been most unkind to you." She shook her head as Anne protested. "Let me speak truthfully. There are things I must say and things I must ask while I still have the time. Do they bury him today?"

Anne nodded, fearful of interrupting the flow.

"About time in this weather." Again, the dreadful giggle. Then the laughter turned to coughing, a paroxysm that convulsed Aveline's whole frail body. "You must know I stabbed him, Anne, but look, he cut me first." And she turned her face toward the other girl. "He did this to me and for the first time I found the strength I needed. Our Lord gave it to me. He told me, in His Mother's chapel at my churching. He said I was His handmaid and that He would show me very soon when I could best do Him service. You must believe me. Our Savior told me that I was to be the instrument of Piers's salvation—unworthy though I am. Therefore, how could what I did be wrong?"

Anne was silent. Aveline's tone was completely rational, but she was doomed by her own words. Soon John Lambert would come and Anne would have to tell him, if he asked her, what Aveline had said, and that would be a terrible burden to carry: she would be the one to condemn this poor tormented woman. To gain thinking time, Anne changed the subject: "Aveline, will you let me look at your face? I think I can clean the pus out and help it heal."

Aveline smiled at Anne. "Do not waste pity on me, child. What I did was God's will and I am in His care. And it's fitting I should bear the mark of my husband's blade; after all, he bears enough from mine . . ." Then, suddenly, Aveline was on her feet and running through the garden down to the river before Anne could stop her.

At the end of the garden there were steps down to the bottom of a wall with a water gate, beyond which barges and wherries could be moored. The wall had great, black iron spikes along the top, and as Aveline ran to the top of the steps, Anne saw what she would do.

"Noooooo!" she screamed as she ran, but she was not fast enough.

There was a hot dazzle of brilliant red from Aveline's underskirt as Piers's widow hurled herself, down and down onto the spikes that lay along the ridge of the wall below.

Effortlessly, those metal spears pierced that fragile body and passed through Aveline's heart. One terrible scream was all Anne heard and then she saw what lay below. All that was left of Aveline was a pitiful bundle of bloodstained cloth flapping gently in the slight breeze from the river. Anne fell to her knees and was violently sick into the expensive double-white roses planted in a border above the river steps. Then everything spun to black.

Chapter Sixteen

It was only for a moment that Anne lost consciousness. Soon she felt herself lifted up and opened her eyes as she was carried away from the top of the steps, away from the dreadful sight of the blood and Aveline's fragile corpse.

It was Perkin Wye who had found her. He'd been on his way down to the storerooms under the house to personally count the sacks of stored grain recently purchased for the stables; he wanted no "misunderstanding" about the tally this time. Preoccupied, he'd glanced over toward the pleasaunce and seen Anne lying on the flags above the steps, and had hurried over to find out what was wrong. Melly, Edward's nursemaid, arrived a moment or so after Perkin and had screamed to see him carrying Anne, apparently lifeless, up from the river. Then she'd seen Aveline hanging on the spikes and, yelling loudly for help, she'd run back to the house.

Alerted by Melly, Mathew Cuttifer and John Lambert hurried out into the blazing light.

"Enough!" barked Mathew. "All of you, back to your work. Now." His voice had the crack of a whip and the desired effect: the members of the household who'd come to look after all the screaming scuttled to the safety of the house.

By this time, Perkin had deposited Anne on one of the stone benches. She was fully conscious again though very pale and she could not look toward the dreadful sight of Aveline's body impaled below them on the spikes.

Mathew took charge. "Perkin, you are to take Anne back to the house and ask Lady Margaret to join us here. Also, send Mistress Jassy to me—she must bring Father Bartolph. And we will need ropes and a large sheet as quickly as possible, if you please. Anne, you will wait for me in the solar."

Perkin bowed silently and picked Anne up again as if she'd been no more than a sack of chaff. The stablemaster was impressed by the lack of fuss the girl had made since he'd lifted her up from the hot stone path. And, too, he'd savored the feel of the sweet-smelling, pliant body lying in his arms—small, but unexpectedly rounded in the breast and hips. Quite happily he strode off toward the house, but after a few steps Anne stiffened and insisted on being put down.

"Enough, Perkin. I can walk. Thank you for your kindness but you must put me down." And though he'd ignored the request at first, after a short time he found himself complying. There was something in the manner of her saying it to him that brought almost automatic obedience . . .

Above the water gate, Aveline's sightless eyes looked down on the river and the gauzy veil on her low-crowned hennin fluttered in the breeze like a flag. Mathew and John Lambert stood in silence, each contemplating how to remove the body of the girl from the spikes.

Thoughts chased themselves through Mathew's head as he looked at what was left of his once beautiful daughter-in-law. He did not know it, but one of the underpinnings of his life had lurched away with the death of this woman; no longer was his faith in God a solid rock. How could the benign Creator of the Universe allow such terrible things to happen? And if it was not God, must he, the man who had insisted on this marriage, be held accountable for these last terrible months and the fact that there were now two bodies to bury—one of them a suicide?

Father Bartolph arrived, trying not to pant. Jassy's garbled tidings had made him run for the first time in many, many years and his black habit was now sweat soaked. He was followed quickly by

Margaret, Jassy, and Perkin Wye, returning with a big, stolid man from the stables, Cob of Linton, slow in his wits but strong.

"Father, we have need to move . . . the body. But first, I think there should be a prayer for this poor woman's soul."

The priest looked most unhappy. Naturally, Jassy had told him what Anne had passed on to her—that Aveline had killed herself. Now, of course, he had a terrible dilemma. Self-murder was a mortal sin and this poor woman could not now be buried in consecrated ground. And since she was dead, it was too late to administer the last sacrament. It was a dreadful fact that, most probably, as they stood there, the soul of Aveline was being taken straight to Hell, for not only was she a murderess but now she had taken yet another life, albeit her own. He shuddered, standing there in the hot sun: it was a fearful thing to contemplate, the eternal lakes of fire in Beelzebub's domain.

"Master Mathew, this woman has died unshriven and, it seems, in the most terrible mortal sin. I cannot administer the comfort of the church, especially after the fact of her death. But the Lord can be merciful, even to the most grievous of sinners. Perhaps what is left, therefore, is our ability to show compassion as He did to us all." The priest knelt for a moment, followed by the others around him, and holding up his hand in blessing over the corpse below, murmured a prayer, asking for mercy for the soul of the poor creature.

In the end, taking the body from the spikes had proved easier than any of them expected. Cob, under Perkin's instructions, had set two ladders up against the wall—one at the head, one at the feet. And when he and Perkin took hold of each end of Aveline's corpse, they'd been able to lift her off almost immediately.

Now, in the kitchen, when the staff of Blessing House were eating their main meal of the day, Perkin was being pressed for all the gory details, and he was able to say, without exaggeration—which displeased some of his listeners—that her body had come off the spikes with more ease than a pike off a hook. She'd been light, of course, no flesh on her, that's what had made the difference. Now, if she'd been fatter, or if she'd been wearing one of the new fashionable corsets—work of the Devil, in the opinion of Perkin, women's natural shape should not be interfered with—it might have been a harder matter and the spikes may not have wanted to give her up so easily.

In the shadows at the back of the kitchen, Anne did her best not to listen. She'd been asked to fetch some food and bring it to the solar, and that had meant she must brave the stares and whispers of the other servants.

Maître Gilles was sensitive to her predicament, as usual. He kept her busy talking as, with his own hands, he quickly assembled the food. Loud discussion over the relative merits of seething freshly slaughtered hens' flesh in saffron broth or milk with a little French tarragon successfully took up the time needed by Anne to prepare Margaret's special brass tray with fine white bread and a small pewter tankard of ale. Gilles then dished the chicken breast onto a pewter charger and personally escorted Anne to the door in the kitchen wall so that she was not waylaid by any of the kitchen staff. He assured the girl that he would keep something for her when she was ready to eat and she was not to fret about wagging tongues.

The kind words from the cook threatened to break the knot in Anne's throat as he handed her the tray and she went up to the solar. But tears would not help now, so she concentrated on keeping the ale in its pot as she climbed toward the crack of light that edged around the solar door.

She had been dismissed to go to the kitchen after an extensive and rugged interrogation by Mathew and John Lambert—so exacting that for one wild moment she thought they were accusing her of causing Aveline's death. Mathew, in particular, had been harsh, relentlessly probing the exact order in which things had happened, but in the end he agreed she'd had no hand in the tragedy and, catching John Lambert's eye for agreement, had sent the girl to get food for her mistress while they talked further.

When Anne returned the men were gone. Margaret was holding little Edward, fast asleep from a recent feed, and Jassy's household account books were spread out around her. Melly was sitting near the hearth, embroidering a dress for the baby. She looked at Anne fearfully, thinking on the wild rumors that were flying through the house—some said Anne had pushed Aveline onto the spikes.

"Put the food over there on the coffer, Anne. Now, Melly, that is well done." Margaret looked with a critical eye at the stitches so delicately set around the hem of the little garment. "Gather up your work and take Edward back to his nurse. I shall visit him later in the day when he has woken."

Lady Margaret carefully handed the sleeping baby to Melly. *He looks so peaceful, poor little thing,* thought Anne, busying herself spreading out a damask napkin over the coffer at the foot of the bed and disposing the simple meal attractively.

"Madam, the food will be cold in a moment if you do not eat." Anne could see her mistress needed food. After all the stress of the last few weeks there were familiar blue shadows beneath her eyes and her face was very pale. She, like Aveline, had lost a great deal of weight and Anne was concerned that her strength might fail again.

Margaret looked at her serving girl and had many of the same thoughts. To please Anne, she tried to eat some of the delicately pre-pared food, but after one or two mouthfuls she put the knife and spoon down. "Did you eat in the kitchen, Anne?"

"No, madam, truly I do not think I could. I was sick you see, after . . ." She couldn't finish the sentence and, much to her shame, hot tears slid down her face.

"Ah, child, come here."

Anne ran to her mistress and sobbed in her arms as if Margaret had been her mother. The older woman cried as well, broken-hearted tears for all the sadness of the last few months, as she stroked the girl's hair. Anne quietened eventually, but she stayed kneeling beside Margaret, and a little peace came to them both. After a time, they heard the Abbey bell call the brothers to prayer and Margaret sighed.

"We must go down to the chapel soon. Dermot should have fin-ished his work . . ."

Margaret sighed again as she eyed her unfinished household accounts. Expenditure was very heavy currently and would get heavier, especially since the funeral expenses for Piers would in-clude a new set of black mourning for each member of the household. Mathew, in the depths of his grief, had also talked about endowing chantry Masses to be said for his son, to pray for the repose of his soul. If he went ahead with the plan, he would have to find the twenty pounds it would cost each year from the proceeds of his business, because what he gave her to run Blessing House would not remotely stretch such a great way. And there was also the monument for Piers to be designed and made, which would be very expensive, and the price of Soul-Scot for his son that must be paid to Father Bartolph and his helpers after the funeral Mass, in recognition of their prayers to help Piers's soul find peace.

So many decisions, decisions for Mathew, and then, as if the thought had conjured up the man, her husband joined them in the solar. Discreetly, Anne curtsied to Mathew and hurried to tidy up the little room, quietly making it ready for the night.

"Husband, I would like to make a suggestion—about Aveline."

Mathew frowned and dropped into his chair beside the empty hearth. After the events of this morning, the day had moved so fast that he'd not thought of what needed to be done for some hours. He sighed. "Very well. Speak on."

"I believe she should be buried at Burning Norton."

Mathew considered her words. Burning Norton was a symbol of his success; it was the house and estate he had purchased only some few years ago in Yorkshire, in the moors near the Cistercian Abbey of Rievaulx. Sheep country mostly, open moorland that even a few years ago had not been worth very much even to the most land-hungry noble. But Mathew had seen the possibilities as the monks had done, and when the impoverished baron who owned Burning Norton had died, he'd been able to persuade the widow to sell after he had agreed to settle an annuity on her.

His venture in the north had been remarkably successful and, over time, he'd expanded his holdings as much as he could, while the tough little sheep who grew such good wool browsed through the heather, and each autumn as they were shorn, made him a little richer.

His daughter, Alicia, and her husband—one of the powerful and influential Raby family, a landless younger son, who was, unusually, not very war-like—lived there, though they were guarding his interests. In his will he had settled the estate on both of them for all that they had done to make the place prosper, but he'd not told them yet. Time enough to learn their good fortune after he was gone.

Yes, it was a good decision that Margaret had made. The parish priest, whose church was close by the estate, was ignorant, barely knew his Latin, and with a suitable "gift" to his parish, he might be amenable to their wishes.

He grunted, and Margaret took that for assent. "I do not believe that we will be permitted to have her buried in consecrated ground, but perhaps the priest might be asked to bless her grave if we were to bury her in the grounds of the house. The little copse of trees that looks down on the valley there? It's very peaceful."

It was strange that the subject of Aveline provoked no heat in either of them. Mathew had not once, in all his agony watching over Piers's body in the chapel, spoken one word of reproach of his daughter-in-law. How she died was impossible to think about—or indeed talk about—because each in their own way felt responsible. All they could do to end this tragedy was bury Piers and his wife, as honorably as they could. And try to get on with looking after the living.

"It's settled then?"

Mathew nodded heavily. Yes, he would agree. For a moment a lonely picture nudged his mind: the plain coffin of his daughter-in-law, bouncing in the back of a cart on the rough moorland tracks as she made her long last journey, alone.

Later in the evening, with Margaret's words echoing in her mind, Anne saw that lonely picture, too, as she stood beside the old open arrow chest in the cellar under the kitchen that contained Aveline's body. The rest of the household were at prayers but she had avoided going, pretending to be ill again after the events of the day. Now, as the light she was holding picked out the lines of the dead girl's oddly peaceful face, Anne placed the iron knife that had killed Piers among Aveline's skirts.

"Iron for defense, from the hungry spirits of the night," Anne whispered.

Now she placed a little parcel of salt, twisted up in a scrap of cloth, in the dead woman's clasped hands. "Salt for the light I will burn for you." For the next seven nights, Anne would cast salt over a candle flame held up in a window; the blue flame would tell the soul where her home was, until it was time for her to leave.

"And when the time comes, this is for your journey, to pay the waymaster . . ." Carefully, Anne put two copper pennies, hers to give from her wages last quarter day, over Aveline's closed eyes. "Blessed Mother, take my sister's soul, guard it well, let her find happiness in your garden."

There was more than one Mother to pray to—and it was not the Mother of Christ to whom she prayed now.

Lady Mary was gentle, but Aveline's death had not been a gentle thing. Better, then, to pray to Aine: she at least would understand the bitterness, the injustice of this girl's passing, for she was the goddess of the displaced and conquered people, those who had been driven to the west of England by long-ago invaders. Aine was mother to the motherless and defender of the lost; she would light the way for Aveline's soul when it was time to journey to her long, last home.

"Sleep, Aveline. Sleep well in the Mother's arms. You will not be forgotten while I live."

Chapter Seventeen

It was the night of the Feast of the Visitation of Mary and all of England held its breath: the queen was finally in labor.

Warwick knew that his power would be diminished if the coming child was a boy, the heir that all England wanted, and so he had bribed a number of the queen's ladies to ensure he would hear news of the birth as soon as it was accomplished—if it was accomplished, for his informants had given him interesting news. The queen was ill, semidelirious, and the doctors were worried. He rubbed his hands. Perhaps, in time, there'd be a French marriage, after all.

For Doctor Moss, these were very frightening times. At the king's insistence, he'd visited the queen three times a day during these last weeks, and each time after the examination, he'd debated telling the king the truth.

This pregnancy for Elizabeth Wydeville had been unlike those of her two sons with her former husband, Lord Grey. This time she had stored fluid in the last months of pregnancy, and while it made her famously delicate face puffy, it also placed strain on her heart. He could tell by her racing pulse and the headaches that were plaguing her. Further, when the heart was disordered, dropsy could result, grossly swelling the arms and legs until the patient could no longer move. Fearfully, in the last few days he'd observed the signs in her fingers. Her rings were sunk deep into the flesh and her feet were so swollen she could no longer wear her favorite slippers. If the child did not come very soon, he was afraid the queen's life would be in serious danger—and that made him sweat, for the king would no doubt fix blame if she died. He, the celebrated Doctor Moss, would be the logical candidate.

At night in his room at the palace, which had a glimpse of the river and a sideways view of Westminster Hall, he'd pored over books from his student days. His library included the works of Galen and texts from Alexandria—banned by the church as the work of Muslim physicians—plus drawings of the illegal post-mortem of a pregnant woman in Milan.

Except for the accepted remedies of leeching and cupping, nothing had suggested how he could alleviate the fluid buildup, so he'd resorted to wrapping the queen in hot sheets and blankets to make her sweat as much as possible. He'd also administered a mash of juniper berries steeped in equal parts of hot wine and the piss of a pregnant mare as an encouragement to the body to expel urine. The queen had not been an easy patient either. Everything he tried to do was only barely tolerated to speed the birth of the prince Elizabeth was convinced she was carrying. God help us all, he thought, if she has a girl. There'll be hell to pay.

It was late now, and cold. Capricious summer had replaced the heat of late June with gray rain and a dank wind that moaned around his small windows. The summons to the queen had finally come on this dirty night after two weeks of false alarms, and he had the dizzy feeling of being strapped to a runaway horse. Events were moving too fast now and he feared a terrible fall.

The eyes of the court were on him, too, for there was scandal that the king permitted his personal physician to attend the birth and lay hands on the queen's body. Most women were uneasy about men in the birthing chamber; they saw his role as giving out advice from behind a screen so that the queen's modesty could be preserved. But the king was a forward-thinking man who had, in his early life, lived abroad in exile where new ideas flowed freely. He was anxious to make use of the all that modern medicine offered, as an example to his subjects. It was Edward who had talked Eliza-beth into allowing Doctor Moss to attend the birth, but now, standing in the queen's rooms surrounded by a pack of frightened women, Doctor Moss was wishing himself almost anywhere else. The queen was in hard labor, screaming and writhing, but her color was shocking. She was immensely hot to the touch and her hands, feet, arms, and legs were hugely swollen. The physician's heart sank; her condition was extremely grave.

Meanwhile, in his private quarters in the palace, the king sat late with William Hastings waiting for news of the queen. Now that the time had finally come, his excitement was tempered by fear. To distract Edward, Hastings had arranged for mummers to be brought to Westminster earlier in the night, and for a time their silly jokes and lewd byplay had pleased the king. It was a scandalous entertainment from France retelling the myth of Leda and the Swan, but as the hours wore on the king's mood had darkened. He genuinely loved the queen, in his way.

"Where is Moss? We've had no news for at least this hour."

Hastings did his best to calm his master. "Sire, we can send for him again if that pleases you."

The king, pacing up and down, looking onto the black-flowing river below his casements, nodded sharply, and a page, catching the look, scuttled from the room to fetch the doctor.

But in the birthing chamber, Doctor Moss was sweating almost as much as the mother-to-be. His greatest fear was that the strain on the queen's heart would prove too great for her to bear. If he could not induce the birth very soon she would collapse into fits and quite probably die.

The doctor was not a religious man, but in the eye of this storm, he found himself praying, asking God, asking Saint Hippocrates, Saint Anne, anyone, to help him birth this child, for surely his skill did not extend so far. He needed help. Two frightened brothers from the Abbey had already witnessed his fear and confusion, since last night he'd had them bring the precious relic of the Virgin's Girdle to help the queen—a supposedly guaranteed aid in even the most difficult childbirth.

The faded strip of cloth had done nothing: but now, at last, he remembered something, something unlikely, a long shot, but like a drowning man he clung to the thought—it was all he had. Anne, the girl at the Cuttifers'. The housekeeper had said she'd made something, a pessary, and it had helped that other tragic woman, the one who killed her husband—Alyce? *Aveline,* that was it— birth her child. It had opened the canal.

Galvanized by terror, he dispatched his apprentice Tom with a mighty clout to the ear to ride to the merchant's house and return with the girl, never mind that it was deep in the night and the household would be asleep.

Tom was more frightened of his master than any merchant, so somehow he talked his way in past the door-ward of Blessing House and was brought to the housekeeper. For Jassy the sight of Tom's escort, four liveried soldiers from the palace, changed her skepticism to conviction as the boy's story of the queen's birth pains tumbled out. And Mathew was likewise convinced when Tom was taken to speak to him.

So it was that Anne, in hastily thrown on clothes, was pushed up onto the back of a horse behind this lanky boy. Jassy was with her, bouncing along behind one of the other men, and in answer to her gasped-out questions, the soldier just kept saying, "We must hurry, woman!" as the horses raced through empty, rain-lashed streets.

For Anne, strange images of the vast, brooding mass of court buildings flashed past in a waking dream. Through one of the gates, hurried down from the horse by strange hands, she and Jassy were rushed past the guard into an inner ward of the palace, then, on foot, they fled up winding stairs and through the endless dark courts, through doors, down corridors past the sleepy white faces of guards and servants, and buzzing knots of hastily dressed courtiers, avid for news, until at last they arrived at the queen's rooms.

Jassy was forced to stay in the outer chambers, while inside, Moss hurried Anne into the little birthing room, yet again closing the door in the face of the king's page, increasingly impatient for news, any news that he could take to Edward. Moss spoke to the girl urgently but quietly, not wanting the ladies around the bed to hear, his fingers so strong on her arm, the grip so intense, she could feel it on her bones.

"The pessary, girl, what was in the pessary you made? Quickly,

quickly." Anne, her mind spinning with all she'd seen as she'd run through the palace, took a moment to understand what he wanted, but the groaning queen brought back that dreadful night with Aveline, so few weeks ago.

"Honey, poppy, and this . . ." She fumbled in her little skin bag, the one that Deborah had given her, and brought out a handful of the same dark seed pods she had used when Aveline had given birth to Edward. Elated, Moss snatched them out of her hands just as the king's page knocked at the door of the birthing chamber, again asking urgently for the doctor.

"Tell the king I shall be with him directly—and that I hope to have good news." Moss knew that he walked a very thin line toward his fate, but he had no more dice to throw, short of hauling England's heir from his mother's womb. However, he would only try that if the queen died. Moss urgently dispatched Tom to find honey and the things they would need to make the pessary, while Anne waited quietly in the shadows behind the press of women crowding around the queen.

The woman on the great bed was howling like an animal now, eyes rolling back in her head, as Moss conferred nervously with one of the queen's sisters and her mother, Duchess Jacquetta. Tom returned quickly, however, and the doctor hurried him over to Anne, thrusting a large mortar into her hands, his voice urgent with fear.

"Do it now. Every moment brings her closer to death." And he whirled away back to the bed. "You must try to push, Your Majesty. Please . . . just try." The women around the queen were wide-eyed with terror, for now the queen was suddenly immobile, shuddering, no longer screaming. Clearly the end was near and there was no sign of the child.

Desperate for help, Anne found herself praying to both Saint Anne and Aine as she worked, as fast as she could, to bind the crushed seed pods and powdered poppy seeds into the honey until she'd made a creamy paste. Hurrying over to Moss, she thrust the mortar toward the doctor's hands; quickly he scooped up handfuls of the sticky paste and pushed it up between the queen's legs.

What happened next seemed a miracle to all in the room that night. In the space of ten heartbeats, the queen gave a great groan, while blood and clear fluid gushed out of her, and moments later, the child's head crowned.

And when the face was delivered, it gave a cry before its body had even properly left its mother's. The rest of the baby quickly followed.

The queen's mother herself cut the umbilical cord, but then there was a moment's stricken silence before Moss gathered enough courage to announce, "A girl. A fine girl. See, Your Majesty—your daughter." The baby's lusty cry brought the queen back and she opened her eyes wearily when they placed the baby on her belly.

"A . . . girl? Where is my son? Who has taken my son?" The queen's anger brought back the life force to her swollen body but it was almost too much. She spasmed, her back arched, and in that moment it appeared that she would die.

Quick thinking by Doctor Moss saved Elizabeth Wydeville. He thrust his hand into her mouth and held on to her tongue so that she would not choke on it—even though she bit him hard—while he bellowed for attendants to hold the queen's arms and legs. Duchess Jacquetta snatched the new princess from her daughter's convulsing belly and wrapped her in a costly velvet cloth edged with miniver embroidered with the leopards of Anjou and the fleur-de-lys of France, the cloth in which they'd thought to wrap a prince. In the frenzy surrounding the queen, Anne was forgotten by everyone except the doctor.

When Elizabeth regained consciousness, she wept bitterly in her mother's arms at her ill fortune, and then the doctor, sure the queen was out of danger, checked the new child. She was a healthy pink now, screaming her head off as the wet nurse was hustled into the room quickly opening the bodice of her dress to feed the new princess. Moss then signaled to Anne to join him outside the birthing chamber.

On the other side of the great doors of the queen's suite there was a monstrous crowd of courtiers, all eager to be the first to hear the news of the sex of the child. The doors might have been of thick, carved oak, but they could not muffle the cries of a newborn baby. The doctor bowed and smiled and accepted congratulations on all sides but strode on resolutely, answering no questions, with

Anne and Jassy trailing in his wake. "Lords, dear ladies. I go to the king. Yes, the child is healthy—and the queen. But please, do not delay me."

There were curious glances for the young girl who followed the doctor, accompanied by the older, respectable-looking servant woman. The court was small enough for strangers to be noticed, though they were quickly forgotten in the excitement that followed the birth of the princess.

The doctor strode quickly toward the king's apartments still buoyed by the wave of exhilaration the birth had brought, as Anne, Jassy, and Tom hurried to keep up. A live child, even if it was a girl—and he, Moss personally, had saved the queen! Of course, the two women with him had played a part—a small part—in that moment, but it was prudent that that knowledge remain his, and their, secret alone.

"Tom." The doctor stopped in a dark, empty passage as his boy scuttled to his side. "I want you to take these two ladies back to their home. Look sharp now." Moss turned with a charming smile to Anne, and swept her a very deep bow.

"Little mistress, I have to thank you but now is not the time. I would ask that you and Mistress Jassy say nothing about the events of tonight, not even to Master Mathew and Lady Margaret, until I have been able to speak to the king. Then I shall call at Blessing House after I have slept and once more seen the queen and her child." Another bow and he strode off.

Tom pulled urgently on Jassy's sleeve. "This way, goody."

That was enough for the housekeeper. She was no one's good-wife and the events of the night, awesome though they'd been, were not so impressive that she would tolerate this boy's offhand tone now.

"I am Mistress Jassy, if you please, and I shall trouble you to re-member that, young man. Come, Anne." And with that she stuck her nose grandly in the air and picked up her skirts with an all-encompassing sweep of her hand, just as she had seen Lady Margaret do. Meekly, Anne fell in behind Jassy and cast her eyes down, clasping her hands at her waist.

Tom shook his head. These two confused him mightily. He

knew that Jassy was the merchant's housekeeper, his master had told him that, but from her bearing and clothes one would have thought her a lady. Anne looked for all the world like the daughter of the house, yet she behaved like a well-schooled servant.

Women. Very confusing creatures. He yawned deeply as they walked quietly back through the palace, sounds of celebration of the birth of the princess coming to them from a distance as all the church bells in London began to peal and cannons fired the salute from the Tower. Well, Tom thought, it had been a big night and he needed his bed.

Anne, too, was exhausted, but as she listened to the commotion spreading through the city, the commons outside the walls of the palace shouting the news from house to house, she felt very worried. Her earlier mistrust of Doctor Moss had returned. It was an odd thing to be summoned in the middle of the night and then dismissed and hurried away from the palace as if they'd been thieves. And then there were the implications of the birth itself. Of course, she was grateful that the salve she'd made had accomplished what it needed to, but if Edward were to keep the country safe from the bitter wars of succession they'd all lived through, he must have sons. Court politics did not greatly interest her, but the consequences of a girl being born had been discussed in Blessing House, and Anne knew that Warwick would do all he could to foment unrest now that a princess, not a prince, had been given to the king and queen.

"Please, Aine, please, Mary," she prayed as they hurried through the chaotic streets, among the people lighting bonfires in the squares and passing ale jugs from hand to hand. "Please preserve King Edward and his little daughter and may we have peace . . ."

Chapter Eighteen

It was four months since the queen had been delivered of the Princess Elizabeth and in that time much had changed at Blessing House. The first breath of winter could be felt as the last yellow leaves dropped in the pleasaunce, and Anne was in the solar packing her few possessions into a small, iron-bound coffer as Jassy hurried into the room.

"Not done yet? They're waiting for you below."

Anne said nothing as she folded the last of her three dresses carefully—it was her best, the green gown given her by Lady Margaret—and placed it on top of the other two. Jassy bustled forward as the girl closed the coffer and helped her put the pin through a simple hasp to keep it shut in transit.

Anne took one last look around the lovely room, her home and refuge for more than a year, and as her eyes dwelled longingly on each familiar thing she saw, she shivered. Perhaps she'd never see this place again. Her eyes filled with tears.

"Now, now. None of that," Jassy said. Clumsily, because she was unaccustomed to offering affection, the housekeeper pulled the girl into her arms and rocked her for a moment as if she had been a small child, and then dropped the embrace, embarrassed. "Anyone would think you were off to your death, you silly burde. This is a great opportunity."

Anne understood the unconscious note of envy she heard in Jassy's voice—she'd heard it often enough over the last weeks from most of her friends, and some who didn't like her—for the queen had requested, personally, that Anne join her household.

It still seemed the most remarkable thing. After the night of Princess Elizabeth's birth, Doctor Moss had informed the queen of the role—the very minor role, in his estimation—the girl from Mathew Cuttifer's household had played in her survival, and that of the royal child. Then the story had been told of Anne's part in the cure of her mistress, Lady Margaret, and that had been enough. Such knowledge of plants would be useful in the royal household, and the queen had petitioned the king for Anne's services so that she might teach her ladies the skills she possessed. But the decision to employ the girl permanently within the palace was sealed when Anne prepared a herbal tea for Doctor Moss to give to the queen. With its help Elizabeth had shed the excess fluid of pregnancy and greatly enhanced the clarity of her skin.

So now, after saying her good-byes to all her friends at Blessing House, Anne curtsied to her master and mistress as they sat formally on a dais at the end of the great hall accepting her farewell.

"I will send word to your foster mother of your good fortune, but we expect that you will serve the queen with the devotion you have extended to my own family, Anne. You will bring honor to us in this way." Mathew was perplexed by the degree of sadness he felt at the departure of this girl. Servants came and went from his house as they did from any other, yet he had come to appreciate that Anne was kind, and had courage. Rare enough qualities in someone so young, but it was still odd to feel bereft in the face of her departure. She was not his daughter, after all.

But Mathew's wife understood her husband's sadness better than he did himself, because she felt it too, and had thought about its source.

When the summons had come from the court she and Mathew had not hesitated to release Anne, though for different reasons. If Mathew, on one level, felt it was great good fortune that a servant of his should now be so close to the queen—and he had lectured Anne at length on the duty she owed for all the opportunities Blessing House had given her—Margaret recognized something else.

Over the last year and more, Anne had grown. She was tall

now, moved gracefully, spoke softly, and seemed as well bred as any court lady. Her unusual degree of learning, her often demonstrated loyalty, the warmth she and the girl had for each other after all the terrible events of the last few months, made Anne different from any other servant in the Cuttifer household. She was gentle and strong at the same time: a green willow, reaching down to a still pool . . . And when she left, a small light in the gloom of this great old house would be gone. She would leave a hole in all their lives that would not easily be filled.

Determinedly, Margaret shook off the wistfulness she felt as the girl bowed before her, and then she did something that surprised her husband. She got up and embraced the girl as if she had been her daughter, about to leave home. "Dear child, we are not far away. You must remember that. If you have need, we will always listen."

Anne's heart brimmed with unshed tears as Margaret gently kissed her and then gave her a little cloth packet. "This is something we want to give you. It comes from us both. Open it, to please me."

With careful fingers, the girl undid the scrap of ribbon that bound the black velvet and opened the material wrapping. Inside there was a fine gold chain and on it swung an exquisite filigree cross, with a delicate pattern of tiny alternating garnets and pearls.

It was unusual, this cross, for behind its arms there was set a circle, such as was often seen in stone crosses of the west and the north of the kingdom, the parts where Christianity had come earliest and found an accommodation with the ancient beliefs of the people there. Anne looked up into Margaret's eyes, tried to say something, a word of thanks, but nothing would come.

Margaret slipped the chain over her head and gently arranged the cross so that it nestled down inside the bodice of her black gown. "There. Now you will always have something to remind you of your time here with us, something familiar that will give you strength when you pray. I know you have a special dedication to the Mother of us all, for I've heard you pray to her often—she will hear you."

Margaret smiled at her and gently laid one finger on the girl's lips, as if to stop her speaking. Anne guessed that Margaret somehow knew of her belief in the strength of the other gods, the gods of her childhood in the forest, and she was grateful for Margaret's approval and understanding. The circle and the cross would indeed give her strength when she prayed.

Now Anne knelt before Mathew and Margaret and formally kissed their hands. "For all that you have done for me, for all your kindness, I shall always be grateful."

Then at a signal from Margaret, Jassy raised the girl to her feet and Anne left Blessing House. One last look back as she passed through the great front door, and she saw them both as distantly as effigies of Mary and Jesus in the great Abbey.

The door closed behind her as she was swung up onto the back of the sturdy cob being held by a man-at-arms arrayed in the queen's colors of murrey and black. There were two other soldiers to provide a guard for her on the short ride to the palace, and one of them, a sergeant, picked up her coffer and placed it behind her in the saddle. "Shove up, lass, don't fancy carrying this to Westminster."

He groaned extravagantly at the weight of her possessions and grinned at her engagingly. He knew he wasn't bad-looking even though he'd lost one of his front teeth recently in a fight. He quite fancied his chances with this new and tasty bit of girl flesh in the queen's household. But he changed his mind when she spoke.

"I apologize for the inconvenience, sir. I was not aware that my things were so heavy."

Her accent was refined, faintly French, and she looked at him with such seriousness that for a moment he wondered if they'd been told wrong. This girl couldn't be a servant, could she? More like a poor relation. He smartened up rapidly, fearing he'd given offense. "Lady, er, nar, I . . . that is to say, it's not really heavy. I was joking . . . Men! Stand up there. I'll take that." The sergeant wrenched the reins out of the other man's hands and prepared to lead the horse, and its rider, himself, through the throng toward the palace.

The other two guards smirked at each other as they fell in before and behind the horse, but they marched smartly and with some self-importance through the crowded streets, calling out to make space for their passage. Sergeant John-at-Hey had got it wrong, hadn't he? This was no juicy little doxy—this was a lady. And wouldn't they enjoy telling the story tonight at the Wheel and Dragon, the inn the queen's men favored just nearby in Chepeside?

There was much bustle at the palace when the little party arrived in the outer ward. The king was just returning with a group of magnates, and the queen and her ladies, from a month in the country at Windsor, where they'd been hunting in the brisk autumn weather. The vast courtyard was a seething mass of horses, men, dogs, and servants running back and forth as the king and his party dismounted from their ride. While his squire, Loren, held the head of his destrier, Edward slipped down easily and strode over to the queen's curtained litter, ceremoniously handing the queen onto the cobbles.

Anne's breath caught in her throat when she saw him, but then her eyes widened even more when she saw the queen. Elizabeth Wydeville was smiling glintingly up into her husband's eyes. This radiant woman with the white skin, the slender body, and the stem-like waist could not be the same creature as the red-faced bloated mass she remembered in the great bed on the night of Princess Elizabeth's birth. She was as beautiful as everyone said she was.

"Yes, a miracle, is it not? Witchcraft, some say." Doctor Moss had silently joined Anne and she jumped when he spoke. Now, she watched awed as the brilliant royal party ascended the wide stone steps that gave up into the great hall of the palace. "Nonsense, of course. But you had something to do with it, I'll be bound. Or rather, the teas you made did. And that woman has discipline, I'll give her that. She's eaten like a bird since the birth, and now she has you. Look what you did for her skin."

Anne frowned. "Sir, I feel so . . ." Moss looked down at her and smiled slightly at the anxious look on her face as she continued. "I know so little. It may be that the queen believes I have abilities that I do not have and I may disappoint her . . ."

"Now child, you will serve the queen and I will help you. I believe you know more than you think you do—and it's just a question of learning to please her." Which would not be easy, as he knew. "And then, well . . . who knows?"

At the top of the stairs the royal party paused for a moment as the king made a joke. Elizabeth Wydeville's bright laughter floated

through the still cold air, but a sudden whinny from the king's destrier competed for Edward's attention, and he glanced toward the
source of the noise in the courtyard below.

Catching the king's eye as he looked down, Doctor Moss swept
off his flat velvet hat with its trailing liripipe, and prompted by a
businesslike poke in the ribs, Anne dropped down into a curtsy.

The king grinned and waved cordially at his friend as he
turned back to the queen: "There's Doctor Moss, my dear, and he's
brought the girl from Mathew Cuttifer's that you asked for. Now,
let us eat—and quickly."

The court party strolled inside after the king and queen, leaving the courtyard deserted except for Anne and Doctor Moss. A
wave of loneliness came over the girl and she felt like crying. The
doctor, who was not insensitive, saw her distress and patted her
shoulder gently.

"Come now. I shall deliver you to the serving ladies' dorter
where you will find Dame Jehanne. She has charge of the queen's
body servants. She'll know what to do with you."

Chapter Nineteen

Anne's first day in the palace began in a confused blur from the moment Doctor Moss brought her to the dorter of the queen's body servants and abandoned her there.

Timidly, she knocked at the door, which was hurled open with some violence.

"What?" A red-faced, strong-bodied girl of about her own age glared at her fiercely. "Yes? Speak, girl."

"That will be quite enough, Rose." An old woman appeared behind the angry girl and spoke to her sharply: "Be about your business. The queen will be waiting."

Muttering something dark, Rose pushed past Anne and hurried away. The older woman shook her head, clearly annoyed, and then turned her attention to the girl standing before her. "Yes? And who are you?"

Something odd happened as Anne dropped into a curtsy: the stern expression of the imposing lady shifted momentarily to uncertainty before it was recaptured.

"Get up, girl, there is no need to curtsy to me. Tell me your name. Quickly now."

Anne gulped with nerves: everyone seemed so unfriendly. "My name is Anne, if it please you, Lady. I have come to be a body servant to the queen and I am to ask for Dame Jehanne."

The old woman said nothing, but slowly, very slowly, walked

around her, even tipping her face up so she could see it more clearly. Then, shaking her head briskly as if to banish some unwelcome or confusing thought, she grabbed Anne by the wrist and pulled her inside the room.

"Very well. Come in, come in quickly. I am Dame Jehanne and we've been expecting you this hour past. They took their time sending you from Blessing House, I'll say that! Now, there is no time to dally. Where *will* we put you?"

The little room seemed entirely full of women getting dressed—and smelled strongly of sweat and burned hair from the curling tongs because the one little window was firmly closed. Five pallet beds jostled for space between the coffers that held the women's clothes, and now Anne was to be added to the chaos.

"There, put it down over there." Dame Jehanne nodded to the man-at-arms who was carrying Anne's small coffer, and much abashed to be in a room full of women, the overgrown boy did as he was told.

"Oaf!" The tone was not forgiving and the expression of the girl who'd snapped at him was even less so. The boy had managed to stand on the hem of her dress, and even though she was a little thing, barely up to his chest, she had eyes so dark as to look black in the gloom of this chamber and they flashed at him nastily.

"Sorry." The soldier plumped the coffer down and backed out as fast as he could, though not before Anne handed him a groat for his pains, which he'd not expected. He blushed and smiled and then was gone.

"Now, girls. Girls! Listen to me." The noise of four girls squabbling stopped dead—it was as if a whip had cracked. "This is Anne, she's come to join us in waiting on the queen. She will sleep here in the dorter." A collective groan. "Well, it can't be helped, we shall just have to make room."

"How?" said someone sotto voce.

"By tidying this place!" Dame Jehanne looked piercingly at the girl with the dark eyes. "You especially, Jane, your things are everywhere I look. And I expect that you'll make Anne welcome, she will make our load lighter. Now, finish dressing, there is very little time before dinner. When I return, I want you all neat and presentable—

and this room made straight!" Dame Jehanne bustled out with a small nod to her newest charge, and Anne stood at a loss for a moment.

But then one of the others took pity. "Anne is your name?" Anne nodded shyly. "Well, Anne, we shall have to do something about that." She was pointing to the ink-black dress that Lady Margaret had given Anne after Piers's murder. "The queen expects us in livery unless the court is in mourning for someone important. We'll have to lend you something."

"That is very kind."

"I am Evelyn," the girl said as she picked her way over to the wall where a number of dark red dresses hung from pegs. "And this is Lily and Dorcas." A girl with her forehead plucked fashionably bare nodded to her, as did her friend whom she was helping to dress. "And, finally—"

"Jane." It was said as a challenge. The dark-eyed girl who had screamed at the boy was daring Anne to forget her name.

"Yes. Jane, I was coming to you."

Jane scowled at Evelyn and rudely turned her back, crushing geranium petals and rubbing them onto her lips to heighten their color while peering at herself in a small precious square of burnished silver to see the effect.

Evelyn decided to ignore Jane as she went through the hanging dresses looking for one that might fit Anne. "What about this one? Length looks about right." She was correct but the size was clearly made for someone much bigger.

"That's Rose's. She won't like it." Dorcas had spoken up, engagingly giggly.

"Oh, well, at least it's clean," said Evelyn cheerfully. "Hurry up, Anne, the old bitch'll be back soon and there'll be hell and damnation if we're not ready."

Willing hands helped Anne strip off her black, high-waisted gown and then dropped the red dress with the queen's badge embroidered on it over her head. The dress was far too big on her slender body but Evelyn pulled the waist in by binding a wide black belt high under Anne's breasts, and since the gown was made of quite fine wool it draped becomingly. The simple coif she was wearing was removed and her thick gleaming hair combed out and pulled back tightly.

"Headdress?" Evelyn was freely looting the others' possessions again. "Ah, this now—this will look very well." She'd found a low-crowned hennin made from stiffened ruby-red velvet plus a fine gauze veil to attach to it—both out of Rose's coffer.

Dorcas snatched them from her. "Here. You're never any good at this." Carefully, the girl placed the hat on Anne's head and arranged the veiling so that it draped around her shoulders and fell down the back of the gown nearly to the floor.

"She looks far too fine—for a servant. Careful she doesn't make the queen jealous." Jane was looking critically at Anne.

"Don't pay any attention to her." Evelyn stroked her new friend's arm gently. "Indeed, though, you do look very nice."

"Do I?" Anne was startled by the kindness in Evelyn's voice and the admiration she saw on her face.

Dame Jehanne hurried back into the room. "Now girls, Rose has just about finished with the queen and so she'll meet us down in the great hall. Hurry, hurry." She clapped her hands sharply.

Obediently, the girls formed up in pairs, but Anne, not sure what was expected, stood uncertainly to one side.

"Come, child, join me—here." Jehanne beckoned Anne to stand beside her. "Remember now, no unseemly gawking at the men, and no exchange of light comments. Is that clear, Jane?"

Jane scowled and did not answer. "Jane, I was addressing you. What do you say?" The authority in Jehanne's voice was unmistakable.

The girl sketched a curtsy. "Indeed, mistress, I am sorry you think I would."

Jehanne made a little snorting sound but was satisfied that Jane understood her meaning. "Very well. Now, quickly, girls." She led the small flock out of the dorter and into the endless flow of courtiers and servants who were crowding to the great hall of the palace for dinner, since it was late in the morning.

As they were the queen's actual body servants, as opposed to the ladies who waited on her but whose chief role was to be amusing companions, Jehanne led the small band of girls to their position at the board well below the queen's highborn servitors, yet above the minor court functionaries who did not work directly in the king's or queen's chambers. There were appreciative glances and comments from the milling throng of men-at-arms and even some gentlemen as they passed into the great open space of the hall.

Anne was daunted. At Blessing House she'd become used to seeing members of the court and she was no longer frightened of crowds, but this gathering and the noise it generated was intimidating. They seemed like a great hive of bees, buzzing hungrily before they gorged and swarmed. Everywhere she looked there was flashing, moving color. The clothes of the courtiers were magnificent, the men often gaudier than the women; rich tapestries lined the walls and beckoned to be looked at more closely, while the glittering gold and silver plate arrayed behind the dais where the king and queen would sit were the most costly she'd ever seen. Indeed, Edward had his own great golden salt in the shape of a castle besieged by giants. And there was music, too: above the hall, in a gallery, a choir of singing boys accompanied by a small orchestra of viols, sackbuts, and tabors sang with piercing sweetness a French lay of the Green Knight and his fair beloved, lost forever.

Anne wanted to stand and listen. A shiver ran down her spine and her eyes filled with tears at the sweet sadness of the words, but a sharp tug on her sleeve called her back. Jehanne pointed silently and Anne hurried to obey. The group now stood beside the long bench they would sit on to eat their dinner and Anne sat down quickly; Jane laughed contemptuously but stopped dead when she caught Jehanne's eye.

"Not now, Anne. We wait for the king." Blushing a bright, hot red, Anne scrambled back to her feet just in time to hear the hard brass bray from the four trumpeters who had marched into the hall, dressed in the king's formal livery, which bore the leopards of Anjou and the lilies of France.

All sound in the hall ceased as the court waited decorously in silence for the entrance of Edward and Elizabeth. Hearing another blast from the trumpeters, Anne looked up quickly toward the high dais and was scorched by what she saw. All that Deborah had said to her was gone in a fireflash—Edward filled her eyes. Forcing herself to look down, she fought to suppress the fever of yearning as the gathering slid to its knees in the rushes.

Edward's night-blue velvet jerkin was slashed to reveal the lining of white cloth of gold, and on his shoulders lay the golden collar of double S links from which hung an enormous misshapen pearl, curiously like a woman's headless torso. Long, hard-muscled legs were tightly sheathed in hose of a plum color and under his left knee was the garter of the knightly order founded by Edward III. On his head there was a light crown studded with topaz, crystal, and rubies.

Elizabeth Wydeville's magnificence was yet greater than her husband's. Though she had a naturally high forehead, her blond hair had been plucked back so that her brow shone, round and high and pearllike. Under her small crown, silver netted cauls, dotted with diamonds and amethysts and lined with rich purple velvet, completely hid her hair. Daringly, the neckline of the bodice of her tissue-of-silver overgown plunged deeply between her breasts and was caught to her high belt by another amethyst the size of a bantam's egg, calling attention to the pure white of the skin of her breasts, shoulders, and neck. And the purple velvet underskirt of her gown formed a long train that was carried by the daughters of six earls as she and Edward processed toward the high table through the kneeling crowd.

She looks like the queen of Heaven, thought Anne, deeply humbled. *And she is his wife.*

"Beautiful, isn't she?" whispered Evelyn beside her. Anne nodded silently.

"Pity she's such a bitch," Jane sneered. "She'll never keep him, he likes warmer flesh . . ."

Anne turned and looked at her companion in astonishment. It was as if the other girl had spat upon the image of the Mother of God.

Evelyn, amused by Anne's expression, patted her on the hand. "Oh, don't listen. She just thinks the king fancies her. Delusions!"

"But how . . ." Anne was about to screw up her courage and ask Evelyn why Jane thought such things, when she was forcibly interrupted by a heavy hand thumping down on to her shoulder and a snort of rage.

"That's mine! And that!"

Someone was tugging at the velvet cap, which, in a reflex action, Anne tried to hold to her head as the pins holding it to her scalp ripped at her hair.

"Dame Jehanne, she's wearing my dress *and* my hat!" It was Rose, late and even more unfriendly than she was at their first meeting.

"Rose, you're late! Stop that! Anne had to wear something and yours was the only clean spare dress. Hurry now, kneel. Really!" snapped Jehanne in an angry whisper. "Some days managing you bunch of girls is worse than trying to be the keeper of the king's lions at the Tower."

"But madam." Rose was close to angry tears.

"Enough, Rose! Anne, who is your new colleague, will be provided for in the next day or so. For now I expect you will be gracious enough to share what you have with her. Now, that is *enough*. Kneel!"

The cutting look and fierce undertone finally silenced the mutinous Rose as she crowded in beside Jane, who laughed slightly, making her angrier still. She shot a poisonous glance at Anne just as a signal from the Lord Chamberlain, William Hastings, gave permission for the court to sit. Instantly the hall swarmed with servitors as the first dishes were brought out. However, though the singing boys above their heads wove melody through the air like incense, no conversation resumed. Anne had not realized that court meals were customarily eaten in silence.

Evelyn guessed at her confusion and dared to whisper, "Ha, this is nothing. Sometimes, if the queen feasts without the king, we all have to kneel without speaking while she eats, right through the whole meal, even the duchesses—even the king's own sister, the Lady Margaret. At least we're being allowed to sit today. You watch, the king will get sick of this. He likes good cheer."

And it seemed Evelyn was right, for shortly the king murmured something to the queen, and when she responded, smiling,

Lord Hastings to the king's right in turn spoke to Duchess Jacquetta, the queen's mother. Soon conversation flowed up and down the body of the hall. It was a long banquet, and as course followed course more than two hours flowed past, and for all that time, Anne did her best to avoid looking at the king while she tried to grasp the customs of the court from the chatter of the girls around her.

"Dorcas, it's your turn to do the personal linen. You know it is!"

"God's blood, it is not. I am Her Majesty's silk woman: I clean the silk only. I do not touch body linen!"

"You'll wash what I say you wash, my girl. Since when have you become so high-stomached that the queen's undergarments are not good enough for you to handle?"

Jehanne fixed Dorcas with a look, and the girl subsided, muttering, "It's not fair," under her breath.

Evelyn just shrugged and cut herself another large slice of oyster pie "Here, Anne. Try this, it's really very good. You will need your strength, we work hard, believe me. After all, we're not the lady servants."

Dame Jehanne, picking up on the conversation, agreed: "You will be expected by me, Anne, and the queen, to work diligently and well. It is a sacred trust to be about the person of the queen. I shall watch you closely."

It was not said unkindly but Anne was worried. She wasn't afraid of long hours and many tasks because she'd been well trained, but she was frightened of doing the wrong thing through ignorance.

"Settling in, is she, mistress?" Doctor Moss's calm voice interrupted Anne's thoughts.

The openness of the girl's smile shamed him for a moment. He knew it was gratitude for a familiar face that made her look up at him so happily, but, he reflected, if she ever smiled at him, or any man, with true, loving intent, well, the great world, or his master, might give her anything, anything at all.

"She will do soon enough, I'm sure, Doctor Moss." It was said with a certain cool asperity. Dame Jehanne did not like Doctor Moss. The feeling was mutual. What she saw was a man who had risen too fast, was too well dressed for his station; a man who was morally ambiguous for all his graceful ways and warm eyes. And he looked down on a sharp-faced old woman who hid her wiry gray hair behind a nunlike coif and knew far too much about the court and everyone in it. They each had their sphere of influence but the difference between them was that he wanted more, much more.

At court, it was said that Dame Jehanne had been a favored servant of Henry VI and his queen, the French she-wolf, Margaret of Anjou. She knew the secrets of two kings and, now, two queens, for, most unusually, after Edward had won his throne she'd been kept on at court when so many other of the Lancastrian faction and their servants had been banished. But after a period spent waiting on Cicely, Duchess of York, the king's mother, Jehanne had been handed on to the new queen.

Perhaps it was not so surprising when one thought on it. Elizabeth had been the widow of an obscure Lancastrian knight; perhaps it was natural she should want someone from the old regime about her, one who knew court ways. But while Moss's standing with the queen was high at the moment because his was the credit of saving her life, and that of the queen's daughter, the Lady Elizabeth, this old woman still had a disproportionate amount of influence on the queen, in his opinion.

But perhaps her time is passing, he thought as he rubbed his hands happily inside his sleeves. And this girl might be the key, if she pleased the queen—and the king. He'd make sure he received the credit as her sponsor, but these things were to be done carefully and discreetly. "Mistress Anne, with Lady Jehanne's kind permission, I have been asked to present you to the queen."

Jehanne frowned. He'd added the honorific to flatter her but what he was proposing was unusual. Of course she'd expected to take Anne to meet the queen in her chambers after the dinner, when Elizabeth retired to change for the afternoon. But this child was not gentry, after all—not someone's daughter to be presented by an influential sponsor—so it was odd she should meet the queen in public as if she were. "And who has asked this, Doctor Moss?"

"Lord Hastings, madam. However, I believe the queen desires it." The queen knew nothing, of course; it was the king who had arranged this meeting today, with Moss's connivance. Moss was pleased that Anne looked so appealing in the mulberry-colored dress—a tricky color, that, for most women to wear . . .

"Very well. Anne, please go with Doctor Moss, and when you make your curtsy to the queen, remember to speak only if she speaks to you and keep your eyes lowered unless she commands otherwise."

Stomach tight, with knees that barely held her up, Anne stumbled after Doctor Moss as he sauntered toward the high table on the dais. The king sat under an embroidered cloth of honor and he was her lodestone; closer and closer she came, the sound of her blood hammering so loudly it seemed those she passed must hear. But then she was there, in front of the line of opulently dressed men and women behind the high table. And all she could do was sink to the rushes on her knees, head lowered, veil pulled forward to hide her face.

Richard Wydeville, the king's father-in-law, was bored and annoyed. Somehow, he'd been placed several seats away from the king. His wife, Duchess Jacquetta, was seated next to William Hastings, the man who every day seemed more and more inimical to his family's interest. And unfortunately, while he brooded, he'd eaten and drunk far too well: he could feel it. His beautiful tight new jerkin of fur-edged brocade was straining at the pearl buttons round his middle, which, he had to admit, was feeling increasingly soft these days. If he wanted to keep his famous looks, he knew he'd have to be more attentive to fast days, but tension always made him hungry. He needed diversion; that would stop him eating.

Then something odd happened. A servant girl was being presented to the queen, his daughter. He frowned. It was an unusual breach of protocol. And then he saw the expression on Edward's face and frowned deeper still. For all that he tried to hide it, the king was very interested in this girl. Too interested.

Ever alert to the way the winds were blowing at court—because the future of his vast, expensive family depended on the queen's keeping the king's favor—Richard Wydeville looked coldly at the girl kneeling before them. She seemed innocent enough, head bowed like a little nun, but that was no guide. The most notorious doxies were good at that. Then, at a signal from the queen, the girl raised her face and got to her feet. Wydeville sucked his teeth. Very appealing, this child. Very. He'd have to warn Lizabet—he corrected himself—warn the queen.

But his daughter hardly registered the humanity of the girl standing in front of her, though she was surprised that Moss had asked to present her. All she cared about was if Anne could make simples and creams to help banish the few, the very few, lines that had made a first faint appearance on her face. She'd seen them this morning in the pitiless eastern light of dawn as she was being bathed and her servants had held up her great mirror—silver, covered by precious Murano glass—so that she could inspect the skin of her face and neck.

Something cold had brushed against her heart. She'd had three children—her luck could not hold forever. She'd have to work hard, very hard, if she was to retain a succulent body, sweet enough to keep the king in her bed. Of course she'd heard rumors of the women he'd had during the last part of her pregnancy, but perhaps they were only rumors. That's what her women said they were, just gossip. And she knew his passion for her was still hot, really hot; she shivered still when he touched her and that delighted him, she knew. Elizabeth looked consideringly at the girl before her, waiting with downcast eyes, to be spoken to. "Step closer, Anne. So, Doctor Moss, this is your competitor."

The doctor laughed heartily, though Wydeville, ever the cool observer, saw a watchful look flit over the man's face. "Your Grace, that is why I recommended her to you. Anne has never been formally trained and, of course, women never will be, but I count her as a colleague in some ways. Her knowledge of herbs and simples is, as I believe you know, remarkable. She will serve you well."

With the queen's attention caught as she talked with Doctor Moss, the king allowed his eyes to roam over the girl's body and he was amused by the blush that spread over her face and neck and down into her bodice. Even though she was looking at the queen, he knew that Anne could feel his look because, unwillingly, for just a moment she'd flicked her eyes at him and he'd smiled, just a little. She nearly smiled back but caught herself, and in horrified confusion looked earnestly at her feet again as the queen continued to talk to the doctor. Edward laughed out loud, enjoying his little game, and the queen, reflexively, laughed as well, as did the whole royal table, happy, as usual, to oblige the king. Then the king became impatient for there were other things to think about: there was just time to go to the mews to inspect one of his favorite gerfalcons, who was ailing, before he had to receive an emissary from Burgundy. The girl could wait for later, there was time now she lived in the palace.

"My dear, perhaps . . . ? " Edward caught the attention of the queen and she waved dismissal to Anne and Moss. Carefully the doctor backed away, bowing, and Anne did the best she could to follow, terrified that she would catch her heels in the gown or the rushes and fall like a fool. But she kept her feet and soon the sense of exposure she had felt standing before the high table evaporated as the trumpeters blew once more, the singing finished, and the royal couple departed the hall. The meal was finished.

Quickly, Anne found her way back to her companions and hurried with them out of the hall and up to the queen's rooms overlooking the river, as servitors gathered up the scraps of the meal that would be taken away to the palace gates and given to the poor.

Issuing instructions over her shoulder, Jehanne rushed into the queen's robing rooms. "Dorcas, find me a fresh linen shift. Jane, hurry now, bring the russet velvet, and the green as well. Gloves, where were they put . . . Evelyn! Don't just stand there—water, get the water. And Rose, you help her, two ewers apiece mind, and hot. Anne, keep silent and learn."

On the heels of this breathless speech the queen swept into the robing room, surrounded by other magnificently dressed women chattering brightly in French. Among them was her mother, Duchess Jacquetta, and two of her younger sisters. Jehanne bobbed a curtsy with the ease of an old and trusted servant, and calmly moved forward accompanied by Jane carefully carrying a trailing gown of russet velvet, the color of fallen oak leaves, which she draped becomingly over a large settle.

"What's this?" The queen frowned at Jehanne. "I said I wanted to wear the green velvet today."

"Aye, Your Majesty. We have that too. Jane!" And the girl hurried forward again, this time cradling another gown made of deep, verdant green, the underskirt fashioned from panels of red and cream damask.

The queen looked at the dress and then walked very slowly over to Jane. The room fell silent; there was something in the queen's face that held them riveted with formless dread. "Jehanne. Come here. Look." The older woman peered carefully at where the queen's finger was pointing. "Who is responsible for this?" There was a groat-sized fleck of mud on the hem of the underskirt and the queen's voice was ominously soft.

"I am, Your Grace," said Jehanne quietly. "It shall be seen to immediately."

Once, twice, the queen hit Jehanne across the face with her open hand, the rings on her fingers drawing blood in long scratches. "Too late," said Elizabeth Wydeville casually.

Anne stood in silent shock, as did everyone in that room, though there was a rush of indrawn breath.

"So, I shall wear the russet, but this will not happen again."

The older woman shook her head as, with steady fingers, she began to unlace the back of the queen's silver and purple gown. "Will you wash, Your Majesty?" she asked in a voice that was rock calm.

"No."

Rose and Evelyn backed quietly out of the room, doing their best not to slop the water in their ewers, as the other women crowded around the queen, exclaiming how well the russet gown would set off the color of her skin. Stoically, Jehanne removed the silver cauls and the crown and brushed out the queen's hair to its full length, which made Anne gasp. It fell nearly to her feet in a mass of fine crimped gold.

"You, girl. Come here." The queen was talking to Anne. "Are you blind as well as deaf?" The edge in Elizabeth's voice was dangerous. Hastily, Jehanne seized Anne by the arm and dragged her forward to the queen, where some blessed reflex made the girl drop to a deep curtsy. "Here, look at this . . ."

Anne looked up warily. Elizabeth had a handful of her own

hair and was holding it up to the light. "See, here—and here. It's darkening. It'll be tow-colored soon." She was right. Looked at closely, the fine strands were not uniform in color at all—especially near to the head where they were noticeably darker.

"Well, daughter, you've had three children now. It's well known that childbirth darkens yellow hair . . ."

Elizabeth froze her mother with a look and Duchess Jacquetta shut her mouth with an audible snap. The queen then turned back to Anne. "Well? What do you say?"

Anne dared to speak. "There is a wash I can make, Your Majesty. I believe it may prevent the hair from darkening further." Anne looked up and the words dried in her throat, constricted by fear; the queen's eyes were very cold.

"Very well. I shall accompany the king hawking after he has seen the ambassador from Burgundy. When I return you will apply this wash and we shall see. Jehanne!"

There was an immediate flurry to dress the queen in the russet velvet gown and hide the offending hair under a gold silk padded turban the size of a small pumpkin, bound with silver wire and tied upon her head and under her chin by trailing green ribbon. As the six serving maids helped Jehanne lace and array the queen, Anne marveled at Elizabeth's body. It really was firm and slender, delicate breasts and arms, and a little, softly rounded belly like an inverted bowl. Truly God had given the queen many natural advantages over other women. Then as the chattering mass of court ladies trailed out of the robing room in the queen's wake, leaving the body servants to restore order, Jehanne gingerly touched her cheek. The queen's rings had cut down almost to one cheekbone.

"Come—no time for chatter. Anne, gather the linen and please search through the larger coffer for mending to be done. Jane, make sure that no mite of mud remains on the green gown. Brush and cleanse it well." A brief fierce look hit home and Jane had the grace to blush. It had been her inattention that had caused the outburst from the queen. "Rose, Dorcas, Lily, dust everything, and these tiles will need waxing again, please. Evelyn, alert the laundresses that we may need their services also. Go now."

The girls worked silently and quickly, nobody brave enough to offer Jehanne assistance, but there was an undertone of things not said in the room that Anne could feel. Under Jehanne's watchful eye all was made neat, and finally she declared their work was done. The chamber was burnished and smelled sweetly of wax and the last white roses and gillyflowers from the palace gardens that Jehanne had arranged in a silver jug.

"Very well. Rose, there are the three silk shifts to be mended. That will take all your time until we must change the queen for supper. The rest of you may now go, and I shall inspect that purgatory you call a sleeping chamber before the nones bell rings."

Quietly, the others filed out and Anne waited to be spoken to. Now, at last, Dame Jehanne allowed herself to sigh, and with a grimace, touched her cheekbone. "What do you need to make the wash for the queen's hair, Anne?"

"I have everything except lemons, Dame Jehanne. I shall need juice from quite a number because the queen's hair is so long and thick."

"Very well, we shall see what we can do." The old lady seemed to be taking her time now, carefully smoothing the counterpane of the queen's bed with Anne's help, almost as if she wanted to delay the girl's leaving. "Now . . . tell me something of yourself. How long did you serve Lady Margaret Cuttifer?"

In telling her history at Blessing House, Anne, being young, told Jehanne more than she thought she did, though she was careful to be discreet about her former employers.

"You were brought up in forest lands, did you say?" Jehanne was unexpectedly sharp with the question and startled Anne.

"Yes, I was . . ."

At this answer, the old lady abruptly waved her hands to indicate the conversation was finished. It was almost as if she could bear to hear no more, which puzzled Anne. Why had she upset Jehanne? She'd seemed so interested a moment ago. Perhaps she was in pain. The older woman had turned away from her now. Anne spoke quickly, before she lost the nerve. "Will you let me help, Dame Jehanne? I could clean the cut on your cheek?"

Jehanne turned, dignified. "That is kind but I shall just use a little warm wine. That will be quite sufficient." And since, clearly, Jehanne did not want her sympathy—or her help—Anne said no more as the two women left the queen's rooms to their unaccustomed silence.

Chapter Twenty

Dank, darkening October had turned to November and now cold flurries of sleet-ridden wind off the river made for a bleak morning as William Hastings, the king's closest friend and palace chamberlain, finalized plans to move the court to Windsor for the Christmas Court.

He was looking forward to the change, though it meant a great deal of work for his office. It was a fact that most courtiers liked Windsor more than London, for even though the castle was still a formidable fortress, it seemed more intimate somehow than the great drafty barracks of Westminster. Hastings was determined to make this Christmas Court as merry as possible to distract the king from the increasing tension of his relationship with Warwick. And if it was true, as was rumored, that the queen might be pregnant again, then there would be double cause for the king to celebrate, and his court with him.

So there was much to do, and most mornings found William out of his bed before dawn, even though the evening revels rarely finished until the dead part of the night. A monk once told him that if he wished to banish the aftereffects of wine, he should drink as much water as he could before he slept. This advice had sounded like certain suicide, because everyone knew that London water was foul and a potent source of contagion since so much filth poured into the Thames. But this clever monk had added good advice. "Boil it first, sir, boil it and have the steam condensed off the pot with a cold metal plate. That is what you must drink—the water from the steam. It is very pure." So it had proved, and while there were those who scoffed and said that drinking water was a sure way to the Devil, that's what William put his lack of headaches down to—drinking his metal water.

This cold morning he sat in his room in the fine new black-and-white house at Saint Paul's wharf, less than ten minutes down-river from the palace by fast barge, comparatively clearheaded, while a constant stream of court servants ran in and out with papers for him to sign: bills of instruction and command that would put the court on the muddy roads and autumn river to Windsor within the next few days. But for now there was a lull and the chamberlain stretched mightily and strolled over to his casements dressed only in his hose and linen undershirt, casually scratching the recent flea bites on his belly.

Thoughts chased through his head as he looked down on the gray silent river rushing past below. The queen didn't like him, that he knew, but then, what wife liked her husband's best friend? They'd had a history together, he and Elizabeth Wydeville, before she married the king. When she'd been plain, widowed Lady Eliz-abeth Grey, her husband's meager lands had marched with his and he'd had occasion to help her with preserving her son Thomas's in-heritance from her dead husband's grasping mother, the dowager Lady Grey. But perhaps he'd extracted too high a price for his ser-vices and that underlaid her hostile feelings for him now.

As Lady Elizabeth Grey she'd signed an indenture that if either Hastings or his brother Ralph had a daughter within five years of their agreement, she was bound to marry her son, when of age, to this girl, or forfeit five hundred marks—a large sum for a widow in tight circumstances. She'd not liked signing that deed, but at the time it had made good business sense. Quid pro quo. But then, if he allowed himself to be honest, he'd known that he had had the best of the bargain at the time.

And for all her beauty, her flesh had not tempted him, so he'd not been swayed from good business by that obvious appeal. She'd seen that when she'd tried to soften the contract conditions and she'd not liked it at all. And she'd never forgotten it. Strange how the great wheel turned.

He walked away from the window, sighing. Their agreement had been made little more than a month before the now-famous secret wedding, and he would swear that, even then, she'd not known just how much things were about to change.

He was aware of the king's lust for her, of course, but thought it would pass as it always had—perhaps, in the end, to the lady's advantage. But Elizabeth and her formidable mother, the widowed former Duchess of Bedford, daughter of the Count of Saint Pol— who'd later so scandalously married Lord Wydeville—had played the king well. Elizabeth must have finessed the virtue card; there was no other explanation. She would not be his whore—if he wanted what was between her legs, Edward would have to marry her.

So there'd been the secret wedding on the night of April 30; the witches' sabbat said those who wished the queen ill—and they were many. Scandalmongers wittered that she and her mother must have bewitched the king. The even more credulous pointed out that Elizabeth and Edward had first *met* under an oak tree and oak groves were haunted by black rites still, in the minds of many. William Hastings thought it all so much nonsense. He shook his head impatiently—he was a modern man. The king was led by his privates, it was simple as that. Certainly the great rise of the Wydevilles after Elizabeth had got the ring on her finger was extraordinary. But witchcraft? No, the woman had an amazingly fair body for one near thirty and an angelic face. And a tongue like a stabbing sword, which he knew now to his cost.

Yes, the wheel had turned and if he was to protect Edward, guard his back, he'd have to step carefully. The queen had been politically weakened lately by the birth of her daughter, but if she was pregnant again the die of the succession was in play once more and his own position would be strengthened, or weakened, by the sex of that coming child.

Hastings shook these troublesome thoughts away with something much more pleasant: the king's entertainment must be particularly fine during the Christmas Court at Windsor. Perhaps, as well, it was time to send his own wife, Catherine, back to their estates, because she, too, was pregnant and surely would not enjoy the rowdiness and the late nights.

He was honest enough to smile slightly at the lie he so conveniently told himself. Catherine would have liked to go to Windsor, but if she did, he would not be free to accompany the king in his enjoyments without reproach. His wife was a good woman, a good breeder, and he was very fond of her, but she had more than a small share of her brother the Earl of Warwick's formidable temperament, and rage at his little enjoyments would be certain to harm the child she was carrying. He'd bring her round to his way of thinking. Somehow.

He dismissed the thought of the confrontation to come. The time had fled while he'd been ruminating; he'd have to move fast to be dressed and into his barge to get to the palace before Edward awoke. It was important, for his continuing political dominance at court, that he be the first man Edward spoke to each morning, that he heard how the king was thinking, for that first conversation always had a bearing on the king's humor for the rest of the day—and on how his own influence might affect events at court.

Down by the river the bargemen waited, stamping their feet and blowing on their fingerless gloves. The first faint streaks of watery gray light could be seen in the eastern sky but the dank river mist made for a miserable wait.

There was a sudden stirring in the dark air as Lord Hastings arrived among them, warmly dressed in a fur-lined cloak with a large, flat velvet hat on his head, lappets hanging down to protect his ears from the cold. The bargemen liked their master. He never forgot their service on these cold mornings and was free with groats and, sometimes, pennies—and he knew their names.

Today, though, William was abstracted, barely acknowledged the men on his barge. In the haste to leave he'd not had himself shaved and there was at least a day's strong black stubble on his face that the torchlight picked out as he jumped down onto the little back deck of the gilded and painted craft. He looked tired, and for a moment, in the torchlight, it was possible to see the old man he would become in time. Then he yawned mightily and dispelled the illusion—all strong white teeth and red mouth and not one gray hair in his head.

Once settled in the barge, brooding on all he had to do, the journey up the river against the tide was as swift as his men could make it, but even so, it was nearly full light before they docked at the palace water stairs. William was cursing roundly as he ran toward the king's chamber surrounded by his retinue of trusted palace servants and friends.

Fortunately, the king, though awake, was finding it hard to leave his bed this morning and it wasn't just because of the sharp winter air that had penetrated even to his private room, the great painted chamber of Henry III. He loved this room—its walls a riot of illustrations from the Old Testament, depictions of Virtues and Vices personified, painted soldiers standing at each side of his great carved bed of state—but its vast size was hard to warm on these cold mornings, even with a fire roaring in the great chimney breast.

Beside him, buried in the fine sheets and sleeping sweetly, was a girl. He watched her breathing gently and smiled, stretching languorously in memory of last night. She'd been very enjoyable—and eager—but then, of course, most of them were. He was conscious that shortly his rooms would be crammed with his closest friends, including William, but he was loath to wake her, because after he did he'd probably never see her again. That thought caused a certain slight but enjoyable feeling of sadness. She'd been a pleasant diversion but it was time to dispense with her services. He wasn't going to take her to Windsor because, frankly, he was getting bored. He'd let Moss handle telling her.

Edward sighed, and then crossed himself. Sometimes, his enjoyment of women—their company, their smell, their flesh—seemed excessive even to him. Surely the good Lord understood? He'd been chosen as king and had held his throne—the image of Warwick came unbidden—and women relieved the constant tension he felt, the need to dissemble all the time. And most kings did as he did; think, after all, of Solomon, of David. Warriors, thinkers, and lovers, both of them.

"Jane . . . Jane, sweet. Wake now . . . they'll be here soon," he murmured gently.

The girl beside him mumbled something and stirred. He smiled. She really did look very sweet—tumbled hair, one round breast exposed among the pure white linen. He felt himself harden. Perhaps there was just enough time; after all, he was the king. Gently he stroked the breast and slid down beside her, under the sheet, matching his body length to hers. "Jane, ah Janey . . ."

She was awake now, but barely, sleepy eyes half opened as she felt him push her thighs apart. She smiled. "Yes, Your Majesty?"

"Shush, lie still."

Now he was in her, covering her body, pushing hard. She relaxed and let him do what he liked, rocking with him, smiling triumphantly—though he didn't see that—as her thoughts wandered, detached from the man above her. *Time to ask for a few favors,* mused black-eyed Jane Fuller, *and time to get out of that dreadful dorter. And maybe, time to stop working for the queen . . .*

Edward was close, so close—heat building, pleasure burning, the whole world centered on the moment and the movement—as he heard William knocking gently on the door—and that was enough. He came roaring, slamming home into the willing, warm girl beneath him.

Outside the door of the painted chamber, William paused. He smiled slightly to Moss and Davis, the king's Welsh valet who was stationed outside the door. They'd all heard that sound more than a few times; they knew to wait.

"Moss, a word." William drew the doctor aside from the small group of men who were waiting to enter the king's bedroom. "I believe that the king will have private business for you to contract shortly." He nodded toward the closed door from behind which could now be heard the low murmur of two voices.

The doctor nodded, face carefully neutral; he was used to these little tasks, was glad they made him useful to the king. "What shall we say to the queen?"

"I shall tell you shortly."

Both men turned as one of the great doors to the king's chamber was thrown open and the king himself stood there, smiling broadly, draped in a fine, furred velvet cloak but plainly naked underneath. "William! Good morning to you."

"And you, Your Majesty." William bowed low before Edward, noting the healthy, glowing look, the clear eyes, as did all those with him. He grimaced slightly; how did the king sustain himself on so little sleep and so much wine? And so much sex. Youth, he thought wearily for a moment. Youth.

"Well now, enter, enter . . ." The king was impatient to begin the day, and the courtiers flocked into the great room as Filke, the king's Flemish barber, offered hot scented water and curds of soft soap made with the best fat and almond kernel oil, for shaving.

William saw that the rumpled bed was empty. He was one of the very few who knew about the door behind the large modern arras that portrayed the labors of Hercules—a door he'd often used himself.

As the king sat for the barber in the light from the three large casements—and William held the shirt to warm by the fire—gossip was quietly exchanged between them out of the hearing of the others. Edward loved picking over the bones of people's lives and not just because he enjoyed the peccadilloes of his courtiers. It was a vital source of information about the shifting alliances around his person that both he and William, his closest friend, valued greatly.

"So, William, tell me. My esteemed mother-in-law, Duchess Jacquetta: what rumors today?"

William was careful to speak softly and lightly in reply: they were on dangerous ground here and both men knew it. "The duchess has a new confessor, sire, but I'm afraid it won't do any good."

"Who is he?"

"A Dominican, I believe. A most holy man, it is said. Father Bruno. French, I understand."

"So, smokescreen of holiness, is that it?"

Cautiously, William allowed himself to nod as he proffered the shirt to the king now that the barber had finished and was bowing himself out of the room. Both men knew that recent court gossip about the queen's unpopular, grasping mother talked up her supposed connection with the black arts.

"And my father-in-law? What of him?"

"Lord Rivers is ill, sire, he's asked to be excused Mass this morning. Something he ate, I believe."

Edward laughed, unexpectedly harshly. Like all the court, he had been astonished by the plague of Wydevilles that had descended after his marriage to the queen, and Hastings kept him informed of the rumblings of discontent about their high-handed behavior. But Edward was confident he could control the queen, and through Elizabeth, her rapacious relatives. Hastings was much less optimistic than the king. He had great respect for Elizabeth's powers of persuasion, so clearly linked to the beauty of her body and face. These were formidable weapons for any man to fight when the queen wanted something. Besides, the king was notorious for getting others to do his emotional dirty work. A decisive general, a good administrator of his kingdom—as he was beginning to prove himself—yet he hated the mire and complexity of intimate human relationships. What he wanted were friends, laughter, and music; loud voices, reproaches, and tears filled him with unease such that, when women cried, he walked away and Hastings picked up the pieces.

The queen understood the king well, far too well, and, where her family was concerned, she exploited his impatience and discomfort about emotion. She made it easy for him to say yes when she asked him for favors—she never clamored or begged—and she rewarded him with sex. The sorts of games they played together were unlike those of any of his other lovers, for she played his body like a viol—delicately and well. He'd always returned, thus far. William sighed. Women!

"Ah, women." Edward breathed the word reverently.

William was startled and then saw that the king was looking out of the window as Davis dressed him. Down below them on the river was an open wherry, and sitting in the stern, a young woman and her serving girl were being rowed upstream. The hood of her cloak had slipped back and they could see her pretty face, veiling fluttering in the damp wind.

The king grinned at his friend. "Ah, William, so many plump little coneys. So little time, eh? Now, to work. What are the plans for Windsor?"

The valet finished dressing his master, and the group of men in the bedchamber, taking a signal from William, fell in behind the king as he left the room to go to Mass. As they walked out into the king's general reception rooms, William drew Moss aside and slipped a small leather pouch into his hands, a pouch that clinked, and an exquisite, tiny enameled box. "Jane Fuller. The pouch is for her."

The doctor nodded.

"See she leaves the court before we go to Windsor."

Moss bowed his head. The king would see that Jane was well looked after. Most likely she would be sent north to York, the king's family stronghold. A dowry and marriage would be arranged for her, perhaps to a prosperous brewer or merchant, and Moss could feel by the weight of the purse in his hand that Hastings had provided money for her trousseau. All that remained now was to let the girl know her good fortune.

The doctor sighed. It was never easy. William clapped him on the shoulder with a certain sympathy. "Come to me after you're done. There is much to speak of. And by the way, the box is for the queen, a gift from the king. Please take it to Her Majesty without delay."

Chapter Twenty-one

It had taken Anne a number of weeks to make sense of the Palace of Westminster's huge maze of bewildering passages and chambers and find within it landmarks she could recognize when she got lost. But though the vast building began to feel more familiar, the protocol within the court continued to be a severe trial and she lived with dread every day: dread that she would say or do the wrong thing and find herself banished from the palace and the life of the queen and, if she was honest, the king.

Court life intrigued her, and as she learned who was ascendant and who was in decline within the circle of royal favor, she found herself thinking about the real nature of all these mighty people and how she could find a secure place among them.

The queen was the hardest to read—one minute warm, laughing, and friendly; the next, an icy tyrant who would act on a whim, a whim that could unleash a cataclysm upon the life of the person concerned.

Fortunately, at the moment, Elizabeth was extremely pleased with Anne. So pleased, that within two weeks of her arrival at court the queen had caused the girl to be moved out of the dorter she shared with the other body servants—to the great relief of Rose, Dorcas, and Lily; to Evelyn's sorrow, and to Jane's intense jealousy—into a tiny room all of her own, barely a cupboard, next to the queen's own suite of rooms.

The reason for this unheard-of favor had been the glorious living gold that Anne had restored to Elizabeth Wydeville's hair. She'd made a wash with lemon juice and then applied a hot paste of fine, white clay. The clay was from a rare seam in the heavy red London earth that brickmakers near the castle had found; Anne had heard of it by chance, tested it, and found that it, too, had bleaching properties when mixed with almond oil and the urine of a lactating woman.

Everyone at court commented on how radiant the queen now looked, and how she and the king were more in love than ever.

Today, so as to make herself particularly attractive to the king, Elizabeth had spent fully an hour sitting in the deep brass tub placed by the fire in her robing room, as her servants filled and refilled it with hot milk. Anne, Dorcas, and Evelyn had run back and forth to the kitchens in relays with heavy copper cans, until at last the queen was satisfied that the milk really had increased the smoothness of her skin. Now her servants were rushing to dress her in time to join Edward at Mass.

Anne stood waiting quietly with a basket of ivory hairpins as she watched Jane brush the queen's hair. Jane was smiling pleasantly enough as she went about her task quickly and methodically, sectioning Elizabeth's hair and being careful to brush with long, steady strokes from the roots to the ends. But in her heart Jane was thinking how much she hated this woman and how little the queen knew of what her husband *really* liked, when Doctor Moss was announced with a message from the king.

"Jehanne, see what he wants. Jane! You're ripping my scalp!"

The queen was testy and Dame Jehanne saw the flush mount up Jane's neck as she herself hurried away to obey Elizabeth. Jehanne was convinced the queen was breeding again. There'd been no bloodied rags to remove from the garderobe for two months now, and the flightiness of her moods suggested it too. But of course, she was careful to keep her suspicions to herself. It would be dangerous to speculate until the pregnancy was confirmed.

In the outer receiving chamber, Doctor Moss was sauntering up and down as he waited for the summons, the only outward sign of his impatience the slapping of one pigskin glove on the other from time to time.

Jehanne bustled over to him. "The queen is dressing, Doctor Moss. I'll take your message."

The doctor bowed low but he was implacable: "You are most gracious. However, I fear that I must speak to Her Majesty. I have been asked to, personally."

"By the king?" Jehanne was sharp. She was sometimes difficult about granting access to the queen, especially to Moss whom she did not trust. Too smooth by half, she thought him.

The doctor tried not to frown in annoyance at her tone, but felt it prudent to confess the truth. The old witch would be bound to check.

"The Lord Hastings. But still . . . the king especially asked him." And he smiled his most charming smile.

To which Jehanne was impervious. "Wait here," she said as she closed the door of the dressing chamber with something of a snap.

He smiled faintly: a tilt to him he rather thought.

Anne and Jane hardly dared breathe as they lowered the queen's headdress on to her head; it had a daringly wide, delicately starched butterfly veil that they were both desperate not to disturb. Rose watched them with an eagle eye. She was the queen's gofferer, and this was some of her best work, so woe descend on both if they creased or broke those perfect gauzy folds. But there, it was done, and as Evelyn fixed the cap that supported the veil with long gold pins topped by pearls, all the girls sighed in relief.

Carefully, the queen moved her head back and forth, testing the weight of the starched veiling above, and then, unexpectedly, she smiled. "Excellent, Rose. You have done well."

Smiles broke out around the chamber—it was a good day, after all. Emboldened by the change of mood, Jehanne approached the queen and bent down to whisper something that Jane, as close as she was, could not catch.

Elizabeth smiled radiantly and stood up. "Come now, I am eager to join my Lord the King at Mass." Sweeping forward confidently, she crossed swiftly through the carved doors of her robing room and out into her receiving chamber.

Doctor Moss looked up to see an enchanting sight. The early sunlight flooding the eastern walls of the palace glowed through the veiling on the queen's headdress and caught and magnified the brilliance of her jewels. Not for nothing had she snared Edward, thought Moss, for sometimes her beauty was otherworldly. He crossed himself discreetly as he bowed to one knee. Perhaps what they said was true and she *was* a servant of the devil: such lustrous flesh could not be honestly begotten surely?

The queen saw the effect she had on the handsome doctor and was pleased; it warmed her tone when she spoke to him. "Doctor Moss. I believe you have a message from my lord the King?"

The doctor finished his bow gracefully and just as gracefully moved forward, bowed again, and offered the exquisite little enameled box, without comment. Eagerly, the queen took it from his hands, prised the lid open—and gasped. There, resting among black velvet, lay a great emerald ring, the immense, glowing stone like something out of legend. Triumphantly, the queen pushed it onto her forefinger and held it up for her people to see as Doctor Moss spoke.

"There is a message, Lady Queen. From your husband the king. Green is the color of true love and I am commanded to tell you that the beauty of this small token"—the great ring flashed and burned as the queen held it up to the light—"dims in the blaze cast by the the fairest jewel in his kingdom. And besides, he thought it might match Your Majesty's eyes."

The queen laughed delightedly. "Bravely said, Doctor Moss. Bravely said. But now we must hurry." She swept out, surrounded by her women, all vying to admire this present with its testament of the king's love for his queen. But Doctor Moss stayed back, allowing the ladies to flow past him, and his not unsympathetic gaze strayed to Jane Fuller, as she, Anne, and the other body servants tidied up the robing room with Dame Jehanne.

After a moment, he strolled over to Dame Jehanne and spoke quietly. He nodded toward Jane as she stamped to and fro, angrily dropping clothes into hoppers and getting in everyone's way.

"Sir, perhaps it can wait until after we have finished our tasks here."

"No, I think it cannot."

There was something in his tone that gave Jehanne pause. She looked at him uneasily, then folded her lips when he raised his eyebrows. "Jane. Come here," she called. Sulkily the girl did what she was told.

"With your leave, Dame." Doctor Moss took Jane firmly by the arm and led her out into the corridor beyond the queen's rooms.

"Well now, don't stand there gawping, girls. Get on with your work," Jehanne snapped.

A moment later, as Anne and Evelyn struggled to carry away the cans of cold milk drained from the bath, they heard Jane cry. "No!" Great, heartbroken sobs followed and nearly drowned the doctor's low voice as he spoke to her. And when the queen's women had finished their allotted work in the robing room and hurried away, chattering, to break their fast, Anne and her companions saw that Jane and the doctor had disappeared.

The rest of that day was crammed with work. Between them, the five girls—for Jane never came back—supervised by Dame Jehanne, packed all the queen's clothes, her shoes and headdresses and cloaks, her cosmetics, her bed linen, her favorite furniture, and even her plate, ready to be taken up the river to Windsor in the afternoon. They received word during the morning that the queen had decided Anne was to travel with her and attend to her needs on the journey, and if the others were envious, they didn't let it show, apart from Rose, of course.

Evelyn was full of practical advice for her friend. "Take some sugared almonds with you, Anne, and the candied violets—she loves them and they might sweeten her temper, especially if she is breeding again." The two girls worked swiftly as they packed the last of the jewels away, wrapped in silk and deposited into a specially made plain iron strongbox for which Dame Jehanne held the key. "Oh, and carry a choice of muffs. She likes the miniver one best at the moment but you never know."

Finally, when Dame Jehanne was out of earshot, Anne plucked up the courage to ask the question that had been burning in her mouth all day. "Evelyn, where do you think Jane has gone?"

The other girl turned to her friend and looked at her seriously for a moment. "Away. She won't be back."

"Why?"

Evelyn was uneasy. There was so much she took for granted, and so much Anne didn't yet know. "The king. He..." She stopped because Jehanne was within earshot again.

"Come along, you two, you've had more than enough time with the jewels. Here, out of my way." Jehanne riffled through the bunch of keys hanging at her waist, checking that she still had the little one needed to unlock the jewel coffer when they reached Windsor. Finally, she found it and, reassured, she dropped the hasp over the hoop of the holder before padlocking it. "There. Now, Evelyn, I want all these other coffers taken down to the oxcarts. Would you fetch the men, please. I shall take this personally."

And in the rush and hurry to be away, Anne never did get an answer about Jane.

Now in the second hour after noon on this bleak November day, Anne stood waiting beside the palace water gate along with a press of courtiers and servants. The royal barge, bravely tricked out with scarlet and gold, leopard pennons flying, was tied fore and aft to creaking elm posts, and its crew of twenty strong watermen was impatient and cold. Behind the king's barge another was moored, painted with the royal arms but more workmanlike in appearance. This was where the baggage and some of the body servants would travel.

"Anne? There you are." The girl turned to find Doctor Moss at her shoulder. "Excited?"

"Oh, yes, sir. I've never been to Windsor. They say it has very beautiful country. I shall look forward to walking in the park, if I am permitted."

"We must see what can be done to fulfill your wish." The doctor spoke more warmly than he'd intended but he couldn't help himself. The little girl was growing up. Court life was adding a polish to her and some conversation also; she seemed more at ease with him now and that would be useful to them both. He found he approved of her looks: the dark red of her livery contrasted happily with the gray of her cloak; plainly she was one of those girls who could wear almost any color and look well in it. Making an effort to appear avuncular, he patted her on the shoulder, though a quick flash of lust pushed his thoughts in another direction. She really was very appealing.

Anne smiled shyly, though she was a little surprised. Doctor Moss was most often distant when they met by chance, and so the warmth of his tone today, his genuine interest in her, was unusual.

"Doctor Moss, do you know Anne? One of the queen's body servants?" A young squire, wearing the badge and livery of Lord Hastings, had appeared at the doctor's side.

"You see her here, young man."

The boy turned self-importantly to Anne and then blushed—and his words came out in stumbles. "Er, my master, that is, Lord Hastings, commands on behalf of the queen that you . . . that you . . ." He stopped because he was abashed; no one had said to look for a *beautiful* girl.

"Well, boy, spit it out." The doctor was amused.

"The queen approaches, girl." Inadvertently the boy bowed and then cursed himself for a fool. His name was Roger de Lascelles and he was wellborn. This girl was just a servant; good for a tumble but hardly meriting courtesies he'd extend to a knight's child or a lady. Reborn pride and a sense of his own superiority made his next words curt. "Find your place on the king's barge."

Silently Anne curtsied to the red-faced boy as he strode away. She was confused by the change in his tone, but looking forward too much to this trip on the river to pay attention to his odd manners. The doctor laughed and she turned to him. "Why do you laugh, sir?"

"Oh, at us, Anne, at us. We're a curious breed."

At that moment, a great mass of people surged down toward the water gate and in their midst were the king and queen. William Hastings was conducting them to their barge. In the press of bodies, Doctor Moss was separated from Anne who, being polite and relatively slight, was swept closer and closer to the edge of the water stairs by the crowd. As yet more courtiers pushed down through the gate, Anne's feet slipped over the stone edging and she lost her balance. Below her the black water of the Thames sucked and beckoned and for one dizzy moment she felt herself falling between the quay and the royal barge—but a strong hand grabbed her wrist, then her waist, and hauled her back by main force.

Anne found herself looking up into the face of the king. He smiled down at her, pressed so close by the crowd that her body was measured against the length of his. With one strong arm he turned her round, away from the edge, neatly and swiftly, and then he let her go. "That was dangerous, girl. You could have been crushed." And he was gone, back into the press of courtiers.

Doctor Moss pushed his way to Anne's side, smiling grimly. "The king speaks truth. Let me escort you to the barge this time."

Was it the water on the flags that made them so slippery or would her legs not hold her up? Anne was grateful for the doctor's hand gripping her arm as she made her way uncertainly toward the gangplank across to the king's barge, for she saw that tumultuous moment again and again: Edward's mouth had been so close to hers, she was certain that . . . what? He would kiss her? Had she really seen that in his eyes? She closed her own for a moment as dread and delight ran deeply through her body. Thunder muttered, far in the distance. Soon there would be rain and it would be a cold journey to Windsor, yet Anne was sweating, her heart beating as if she had run all the way through the palace to reach the wharf.

The queen, who was being handed onto the barge by Hastings, wondered what the sudden noise had been behind her as the king arrived at her side. "Nothing, sweet burde. One of your servants nearly fell in the river. Silly girl."

Doctor Moss just succeeded in guiding Anne onto the barge as the watermen, impatient to be away, cast off and dipped their painted oars into the cold river water, and the court floated away, up the Thames to Windsor.

Chapter Twenty-two

The Christmas season was always kept with great state by the court at Windsor. Every day as it grew nearer and nearer the time of the Savior's birth, the king went out hunting seeking stag to bring home to his subjects for the Christ-Mass wassail. It felt very ancient, this ritual: the king, anointed by God, riding through the great depths of the silent forest dressed in green, surrounded by his knights, their horses' hooves muffled by the fallen leaves, hunting the lord of the trees and the high hills. And when Edward had made his kill, he rode back on his destrier, the dead stag following him slung across the back of another warhorse, led by the king himself. An honor from one monarch to another.

As the days grew shorter and the red sun set lower behind black trees, the inside of the castle was a warm, roaring haven against the cold winds, the sleet, and the rain this season always brought.

Everyone in Windsor Castle looked forward to the Christmas time. Long winter nights, rich venison, and much wine bred license among the court and, despite what the priests might say, there was a sense of old rites and pagan memories of wilder times in the air. They had a young king and queen and most of the courtiers were of a like age. What else does youth do in winter but lay down fat and try to breed?

Each day Windsor felt more and more alive as the magnates

and their people arrived from all over England, but Anne was rest-less and increasingly she slept badly, her nights haunted by heated dreams laced with dread. Whatever she did, sleeping or waking, she could not avoid the king. In her dreams she saw his face, writhed under the touch of his hands, woke sweating and guilty, and then, during the day, she could not help being present in one or other of the great solars where Elizabeth spent most of her time— and which the king enjoyed visiting.

Edward particularly liked to arrive as the queen was being dressed in the morning and would sit behind a screen as his wife was bathed, joking with all her attendants, the ladies and the ser-vants. It was very relaxed and the women surrounding Elizabeth vied for Edward's attention. But not Anne. She lowered her eyes and tried to make sure she was on the opposite side of the room from where he sat.

It was on the feast of Saint Thomas, four days before Christ-mas, that the new pregnancy of the queen was deemed safe enough to be announced to the court. The king signified his pleasure and satisfaction with Elizabeth by holding a special High Mass with prayers dedicated to the child, and for the safe delivery of the queen. Afterward at supper that night it was decreed that a special tourna-ment would be held at Windsor in the new year to celebrate the coming baby. Edward himself would take part; he, with Hastings and eleven other picked knights, to make up the same mystic num-ber as the Lord and his disciples, would challenge a team of knights to be led by the Earl of Warwick.

There was a moment's silence before the court applauded, but afterward conversation buzzed with what this could mean. Was this an honor that the king was bestowing on the earl, or was it meant to be a sign of some sort? Whichever team won, there would be much at stake and that would add piquancy to the contest.

Anne, sitting silent with her companions in the shadows at the end of the board during the feast, felt her heart squeeze with fear. She'd never seen a tourney but she'd heard about them. Staged combat was a sport that everyone discussed, but it was dangerous, even with blunted swords, and she was frightened for the king, and the kingdom.

Perhaps it was the strength of the wine that night, perhaps it was the unrelenting tension of being in the king's presence and the emotional exhaustion she felt, but when Anne slipped into sleep after the feast, black terror stalked her. In the otherworld of night, men hacked each other with swords and axes, sharp blades bit bright steel as blood soaked the ground. The screams of dying horses drenched the air with formless agony and Anne could not look away, she was the center of the conflict, and through it all, through the terrible carnage, there stalked the figure of the Sword-Mother, Aine. Anne was grateful, so grateful, that Aine's face was turned away, because the Mother's forearms and breastplate were red with blood, and if she turned and saw . . . But in the midst of the shouting and screaming, Anne stumbled away unscathed, one thought only in her mind: find Edward, find him before it was too late . . .

Too late for . . . what? Suddenly the Sword-Mother was standing in front of her, slowly, so slowly turning her face, turning it toward Anne, and with a breaking heart, the girl saw Edward lying beneath her feet, wounded, bleeding . . .

Heart hammering, breath burning in her lungs, Anne forced herself to wake. The vast building was silent around her, and black, yet the resonance of terror remained, the overwhelming certainty that Edward was in danger and needed help.

As the beating of her heart settled, Anne knew what she had to do. Quietly, stealthily, she stole away from her bed among the queen's body servants dropping a shift over her naked body, and wrapping herself in a thick cloak with a hood. In felt slippers she ran soundlessly down to the little Norman chapel used by the court at Windsor. Kneeling at a stall in the dark choir, she began to pray for Edward's safety in the tourney as tears slipped unheeded down her face.

The chapel was dark but for the light kept burning before the pyx, and the stone walls breathed cold. Anne shivered, wrapped the thick cloak tighter, and set her mind on God, the Christian God, but it was hard to concentrate on prayer, to reach the Lord, when images of the king's face, eyes closing as he died, were all she saw. In terror, she squeezed her eyes tight shut, but then something odd happened. She heard voices whispering.

There were two others with her in the chapel now; men, from the bass tone of their quiet conversation. She shrank back into the stall, desperate not to be seen, then, when she dared to look again, she saw a flash of gold close to the altar as one of the men threw back the fold of his cloak and turned his face into the light. Her heart lurched. It was the king! Then she saw her mistake. This man was the Duke of Clarence—George, the king's younger brother—and the other was the Earl of Warwick.

Anne prickled with fear. The earl was standing with his hand on the prince's shoulder talking to him urgently, and from the scowl on Clarence's face it was clear the duke did not like what he heard.

From a distance, it was easy to mistake the younger brother for the king—they were both tall and fair—but close up the resemblance faltered. It was as if, when Clarence was formed, the mold that minted his brother had blurred just slightly. His hair was not so bright, he had bad skin—unlike Edward—and a petulant mouth. He was also easily upset and—a foolish thing at court—showed it.

The gossip said he was hot to marry Isabelle, Warwick's eldest daughter and a great heiress since the earl had no sons. She was only fourteen and Clarence was older by some seven years, but he'd lusted after her since she was twelve.

"He will not permit the marriage."

"Why not?" The duke almost stamped his feet, and Anne could see him clearly as he turned to stare angrily off into darkness—as if his brother might be lurking in the shadows ready to challenge him. Warwick shrugged, eloquently. Not for him to speculate, that shrug said.

"I see his game. He's frightened of me!" Clarence had a penetrating voice and Warwick looked around nervously, worried they would be overheard.

"Frightened?" the earl queried.

"Warwick, how can you be so dense? Edward, my precious brother, knows he's none so secure on this throne. Everyone hates the queen even if she is pregnant again. But if I were to wed Isabelle, why, the whole of the north would be ours. I'd be a real threat, wouldn't I? You've put one brother on this throne—why not the other?"

Warwick mumbled something in reply, something Anne could not catch, but she saw his face—for a moment it flashed with something like triumph. "Wishful thinking, I fear, Your Grace. Still, it's true that the people are murmuring again. Lawlessness is on the rise. Men say your brother spends much time in the bed of the queen."

The duke snorted. "And plentiful others."

Anne flinched, unwilling to hear what so many people took for fact.

Again the earl shrugged smoothly and changed the subject. "However, the case is that the country needs governing and our king seems tardy learning the art of good governance."

"And the cursed Wydevilles are a plague of locusts consuming the substance of this kingdom. Warwick, I will not bear it."

"We shall need to move carefully, Your Grace. Gently and slowly. However, by some means I shall contrive, you shall have Isabelle. That is my promise."

As the two men moved away together out of the chapel, the earl's words hung in the cold night air like smoke. Anne stayed where she was in the dark, all thought of prayer banished, until she was sure the two men were gone, and then she slipped out the way she had come, her mind even more troubled than when she had arrived.

Anne was abstracted as she approached the little room she shared with the others, until she cannoned into someone dressed in a fine velvet dressing gown. Edward. He was leaving the queen's bed, tousled and sleepy, to go back to his own quarters, holding a candle to light his way. Her anguished dreams were suddenly made flesh, and before she could stop herself she signed the cross, tears in her eyes, as if to keep him safe. Then it came to her; he was real, this was no dream, and she snatched her hand back, hoping that in the confusion of the moment, he'd not seen. Shakily, she bobbed a panicked curtsy, then tried to hurry toward the dorter, and safety, when he put out a lazy arm to stop her.

"Well, now . . . it's dark, and very late. Or rather, very early. What have we here? Anne, returning from a tryst?"

"No, sire!" Anne was glad he could not see her clearly in the darkened passageway—she felt the blood heat her face and neck.

He was amused. "Oh? What, then?" Anne was silent. "Very enigmatic, sweet child." The hand he'd put out to stop her flight was resting gently on her shoulder now, and he moved a step closer, his body between her and the door of the dorter. He spoke softly, as he would to a hawk unsettled in the mews. The girl shivered, unwittingly closed her eyes and swallowed. He smiled, moved nearer, smoothly pulled her closer so that she stood against him as he stroked her back. "So, where have you been, hmm? So late?"

For a moment, Anne was lulled by his words and relaxed against the broad chest, the pleasure of his touch running through her body; wanting, oh, wanting so much that he would lean down and . . . But then, in a flash, as one of his hands slipped inside her cloak and slid down to her waist, pulling her tighter against him, she realized she had to stop what was happening. "No . . ." It was agony to whisper the word when she so wanted him to go on, but she found the strength, though her throat nearly closed with the effort of saying it.

"No?" he murmured. But he stilled his hand, which had found its way to a breast and was stroking it, so gently, so lightly. "So be it—if you make me a promise." He dropped his hand. Quickly she pulled the cloak around her and nodded.

"Tomorrow, when I ask it of you, you will tell me the truth."

"What truth, sire?"

"The truth of where you've been tonight. On your honor." He smiled down at her. "Good night, Anne." And then he stooped down, pulled her to him, and kissed her on the mouth. She was overwhelmed, beyond conscious thought; her mouth opened under his and for one dark, sweet moment, as he held her so tightly, the world snuffed out. There was only this man, this girl. Then he let her go.

"Tomorrow." And he was gone. And she was left alone to find her bed, mind spinning, body shivering from fear, love, dread, and cold.

Chapter Twenty-three

 The next morning dawned freezing and wet. It was as if the earth mourned, the sleet of frozen tears hitting the windows in the royal apartments of Windsor like pebbles.

The queen had slept badly after the king's visit, so she'd been pleased with nothing this morning, and then, just as they'd finally got her fully clothed, she'd rushed to the garderobe to vomit but had got there too late and sprayed green bile down the front of one of her favorite gowns. Then it had been frenzy as all five of the girls, and her gentlewomen servitors, cannoned into one another as they tried to find something else Elizabeth would agree to wear.

So it was a miracle that the queen had arrived at Mass on time, and now, after the court had gone out hunting—the queen with a green face but determined not to give in—the servants sat companionably together at mending and embroidering in the queen's smaller solar. Anne was brooding and tense.

"Anne! Pay attention to your work. You've not set a stitch for ten minutes—what can you be thinking about?"

Embarrassed, Anne tried with all her will to banish the memory of Edward's body against hers, the hard muscles in his arms, the softness of his mouth on hers, as she went on with repairing the lacing holes in one of the queen's dresses. Morning had made that moment distant, surreal, something that might never have happened, except that it had. And it was wrapped around by the fog of treason, the things she had heard in the chapel, her anguished fears. Agitated, she automatically plunged the needle into the material, misjudged, and rammed it into her finger on the other side. She yelped and blood seeped onto the expensive yellow velvet.

"Now see! Foolish girl! Give it to me, quickly, quickly. We must not let the stain set." Jehanne snatched up the gown and ran into the garderobe with it, followed by Anne sucking her finger, anxious to make amends. "Fuller's earth: the special white. Quickly now! Oh, we have no old urine! Cold water then, quickly . . ."

Carefully and quickly, Jehanne dampened the area of the cloth that had blood on it, and then, making a thin paste of the finely ground white clay, pressed it on to the blot. "There now, it needs to be left alone to dry. And then we can brush it out and perhaps . . . only perhaps, mind . . . it will take the stain with it." Anne nodded dumbly and then sat down abruptly on a coffer, the strength in her legs draining away. Jehanne looked at her sharply. "Very well. What is it?"

Anne felt defeated. Where should she begin? she wondered, even as she spoke. "Last night. That is, I was in the chapel and they were there. I was so frightened, for the king, and then he, well . . . he . . ." Anne stumbled to a halt but her face said it all. Fear and confusion and . . . something else. Jehanne's eyebrows went up. Something serious had gone on.

Jehanne helped Anne to her feet and led the unresisting girl out through the solar as she issued orders to Evelyn. "Evelyn, Anne is not well. I'm taking her to the dorter to give her some physic. You will be my deputy here, and when you have finished your current tasks, we must prepare warm, dry clothes for the queen. Rose, come and find me immediately if you hear the hunt returning. They surely can't stay out long in this."

She led the girl out of the room and closed the door on the cosy warmth. The passage outside was icy as a bitter wind chased itself through a badly shuttered window; it was colder inside the building than out.

When they reached the corner tower near the queen's rooms where the dorter was, Jehanne wrenched the door open, and for once, Anne was glad it was so small. There was even a brazier with a few coals still burning, so the room was not entirely frigid. Jehanne struck flint and lit the wick of two small oil lights that struggled to make an impression on the winter gloom.

"Now, Anne, I can see something is bothering you. Let me just find the tonic Doctor Moss gave me for the winter ills. You need something to give you heart, I can see that. Now, where is it . . ."

Anne watched as the old woman bustled about, wondering how she would find the words to voice what she knew. And realizing that if she confided in Jehanne about the king, she would be prevented from being close to him ever again. She closed her eyes. That thought was too much to bear.

"Here it is." With a triumphant flourish, the old woman produced a small stoppered clay bottle and pulled out the rag plug. "Here now, just two swallows." It was an effort for Anne to sip the bitter fluid from the little bottle. "So, now. Tell me."

Anne sighed and closed her eyes, seeing it all again. "Last night, I was in the chapel—"

"The chapel . . . but . . ." Jehanne stopped herself. Best let the girl find her own words. "Go on. You were in the chapel . . ."

"Yes, and I saw the Earl of Warwick and . . . the king's brother. The Duke of Clarence . . ." And then it all poured out, the exchange she had heard between the two men, the implied treason, and the enmity of George for the king. When she had finished, Anne was rocking herself back and forth, a child needing comfort.

Jehanne was silent for a moment as she thought. Clearly Anne was speaking the truth and somehow the king needed to be warned. But how to do it and ensure both Anne, and she, survived the telling? "I think I shall speak to Lord Hastings—but I'm afraid he will need to speak to you also."

Anne was no fool. She could hear the unacknowledged fear in Jehanne's voice, and she knew that what she'd heard was potentially explosive in the overheated atmosphere of the court and its maneuvering factions. "Oh, I wish Deborah were here, she would know what to do," she whispered.

There was silence for a moment and then Jehanne said, in an odd strangled voice, "Deborah?"

Anne, who was screwing up her courage to tell the next part of her story, didn't hear the odd tone. "Deborah is my foster mother. She took me in after my mother died having me. She brought me up."

Jehanne was staring at her now, her face fixed and white in the gloom. The intensity of the look was arresting. "This . . . Deborah. Is she alive?"

"Oh, yes. She found me my place at Blessing House. She taught me everything I know of simples and healing."

"Where did you live, girl?"

"Our house was in the forest. It's close to the marches of Wales, away to the west."

"Are there king's lands near your home?"

"Yes. There's an old lodge and a hunting preserve. But Deborah says it was last in her mother's time that the court came there to hunt. There's just the game wards and a reeve to look after the king's lands. They never bothered us."

"Yes . . ." The word was breathed out, like a long sigh. Quietly, Dame Jehanne got to her feet and with a shaking hand picked up one of the oil lamps, holding it close to Anne's face so that she could see her clearly. "Turn your head, child. Now the other way. Now look me in the eyes."

Obediently, Anne did as she was told, questions hovering on her tongue, as Jehanne, apparently satisfied by her inspection, put the lamp down very carefully and sat looking at Anne in silence. The silence stretched to an uncomfortable length until at last Jehanne sighed. "How may I contact your foster mother, child? Does she ever come to London?"

Anne was alarmed. "Will I have to leave the court?"

Jehanne laughed a little; it was a harsh sound. "I do not know, girl. What you have told me is serious indeed, perhaps much more serious than we can imagine. But . . . perhaps you hold a key to this puzzle. I think she will want us to meet."

Poor Jehanne. For a moment, as she gazed at Anne, her face crumpled and it seemed as if she would cry. Anne rushed to comfort her. "Ah, do not upset yourself, mistress. There will be a way to tell the king, I am sure of it." Gently, she gathered both of Jehanne's hands in her own, making soothing little noises, the kind a mother used to comfort a child.

The warmhearted gesture seemed to shock the old lady even more. Grasping Anne by the shoulders, Jehanne looked searchingly into the girl's eyes and nodded fearfully. "Yes, I have seen your kindness before now. My God . . . oh, my God. You've never been like the others—now I see why."

Anne was even more perplexed. "What do you mean, Dame Jehanne? Which others?"

But Jehanne only shook her head. "Your foster mother. How can I get her a message?"

Why did Anne feel such fear as she replied? "It's hard to get messages to the forest. Sometimes I've been able to send word with a tinker who's our friend. He buys his stock in London and stays at an inn called the Angel, in the east Chepe, when he's here."

"And when will he be in London next?"

"He may be there now. Sometimes he winters over and goes back on the roads in spring."

Jehanne got up briskly, all emotion banished. "I shall return later but in the meantime you are not to leave this room. I shall think on what you have told me."

It was only after the old woman had left the dorter that it occurred to Anne that she had not told Jehanne about the king. She hugged the thought of him, the sense of him, to herself. And then, without being aware, she fell back on the bed and slept well, for the first time in many days.

Meanwhile, Jehanne hurried through the castle to where the queen's guard was stationed in the outer ward, looking for an old friend of hers, a certain sergeant she'd known since she was a girl. He came from the same area she did, just outside Patrington in the Holderness of the north. She found him, muffled in his old campaign cloak, down in the enormous stables that housed the king's and queen's horses. It was said these stables were big enough to keep and feed over two hundred animals, even in winter.

"Sergeant Cage?"

The man turned toward the voice—a lady's voice but familiar. "Dame Jehanne. Why, it's a pleasure to see you here." Then the sergeant frowned; it was not fitting for a woman to be around the stables.

"Yes, Sergeant, I know. I shouldn't be here but I need you to do something for me, if you can. Urgently. I need a trusted man to be sent to London with a message." The old lady pulled out a purse and carefully counted out a number of groats and two silver pennies. "I hope I shall not inconvenience you too much. You know I would not ask if it were not very important. Will this be enough?"

His hardened hand closed over hers. "Put thy money away, lass." He said it softly and crossed social bounds to speak like this, but there'd been a sweet tenderness between them once, when they'd been young, and he'd never forgotten it. Neither had she. And he remembered her as she'd been, the fairest thing ever to be born on her father's small holding. "Now, where is this message? And who am I to send it to?"

Jehanne gave him the message then, warmed by old memories, hurried away, back to the solar. There she found the queen's rooms in an uproar; Elizabeth had indeed found the hunt too much and had returned to the castle ahead of the king. She'd managed to put a brave face on things until she'd got to her rooms among her own people, and then she'd collapsed. Immediately, Jehanne set about getting her undressed and into bed—if only the queen's lady attendants would get out of the way. She dispatched Evelyn to bring Anne from the dorter, for every pair of hands was needed now.

The queen was lying, eyes closed and white-faced, across the lap of Lady de Sommerville, the wife of a powerful northern landholder and staunch supporter of the House of York, as Jehanne tried to unlace the dress without further disturbing her mistress. The rest of the lady servitors in the room clustered around, each offering conflicting advice.

"Well, I think a hot posset mixed with egg, a little malmsey, and nutmeg would be the best thing . . ."

"Not at all—spices would be very bad for her in this condition . . ."

"A hot brick for the queen's feet?" It was the most sensible thing Jehanne had yet heard and she looked up gratefully to Anne as she hurried into the room ahead of Evelyn.

"Yes, child. Quickly. Now, Your Majesty, we're unlaced. Lady de Sommerville, if you would just help Her Majesty to stand." With the last of the lacing free, the gown could be loosened and slipped off as the queen got to her feet and stood there swaying, eyes closed. Quickly, Evelyn stepped forward with a velvet dressing wrap furred with bands of marten and lynx, and Jehanne swathed Elizabeth in its folds. "There now, madam. Lean on me, and we shall have you in your bed in no time . . ."

From under closed lids, slow fat tears slid down the queen's face. Her ladies looked at her in astonishment: the queen must be seriously ill, no one had ever seen her cry. Except when the Lady Elizabeth her daughter, had been born, of course, but that was just natural disappointment.

"Ah, Jehanne, I am so cold, so cold . . ." The queen put her hand on her belly fearfully. "Do you think I have injured him?" The ladies looked at one another, momentarily uncertain.

It was Anne who spoke. "No, Your Majesty. You are healthy and strong. All you need is rest and warmth. And to sleep. See, we have the bed prepared." She spoke quietly but the calm authority in her voice worked. Meekly, the queen nodded and climbed up into the great bed amid perfect silence. The others were so amazed that a servant had spoken uninvited that they had nothing to say.

Settled under the counterpane, snuggled up with her hair neatly braided like a small, clean child, the queen looked just like any other young woman, and compassion flooded Anne's heart. The life of a queen was hard. Everyone watched you all the time, and who was there to trust, really trust? Courtiers sought your friendship for advantage, not because they liked you. No wonder Elizabeth was difficult to deal with.

As she pulled up the coverlet of finest winter sables backed with silk, Anne wondered what the queen would see if she opened her eyes now. Would she see a servant? Or would she see through the façade to the slattern who lurked beneath? But the queen did not open her eyes and soon drifted away, soothed and warm, into a deep sleep.

The lady servitors were drifting out of the room as Jehanne signaled the body servants could leave as well, but as Anne turned to go with her friends, Jehanne held her back. "I want you to stay here with the queen until she wakes. There are things I must do before the king returns."

Now Anne was alone with the queen as the rain beat against the windows and the fire sputtered quietly in the corner hearth. She stood at the foot of the great bed for a moment watching the queen breathe. Without all her fine clothes Elizabeth was just another woman—as she was. Anne sighed deeply and walked away to a stone seat built into the wall under one of the windows. Slumping down, she closed her eyes and leaned her forehead against the cold glass. Perhaps the icy feel of the panes would restore some sense. She had to think her way around the present situation. What would she say to the king when he asked her about last night? And how would she deal with her feelings?

"Lady Mary, give me strength. Oh, please . . ." The whispered prayer was fervent but not sincere—she could not lie to herself. Yes, she needed strength, but she did not want it. "Ah, Jesu," she groaned aloud, and the woman in the bed stirred. Anne held her breath. The queen settled back into sleep and the girl was alone with her thoughts once more, thoughts of Edward, pray as she might. Then she heard voices outside the door—a quiet exchange, two men—and a moment later the door eased open and there stood the king, muddied and wet from the hunt.

For a moment he did not see her, his attention was on the woman in the bed, but unconsciously Anne moved slightly, and he turned to find the source of the tiny sound. Their eyes locked. And very slowly he smiled.

She could feel her heart pound as he walked toward her like a hunter, his eyes fixed on hers, almost, it seemed, willing her not to move. Finally, he stood a pace away and she could smell him. Wood smoke and wet leather and horses, and she knew that if she reached up to touch his face it would be cold. Her throat was tight and she was breathing fast; if she did not get up and walk away, the die would be cast. It would be too late.

He moved a little closer and she could hear him breathing. Leisurely, he stripped off one hunting glove, very deliberately, very slowly, silently. She dropped her glance away from his eyes.

"Look at me." It was said in a whisper but it was an order. She looked up and he must have seen the fear in her eyes because he laughed, very softly. "We must still have our conversation, you and I. But perhaps it should not be here." And then with his free naked hand he touched her face and allowed a finger to linger, for a moment, on her mouth. "Pretty." Then he turned away and walked over to his wife's bed. "You may leave us, Anne. Send for Jehanne, if you would."

He was the king now, formal and distant, and she could not have been more grateful. Quickly, she sprang to her feet, curtsied, and almost ran out of the room—straight into Hastings's arms. He had been waiting for his master outside the door, and he, too, was filthy from the hunt. "Holla! In such a hurry, the Devil must be on your tail."

It was meant as a joke, of course, but for Anne it rang too close to the truth. "Pardon, sir. I must find Dame Jehanne, the king has asked for her . . . Perhaps you have seen her?"

William shook his head. "We are not long back from the hunt."

"So she has not spoken to you, sir?" Anne asked urgently.

"No." William was puzzled by the girl's reaction: she looked first disappointed and then greatly relieved. But she hurried away when William let her go, before he could quiz her further. Thoughtfully, he watched her leave. His master's taste ran to women of all kinds, but he felt a twinge of conscience about this one. He knew of Anne and the king's interest in her; she was very young, many of them were, but it would be sad if she lost her unexpected and shining openness as a result of the king's favor.

He sighed and then became impatient. He had many more things to think about than the fate of one servant, no matter how charming she was, not least the health of the queen now that she might be carrying the heir to England's throne.

Chapter Twenty-four

Richard II's great bath-room on the ground floor of the king's lodgings was filled with steam, and much water had slopped onto the painted tiles as Edward and William enjoyed a scalding tub together after the hunt.

"Heat, Dickon, more heat! Bring us more hot water, the taps have given out . . . and ale. What do you say, William—hot or not?"

"Hot what, Your Majesty?"

"Ale, you fool. Hot ale?"

"Aye. And a hot bath maid or two as well. If I'm to endure yet another stew with Your Grace there must be some compensation, at least."

The king smiled, wolfish for a moment. "Dickon!" The man scurried back, bringing yet another pitcher of fiercely hot water that he tipped into the bath, accompanied by howls from both men, and much laughter. The king, a wicked look on his face, called William's bluff. "My chamberlain has requested aid in his ablutions. Any handsome young laundresses you can recommend?"

Dickon smiled. "Perhaps. Give me but a moment, Your Majesty." And Dickon scurried out, a man with a mission, as the king grinned at Hastings.

"I know that smile!" William grabbed one of the larger bath sponges and lobbed it, full of water, at the king. With a roar the king threw it back and it caught William full in the face. So with great gusto the two men hurled water and soap at each other and fell to wrestling in the huge stone bath as water sprayed everywhere, some of it catching Dickon and the girl he'd brought back with him. She was attractive: curly hair held back behind her head in a thick braid, and a small, tight waist under high, round breasts—modestly enough covered with a household kirtle and apron.

"Turn your eyes, girl." The king hopped out of the bath as Dickon rushed to wind him in a linen bath sheet. "Yours is the field, Chamberlain. I shall see you presently, when you are clean." And with a wink to William, the king left the shambles of the bathroom behind him to dress in an outer room beyond.

"Close the door, girl. And tell me your name." William liked what he saw, and it seemed a shame to waste what the king had so courteously provided.

"Mary is my name, sir."

"Well, Mary, bring the pitcher over here." William drew up his knees, a gesture at modesty, as she closed the door and lifted the pitcher. "Pour it in behind me." He sighed with contentment as the hot water mingled with what was left in the bath. "They say you're a good laundress, Mary. Tell me, have you ever washed a man?"

The girl giggled as she poured. "No, sir. It's not my usual trade."

"So what is your usual trade, girl?"

"Starch, sir. I prepare the starch for the queen's gofferer—and I'm in charge of washing all the really delicate linen for Her Majesty, with Rose, one of her maids."

William was fishing around in the water as she talked, and he finally found what he was looking for. "Ah, here it is." It was a large piece of fine white soap made with oil of almond kernel from Castile; fine soap was an eccentric indulgence of the king. "Well, Mary, let's see how good you really are. Wash my back, if you please."

For a moment the girl said nothing, then he heard her put the pitcher down. William handed the soap up behind him; tentatively, Mary took it and started to rub his back.

"You'll likely get quite wet, you know," he said. The girl looked at him and then dropped her eyes. "Perhaps you should take them off. Your clothes." One of her hands strayed to an apron string but then dropped, uncertain. "Of course, you don't have to. If that's not what you want . . ."

Mary smiled slightly. It was enough. "Turn around, girl, let me help you." William's throat was tight, his breathing faster, as she obediently turned her back to him. Carefully, he undid her apron and then gently and slowly he pulled the laces from the back of her dress. As he pulled the sides of the garment apart he could see the smooth skin of her shoulders, and her back, down to her buttocks—she was naked under the dress, of course. The warm water and the closeness of the girl made him stir languorously, in anticipation. "Well, Mary, I can see you have a way with starch." His voice was husky.

"Why is that, sir?" The girl turned around quickly and neatly, her clothes modestly held in front of her, but she'd allowed him to glimpse the side of her body, a hint of breast.

"Look at this."

The girl laughed when she saw what was poking up in the soapy water and then, deliberately, one by one, dropped her garments on the floor and stood before him, naked. She let him look at her for a moment and then climbed the steps that led up to the bath, easing herself over the rim. Then very slowly, she slid her body over his in the hot water until she lay on top of him, allowing herself to rock gently up and down, up and down with the water. William was impatient, and as she allowed him to kiss her, he pushed his hand between her legs to open her thighs, then, his fingers feeling no resistance, eased himself, slowly, deliciously, up inside her body. She felt so good, hot and soft as butter. She gasped as she felt him enter but then slid herself down, panting slightly, so that he was firmly planted between her legs.

The hot water sucked and gushed between them as he began to move her up and down on his belly, almost weightless in the water; she was slick and the heat of the water surrounding them was almost too exquisite.

"A thorough laundering . . ." William wanted to prolong the pleasure as long as he could but he was close, especially when she slipped her hand down between them both, her fingers sliding back and forth, first on him, then on her. She was pleasuring them both, something he found deeply exciting and slightly shocking.

Edward had nearly finished dressing in the other room outside the great bath but he could hear what was going on, as the door was slightly ajar. "Thank you, Dickon. I'll call if I need you." The man bowed and left the room, face carefully expressionless, as Edward sauntered over to the bathroom door and peered through the opening. It was erotic watching other people make love and, although it wasn't the first time he'd seen William with a woman, the sight of the couple in the bath set his blood racing: William was riding the girl now as she held on to the taps, eyes closed, her mouth open in pleasure.

The king gently pulled the door closed, deeply aroused. And thought of Anne. And smiled. There would be revels tonight, and the queen, exhausted as she was, would surely need to keep to her bed; he would instruct Moss. And it was time for Anne to answer the question he had asked of her; there was a mystery there and he would enjoy the solving of it . . .

As with all Christmas revels, of course, the most important thing was that the hall was warm but not so well lit that certain assignations could not take place in the shadows, supposedly unnoticed.

It was late in the evening now but the king had been drinking lightly, just enough, and was increasingly of the mood to enjoy himself. The queen's chair of state, beside his, was empty; Moss had hurried to obey the wishes of his king and now, after the administration of a draft, Elizabeth would sleep until morning.

Anne, too, was sleepy because she was pretty close to drunk; in her fever to deal with the conflicts raging in her heart and her conscience, she'd gulped down whole wine—usually she drank it watered—and it had gone straight to her head. And when she tried to eat to balance the increasingly heady feeling, she'd found she had no appetite because there, at the head of the hall, was the king—and all she knew was that she must, absolutely must, avoid looking at him.

But the night wore on and from time to time she'd stolen a glance at Edward, and, just now, she looked up to find his eyes on hers. He raised his cup, bowed slightly, and drained it completely—without looking away.

Anne, feeling the heat rise to her face, dropped her glance. The whole room must have seen the king. But Evelyn was flirting with the man who was serving them yet more food—gobbets of pork in a sauce of pickled walnuts and cinnamon and cloves—and Dame Jehanne was talking brightly to her neighbor, one of the queen's underpantrymen. No one at her table had seen.

Suddenly, there was wild applause—the Torch Dance! With a nod from the king, the musicians struck up the opening as servants brought lit tapers to the courtiers.

In the dance each lady carried a light and it was the job of her suitor to blow the candle out. But there were rules to what was, effectively, a dance of stylized seduction: the lady could shield her candle with one hand and the gentleman was not allowed to touch her—he could only use his mouth to accomplish his task. If the candle was blown out, that couple retired until, at last, only one pair was left who danced closer and closer to each other until the flame was finally extinguished. The music was provocative, too—a quick, insistent beat from the tabors underlying a gliding, sinuous rhythm from the viols with the melody of a single flute that worked its way into the blood.

Anne saw the king stand. He was going to join the dance. She didn't want to watch him flirt with the court beauties and so she wriggled off the tightly crowded bench with a mumbled excuse to Dame Jehanne that she was going to the garderobe.

Rose cast a sardonic glance at the girl as she hurried, a little unsteadily, out of the hall. "Ha," she said to Dorcas resentfully, "thinks she's got us all fooled, Mistress Mealymouth."

"Who'dya mean?" Dorcas was fuddled by the wine, the heat and, the food.

"That one. Anne. Gives herself airs, thinks she's too good for us. Plays at being the virgin. Bah!"

"Isn't she?" Dorcas was really confused now.

"What?"

"Anne. Isn't she a virgin?"

Rose snorted, and Dame Jehanne, who had heard the last exchange, sent a quelling glance down the table at them both. "She's always down on me," hissed Rose to Dorcas, "just because I speak the truth, unvarnished . . ."

But she forgot her anger the moment the good-looking servitor leaned over her shoulder, saying, "More pork, young mistress? Tastes just like man's flesh, I hear." And he dared to wink at her.

That made Rose feel much better, until Dorcas, in a loud beery whisper asked, "Are *you* then?"

"What?"

"A virgin?"

Rose choked. The servitor heard her and as he leaned down to ladle some of the dish onto her trencher he said, "Always at *your* service . . ." And he winked again, lewdly, so the warm thoughts that flashed into her head—plus the tight buttocks she saw under his short jerkin as he swaggered away—drove Anne from her mind.

Anne's thoughts, though, were anguished as she hurried from the noisy hall. The king—the way he had looked at her, so steadily. He must just be playing with her; surely it was just another diversion, if all they said about him was true? But she wasn't going to do that, be a diversion. Was she? She felt like crying, felt like laughing, as she ran. Felt like—

"So, now it is time to redeem your promise." Anne had rounded a dark corner and there, standing in the light of the wall sconces, alone, was the king. He held out his hand. "Come."

For one frozen moment she stood there and then, slowly, one hesitant foot after another, she walked toward him, heart pounding, throat dry until she stood no more than a foot away.

He was not smiling. "Give me your hand." The voice was low, the words a breath, and for a rational moment her mind cut through the clamor of her body urging caution. But then she looked up into his eyes and what she saw there, the intensity, drew her like a magnet. Silently, she held out her hand; he clasped it and then drew her to him inexorably. For a moment they stood there, locked by each other's eyes, but then he bent down, slowly, slowly, and gathering her to his body, kissed her so softly. And then again. Deeper. Slower.

Her eyes closed as she let him take her mouth and then he kissed her throat, and her mouth yet again. Urgently, her body held tight to his, his kisses came faster and faster, deeper and harder—until Anne's blood hammered so noisily she felt she would faint.

But now they could hear revelers leaving the hall. Quickly, Edward slipped off his handsome three-quarter cloak and draped it around Anne's shoulders—on her it brushed the floor. Lady Margaret's gift, the distinctive green dress, was covered and the deeply furred hood put her face into shadow, only her eyes gleamed. And then they were running together, his arm around her waist, hurrying away from the hall and across one of the inner courts toward his suite of apartments.

The cold outside was vicious; it was a wet, wild night. Even the sentries guarding the outer entrance to the king's rooms were huddled together around a brazier under the overhang of the porch shadowing the iron-studded door. But Edward had a private way to his quarters, a small door beside one of the great, multipaned oriel windows he'd added to the ancient building. He pulled back a hanging curtain of cold, wet ivy and there it was, unlocked. A deft twist of the iron handle and they were inside in the dark, unseen by the men guarding the main entrance.

"Come here."

She could see very little as her eyes adjusted after the flaring light of torches outside, but she knew he was close, she could smell him. And then his hands were around her waist and he'd plunged his mouth down on hers again, her body crushed to his. It lasted for a moment but in that moment her hands slid up around his neck, her breasts flattened against his chest, and he felt her heart hammering.

He laughed in the darkness—it was a warm sound, happy from sheer delight. "Close now, my darling."

He was beside her now and a moment later he'd pushed another small door open and they were in his private apartments, alone in the softly lighted room with a fire burning gently in the huge corner hearth. On a table was a large silver flagon of wine, two golden cups, and food enough for ten. There were tapestries on the wall and a great carpet, glowing like a pool filled with dark and gorgeous jewels on the boarded floor.

The king unclasped his cloak from around Anne's throat and tossed it aside toward the bed, which lay with its snowy white sheets, its ermine counterpane, in the shadows of the room. And he led her toward the fire, saying, "Come, warm yourself. Eat. You have nothing to fear."

As if in a dream—perhaps she would wake soon, and it would be tomorrow?—she allowed herself to stand in front of the flames holding up her hands to warm them.

"What are you thinking?" He spoke quietly.

She looked up at him trustingly. He was leaning on the carved chimney breast, close by but not touching her. She sighed. "Ah, sire, wondrous things. Terrible things."

"Are you here willingly?"

She stared into the heart of the flames, into the glowing coals, as she thought of her answer and then looked up into his eyes fearlessly. "Yes. God forgive me."

He frowned slightly but then his brow cleared as he stretched out his hand and softly touched the veiling covering her hair. Gently, he searched for the pins holding it to her head and, one by one, removed them. The gauzy fabric floated to the floor. Now his hands were busy in her hair, unraveling the thick coils.

"Shake your head." He spoke softly, his voice husky. Hesitantly, she did as he asked and the rich, shining strands tumbled down past her waist, glinting where the fire caught deep red and gold lights in the darkness of her hair. There was silence, except for rain beating on the windows. The two of them, man and woman, gazed at one another.

"I've wanted to touch you, see you like this, ever since that day in the Abbey."

"You remember?" She was humbled by the knowledge that they truly had reached out to one another, more than a year ago.

"Come here." She took a step toward him and it was as if she crossed a great divide—she would not turn back now.

Carefully, deliberately, he picked up a handful of hair and held it against his face. He closed his eyes, breathed in her smell. "Silk. Living silk."

She giggled, and he grinned at his own extravagant language. But then his finger traced the contour of her cheek, down to her mouth, and his expression changed. "I want more than touch," he whispered. "I want . . ." He pulled her to him with strength she did not want to escape. And looked down into her eyes, his own shining in the light of the fire. "Your heart and soul. And body."

Helpless, she was suddenly frightened by the power of what she felt, and did not dare to look up. He laughed, deep in his throat, and she felt him unlace the back of her gown before he picked her up as if she weighed nothing.

He strode over to the bed and then, before he put her down, dropped his mouth to hers so that she, intoxicated, hardly felt it when he placed her against the mound of pillows and eased her dress off her shoulders to reveal her breasts. Instinctively, she sat up and crossed her arms, hiding them from him, blushing.

Her modesty was a powerful erotic charge to him but patiently he leaned forward again and softly, gently, kissed her throat, the hollow at the base of her neck. Gradually he felt her arms relax and then, tentatively, steal up around his neck so that her naked breasts were soft against his chest.

Delicately, not disturbing her embrace, he sat on the bed beside her, one hand sliding around her waist, the other lightly tracing the line of her spine, the touch like a velvet glove over the smooth, shining skin. She was breathing faster now and returning his kisses more passionately as he found the last of the lacing on her gown and eased it loose. "Let me look at you." He sat back, smiling into her eyes, deliberately not glancing lower than her face.

Again, the bright blood flushed her face and neck—and, he was sure, her breasts—but then she nodded slightly and he allowed himself to drop his eyes. Her breasts were beautiful, fuller than he had thought and gleaming like the surface of pearls in the light from the fire. With one finger, he traced the line of her jaw, then her throat, then down, down to the cleft between and underneath one and then the other—up to a small hard nipple and then, without warning, he closed his mouth around the little mound, sucking and biting very gently.

She squirmed and gasped but then, after a moment's hesitation, closed her eyes and lay back against the pillows as his hand caressed the nipple of her other breast.

"Give me your hand." With closed eyes she let him guide her, down his body, across his belly, and on to where she felt the hard bulge in his hose. Her eyes flew open. "You see, Anne, what you do to me?"

He was bent over her, a dark shape, his head and shoulders outlined by the light of the fire, and for a moment she was frightened by the power and the strength of his body. But she knew that the time to say no had long passed. Then, as he slid out of his jerkin and she saw the beauty of him, all fear departed. He was perfectly made.

"You are perfect." His words startled her; had he picked up her thoughts, were they so close in mind? But the liquid, dreamlike warmth that was spreading through her body as he ran his hands over her banished all but physical sensations.

Deftly, he lifted her slightly in his arms and eased the dress completely off so that it dropped to the floor. She was naked now, lying trustingly, skin to skin, as one of his hands traced the contour of her spine down to her small, round buttocks.

Now she was on her back and he was stroking her belly, the strokes becoming firmer and longer, then lower, slower, and more deliberate as delicious shivers ran from her breasts to her groin. She was panting and so was he, as, unconsciously, her thighs began to part, allowing his hand to find its way between her legs. That pleased him, she could tell, for he growled deep in his throat, but the shock when his fingers found the opening in her cleft was still great and she tried to sit up away from his questing hands.

Her patient lover was completely naked now and becoming less and less restrained. He smothered her protests with his mouth as she felt him slide over her so that his body covered hers completely. And between their sweating bodies, pinioned against her belly, she could feel him hard and hot against her pubic bone, impatient to be inside her—just as a discreet knocking began at the door of the room.

For a moment, the universe of flesh held them, but the insistent knocking became too much. Edward slid off Anne's body with a muffled curse and strode naked to the door of the chamber.

Anne was distressed, shocked, and then a great wave of guilty shame and confusion lapped high as she saw the disordered bed, her abandoned clothes. She was naked, in the king's room, and he was about to open the door!

As quick as thought, she snatched up her dress, found her veil, and ran through the little door behind the arras and out into the passage behind the king's room before he had fully crossed the chamber. Her last thought, as she fled, was how glorious he looked, but then the cold of the dark passage hit her and all she could think to do was drop the dress over her head and keep running, stumbling to find the way out.

The journey back to the dorter was humiliating. She did her best to tidy her clothes but she could do little with her hair and she had lost her shoes. Also, trying to relace her gown, by herself in the dark, was close to impossible.

Hurrying across the inner court near the king's lodging, she couldn't avoid meeting a number of sentries—though, mercifully, she knew none of them by name or sight—and their faces mirrored what they saw. She looked like a girl who'd just been tumbled. Blushing fiercely and trying not to cry, she gathered her dignity as well as she could and walked the rest of the way to the dorter on freezing feet, calmly and quietly. But her mind was a welter of disordered images, images she shrank from.

She was wanton. A slut. There was no other explanation. True, she was still technically a virgin, but that was all. In her heart she had wanted the king as badly, as fiercely, as he had wanted her. God knew, she still wanted him, and if they had not been interrupted, she would by now be, irrevocably, his whore, his leman.

Edward, however, wasn't thinking of Anne. When, in a rage, he'd flung open the door of his room—hot words ready to blister whoever was standing on the other side—he'd found William Hastings fully dressed with a sword on his belt.

Brusquely, he strode past his naked king into the room, not bothering to apologize. "They've gone."

"Who?" Edward had fighter's instincts—he hardly had to ask.

"Warwick. And Clarence."

"When? Davis!" He needed to dress. Where were his clothes? Davis, his body servant, entered the room at a run and, prescient as usual, had a fresh linen shirt over one arm and hose in the other. The king dressed rapidly, dragging a hand through tousled hair as Hastings filled him in.

"Straight after the revels. Packed up stealthily, gathered Warwick's affinity, and left. Must have had it planned." As he talked Hastings took in the evidence that the king had had a visitor. There beside the fire was a red ribbon, and half hidden near the bed, a pair of small, fine leather shoes. He sighed. Edward was an extraordinary young man, a fine fighter, and he had the makings of a great king, but sometimes even he, Hastings, thought his fondness for bed sport verged on the obsessive.

It dawned on Edward, too, as he dressed, that Anne had fled and with a spare part of his mind he was both glad and sorry. He knew she'd been as hot for him as he for her, but it had taken a lot of patience to make her so receptive. Still, he'd enjoy trying again, when he had the time. Now there was work to be done. "Do you have knowledge of where they're going?"

"They took the north road, sire."

"Well now, we must find my wretched brother and entice him back. Really, all this fuss just because I said he couldn't marry Isabelle. One thing, Hastings . . ."

"What, sire?"

"Warwick. He's overreached himself this time."

Chapter Twenty-five

The queen was feeling better. She'd slept well through the wild storm of the previous night and was determined to reclaim her husband's attention. Edward was so robust that physical weakness in others made him impatient, so particular care went to her appearance on this brilliant, crisp winter's morning, and not one of her servants—base or gentle—was spared a tongue-lashing in Elizabeth's quest for perfection.

An unusual entertainment had been planned. After Mass, instead of eating the main meal of the day in the hall, the king had decided that a winter picnic would take place at which the most adventurous members of his court could assay the newly introduced sport of skating on frozen ice, using split beef shinbones strapped to their shoes. He'd learned the skill when he'd lived abroad, in Brugge as a boy.

Time, however, was not an ally as Elizabeth caused havoc by rejecting gown after gown in her search to find the most flattering ensemble in which to learn to skate. "The red velvet, Your Majesty, with the beaver tippets? Now that will stand out."

"You're a fool, Jehanne. I'm too fat now." The queen scowled as she looked into her glass.

The women of her suite rushed to reassure her.

"Fat? Oh, no, madam!"

". . . waist like an eel . . ."

" . . . such a good color for your complexion . . ."

"Enough! I'll not wear it, the velvet is worn. See, here—and here." No one but the queen could see anything wrong with the lustrous fabric but no one ventured an opinion.

Anne had been completely silent as Jehanne and the other women did their best to pacify the queen. She'd not slept in the few hours between leaving the king and getting up in the cold hour before dawn to brush the queen's clothes, in preparation for dressing her. And in her bed, she'd hugged her belly against the cramps that assailed her as she played, over and over, images from her time in the king's rooms. Burning with fever, shivering with cold, anxiety running acid through her bones—what would happen when she met him again? How could she look him in the eyes feeling the shame that she did? And also, the fear remained. She had not spoken to him about what she'd heard and seen in the chapel the night before; danger remained and he did not know it. Or so she thought.

"Anne, you have nothing to offer?" The queen was icy. Recently, Anne had not pleased Elizabeth. Previously, the girl had attended on her cheerfully and made lotions and other cosmetics that had pleased her, but in recent days Anne had become more and more silent and evasive.

The whip of the queen's tongue brought Anne out of her fog of misery and she saw the startled concern on Jehanne's face. Buying time to think, she curtsied and then, grace of God, inspiration struck. "The white brocade, Your Majesty, with the ermine. And your emeralds with the pearl and silver hair cauls. You will look like the Winter Queen. And you should ride your white palfrey with the silver harness—the Arabian that the king gave you on your name day."

The picture that Anne conjured up—a mystic, almost fairy-tale figure—pleased the queen against her will. The girl was right, for the good thing about the white dress was that she'd only worn it once, months before. No one would remember it if she teamed it with one of her new cloaks—perhaps the one of white velvet from Venice.

Grudgingly, Elizabeth gave her approval, making a mental note not to forget Anne's odd behavior lately. That would have to be addressed, though there was no time now. She would speak to the king when she had a moment alone with him.

Finally, the queen and all her women were assembled in a cavalcade accompanied by selected gentlemen—including Doctor Moss—and were on their way to meet the king and his men at a specially created winter bower in the greenwood. Everyone had cheered up considerably, including Elizabeth.

Jehanne and Anne were traveling behind the party in a bullock cart, one of several that contained provisions for the picnic. It was a fine, brilliantly cold day, with a high blue sky, though the driver of the cart, a battered veteran of many Yorkist campaigns of the past, foretold snow before the evening. "And, if I'm right in this, much more after that. We'll be snowed in for Christmas, mark my words . . ."

"But we've still two days to come, man. How can you know what the Lord will send for his birthday?" Jehanne scoffed.

"Well, lady, I recollect the campaigns I fought with the king after the scurvy death of his father, the good Duke of York that was, at Wakefield, rest his soul. Towton now—when we saw off that she-wolf of Anjou—freezing that was. Fine and crisp the day before—just as this—and a blizzard for three mortal days after. All the snow ran red but we fought on."

Anne shivered and wrapped herself tighter in her dark red cloak as the man maundered on. Red . . . the blood-colored cloth fluttered at her feet like a spreading pool, fluttered and rippled like a battle flag. And then there were screams, other voices—and she heard the whistle and thump of arrows, the bray of wounded horses. Her throat closed with fear as she tensed, ready to jump from the cart, ready to run . . . But as she looked ahead and to the side, there was nothing. No battle: no marauders dropping down from the trees or in their path. All around were the same happy, unconcerned people, excited by the treat that today had in store.

Anne felt dizzy and sick—and shattered by the terror she'd felt. Her heart still surged with fear . . . and the certainty that it was Edward who would have to face the battle to come. There could be no escape, the conflict would have to be played out; the danger to the king and his kingdom was still as strong as the smell of blood on the wind ... And then she remembered. To tell him what she sensed—even if he believed her—she would have to speak to him alone, and after last night, how could she face that? Desperately she prayed, *Oh, Lord, let this journey last forever. Let him not be there. Let him not see me* ... But a moment later they rounded the last bend in the forest track and there in front of them was a pleasure ground with tented pavilions and fires burning, all laid out around a good-sized lake that had frozen solid overnight.

It was a bright, happy scene, all the brilliantly dressed young courtiers milling around the queen as she was helped down from her horse, laughing, joking, bantering, no thought of anything but pleasure in their heads. Of the king there was no sign.

Jehanne, Anne on her heels, hurried over to tend to her mistress; nothing, no stray hair or speck of mud, would be permitted to spoil the lovely picture the queen made in her shimmering white. Anne smiled ruefully. The white dress was an inspired choice, for Elizabeth seemed angelic, hardly made of human flesh, surrounded by the ruddy faces and myriad colors of the court—and she knew it. Knowledge of her beauty added an extra glitter to her smile as she settled herself in a gilded Italian folding chair outside her pavilion to await the king. And yet, when Anne looked at her triumphant mistress, a shiver ran through her, for suddenly she saw the skull beneath the skin of Elizabeth's beautiful face, just as she had with Piers. Then the image slipped and blurred and she saw the queen again, much older, dressed as a nun, all beauty lost and despair her dark companion. And that overwhelmed Anne with misery and fear. Why did she see these things? She turned away, desperately unhappy, only to find Doctor Moss blocking her path.

"Why so sad, maid?"

Before she could control her reaction she grimaced at the word "maid." "Nothing, sir. I'm tired. It's hard to sleep well in a strange place."

Moss's eyes narrowed. So, events had moved on; this was useful knowledge. "Yes. The king's court makes rest ... difficult, for Edward needs no sleep, it seems."

It was said lightly but Anne, hypersensitive to every nuance of speech, heard something in his tone that made her look up at him defiantly. "Not all are suited to this life, sir."

She curtsied and walked back toward the court party, proud and contained but aching, desperate to cry. Moss looked after her thoughtfully and felt a surprising flash of pain. Then he dismissed the thought impatiently. She'd been brought to court to please the queen, and the king. Well, let that be so in each case. For both their sakes—and for his.

Yet as he turned away he saw that men's eyes followed Anne as she made her way to Jehanne once more. He saw the way they nudged each other as she passed, saw the hot gleam of lust in each face. For one moment he allowed himself to feel what they felt, then anger washed through him. And envy.

Then, resolutely, because he was a man who could control himself if others could not, he closed his eyes and locked all feeling away. To covet a woman's body was one thing, to act, quite another. He could not afford to see Anne as anything but a useful device, a tool. He would meditate on that until he found strength to resist the temptations she offered.

Later, Jehanne sent Anne to find the queen's cosmetic box, and just as she was rummaging among the welter of objects that must accompany her mistress on even the smallest trip outside the castle, a man's gloved hand descended on her shoulder. She spun around and found herself looking up into William Hastings's cool eyes.

"I have been asked to bring you to a certain person. He wishes to speak to you."

The shock of what he said nearly buckled her knees, but some part of her wits remained. "Sir, the queen, my mistress has asked that I—"

"You are a subject of the king first, girl," he said, taking the small wooden casket out of her hands and passing it to a man-at-arms who was standing impassively beside him. "For Dame Jehanne, who is with the queen. Immediately," he told the man and then returned his gaze to Anne. "Come, girl."

Anne had no choice but to follow after the chamberlain, heart beating clamorously.

Only Jehanne watched them go, and that by accident. She'd happened to look up from readjusting the netted silver cauls covering the queen's hair, when she saw Hastings swing the girl up behind him on his destrier and canter gently back toward the castle, where the bend in the dirt road soon hid them from view. Startled and fearful, she closed her eyes in prayer for a moment, asking the Blessed Virgin to protect Anne, as the queen laughingly exchanged compliments with a grizzled, smitten baron from the lands around York, her husband's stronghold.

Anne, clinging to William Hastings's lean waist, tried to suppress shamed excitement as she mentally rehearsed what she would tell the king about Warwick and Duke George, using the imaginary dialogue as a tool to banish all thought of what she would really like to say to Edward. It was a short ride, however, and soon William had turned aside from the main road onto a bridle path. He reined in his horse at the entrance to a small clearing where a wattle-and-daub cottage had been built, its back against the dark trunks of the oak and beech trees. There was a destrier tethered there, cropping the withered winter grasses. Hastings slid down from his horse and held up his arms; the horse was enormous and Anne was a long way from the ground. "Here, girl. Jump."

She was suddenly afraid and he smiled. "Come now, nothing's as bad as it seems." That raised the smallest of smiles and, suddenly decisive, she allowed herself to drop down into his waiting grasp. He felt a small, unexpectedly voluptuous body; she, the hard arms and broad chest of a fighter.

"Thank you, sir. For your assistance." It was said with dignity, and not for the first time, William Hastings appreciated the unusual qualities of this girl.

"Well, then," he said and gestured to the cottage, then he swung back up into the saddle, wheeling the horse to leave.

As the sound of the hoofbeats drumming on the frozen ground receded, Anne stood in the clearing hesitating and then, breathing deeply, walked toward the plank door that stood ajar in the dilapidated little building. It was a reflex action to knock as she stood outside but pride made her pause, and before she could change her mind, she pushed the warped door inward, unannounced.

He was standing by the desultory fire burning directly on the earth floor, the smoke finding its way out through a hole in the roof. He turned and smiled at her tenderly, holding out his arms. "Little beloved."

She wanted to go to him, so much. Tears in her eyes, she shook her head.

"Then I shall come to you." The king's voice was tender and he laughed a little as he said it. Even at twenty-four he'd had much experience with women. He was dangerous because he understood what she was feeling. That was a weapon he could use.

He was standing in front of her, very close now. His pupils were huge in the gloom of that little hut.

"This is very disloyal, you know. I am your king, after all." He was being whimsical, that was the tone in his voice—but it's dangerous to play with a king, that was the message.

"No, sire. I'm being loyal. You are married and I was wicked. Foolish. And there is something else. I must tell you——"

His laughter cut her off. "Ah. Such principles. So earnest. But . . . if I should stretch out my hand now . . ." And, taking off one glove, he gently touched her face; she felt that fingertip through her entire body. "Where is that strength?" He pulled her to him, not so gently, mouth descending on hers. For one sweet moment she let the kiss happen, floating down, down into bright darkness, and then broke away.

"No, sire. This is wrong. I am wrong to let you do this."

He could hear the agony in her voice but she was not pleading with him, it was a statement of fact. And while this made him impatient—she wasn't the first, after all, to protest—he heard something he'd never heard before. Certainty. And purpose. And she had not put her arms around him.

Perplexed, he stood back still holding her and looked into her face—he saw a will the mirror of his own, and he was astonished. This girl had nothing to bargain with except her body, but he might have been looking into the face of an opponent before the joust. This made things very interesting. He enjoyed many things in women, but courage was not the first of the things he sought. Nor intelligence.

He released her and turned away, holding his one naked hand over the little fire again, buying time to think. "I am not a cruel man, I believe. I would not force you, but . . . I'll make you a wager." He turned back, looked at her again, warmly, one comrade in the battle of love to another.

She didn't know whether to laugh, from relief—or cry, from loss.

"I believe you love me, Anne." She said nothing, which he approved of—strategy always interested him. "And I also believe you will come to me soon, of your own accord, and make me the gift of your body. Let us both agree on a time. The first day of the tourney, the feast of Saint Valentine?"

Anne shivered with her private knowledge of Warwick. The tourney would be canceled if open warfare broke out between the two factions at court.

"But if you do not come to me and give me what I seek—and I promise you there will be no pressure—then on the day after our agreed day you may ask me for one thing that exists within the bounds of my kingdom and I shall grant it. Whatever it may be."

He smiled at her, and as Anne opened her mouth to respond, with one quick pace he was beside her, so close she was frozen, all thought of warning him about the future she had seen driven away by the power between them. Breath for breath they gazed at each other, closer and closer his mouth came to hers, but as she raised one hand, one finger, to stop him—in a dream of sweet pain—he caught her wrist and kissed the inside of her palm. Softly and very gently.

Then he was gone. Anne felt her entire body shaking as she considered what he had said, and against her will, felt gratitude. By the granting of that one wish it was as if he and she had become characters in a troubadour's poem and, strangely, she was intrigued. And flattered. She'd never had leisure to play the elaborate court games of flirtation, but he'd invited her in to play with him. It was a casual, magnificent gesture he need not have made. She laughed aloud, but then the anguish and the shock welled up, and she stumbled out into the brilliant light of the winter's day blinded by tears. And into the arms of Doctor Moss.

Unthinking, because he was familiar and because she thought

he was her friend, she buried her head against his shoulder as he allowed her to cry herself out. He said nothing as he held the small shaking body with a certain reluctant tenderness, rocking her gently.

"I have come to fetch you back. Dame Jehanne sent me," he said finally.

She looked at him in horror, eyes red from crying, pale face ribboned with tears in the silver light. "No. The king will be there . . . and the queen."

"Nonetheless. You will be missed."

"But Doctor Moss, you do not understand. It is all the most terrible mess."

Moss smiled slightly, he could not help himself. "I have been at court a long time, Anne. Assuredly, I do understand—"

"You do not."

It was said with real power and he'd never heard that before from Anne. It was arresting, transformative. This was a woman's strength, not a girl's. "Therefore, tell me. I am your friend, Anne. You can trust me."

Anne sighed deeply; there was a choice here. Perhaps to speak of what she knew would make it less of a burden. Yes, Doctor Moss was her friend, she was sure of that. It was to him she owed her place at court. And yet . . . it was the king who needed her knowledge, not a courtier.

"Sir, I need a little time to think, for there are things that are sensitive. Frightening things . . . May I ask your advice a little later?"

Moss had to be content with that answer, though he burned to know more. Knowledge was always power at court.

"How did you know where to find me?" Anne had composed herself now, regrets and confusion put firmly to one side. She had to face them all again, face the queen . . . and the king. She could only do it if she were staunch.

"Dame Jehanne saw you leave with the chamberlain. She asked me to follow and so I did, discreetly. The king did not see me."

Anne was puzzled. Jehanne made no secret of loathing Doctor Moss; why would she have asked for his help?

Moss saw Anne's confusion and cursed himself for an idiot. All very well to acknowledge a growing obsession with this girl to himself, but how had he allowed himself to indulge in such risky behavior? What if the king *had* seen Anne and he together? He could have destroyed the patient work of months, all on a whim.

He gestured toward the edge of the glade where his horse was tethered behind a dense thicket of leafless hawthorn. "Are you ready to return?"

He sounded nervous, and Anne was about to question Moss further when they heard a distant clamor from the lake.

"The king has arrived at the picnic I think; we should go."

Anne nodded. Moss was right. Each moment of delay made it more likely she would be missed by the queen.

She was grateful that he asked no questions as they cantered back toward the pleasure ground. When they rounded the bend in the road they saw a glorious sight: the king was gliding gracefully over the ice of the frozen lake, velvet cloak flaring from his shoulders, long particolored sleeves flying. And as they looked on he stopped with a flourish and bowed deeply to the queen, who proudly applauded, surrounded by her ladies.

Anne slipped into the press of women around Elizabeth, bearing a dish of sweetmeats that Doctor Moss had given her: marchpane rolled in violet-colored sugar crystals and preserved rose petals, favorites of the queen. Jehanne seized the dish and presented it, curtsying. "Here, Your Majesty, the girl has returned and, just as I instructed her, has brought the marchpane comfits freshly made at the castle. It is entirely my fault they were overlooked this morning."

The queen waved acknowledgment, her attention elsewhere as she absently selected one of the sweets, her attention on the king as he removed the strapping that held beef shinbones to the soles of his long-toed shoes. Her face transformed into the most lovely smile as he strode toward them laughing and slightly breathless, cheeks ruddy from exercise in the cold air. "Hungry, my lord?"

There was a certain low breathiness in her voice that made the king smile; he liked it when the queen had the wit to joke with him. Out of the corner of his eye he saw that Anne was making sure to be particularly busy handing delicacies to the queen's favorites, her face carefully impassive. Smiling, he raised his voice so that she would be sure to hear him. "Alas, not for food, Lady Queen. I am but a poor knight who has lost his way and may not partake of earthly food again until I have fulfilled a vow, laid upon me by my lady love." To the great delight of his court, the king cast himself, groaning, before the queen. But for a moment, unseen by the crowd, his eyes found Anne's though she looked as quickly away.

Unconscious of the byplay, Elizabeth laughed brightly and proudly. Let the court mock; here again was proof of the king's great love for her. "Sir knight, I am queen of this winter land and I have the power to release you from the vow imposed by your cruel lady. You have but to speak and I shall listen . . ."

The court entered into the spirit of the game with gusto, calling, "Speak, sir knight. You do not hunger in vain . . ."

Hastings watched the pretty charade with a certain cynicism. The king was clever to distract the court from Anne with the smokescreen of his attentions to the queen. As ever, Edward's enjoyment of this new sexual hunt was intense; William had seen the look flicked toward Anne, if others hadn't. The joy of this contest would be deepened by the privacy that his ever-loyal chamberlain would help to contrive, but it never hurt to set the hounds running on the false trail of renewed attention to the queen—and that was Edward's business now. William understood. With such serious events afoot, the distraction of women was pleasant for a short time.

The king still lay groaning. "Alas, alas. I thirst and yet I may not drink. I hunger and may not eat unless I have fulfilled my vow."

The court obligingly took their cue and chanted back, "The vow, the vow. Tell us the vow."

The king knelt in front of Elizabeth and yet, for those with eyes to see, it seemed, for a moment, as if he looked just slightly over the queen's shoulder, seeking someone else entirely. "I vowed to find the fairest lady in all the land, whose beauty eclipses the moon and falling snow, and kiss her sweet lips . . ."

Only Hastings saw that Anne had moved well away from the royal couple now; anyone else who saw her go would find nothing amiss in a servant hurrying away, perhaps to obey an order from the queen.

" . . . and she would give me a token that I might bring to the lady of my quest, to prove that all my tasks had been accomplished. Long I searched, broad lands I traveled, and fair damsels met in full measure but none was so fair as the moon, or falling snow. I grew thinner and thinner, weaker and weaker, and I despaired of ever finding such a one . . . yet now, my heart is alive with hope for I dare to believe that she whom I sought stands before me."

There it was again, that searching look, almost brazen this time, and the queen frowned for a moment. Was the king distracted? A warm laugh from Edward reassured her as he pantomimed being blinded by her beauty.

"Ah, the perilous beauty of the Winter Queen—I hardly dare contemplate this peerless face! May I presume to kiss this fair white hand, O lady of fatal grace?"

The queen giggled happily, holding out one hand, and the king kissed it lovingly. William Hastings sauntered forward to play his part. Quietly, he stepped up to the queen and handed her a little packet. Delighted, she unwrapped it quickly and flourished it for all the court to see.

"Ah, sir knight, you have fulfilled your vow and now you have your token." The queen handed Edward an oval medal, very cunningly engraved with her face in profile, suspended from a golden chain. And hanging below the badge there was a crystal vial stopped with a ruby, and inside that, a lock of golden hair.

The king sprang to his feet, kissed the medal and the queen heartily, and cried, "Thank God for that. At last we eat!"

Shouts of good-humored laughter lapped around them as he escorted Elizabeth to tables burdened with "simple" food of the forest. Hot venison pies with carved pastry lids, pike fritters with saffron and pepper, stewed waterfowl and fresh, fine white bread to sop up the juices, all washed down with hot mulled ale and warm wine. The servants were kept running between the fires and the tables as the ravenous courtiers descended like the plagues of Egypt, consuming the best this winter kingdom could offer.

Anne, too, was kept busy, with no time to eat, much less think. Jehanne saw to it that she was assigned to one of the lesser tables crammed with the queen's relations, rather than the table at which

Elizabeth and Edward sat. Anne was grateful to Jehanne because, try as she might to avoid looking at Edward, his eyes still sought her out. Time was pregnant with his patience; he had the nerve to play this game out, she knew that. Anne had to steel herself to concentrate on the task she had been given. Surely filling her mind with the actions of her hands would give her the strength she needed, the strength to fight her sinful passion and learn to look on the king for who he was, not the man she loved? She would not give in, could not give in; he was wily, she saw that now—each warm look he threw toward her said as much.

And she laughed at her own naïveté. Had she really been frightened for him? The dreadful dreams, the vision today—overheated lust was the answer and the cause, and that could be banished with hard work, much prayer, and penance! Then, in the midst of her work, she looked up to see him watching her, and the loving look on his face nearly undid all her fierce, good intentions. No! She had to concentrate on other things—and she would!

Lord Rivers was astonished therefore, and agreeably surprised, by the attentive service he received that day. It seemed he had no more than to look up and his cup was filled. No more than inspect the tasty dish being offered to one of his neighbors but that it was offered to him. And all from the remarkably pretty girl dressed in his daughter's colors, who seemed to have made it her mission in life to please those whom she waited on. And so gracefully too. It gave him pleasure to watch her move so adroitly around his table, as if she were part of a complicated dance in some tableau.

So much so, he decided he would ask his daughter for the girl's services after Christmas. As a New Year's gift perhaps. God knew, his wife was hard to please—that's where Elizabeth got it from, of course—but the duchess had not been happy lately with all the nasty rumors flying around the court and this might cheer her up. Perhaps he could soften Elizabeth to his will by approaching the king first? Yes, that might be a good plan, he thought complacently as he accepted yet another piece of lark and goose pie, and looked over toward Edward and his daughter. But then he saw the king watching the girl as well.

And then he remembered all over again his instinct on the

night that Moss had presented this same girl to the queen. Very odd that had been. Moss had a reputation for sexual dalliance to rival the king's—before he'd married of course. Yet, if he remembered it rightly, it had almost seemed as if the doctor was making a gift of this girl to his son-in-law. He frowned. And there it was, that look again, from the king to the girl. He was too interested. Better move quickly on this, he thought, don't want anything unseemly to mar Elizabeth's triumphal progress.

Chapter Twenty-six

It was Christmas Eve and the half-built Chapel of Saint George, to be dedicated to the Knights of the Garter, glowed like a massive lantern, though building materials still lay everywhere. By special license of the king the court had been allowed to see and worship in his partly made masterpiece, the building he had commissioned and passionately overseen, for this one night. So many man-sized wax candles had been lighted that the vast space felt slightly warm, a miracle since it was still partly unroofed. And then during vespers, snow began to fall gently but insistently, sprinkling the fine clothes of the courtiers. As the carter had predicted, winter would close in this night.

The world outside the castle was silent, black and white, drained of all color, as the flakes fell faster and faster and piled higher and higher around the dark walls of the keep. Massive drifts rose around the little houses of the town and the roads choked. The river, too, froze, the first time that men could remember it; even the oldest gaffer in the village said it hadn't happened in his time. And around the great trees in the forest there was a pathetic sight: sparrows frozen to death as they roosted in the branches, lying on the ground.

So the world held its breath and waited for the Christ child to be born, and even the most cynical of the courtiers found themselves silent and attentive as the ancient, familiar words were read out from the Bible. Some few of the literate courtiers could even understand what the priest was saying because they had enough Latin.

Near the front of the new chapel, behind the king, William shuffled impatiently as he brushed snow from his shoulders. A long time ago he'd decided that religion was useful for keeping the people in their place but that was about all. He was disgusted by the extent to which many English church institutions had been corrupted by the shameless venality and extravagance of the papal court. And Rome was also the greediest landlord, in England and in Christendom at large. It offended him that a man he'd never met in a faraway country owned nearly a third of his own country, paid no taxes for its use, and allowed his clerks to live so scandalously. Hastings shivered. In time, there would be a reckoning for everything, he felt it in his bones, and moments like tonight when the message of the church—of innocence, of salvation, of justice for all, and truth—was so far from the day-to-day reality only made him angrier.

Still, there were other, more pressing things to think about. After the Mass was finished he'd have to capture the king's attention long enough to tell him about Mathew Cuttifer. All the news from the north was bad and Edward would have to move fast to raise an army, covertly, in time for even a glimpse of better weather and a raid on Warwick's stronghold. For that he would need money from his people—which was why William had asked Mathew to travel to the Christmas Court from London. He'd just arrived this afternoon in a wherry rowed by four nearly frozen watermen, an hour before the river iced solid.

Hastings knew that Mathew was the key to unlocking the purses of the wealthy London merchants; they'd support the king in return for . . . what? Their price was what William needed to find out, and quickly.

William did not know of another visitor to the castle, however; one who was just as fervently expected, though much less powerful. For all that, she harbored a secret that was overdue in the telling, a secret that might have the power to transform or destroy Edward's reign.

Deborah had been surprised when, three days before Christmas, an old friend of hers, Alan the Tinker, had arrived at her small, snug cottage. Though people in the village knew the location of her house and physic garden, and sought her out as a healer, she took care to live quietly. Being known as a healer, locally, was to her benefit, for it brought in a little extra to the pot, but she knew that curing people and animals might be construed as sorcery by unthinking outsiders, so she was not unhappy that few outside the village knew where to find her. Alan, though, was one of that few, and welcome because he brought news of the world on his visits, while he mended her tools and pots and pans.

She'd always paid in kind for the work he did for her and the efficacy of her remedies kept him coming back, for he did well from selling on small stoppered jars of her simples. There were syrups for the winter ague made from honey, rosemary, and juniper, and spirits of wine. When the milk would not let down after childbirth there was dried milk thistle and betony to be made up into a hot poultice to apply to the breasts. For fever in small children there was a simple made from the bark and leaves of willows, and, best of all, a creamy, sweet-tasting mixture for colic that mothers cherished because their children would swallow it without complaint. And for men who had troubles with their heart, Deborah made pellets from foxglove pounded with hawthorn berries that thinned the blood. This remedy was famous on Alan's rounds. Many a fat miller or priest had been saved by Deborah's pellets melting under their tongues, easing the pain that shot down their arms and across their chests. Though often, of course, they put survival down to their favorite saints and made vows to go on pilgrimage for their soul's sake.

This cold day, Alan had had something for Deborah: a little scrap of vellum covered in badly formed characters. She'd read it in the light of the fire with the aid of a piece of a lens he'd brought her the year before last. Her sight had been getting worse lately. As she'd followed the words, her expression had changed to something like fear, which had surprised the tinker very much. Then, quickly, she had thrown a couple of clean kirtles into a drawstring bag of skin and, at the last minute, an unexpectedly beautiful dress of mulberry-colored brocade with a tall hennin, swathed in gauzy silk veiling, which she wadded with clean undershifts to protect from damage.

Then, wrapping herself in a thick but much-darned traveling

cloak, she and Alan had ridden off together on his sturdy cob, leading his packhorse. They had both known it would be a very cold journey east as they rode toward Windsor, and there was no telling if they'd arrive before the weather beat them, but after an achingly stiff ride, Alan and she had reached the gates of the castle on Christmas Eve, nearly frozen, just before the snow.

"Who is it you want?" asked the not-unkind sergeant of the guard when he saw how cold the woman was.

"I'm to ask for Sergeant Cage. He's expecting me."

It took an hour or so to track Sergeant Cage down. The whole castle was celebrating the impending birth of the Savior, green branches of fir and holly were being hung all over the vast building with an agreeable level of chaos, and the place was huge—one individual was never easy to find, unless you knew for certain where to look. However, to honor the conviviality of the season, the sergeant of the guard allowed the woman and the tinker to thaw in front of the fire in the guardhouse of the outer ward. He even permitted the tinker's horses to be taken to the stables for a bite to eat. *Must be getting soft,* he thought. *Christmas. That's what it is.*

Deborah was grateful for the time to tidy herself—as best she could—and at least start the process of drying her clothes, though she longed to take them off and do it properly. She was so tired from the long, hard miles that she was beginning to nod in the warmth when Sergeant Cage arrived in a flurry of dark cold from the outside, stamping his feet to get the snow off his rawhide boots. Though Jehanne had told him to expect the woman, he'd never believed the message could travel so fast from London at this time of the year, so he was quite surprised to find Deborah and the tinker sitting in front of the guardhouse fire. Still, they'd made it, and Dame Jehanne had sworn him to silence, so that's what he was prepared to honor.

Among curious looks he waited patiently for the woman to wrap herself in her slightly less sodden cloak and then held the door open for her to slip through. Having sent the tinker to the stables, he hurried Deborah across the vast inner ward toward the Lieutenant's Tower and the great mass of the keep, even blacker than the night sky. Beyond that lay the king's and queen's apartments, but it was a long, dark, cold walk in driving snow nearing blizzard conditions and the woman looked exhausted. He very much hoped she would not collapse before he found Jehanne.

Luck was with them, however, or else the woman was hardier than she looked. Jehanne was just leaving the queen's rooms after dressing Elizabeth for the evening festivities when he found her. Deborah and Jehanne looked at each other for a long moment. And then Jehanne very deliberately crossed herself and sighed. "It's true then."

"Yes, it is true."

"Then, the good Lord keep and guide us."

Sergeant Cage thought it was a curious greeting between old friends, but he soon banished the thought as he hurried away to a long and busy night in his overcrowded stables. As he left, the door from the queen's apartments opened and Anne hurried through with a number of the queen's gowns.

Deborah spoke. "So, child, have you no welcome since I've traveled so far to be with you this Christmas?"

"Deborah!" Joy transformed Anne's face. "Oh, I'm so glad you're here; there is such trouble . . . the king is—"

Jehanne cut her off, conscious that Sergeant Cage could hear. "Shush now, girl. Take the queen's dresses to the laundry. See that they are extra careful with the spots on the tissue-of-gold overdress, please. And then you may rejoin us for a Christ-Mass wassail."

Long habit of obedience meant Anne did as she was told, walking uncertainly away but casting a glance toward the two older women as they glided off into the darkness beyond the queen's rooms.

The last days had been very difficult for Anne. She knew that there'd been some discussion between the king and queen about her position in Elizabeth's household. With typical capriciousness, when the king had reported his father-in-law's request that he be allowed to "borrow" Anne for the remainder of the Christmas season—to cheer the duchess up with the use of some of her unique skills on an aging, once-beautiful face—the queen had refused permission, which annoyed Edward mightily. Elizabeth had forgotten her displeasure with Anne of a day or so ago, because the girl had made a tea for her from orient ginger that eased the more violent symptoms of her morning sickness.

The king fumed but could say nothing. Undeniably, it would be easier for him if the girl were not under the queen's eye all the time. He found Anne's presence disturbed him intensely whenever he was in his wife's chambers, and that was becoming harder and harder to hide. He wanted to look at Anne, touch her, even talk to her. If she were elsewhere he could continue this patient wooing, this long, slow campaign that was as fascinating as the plan for any battle.

Anne herself could hardly breathe when Edward was present. She knew they were both trapped by a force as strong as a river in flood, and it was addictive, this sensation, and dangerous. So far, for the last two days, she'd managed to avoid speaking to the king on any but the most trivial level. But the game was dizzying—it seemed that everywhere she turned, he was there. She could smell him in the very air of the queen's rooms.

Edward was as conscious of Anne as she was of him. He knew, too, that he'd been very clever with his wager. He had judged, quite rightly, that her infatuation for him was profound, and that it would take a much steadier head than he thought a sixteen- or seventeen-year-old girl such as she might have to resist the charged glances he cast at her, the times he brushed her hand with his as she passed him in his wife's rooms. Yet the strength of her will, her fight for composure was impressive, and made the game deliciously intense. He'd not been so excited by the thought of what was to come for a very long time. He had only to close his eyes to see her naked, that beautiful skin touched by the light of the fire in his chamber, that mouth so ready to receive his own . . . What he wanted most was to take her somewhere, alone, out of the court's eye, for he was hot to touch her, to kiss her, just to look at her. She knew that, and he knew that, and soon she would not be strong enough to deny it.

For now, though, after seeing Deborah so briefly, Anne fled down to the kitchens of the queen's quarters to where the laundresses plied their sweaty trade even in winter, though only for Elizabeth. The rest of the world waited for spring to wash and dry all the dirty clothes of winter.

Anne particularly liked Mary, the laundress who managed to work cheerfully with Rose even when she was difficult. Today she was boiling up yet another copper vessel of spring water as she shredded fine lye soap with which to wash the queen's woolen clothes. Mary had an excellent instinct for the right water heat for such expensive garments: too hot and the material felted and shrank; too cold and the grease didn't come out, nor enough of the sweat smell, which, though most people hardly noticed it, was something the queen was very particular about. Of course, many of the fine brocaded and furred clothes could not be washed at all but had to be dealt with in other ways, and that was why a skilled laundress could enjoy a long and profitable career at court.

"Three tonight, Mary. One velvet, one brocade, and one broadcloth. The queen wants to wear the blue velvet the day after next. Can you clean it in time, do you think?"

Silently, Mary held out her hands for the gown and then looked at it under the light of a wall sconce. There were deep sweat rings under the arms and spots of grease on the bodice, quite a lot of it from last night's supper, even though the queen had such dainty airs.

"Well, I'll have to, won't I? Stinks a bit when you smell it up close." Mary sniffed the seams under the sleeves of the gown and then she laughed. "Your face! Queen's just like us, got a body same as you and me. Eats, sleeps, shits, pisses—don't forget it. Anyway, you know that better than most, I'd reckon, seeing you dress her . . . Want a Christmas wassail with me?"

Generously, Mary held up a stoneware jug. Pressed into the baked clay were the arms of William Hastings. "Little present; sent by a friend of mine." Anne recognized the badge and wondered where Mary had got the jar from but she didn't have time to linger, much as she'd have liked to.

"Have to get back up to the queen's rooms, but I'll see you tonight, after vespers. We'll have our wassail then?" Impulsively, she gave Mary a hug. The laundress had a big heart and was unfailingly generous to Anne. Once, at considerable risk to her position, she'd stuck up for her to Jehanne when Rose had blamed Anne for scorching one of the queen's gowns as it was being smoothed by hot, flat irons on the stone laundry bench. And all because she liked Anne's face, or that's what she said afterward when the shouting had died down.

Now Anne hurried from the laundry back toward Jehanne's room through the vast, nearly empty spaces of the queen's suite. Silently she thanked Jehanne for bringing Deborah to court, but yet, one part of her shrank from the conversation they would surely have. She knew that, after telling the story, Deborah would insist she leave the court and the king's influence, and she was so deep in anguished thought, she nearly ran past the door to Jehanne's tiny chamber.

The two women inside were sitting huddled together on the box bed and Jehanne had a small, exquisite pair of scissors in her hands as Anne entered.

"Come sit beside me here, child. Deborah and I were discussing the past—and how we met."

Anne was perplexed. "You know each other?"

Looks were exchanged by the two other women and no answer was given. "What do you know of your mother and father, child?" Jehanne asked.

Anne caught Deborah's glance; she, too, looked worried and that frightened the girl. "Only that my mother died when I was born and my father was very sick and could not look after me in his house. Deborah took me in and then she became my mother."

The two women looked at each other; Jehanne crossed herself and seemed to summon courage. "Anne, your father is alive."

The girl's face lit up but the older woman held up her hand for a moment. "He's alive but . . ." She swallowed, seemed to have trouble catching her breath. "Anne, your father is King Henry, the old king that was, the sixth of that name. And you are the granddaughter of great King Harry, his father. He who beat the French at Agincourt."

Anne shook her head, the words skating through her brain. What were they talking about? "The old king is a madman. It's said he tried to eat his mattress once!" Anne was incredulous. She was a peasant, a servant, how could she be anything else?

"No, he was never mad. It's just that affairs of state taxed him and he would . . . retire—in his mind. It was always worse in winter and his wife, the French queen, was scornful of him. He is a gentle and confused man. To be a king is not easy. I used to wait upon the old queen, Margaret. She was clever and hard, and very beautiful. Not for nothing do they call her the she-wolf of Anjou. Your mother also waited on her, as a gentlewoman."

"What do you mean? Who was my mother?"

Jehanne sighed, memory arcing back more than sixteen years. "Her name was Alyce de Bohun. She was the only daughter of Gervaise de Bohun: your grandfather was a baron, part of the Duke of Somerset's affinity. He had lands in the West Country but he did not survive the French wars. Out of gratitude for his service, the duke brought your mother to court, to be a lady-in-waiting to the queen. She was not much more than fifteen when you were born."

Slowly the implications of all she was hearing began to seep into Anne's mind. And the questions began. "My . . . father? Why has he never tried to see me?"

"He does not know that you exist. Margaret—the queen—saw to that. She tried to have your mother murdered on the night you were born. That was how we met, Deborah and I. She took us both in, and saved you, hid you, after your mother died."

That silenced Anne. At present Margaret of Anjou was skulking back in France, still looking for an opportunity to lead an army back to Britain to reclaim her husband's throne from Edward. Margaret had never been loved by the English people, because she was French and high-handed from the beginning of her marriage to Henry—but principally because she was barren, or so it had seemed.

"Before you were conceived, the queen took no heed of your father, but your mother became his friend—perhaps his only true friend—in a friendless world. She was gentle and liked to play chess; they would play together by the hour. At the time the old queen was pleased the king was distracted—it gave her more power—but then the king fell in love with your mother and she with him. You were the result and that pregnancy proved that the problem of conceiving lay with the queen, not the king."

"So I am a bastard. And my mother was a slut." Anne's tone

was flat and hard. Perhaps she was like her mother, perhaps that explained her behavior with the king. And to be a bastard alone in the great world was a worse slur than being a servant or a peasant.

Jehanne spoke gently. "Your mother was not a whore. She was a child adrift and unsupported at court, in love for the first time in her life with a man who was kind to her. That is how the king came to be your father. Your father is a very pious man, he was never known for loose living. He adored your mother and felt safe with her."

"Who else knows—about my father?" Anne was calm, perhaps from shock.

"Margaret, the old queen. Some of her affinity would know, and the Beauforts perhaps. But none of them know you are alive. When your mother was sent away from court so that you could be born at the king's hunting lodge, Margaret's men went after her. They had orders to kill you both. You see, even a bastard child of the king could give the people someone to rally around, because they hated the French queen so much. Because your father was gentle and chivalrous, she took advantage of him and surrounded him with evil councilors who leached the country dry. The people saw that. Until she had her own son, three or more years after you were born, she did not feel safe as queen of this country."

Jehanne had been around courts all her life, and as she remembered the battles and the gossip from so long ago, it all rushed into her mind as fresh as yesterday. She remembered the queen's terrible fury when she'd heard about Alyce becoming pregnant by the king, and how, for once in his life, the king had stood up to his wife, protecting the girl as best he could, keeping her hidden from the queen's wrath. But not well enough, not when she thought about the dreadful journey they had both endured all those winters ago, and the girl's tragic death in the forest after the baby had been born. When news was brought to court that both mother and child had died after an ambush, relations between Margaret and her husband had become more and more difficult. It was after Alyce's death that the king began his long decline into deep melancholy as the fits of profound sadness came and went.

Three years later, the queen gave birth to a son of her own, but the king could not be brought to recognize the boy as his heir. Finally, he was persuaded to agree that the baby was his child, but piously attributed his birth to the Holy Ghost since he and the queen had been so long estranged.

And for all these years Jehanne had kept silent, for fear that the queen—or her successors—might still find Alyce's daughter and kill her, for only she and Deborah knew the secret.

"Does this mean that King Edward is my cousin?"

"Yes, in the third or so degree. You are both descended from the sons of Edward III: you through John of Gaunt, and the king through Lionel, John of Gaunt's elder brother."

"Can my descent . . . be proved?"

Again, it was Jehanne who spoke. "I believe it can. I have seen a letter from King Henry, your father, to the Duke of Somerset. In it he endows your mother, whom he expressly names, with lands in her own right so that his child, got on her, may exist in keeping with its station. This was before your birth. I believe it is among the crown documents, though the king may not know about it—may not know about you. I have kept some of your mother's things in trust, as has Deborah. She and I are ready to swear to the truth of your birth."

Jehanne handed the girl the tiny scissors she'd been holding and, after searching through her coffer, a little silk-wrapped packet. "The scissors were Alyce's. I have had them since your birth." Suddenly, the old lady was tearful and Deborah pressed her hand gently. A moment later Jehanne continued. "This is something else, it is yours by right." And she gently touched the package wrapped in faded red silk tied with ribbon.

With shaking hands, Anne unfolded the fragile material. It was the wrapping around a little, leather-bound case, the sides fastened together with a tiny gold hook, and stamped on the outside was a golden crown with "Henricius Rex" engraved beneath it.

She freed the hook gently from its keeper and found inside a portrait, no bigger than the palm of a small child's hand. A beautiful solemn face looked back at her, a girl. At the bottom there was a date, "Anno Domini 1450," and a name, "Alyce de Bohun." She was looking at the face of her mother, unseen for over sixteen years. Hot tears rose in her eyes; her mother had died before she'd even reached the age Anne was today.

"The king had it painted by a Fleming who was at court then. She gave it to me on our last journey together. Asked me to keep it safe if anything should happen to her. And I have."

Again Anne's vision clouded. She'd always been an outsider at court, and that had been her mother's fate as well. And both of them had loved a married king, partnered to a vengeful queen. Suddenly, far away, she could hear a rushing, rumbling sound, the noise a great waterwheel makes when it turns; it filled her with creeping dread. Consciously she forced the sound out of her mind. "What am I to do now?" It was a heartfelt plea.

Jehanne cast a quick glance at her companion. "I think we need advice. We must tread so carefully. That another child of the old king exists means more danger for King Edward and the whole family of York, especially now that the situation between Edward and Warwick and the Duke of Clarence is so unstable. As a Lancastrian of the royal blood, even a bastard, you would be very valuable to Warwick—maybe more valuable even than his own daughter, where the marriage of Duke George is concerned. The king pays you more favor: others have marked it as well. How long before the queen is told? She is as jealous as Margaret of Anjou ever was, and as dangerous. And what if the king should . . . take you to be his leman, and it would be asked who you are, where you come from? Hastings will have to ask, believe me, because that is part of his watch on the safety of the king. There are too many questions that cannot be answered without dreadful consequences for you. Let alone what the queen will do if you become his mistress. Things are moving too quickly—we stand on the edge of chaos."

Anne was appalled as the brutal reality of her situation sank in. She could not, now, ignore the knowledge of who she really was and it was clearly impossible to go on living at court, serving the queen, when her relationship to the king was so volatile.

She needed friends, powerful friends, to advise her. But who? Whom could she trust?

Chapter Twenty-seven

It was some hours before dawn on the morning of Christmas and Edward was with Mathew Cuttifer in his private quarters. The king's most pressing need was money to take troops north—once the weather changed—with a big enough show of strength to intimidate Warwick and his own vain, foolish brother George, the Duke of Clarence.

For several hours he and Mathew had been negotiating tax concessions that the merchants of London would accept in return for helping him raise an army to stand for four months in the new year. Edward was impressed by the merchant's wily reasoning. London was the largest manufacturing center of the whole kingdom and the powerful guilds, the mercers in particular, wanted to keep it that way. If the king would consent to further strengthening of certain monopolies within the city—the manufacturing of needles, for instance, in which Edward himself had a large interest—Mathew felt sure he could help his colleagues see where their best interests lay.

A large army under the king's control could protect London and that was no bad thing in these uncertain times. Mathew also believed that the king was a better general than Warwick; his track record proved he was a formidable tactician with a cooler head in crisis than the earl, though Mathew knew he'd need to work to convince others of his belief.

Like the king, he thought they should try to avoid open conflict—it was bad for trade, coming so soon after the last lot of hostilities—but there was nothing like openly preparing to go to war to convince others of the foolishness of risking life, limb, and, more importantly, property.

It had been a long night and Mathew was exhausted, desperate for sleep. The king was twenty-four, well able to stay up all night after feasting and far too much to drink, but those days were long gone for Mathew. And tomorrow—or rather today—he would have an arduous, cold journey back to London. If the river was still frozen it would have to be on horseback, which, with his piles, was not a thought he relished. He swallowed a huge yawn as the king continued to dissect details of the deal he wanted from the merchants of London when William whispered into his ear.

"Master Cuttifer, forgive me. I've kept you out of your bed far too long. We'll finish our discussion after Mass today and then you're for home. One last thing . . ." The king sprang easily to his feet—and unsheathed his sword from where it had been lying on a table. "Kneel."

For one mad moment, Mathew's disordered brain sent a panicked message: *he's going to cut my head off!* But the smile on Edward's face calmed his bounding heart. The king had something else in mind as William indicated the older man should kneel. Tremulously, Mathew lowered himself on to one knee—the right, which was a little better than the left—and bowed his head as the king came toward him, naked sword in his hand. Dazed, the merchant felt two light taps, one on each shoulder.

"Arise, Sir Mathew Cuttifer, Baronet, for so you now are—knighted for loyal services to your grateful king and to the Mercers' Guild. You'll receive the Letters Patent when I return with the court to London, but for now, good night."

So it was in a happy fog that Mathew followed a silent servant to the magnificent bedroom that had been given to him for the night. It was a vast, tapestry-hung room not far from the king's own chambers, but his tired, exalted mind took in few of the splendors. His one disappointment was the absence of Margaret, his wife. She would be a lady in right of *his* name now, he thought happily, not just her own. And there would be a title to bequeath to little Edward as well, his much-loved grandson. The child of tragedy was a flourishing six-month-old with several teeth now, and spoiled by the entire household.

"Sir Mathew. Sir Mathew Cuttifer." He repeated it several times out loud after he dismissed the man the king had sent to light the way. It sounded serious—a man not to be taken lightly. He was pragmatic enough to know that it was a bribe, but, still, it was a title he felt he merited. Secretly, he was thrilled to be at the center of things and this new honor certainly proved that. Now, however, he needed some sleep. He yawned cavernously as he undressed, hoping against hope that someone had thought to warm the bed, or at least air the linen. There was nothing he disliked more than dank sheets in winter; it made getting up in the morning a severe trial. Then, looking around for a candle snuffer, he noticed that someone had slipped something under the door of his room. It was a small square of parchment sealed with a dab of wax. Curious, he broke the seal and unfolded the note, grunting in surprise when he read the name at the end of the few words: Anne!

The little note, written in a fine, flowing hand, begged to apologize for intruding on his rest but asked if he could meet the writer for a moment after Mass today, Christmas Day. There was something important, and urgent, that she had to tell him.

Thoughtfully, he slid the letter under his bolster and snuffed the candle. It was strange, certainly, and he'd never had a letter from a woman written in Latin before. Had she used it as a kind of code, knowing that, even if it had not reached him, few could have read it?

It had been Anne's idea to try to speak to Mathew, once she, Deborah, and Jehanne heard he was in the castle. Anne had worried that he might not help them, but there was no one else to turn to and Deborah, and she, had faith that he was a good man.

So Anne had nightmares again that night: the king's face, his mouth, and his body, woven through images of loss and suffering.

She was running, being chased, one moment she wanted to be caught and then she ran faster and faster, knowing that if he reached out, if he touched her, if he *caught* her, she would die.

She woke with a jerk, heart pounding, mouth dry with fear, a terrible feeling of dread oppressing her still. It was black and all around in the dorter she could hear the snuffles and grunts of her companions, stirring in their sleep. She lay awake, eyes wide, as the madness of the last twenty-four hours came back. She prayed that Mathew had her note. Surely he would know what to do? There was no more sleep for Anne, not this Christmas morning, and for once she welcomed the cold winter dawn.

Not so the queen. Part of being pregnant was that it was hard for her to wake, even though her room began to fill with women from first light. Moments later the king arrived, full of cheer, as they began to dress her. He gave the queen a great smacking kiss over her protests that she wasn't ready to receive him. And then, among much hilarity, he used the excuse of Christmas to kiss every other woman in the room. Even Elizabeth laughed as, one by one, the king cornered each of the ladies in turn, making it all part of a good-humored game. Anne tried to slip out of the room as the hilarity was at its height and the queen was distracted, but the king saw her and made a hullabaloo.

"Now, now. Here's a pretty hind, Your Majesty, doing her best to slip away into the forest. Shall we hunt her down?"

"By all means, my lord, hunt away."

"What say, girls—after her!" And the giggling bunch, young and old, followed his lead, surrounding Anne and dragging her to the king for a Christmas kiss. She was pushed into his open arms and his mouth found hers for one sweet moment before the game swept on and another, more willing victim was found for the king's sport.

The queen was complaisant; all sorts and kinds of nonsense were part of this season, the twelve days of Christmas. It meant little, and though the king had not sought her bed for a night or so, her spies told her that he'd been working late into the night with William and his other advisors.

Her heart skipped an anxious beat when she reviewed the rumors she'd heard last evening from her mother. The king was raising an army. The time for confronting Warwick was moving closer and she took nothing for granted, having lost her first husband at Towton. She'd been queen for less than three years and she had not given Edward a son. God knew, the wheel could turn again . . . Her morbid thoughts were interrupted by the king.

"Hurry, sweet girl. There is someone I shall want you to be especially nice to after the Mass. We need his help."

She knew he meant the merchant, Mathew Cuttifer. She didn't approve of the king showing such favor to the city merchants; it gave them too much self-importance. But Elizabeth was no fool. They would need money and London was the source. She decided to be gracious. "As always, lord husband and king, I am your most obedient servant."

He grinned. "Obedient? How delightful. And such a change too." He clapped his hands. "Come, children, finish dressing the queen. I need her."

He strode out, leaving a buzzing hive of activity behind him as the girls ran to and fro, tending the queen's hair, face, and clothes. She stood in the center of the room, still as a statue, as they laced and fluffed her gown and pinned jewels into the ropes of her blond hair arranged in a coronet above a serene brow.

She knew that the bloom of pregnancy had made her skin lustrous, and this time, thanks be to God, there was no sign of fluid building up. Perhaps the last pregnancy had been an aberration; she must ask Doctor Moss to cast her horoscope again and that of her child. Perhaps this child had been conceived at a more fortunate time than the princess. There was a knock at the chamber door and Doctor Moss appeared as if she'd summoned him from the ether. He was dressed in his most expensive purple velvet gown furred with beaver. He bowed deeply.

"It seemed to me that I should see how Your Majesty fares this fine Christmas Day."

"As you see, Doctor. But there is no time for talk—the king expects me to join him in a very little while. Perhaps we could speak, you and I, a little later, after the Mass. Tighter!"

Jehanne had made one last tug on the lacing of the glorious

tissue-of-gold dress that the queen had chosen to wear for the celebration of the Savior's birth. Uncertain, Jehanne looked at the doctor.

"Perhaps a little looser is desirable, Your Majesty. For the child." The queen pouted, but, determined not to let anything spoil her sunny mood, grunted grudging approval, and Jehanne allowed the back of the dress to expand just a little.

"Walk with me to the chapel, Doctor—we must be quick. You favor exercise for ladies in such condition as mine, do you not?"

"Within reason, certainly. All things within reason, as the Greeks said . . ."

The queen swept out of her apartments, her ladies trailing after her, and Anne had a moment to herself. She picked up discarded garments quickly and then, daringly, glanced in the queen's glass to see her own face.

A pale oval looked back—at least she had clear skin, not like poor Rose—and she could see that the deep red of her livery was flattering; but her face was the same, nothing had changed. She was who she'd always been, and yet . . . it was also the face of a stranger, the daughter of a king, someone she did not know, could not know. Then she gasped—Edward's reflection swam into focus behind hers.

"Laggard. You look very well." One quick stride and he was beside her, kissing her ravenously.

"Honey-mouth," he breathed, kissing the base of her throat, his hand straying down to her breast. Then he was gone as quickly as he had been there, leaving her dazed. Like a phantom.

Oh, God, she had to leave the court—there was no choice now. Unconsciously, her hand strayed to the chain of the little filigree cross that hung between her breasts. Perhaps Mathew would allow her to return to Blessing House for a while, but would he give her sanctuary when she told him who she was?

Chapter Twenty-eight

Anne waited nervously outside Saint George's Hall, anxious that at any moment, her absence from the queen's chambers would be questioned, even though Jehanne was covering for her. It was close to the Christmas morning feast and her stomach growled uncomfortably, but inside the hall she knew the king was still talking to Mathew Cuttifer and William Hastings. She'd been unable to snatch a brief word with Mathew after early Mass, and now she'd heard that he was expected to travel back to London as soon as possible after this final audience with the king. All Anne could do now was wait in a small deserted anteroom she'd found outside the hall.

She was very cold, for there was no fire in the frigid little chamber, and she thought longingly of the warmth and happy chaos that was going on without her all around the castle. A reaction had set in against all she'd been told yesterday. To truly contemplate herself as the daughter of a king was the stuff of dreams—and nightmares.

She had to speak to Mathew without letting Edward see them talking, but if she succeeded, what could she really say? He would think she was mad.

She was still trying to form a coherent speech in her mind when she heard the doors of the hall groan on their hinges and the sound of male voices. It was the king, accompanied by Mathew and William Hastings. Quickly, she flattened herself against the wall behind the open door of the anteroom and let the small party of men walk past, talking seriously and quietly as they went. She waited until the sound of their conversation receded and then slipped out and ran silently behind them on felt-shod feet, flitting from doorway to doorway so that, should they turn, they'd not see her.

The three men were very close to the gate that guarded the king's lodgings at Windsor and Edward was saying good-bye to Mathew before handing him on to a party of men-at-arms who would escort him back to London.

Anne could not hear what was said, but she saw the king nod graciously as Mathew bowed deeply and then backed out of Edward's presence. The king and William watched him go and then turned back the way they had come toward Anne's hiding place in a doorway. Quick as thought she tripped the latch, and skipped through the opened door into darkness, heart beating like a drum as she heard the king and Hastings stroll past outside, their talk a quiet murmur through the thick oak door.

Eyes closed, trying to control her breathing, she counted to ten as slowly as she could and then eased the door ajar. There, very close, was the gate, guarded by two men-at-arms. From the looks on their faces they were bored, cold, and very annoyed to be on duty when everyone else in the whole castle was having fun. Anne slid through the slightly opened door, blessing good fortune that the wall embrasure just next to her hiding place blocked the line of sight from the gate. Summoning a panicked look she ran toward the guards—startling them to alertness, for she'd appeared as if from the air.

"Oh, sirs, sirs, have you seen a man in a red furred robe with a large black velvet hat?"

The senior pikeman looked at the pretty little thing wearing the queen's colors, hopping anxiously from foot to foot in front of them. The poor child was clearly agitated, wringing her hands.

"Just this moment gone, girl. He was with the king."

"Oh, thank you, sir, thank you. The queen will be so angry if I do not speak to him. She has given me a message for him."

The senior pikeman took pity. Everyone in the castle knew the queen was a very hard woman to please. He could imagine the fate of this poor creature if she didn't follow orders. "You'll catch him if you run. There's been a delay with the horses. They're meeting his party at the king's outer gate."

The girl picked up her skirts and was away before they'd had the chance to exchange another word, but it did his heart good to see the young thing run just like a hind in the spring forest. The senior pikeman sighed. Sometimes being part of the king's guards was a less than glorious position, especially on a freezing cold day when everyone else was celebrating. He'd have liked to talk to her a little more, maybe find out her name. She might have shared a mulled ale with him later, when his duty finished. Then he cheered up. If she wanted to go back to the queen's lodgings she'd have to travel the way she'd come.

But Anne knew that returning to the queen's lodgings this morning might be impossible if Mathew Cuttifer believed her. She had no real plans as she ran across the still frosty ground of the king's ward other than to speak to Mathew, beg for his help, though she was painfully aware that she had little proof to offer of the truth of her identity. Yet, if he did believe her—what then? What would he advise her to do? The inner ward itself was enormous, an enclosed space bounded by the castle's outer walls. As Anne ran, she prayed that Mathew would wait, that he would decide to visit the garderobe before setting out, that *something* would delay him.

Yes! She could see them now! A small party of men wearing the king's livery was milling around just inside the arched gate in the massive outer wall. There were no horses, and she could see Mathew stamping up and down with a frown on his face, slapping his gloves against his thigh. She slowed her run to a decorous walk, breathing hard, a hand flying up to check that her headdress still covered her hair properly as the other smoothed the high waist of her dress. Appearances were important to her former master.

He turned and saw her. She swallowed nervously, hoping none of her fear showed as she walked toward him composedly and dropped to a curtsy from long habit.

"Anne!" Seeing her made him remember the note she'd left in his room; the press of business had driven her request from his mind. "My apologies that I did not seek you out. I was with the king and . . . Excuse me for one moment, if you please." To cover his embarrassment, he glowered at the captain of the king's guard who had been assigned to see him safely back to London. "Captain, where are those horses? Time is fleeting."

Mindful that the inefficiency of this simple task could well be sheeted home to him, the captain strode importantly toward the half a dozen men clustered near the outer gate, bellowing officiously, "Tyler! Send another man to the stables. This delay is unforgivable. We must have Sir Mathew returned to London by nightfall!"

Mathew, secretly delighted to hear the magic "sir" and the automatic respect in the man's voice, called out grumpily, "Is there somewhere I can speak to this girl out of the wind?"

"Of course, Sir Mathew. This way, Sir Mathew."

The obsequious attention of the soldier made Anne even more nervous; clearly Mathew's favor with the king was even greater than it had been. Would that fact further complicate what she was about to ask?

The captain was energetically determined to be helpful. He bowed the merchant inside the gate to a little room that led off the main guard post lit by a cheerful fire. There was a blackened oak settle in the inglenook that Mathew pointed to. "Sit, girl. And tell me what is so important that you had to run like a hoyden in full sight of the king's windows?"

Gratefully, Anne dropped down onto the settle and smoothed her skirts as she asked grace to find the right words. "Sir, have you ever wondered who my parents might be?"

"Your parents?" Mathew was completely bewildered.

Anne realized she had begun on the wrong tack. "I have just been told some remarkable things, sir, things about my . . . history. They seem so fantastic, so like something out of a romance. Yet the person I trust more than any in the world has told me they are true. And if they are, I am in danger and so perhaps is the kingdom. I need your advice."

Mathew, grudgingly, found himself intrigued. "Your parents, child? Mistress Deborah?"

"Sir Mathew, if you remember, Deborah is my foster mother.

My real mother's name was Alyce de Bohun and she had a child with the old king, King Henry. It seems I am that child."

Mathew heard the words, of course, but it took a moment for them to assemble into any sort of pattern his brain recognized as sense. "Can this be proved?" Even as he asked the question, he couldn't believe what he was saying. Surely what Anne was suggesting was preposterous.

"Yes. A letter exists from the old king . . . from my father, though I have not seen it; and there is other evidence. Sir, what should I do?" Anne had been able to speak clearly to this point but now her voice shook and she looked at him imploringly.

And he was dazzled. His wife's little body servant had grown up in the last few months. She was now almost a woman and beautiful. Mathew shook his head to concentrate. He looked at her carefully, allowing his eyes to travel over her face, feature by feature. Then, buying time to think, he walked over to the fire, held his hands out to the warmth. "Was your mother English?"

"Yes, sir. She came from a Somerset family. My grandfather, my mother's father, fought with the Duke of Somerset in France."

Mathew grunted noncommittally. "A lady, then?"

Anne nodded. Yes, it was true, her mother had been a lady.

"Does the king know about you?"

Anne shook her head. "I believe he cannot. It was said I'd died at birth. The old French queen, Margaret, tried to kill my mother—and me. But, as you see . . ."

Yes, he did see. And the more he looked at her, the more her remarkable story had some ring of truth. He searched his memory. As a young child, he had been held up as the great King Harry V, the father of Henry VI, marched past, ten thousand men of London at his back on his way to the glories of Agincourt. He'd been a strong, good-looking man in the very prime of his life and Mathew had never forgotten the image of the king he'd been eye to eye with for a moment—he a little boy on his father's shoulders and Harry near enough to touch in that narrow London street.

The king had smiled at his tiny subject. Strong white teeth, bright blue-green eyes, eyes like those of the girl standing in front of him. And the same dark russet hair, the same fair white skin too.

Then Mathew remembered the first day this girl had come to his house, his unease at having a servant who looked so . . . well, *unlike* a servant. And now she sat before him, as composed as any queen might be—until you looked into those same strange eyes and saw the anguish there, the uncertainty.

"What should I do, Master Mathew?"

For a moment, his vanity wanted to correct her—he was attached to the new honorific—but more serious thoughts were running through his mind. "Yes, I can understand your concern. If your story is true, you have guessed correctly. You would be a most valuable piece in the game being played in our country now. Chess piece I mean," he added hastily.

The room was silent as he looked at her for a moment then strolled over to the little window let into the thick wall of the gatehouse. Still no sign of the horses, he noted, abstracted; that was the least important thing on his mind now.

Yes. An *English* child of Henry VI would be a potent addition to the political stakes in England just now. There were many who did not accept the French queen's son by Henry as his legitimate child and who would welcome a new English princess, unofficial or not. Edward, too, had a girl as his heir, so far—even though the queen was pregnant again. But Anne was of marriageable age; that changed everything.

The marriageable English daughter of the old king—whom many still considered the rightful king—would be a rallying point for all who wished to see Edward's Yorkist family displaced and those who had no love for the rapacious Frenchwoman Margaret of Anjou or her suspect-born son. If Anne's descent could be proved there were many great lords, Warwick among them, who would welcome an alternative to Edward on the throne of England.

A quick, glittering marriage with one of Warwick's affinity—perhaps even Clarence—and the deed would be done. Another royal family could be created, one that Warwick would feel able to control, since Edward had grown too great for his grasp.

But Mathew still had his urgent mission to perform: the raising of money to help Edward fight Warwick and Clarence when the moment for battle came. Mathew closed his eyes. Visions of turmoil, flame, and blood filled his mind, things he'd thought never to see again, please God, in his lifetime.

"Sir Mathew? I shall have to return to the castle soon. *What should I do?*"

"Nothing. For the moment. I shall consult Lady Margaret— she will no doubt have useful things to say on the matter. Meanwhile, I suggest you try to obtain the letters you say the king has and that you tell no one—no one—what you have told me today. If what you say proves to be true, I shall help you. But we must have time to plan what should be done. Do you agree?"

He resisted the urge to bow to the still figure who sat on the settle before him. Strange how a normal person could change into something else—a symbol, perhaps—in an instant. Then it hit him like cold water on a hot day. With this knowledge, he, too, and his family, were in grave danger. He had said he would help her, and he would. The question was, how? And what would it bring him when he did: death or great influence?

Outside, the shouts of men could be heard and a moment later the captain of his guard knocked respectfully at the door of the little room. "The horses have arrived, and if Sir Mathew is quite ready . . ."

Sir Mathew was, but first he strode to Anne and, gently picking up one of her little, work-roughened hands, he said, "Your servant, lady." He meant it. "I shall send word with someone you can trust. As soon as I am able . . ."

Anne heard the noise and bustle of the small party leaving, but the sounds came from far, far away. It was not cold in the little room, but she shivered as she looked into the heart of the glowing coals in the fireplace.

Something moved and for a moment it seemed she saw . . . what? The sea, black and cold, under stars; heard it wash and move on the pebbles of the shore; saw the great ship at anchor, rocking; waiting . . . for her. Her head swam and she closed her eyes, trying to think, trying not to smell the salt on the wind that suddenly buffeted through the little room. Windsor was inland, nowhere near the sea . . .

The fire spat and a log broke apart, its glowing, pulsing heart exposed. Suddenly energized, Anne jumped to her feet. She had no money and nothing but a handful of friends to support her, yet she'd been given a sign, a portent that felt oddly hopeful. The vision of the sea felt right, felt true; perhaps it meant that the great wheel had, indeed, begun to turn. And if it had, there was nothing she could do but hold fast, and try to ride the rim.

Deborah and Jehanne had found a quiet spot in the gallery above Saint George's Hall, looking down onto the revelers beneath them. To please the king, the queen had arranged for the townsfolk of Windsor to prepare a surprise. Tonight they would perform the story of Christ's birth, but instead of the play taking place in the courtyard of an inn, or outside one of the churches of the town, as was usual, the villagers had been invited into the castle because the weather was so harsh.

Deborah looked down on the intent faces of the people below as they scrambled to get themselves ready for the performance. She smiled affectionately; these were people she understood, good people, making the most of a rare day when they did not have to work through the short daylight hours. From above, it looked chaotic, and the village mayor was doing his best to cut through the din in a vain effort to instill some organization.

"Now then, I want all the angels on my right hand, along with you shepherds. I said—Watkin Ireman, that means you as well. Yes! All right now. Magi? Where have you taken yourselves to? That's it, over there, beside Mary. Come along now, for pity's sake, or we'll never be ready in time . . ."

Jehanne laughed gently with her friend. "If only life were as simple as putting on this little play. Just a question of persuading people to find their places and stick to them." Deborah nodded. Both of them were thinking of Anne, Anne who'd been missing for some hours now, though they both knew she'd gone to find Mathew Cuttifer.

"I'm sorry I've been kept so long. You must have been wondering where I was."

It was Anne, flushed from running after talking to Mathew. But before Jehanne could voice her concern, she was interrupted by a huge howl from below. The Devil had appeared in the midst of the townsfolk.

On this occasion the Devil was dressed all in black but was having some trouble managing his large canvas wings and long scaly tail as the crowd thronged close to inspect the details of his costume. The poor mayor looked close to a stroke as he did his best to reassert control. "*Don't* touch the wings, they'll break. Perkin! *Perkin!* I'll not tell you again, there's nothing under his tail, nothing! Drop it, drop it now!"

All three women in the gallery laughed—they couldn't help themselves—as the abashed Perkin dropped the Devil's tail, though not before the long-suffering Lord of Hell thumped him wrathfully with his pitchfork. But then the babble was cut through by a knife of sound—trumpets. The king was coming.

Noisily, the throng hushed and shushed itself into an approximation of silence, as the courtiers, led by Edward and Elizabeth, entered the hall and processed through the bowing villagers to a dais where twin thrones had been set.

At a signal from William Hastings, the mayor stepped forward and cleared his throat bravely. "Your Majesties, we, your loyal and fortunate subjects, wish to present the story of our Savior's birth, enacted for your pleasure—and always by the will of God—by those of us who dwell in Windsor." The mayor uttered his short speech gracefully and bowed with all the aplomb of a courtier when he had finished. A small ripple of good-natured approval ran around the hall, it was Christmas after all. Anne, looking down, felt bitter for a moment. The court was benign on a day such as this when the season made them kind. Another day and this man would have been seen as exceeding his station, but the king was arbiter of all and today he chose to be delighted.

"Greetings to you and yours, Master Mayor. The queen and I thank you most heartily for your kind attention to our pleasure, and the pleasure of all at court. Play on."

Like a puff of smoke evaporating, the space immediately in front of the dais cleared of villagers, and after a moment the plaintive notes of a flute wound their way through the thick air of the hall. As one, the members of the court turned their heads to see a fine-looking young man, dressed all in green, enter the hall playing this melody on a simple pipe made from an ox legbone.

He made his way gravely to the empty space and then he, in turn, bowed low and introduced himself: "I am Robin, Green Robin, and I have come to tell you of the birth of a king, long, long ago and in a land far, far away." The crowd sighed unconsciously and settled in happily, attention hanging on this good-looking boy. They all liked a story, even if they'd heard it before.

As the Nativity play progressed, Anne quietly relayed her conversation with Mathew Cuttifer, and when she had finished Jehanne was insistent. "Of course we've got to find the letter, but I think you need somewhere to hide while we look."

"Hide?" Something cold touched Anne's heart; Jehanne was serious.

"Mathew Cuttifer, you must go to him. I cannot see another way."

"But Jehanne, he may not accept Anne into his house when he's had time to think on it." Deborah's worried face mirrored Anne's secret fears.

The girl's concern grew. "Wouldn't I be putting them in danger? Sir Mathew's family, I mean? Shouldn't we wait? He said he'd send word . . ."

"Too late for that." It was Jehanne at her most practical. "We must send you away, today if we can. To London. You must get away from the king, it's too dangerous for you to stay here any longer."

Jehanne shivered as she remembered a passing exchange between Elizabeth and Edward after Mass. Anne's absence from the service had been noted and though Jehanne had covered for her, pleading ague on the girl's behalf, the queen had turned to the king and laughingly asked if he had any hand in the girl's continuing sickness. She'd made it a game, of course, and the king had laughed it off. But Jehanne knew Elizabeth well. She was letting the king know that she'd marked his attentions to her body servant. Marked—and had had enough.

So now it had come, the thing Anne feared most. Fate had stepped in, the path was in front of her, and in her heart she knew it was right, knew that she had to go. However, the pain of the thought that she might not see the king again—or if they met, that he might think of her as an enemy—was nearly too much to bear.

Unconsciously she prayed, first to Mary and then to Aine, asking help from each of them. Nothing came to her except that, distantly, she could hear a child crying, but then the sound of the Christmas music echoed in her mind; a song of redemption and hope; a song of rebirth in the midst of despair . . .

"If that is what you think best, I am ready." Her voice was forlorn but calm. When she raised her head and looked at them, there was a profound change. Anne's face was pared back, drawn in such a way that the bone structure was clear; no trace of baby fat remained. She stood quietly but held herself with touching dignity.

Jehanne felt an absurd urge to curtsy, which she dismissed impatiently with a quick shake of her head. Time enough for that later. Now they had to get Anne out of the court without exciting comment—but how would they do that?

"Jehanne, Doctor Moss will help me to leave the court."

Jehanne balked at the thought. "Child, he'll only help us if it suits his own interest. We can't trust him. And I don't see why he'd risk the queen's—or the king's—displeasure in this."

Anne was implacable. The roles between she and Jehanne had almost reversed.

"Nonetheless, please ask him in my name. Say I will be most grateful . . . in times to come." It was said with a certainty that made Deborah's scalp prickle, something she only experienced when scrying the future. There were no visions now but she heard the truth in Anne's voice. As did Jehanne, who shrugged reluctantly, then hurried away to do Anne's bidding, leaving the others to watch the last of the play.

Anne herself said nothing more because her head was filled with the sound of the sea and on her tongue there was the taste of salt. Or tears.

Chapter Twenty-nine

His tone was as cold as the day outside: "Impossible. You know that—quite impossible." Doctor Moss was in his room, busily preparing a strengthening tonic for the queen, and he'd been quite pleased with his progress until Jehanne found him and interrupted the tricky process of distillation. He shook his head decisively. Her request was absurd, and, for his own very good reasons, he was heartily disinclined to help. Ask the queen for leave of absence for Anne to quit the court? At Christmas? *Today?*

"But sir, all you need say is that her mother is very ill, like to die, and needs the girl."

The doctor was dismissive. "But why should I say such a thing? And even if I did, why should the queen grant such leave?"

"She may not. But if you try you would be helping Anne very much." The expression on the doctor's face did not alter. Jehanne sighed. This would be even harder than she'd thought. "And you would have my gratitude. And hers. Which may count for something in times to come." It was said reluctantly, but it was said. The doctor looked up quizzically as Jehanne pressed on. "Doctor Moss, you have seen the king. He looks at Anne too much, far too much. She doesn't know what to do about his attentions, and I believe he's turned her head and . . . well, you and I both know, the consequences for her could be most dreadful if she becomes his concubine. I should like to save her such misery if I could—and I think you have a fondness for her."

The doctor glowered. It was not for this wizened old woman to speculate about his feelings for Anne. He turned back to his work and carefully measured four drops of a deep pink tincture into a pot that was boiling on his fire and from which came a truly foul smell. Miraculously, as he added the ruby-colored liquid, the contents of the pot foamed up and the stench cleared, replaced by the scent of roses. Jehanne looked at him with amazement.

Moss was flattered by her astonishment and allowed himself to unbend slightly.

"Yes, remarkable, isn't it? Taught to me by an Arabian, a doctor I met in Ravenna. Most efficacious, this—blood of a pregnant rabbit, purified dung from a lactating donkey, ground seed and juice of the Turkish poppy, and pennyroyal plus milkthistle—and this, the oil of triple-distilled essence of desert rose. Very rare, very expensive. An excellent tonic for the queen while she's breeding, and it may make her cheerful as well."

He took the pot from the fire and set it on the sill of a casement window that he opened, oblivious of the freezing air that swept into the room. The old woman shivered, wrapping her sideless surcoat tighter around her ribs.

"Doctor Moss, will you help Anne, if she cannot help herself?"

"I will think about it. I'll let you know later. Perhaps after supper . . ."

Gratefully, the old woman swept down into a curtsy, which surprised the doctor considerably.

"I didn't say I would, I said I'd think about it."

But Jehanne was gone from the room before he finished his words. Thoughtfully, as he stirred the simple to help it cool, he allowed his mind to wander over a way that the queen might be brought to see Anne's absence as a good thing.

Anne was taking a bundle of bed linen from the dorter down to the laundresses when something made her stop outside the stout door that led into the castle's stone-flagged laundry. She heard someone laugh, a man, and then she heard Mary say, "Don't, sir—oh, you'll tear it."

"I'll get you another," the man replied. Then she heard the unmistakable sound of cloth being torn and she heard Mary cry out, the cry instantly muffled. Then there were sounds like sobbing. Frightened and worried for her friend, heart in her mouth, Anne saw that the door was very slightly open and so she pushed it inward just a little more and then, in a rush, saw the cause of the sounds she'd heard.

Mary was sitting on the edge of the stone laundry bench with her skirts pulled high, exposing her naked thighs, and the man stood between them. Her breasts were naked, too, for the front of her dress had been ripped down to free them. Her eyes were closed and she was panting and moaning as the man, fully clothed, fondled and sucked at each breast in turn, fumbling with one hand to undo the points on his hose.

The couple were in profile to Anne's gaze and she watched in stunned amazement as the man suddenly slid himself, fully erect, between the thighs of the writhing girl, pulling her to him, belly to belly, as she locked her heels behind his back. As he threw his head back, Anne saw it was William Hastings. She wanted to close the door and turn away but the man and the woman held her gaze as he, impatient, pushed Mary down on to her back on the laundry bench and she helped guide him back between her opened thighs with both hands, eyes half closing in pleasure as she felt him slide inside her again.

Mary tried to speak but William stopped her mouth with his; she was moaning louder and shivering now as the man thrust harder and deeper, growling like an animal. Not for nothing was William Hastings's personal heraldic device the manticore, the fabled mantiger. Anne, her mouth dry and legs suddenly weak, closed the door unnoticed. She put her basket down and turned away.

"So, did you see if my friend Hastings was inside?"

Her heart froze. The king. He was leaning on a wall just in front of her. He'd been watching Anne, knew what she'd seen and heard, for even with the door more securely closed, there was no mistaking the sounds from the room behind it.

"Sir . . . I . . . that is, I'm not sure if—"

"If it was him? Surely there could be no mistake. I believe you know Lord Hastings quite well, do you not?" The king sauntered toward her now. And he was not smiling, indeed he looked grim.

Anne thought quickly. "Sir, I am needed in the queen's rooms. If it was Lord Hastings, I am sure he will be . . . that is, he should be available to Your Majesty shortly . . ." She curtsied and cast around for a way past him in the dark, narrow corridor.

But he was too fast for her. Two steps and he had blocked the way she needed to go. "Stay for a moment, Anne. We haven't spoken for a little while." He said it softly, caressingly.

"No, sire. There has been so much to do when everyone's enjoying themselves . . ." She bit her tongue; the sounds behind the door were becoming louder and more urgent.

He was beside her now and her heart was pounding. "What did you see behind the door, Anne? Describe to me what you saw." She blushed deeply and felt, with horror, the heat of the blood mount her neck.

"Nothing, sire. I saw nothing."

"I don't believe you, Anne." She shook her head, desperate not to look into the eyes burning down into hers. "Did you see a man loving a woman? And was she enjoying it too?" He breathed it in her ear but she would not look up, just shook her head, trying to pick the moment to run. But he had grasped her waist with one hand, and was pulling her toward him. She held herself rigid as he buried his face in her neck, kissing her throat passionately, then her mouth, as she tried not to respond.

"I have not forgotten my vow, Anne, and I would never force you." But his hands made him a liar, for they were busy inside the bodice of her dress and then sliding down, and down. She gasped as his mouth fastened on hers again and he slipped her skirts up, finding the tops of her tightly closed thighs, sliding one finger, just one, between her legs. She could hardly bear the feeling as the heat seemed to concentrate where he was stroking her. Unconsciously, she moaned and he smiled.

"Soft, so soft," he breathed. "Open your legs, just a little."

Incapable of rational thought, her thighs parted, and she was aching, yearning, wanting nothing more than to lie on the ground, shameless, and let him to do to her all that Hastings had done with Mary. But in her mind she heard the whisper: *"You are the daughter of Henry VI, granddaughter of Henry V . . ."*

"I can't. It is not possible. Let me go." She tried to break free.

"I don't want to, Anne. Let me, ah, just let me . . . you'll enjoy it very much, I promise you." Now his body was pinning hers against the wall and again the aching, melting sweetness of the moment was palpable between them. His hand moved slowly, deliciously, and she felt his fingers slip deeper inside her.

"No."

He was still. For a moment there was silence and she held her breath, tears starting to prick the insides of her closed lids. She so wanted to please him, but it was not possible—now, or ever. Sadness filled her, such piercing sadness, she wanted to howl like an animal in pain. He sensed it and, sighing, let her go, allowing her skirts to fall back into place.

"Has something changed?" Again there was that prescience between them, as if he could read all her thoughts.

"Your Majesty, sire, it is a long, long story and—"

"And?" He was curious now, and not angry. That in itself was unusual. Most often if he was refused, and God knew that was hardly ever, it made him annoyed, but this girl did something else to him. She made him feel protective, and confused. He was deeply touched by her sadness too—and desperate to understand her tears.

"I cannot tell you."

"What can it possibly be that you may not tell your sovereign?" He was quite startled by her determination.

"Please, sire, I must go to the queen . . ."

Behind them the door to the laundry opened and William Hastings, flushed and disheveled, saw the king. "Your Majesty . . . sire, I had no idea . . ."

"Apparently not. I was told you were doing your washing." The king's tone was dry but he smiled, and William laughed. That moment was enough for Anne to drop a quick curtsy to both of them, dart through the door to deposit the queen's clothes with a startled Mary—languorously dressing herself—and then leave through the laundry's other door, before the king had a chance to stop her.

As she ran back toward the queen's rooms, Anne asked herself if she was stupid to feel that Edward and she had a special connection. Their thoughts seemed so close at times and she dreamed of a sharing of their minds, not just their bodies, though God knew, images of their coupling filled many of her waking and her sleeping thoughts. Could it be he felt some of the same pain she felt when she ran from him? It seemed such an agonizing waste that they could not fall naturally into one another's arms. In another time, if he had not been married, who she was could have been their strength, not their weakness . . .

At the door of the queen's rooms she paused, breathing hard, and carefully tucked tendrils of hair back up beneath her cap, smoothing her gown with trembling hands. She should just have time to lay out a choice of clothes for this afternoon's festivities before the queen arrived with her ladies. But her trip down to the laundry had taken more time than she'd allowed, and she was dismayed to find the queen already in her rooms being undressed. Anne braced herself for a tongue-lashing, and did her best to enter inconspicuously.

"So, you are recovered from the ague?" It was the queen, but much to Anne's relief, she sounded merely faintly curious, not testy.

The girl ducked a hasty curtsy. "I was delayed a little with the laundress, Your Majesty." An unbidden flash of the king's face, bending down to kiss her, the feel of his hand on her breast, almost made her gasp as she said the words.

"Then why are you blushing, girl? You are sure it was the laundress who delayed you, no one else?" The queen was suspicious now as Jehanne hurried over to pour her a distracting beaker of hot, spiced wine.

It was Evelyn who saved the need for another answer; she was presenting a gown of blue cloth of gold for Elizabeth to inspect. The queen had decided that on each of the twelve days of Christmas, she and her ladies would dress according to a theme. Today it was to be the twelve labors of Hercules and she was to be Hera, wife of Zeus, the goddess who had invented the punishment of the mighty hero.

Since the Virgin Mary, the queen of Heaven, wore blue, it seemed fitting that Hera's dress should be blue also. And since Zeus's chief weapon was a thunderbolt, Jehanne had designed a headdress for Hera surmounted by golden thunderbolts.

While helping the queen into the glittering new dress, Jehanne seized the moment, since she had completely lost faith in Doctor Moss, who by his absence had plainly decided against helping Anne. "Your Majesty, I have a Christmas boon to ask."

Elizabeth, looking at herself in her convex silver mirror as she watched Evelyn carefully rub paste of cochineal onto her already high cheekbones, was distracted. "Very well, speak on, Jehanne."

"Anne, come here." Jehanne nodded to the girl standing quietly, waiting her turn to help lace the queen into her new dress. "Your Majesty, this girl's mother is very ill. I ask leave that she be permitted to visit her for a few days."

The queen frowned and briefly glanced at Anne, before returning her attention to the mirror. It was inconvenient to release her, but then she remembered her growing annoyance with the girl over the last few weeks—and her suspicions regarding the king. Perhaps sending Anne away at this time, when she herself was pregnant and finding sex a burden, was an excellent idea.

"Very well." It was said carelessly, with a dismissive wave of her hand. "And I command that after you have visited your mother and done what is needful, you return to Westminster. You may help to prepare our quarters against the removal of the court back to London. Instruct her, Jehanne."

And, from Elizabeth's point of view, the matter was settled and Anne banished from her mind. But for Anne, the die had been cast. She would leave, and she would not tell the king.

Chapter Thirty

To leave the warmth and the light of the castle behind was desolation for Anne as she set out with her companions on the following sullen gray afternoon.

It had been a very busy twenty-four hours as the queen had insisted Anne leave only after replenishing Elizabeth's stock of unquents and the special hair bleach only Anne could make.

Therefore, it was well after the dinner hour, and Elizabeth had dressed and had left her rooms to join the king in receiving Christmas visitors from the court of Burgundy, that Jehanne hustled Anne away to the dorter to pack up the little coffer brought from Blessing House that contained her few possessions.

Then, as the court gathered to watch a bearbaiting in honor of the foreign visitors, Jehanne and Deborah hurried the girl to the stables and into Sergeant Cage's capable hands.

A delicate chestnut mare and a small gray lady's palfrey, brightly tricked out with a red leather bridle and saddle, were waiting for them. Jehanne's eyebrows went up anxiously as she saw the costliness of the trappings and the superior quality of the horses. "Whose are these animals, Sergeant?"

The man laughed. "Never fear, mistress, you'll do their owner a favor riding them to London; they both need the exercise and won't be missed."

Sergeant Cage had solved two problems by a stroke. One of the queen's ladies wanted several of her horses, including the palfrey, taken back to London in advance of the court, since she would be traveling back with the queen and had no need of them. Cage was quite happy for Lizotte and Minette to be ridden to the capital just as well as led. And the two women could join John Slaughter, the man whose job it was to lead the lady's two other horses to London. They'd be protected on the journey by the royal badges on John's uniform.

The little party needed to make the most of the low afternoon light and so the departure from the castle took place in a bustle that left Anne no time to think. She was bundled up onto the pony's back and the cold reins thrust into her hands as Jehanne swaddled her tightly in a thick traveling cloak.

"Anne, keep your hood up as much as you can and please let John Slaughter talk for you both in public places. There'll not be much movement on the roads in this weather but you must be careful, both of you."

Deborah smiled with a calm she did not feel as she hauled herself up onto Lizotte's narrow back. "John here will see us all safe to London, won't you, John?"

John grinned cheerfully, innocently displaying nearly empty gums except for one remaining great front tooth. He'd been expecting a cold, boring ride to London. At least now he'd have someone to talk to.

Anne shivered under her cloak as the little party slipped out of the king's gate on their way to London. She was not yet cold, but she was trying to imagine what the king would say when he found she had left the castle. Her heart and body ached for him with a warm, burning pain, though she scolded herself severely for even acknowledging the feeling, as, mentally, she tried to rearrange what she felt for Edward.

Men, and especially the king, were different from women— she knew that. It was possible for them to love or lust for several women at once, as she'd seen plentiful times at court. She had to get on with her life, come to terms with her strange destiny, and walk away from the entanglements of the flesh, since that interfered with her capacity for sensible action. Perhaps she would never see the king again and perhaps that was best, though if it were so, why did her heart squeeze so painfully at that thought?

Resolutely, she murmured a prayer for strength as they passed beyond the bounds of the village, touching her crucifix but asking that the Sword-Mother guide their steps, and her life as well . . .

The afternoon wore on and the day grew colder and colder as the travelers headed south. Their destination was a village about halfway between Windsor and London in which there was a Convent of Poor Clares. The women would be able to lodge for the night in one of the order's guest cells, while John could sleep at an inn in the village with the horses, for males of any kind, including the animals, would not be allowed in the nunnery grounds.

Fortunately, the fierce cold had frozen the mush of the roads, so riding was easier than it might have been, but the journey was trying for all that. There was a cutting wind from the east, and it took Anne some time to adapt to Minette's short gait. The little horse liked trotting and it helped them make good speed, but the constant jolting of those small hooves on the iron-hard ground hour after hour began to test Anne's patience.

Time passed and the insubstantial daylight of the short, bleak afternoon began to fade with no sign of friendly lights ahead. John Slaughter was doing his best to hide his concern from the two women. He'd ridden this road many times and knew it well, but the delay in leaving the castle and a slower pace than he'd expected meant they were not as far along as he'd hoped. His greatest concern was the stretch of dense forest they would have to pass through before they reached the nunnery and its surrounding village. It was the haunt of brigands in summer. Winter was different, weather like this drove most of them inside.

John was nervous, though, and didn't take his task lightly, especially now he had two women to look out for. It worried him that Anne looked like a lady seated on that expensive-looking little horse. Maybe he should stop and put her up behind him on his sturdy gelding so she wouldn't look like such a useful prospect for kidnap and ransom. It was then he heard hoofbeats behind them on the road.

Turning, he saw a small group of horsemen heading toward

them, covering the ground at an efficient hard gallop that ate up the space between the two parties. The light was uncertain so it was hard to see how they were dressed, but he caught the glint of a sword and his heart sank.

"Ladies, ride—now! Follow the road, it's not far to the convent. Go!" And he turned his horse to block the track as well as he could. Deborah, who had also heard the horsemen, thumped her feet into Lizotte's startled flanks and whacked the palfrey on the rump, hard, as she caught up with Anne.

"Fast as you can follow!" And the two animals sprang to a gallop, sensing the fear in their riders. The trees closed them in as they ran and the gloom increased, but then ahead, around a bend, they saw a faint glimmer in the distance: it was a light, a light burning in a building. Behind, though, they heard hooves and then there were voices calling Anne by name, yelling at them to stop.

How did they know to call her name? It terrified both women so that they put their heads down and urged their mounts on, though their horses could never outrun a destrier at full stretch.

Nearer and nearer to the lights they rode. They could see a cluster of buildings now. The village! But the men were at their heels and the thunder of hooves on the frozen road grew closer and closer. All too soon, as they burst out of the forest. Anne was overtaken by a large man on an even larger horse, but as he reached out to haul on the palfrey's bridle, screaming at her to stop, she managed to hit him full in the face as he bent down. He reeled back to recover and fell from his horse, which, panicked, cannoned into another of the riders—and he, too, fell.

"Ride!" screamed Deborah. "The convent!"

And with a fleeting glance back, in which she saw that her companion was close behind, two other men bearing down on her, Anne did what she was told, urging the terrified little horse even faster toward the looming gates of a large building up ahead.

And then she saw that the nuns were pulling the gates closed!

"No!" screamed Anne. "Wait! God's bones, wait!" Blessed be. One of the women who'd been closing the gate heard her and had the presence of mind to yell at her sister to pull the gate open again.

Anne and Deborah raced through, and there was just time for

the gates to be hauled shut in the teeth of their pursuers with a re-sounding thud as the great iron bar that locked them down was dropped into its place.

The two women fell onto their animals' necks, flecked with mud and breathing like fire bellows as nuns clustered around them, some holding flaring torches, exclaiming loudly.

"Well, and what is this?" It was a cool voice, elegant, slightly nasal, and very controlled.

Anne breathed deeply and sat up first. She recognized that tone: authority. "We crave indulgence, Reverend Mother . . ."

"It is not mine to give and that is not my title. I am the subpri-oress. Well?"

"Pardon, sister, but we had no choice but to arrive as we did. We were attacked." It was Deborah who had spoken, and while she was still short of breath, her composure had returned.

"By whom were you attacked?"

"We do not know. Only that we were riding through the forest, with our escort, and a party of men attempted to waylay our jour-ney. They must still be outside."

The nuns were hanging on every word; nothing so exciting had happened since the infirmaress had run away with a passing friar three years ago. Just then a great banging set up; someone was thumping loudly at the gate and ringing the porteress's bell at the same time with a determined jangle.

All eyes turned to the subprioress. "Well, Sister Michael, don't just stand there, see who knocks. Go on." Sister Michael was a strong girl, a peasant lay sister who'd been given to the convent when her family could no longer afford to keep her. She was one of the two whose job it was to guard the gate during the day and lock the convent at night. With a gulp, Sister Michael strode over to the shuttered hole in the wall through which the sisters generally spoke to the outside world. The banging on the gate had stopped but the portal bell was still ringing vigorously.

"Who is there?" asked Sister Michael, in as stern and intimidat-ing a voice as she could muster.

"An emissary to speak to the girl Anne, lately in the service of the queen."

More sensation among the nuns. The queen's servant? Which one was she? Sister Michael looked back imploringly at the subprioress—what should she say now?

"Tell us who you are." It was the subprioress who spoke.

"I and my party are servants of Sir Mathew Cuttifer. We have come to escort Mistress Anne to Blessing House in London. I have warrants you may read."

Anne could not help herself, the laughter burst out of her like a shower of sparks. Sir Mathew had kept his word—and she'd nearly killed not one but two of his men. A fine beginning to their new relationship.

"Let us see this warrant. You may pass it through."

The sisters parted respectfully to allow the subprioress to join Sister Michael at the gate with Anne and Deborah as a rolled parchment was passed through the hole, the shutters being eased open just a little. As Anne quickly saw, Sir Mathew's seal was on the unbroken wax, and as the scroll was unfurled, she glimpsed his careful signature at the bottom: "Sir Mathew Cuttifer, Bart." It was from him, they were safe.

Deborah embraced Anne happily, and then looked a little guiltily at the subprioress. "May we speak with these men, sister?"

The subprioress nodded reluctantly. "Very well, you may speak through the wall, but if you seek lodging this night, your conversation should be brief and can be resumed tomorrow." Turning to the waiting nuns, she clapped her hands. "Come now, sisters, enough of this nonsense."

And as she moved away, gliding into darkness with the other nuns, Anne crossed herself and breathed in the freezing air as if it had been a great draft of wine. She had friends! Sir Mathew believed her story.

Quietly, she gathered herself and stepped over to the wall with Deborah. Calm confidence clothed Anne like a cloak as the tension breathed out of her body. But there was still an appealing glimmer of vulnerability under the careful, polite words she spoke to Mathew's men, and that was enough to win the day, even with the man whose face she had bruised with a small determined fist.

That night, both women prayed together beside their cots in

the clean, spartan little guest cell that they shared, though Anne held fast to Deborah's hand as, later, she slipped into sleep. And dreamt of her mother: a girl younger than she, who walked, smiling, in a flower-studded meadow and opened her arms to offer love—and call her back home.

Chapter Thirty-one

London was mostly still asleep as Anne's party waited outside the city walls for the gates to open. It was barely light, and while they could hear some stirring of feet on the streets inside the city, it was too early for the vendors of food or small beer to be about.

Anne and Deborah were stiff and dirty, for it had been a cold homecoming along increasingly churned-up roads from which the horses of the men in front and around them had thrown up mud, some of which, inevitably, they carried.

At last, the great iron portcullis was raised, and the gate wardens pulled open the huge gates to the city of London. The impatient crowd that was now milling all around them surged inside. They were lucky that John Slaughter carried the king's badge, for that, coupled with the loud voices and brandished swords of Mathew Cuttifer's men, got them through near the head of the river of humanity. But then they found themselves crammed tight into the narrow, filthy street behind the gate.

Trying to force their way through the people into the city reminded Anne of the first time she'd crossed London Bridge. Now she and Deborah were like the folk who'd pushed them to one side; and she, too, was dressed in fine clothes, much finer than the people all around them. All was never as it first seemed.

The familiar smell of the great city swaddled them too—smoke, decay, and shit in equal parts—as they pressed their way forward in single file under the overhanging buildings, trying to avoid their animals' stepping in the stinking open channel that ran down the center of the street, clogged with filth. At last they were in King Street, and turning down toward the river, they saw Blessing House.

Anne was surprised to find tears in her eyes. Was it really only six months or so since this grim building had been her home? Now she was coming back not as a serving girl but as someone much more enigmatic. And dangerous?

Outside the house at last, she slipped gratefully to the ground, patted Minette's sweat-dampened neck, and whispered in one twitching gray ear, "You don't have to carry me anymore—but thank you. May we meet again." Then, embarrassed that she had nothing to give John Slaughter for all his care of them, she stepped forward and held up her hand for the kind-faced man to grasp.

"John, you have been so good to us. I shall make sure Sir Mathew, and Sergeant Cage, both hear of your service. Go with God." The man touched his flat leather bonnet and smiled happily, his one tooth yellow in the red cavern of his mouth.

"A great and rare pleasure, ladies. Especially since I'll carry the memory of you whacking that great lump off his horse until my dying day." His great gust of laughter cheered Anne and Deborah, though they tried, for politeness' sake, to suppress their own giggles.

The "great lump"—Sir Mathew's trusted lieutenant—scowled as he escorted the women around to the rear door of Blessing House. He'd been instructed to bring the women to Mathew as discreetly as possible and paid extra silver pennies for his and his men's continuing silence, so he swallowed his ire. Since it was early, and the household at Mass, it was an easy matter for him to escort Anne and Deborah through the kitchen and up to the solar with its familiar applewood fire where Margaret was waiting. After a tearful welcome, the women sat for a moment in silence as the warmth from the fire found its way into Anne's and Deborah's bones.

"Water will be brought for you both to wash off the grime of the journey, and when you are ready, there are clean clothes. Sir Mathew will join us after Mass." Anne felt odd hearing Margaret discuss her needs as if this lady were the servant, but her thoughts were interrupted by a faint knock at the door that led down to the kitchen.

Lady Margaret gestured for the two women to conceal themselves in the garderobe as, a moment later, a timid-faced girl holding two large leather pails of hot water edged around the door. "You may leave the water by the fire, Yseul." Without a word, the child scuttled over to the hearth, slopping a little of the water in her eagerness to please. When she had gone, Margaret smiled ruefully as she let Anne and Deborah back into the solar. "Sometimes, Anne, I could wish you were back here with us."

Anne smiled warmly. "But I am, Lady Margaret. Back to serve you, if that is what you wish."

The older woman looked at them both and smiled gently. "I do not think that very likely, if what I have been told is true?" She looked directly from Anne to Deborah, though the words came out lightly enough.

Anne smothered the desire to laugh; it was said with such deceptive, gentle courtesy, as if it had been the most innocent inquiry in the world.

"Mistress Deborah, would it please you to wash?" As Anne smilingly picked up the water pails, Lady Margaret conducted her older guest as ceremoniously to the garderobe as if they were at some great court reception, bowing her through the door. "There is a clean wool kirtle and undershift hanging on a peg. We can take your travel clothes to the kitchen to be cleaned and brushed later."

While Deborah was washing, Anne returned to the fire, grateful for the feeling of warm well-being stealing over her weary body. She looked longingly at the bed for a moment. Last night's sleep had been scant and poor, and both she and Deborah had flea bites from the common dormitory of the convent they'd stayed at outside the city walls, the same one they'd slept in the night before Anne had joined the Cuttifer household. Anne yawned sleepily as Lady Margaret returned.

"I've had beds made up; sleep will be good for both of you." Lady Margaret strolled over to the fire to join her erstwhile servant. "And so, Anne, is it true, your . . . descent?"

Anne looked into the burning coals and a quiet moment passed before she raised her eyes to Lady Margaret's. "Perhaps. There is proof, I have seen some of it. Deborah has some tokens and Jehanne, my mistress at court, does also."

Margaret sighed and sat gently in her graceful, gilded Italian chair, arranging the folds of her simple, elegant housegown around her. "Of course, these are dangerous times . . . again."

Both women were silent. Anne, growing up in the forest, had not been touched by the late wars between Edward's father, the Duke of York, and the Lancastrians, nor the later fighting that had culminated in the battle at Towton and Edward taking the throne. But she'd seen the devastation of the countryside and the villages when she and Deborah had ventured out from their home from time to time.

"Yes, it is so," Anne said finally. "But madam, this was not of my choosing."

Lady Margaret laughed mirthlessly. "Indeed. How can anyone choose their birth?"

Deborah rejoined them, neat and clean in a plain dark blue woolen dress. "There, that looks well indeed," Margaret said. "Anne, your turn."

Anne was itching to shed her filthy clothes and wash the dirt of the journey away, so she needed no further prompting to hurry to the garderobe. If only she could wash her hair as well, but it would take more than an hour or two to dry it by the fire and she needed to speak to Sir Mathew soon, for there was much to discuss.

Anne stripped off her traveling dress and stood shivering in her shift as she washed as quickly as possible. Her face and neck and her hands finally felt clean after vigorous scrubbing with a coarse cloth, and even though the air was frigid in the small smelly anteroom to the cloaca, she stripped off her shift at last and splashed the warm water over her naked body, between her legs, and under her arms. Luckily enough, she was not one of those girls much troubled by sweat, but a long winter journey on filthy roads will make the sweetest body smell rank, and she had learned to be fastidious— both with Deborah and from her time with Lady Margaret.

Teeth chattering, she washed her feet last of all, and then, drying her body on one of Lady Margaret's own linen bath sheets that had been left waiting for her to use, dropped a clean undershift over her head, followed by a neat, plain, dark red dress, made modestly high at the neck, though displaying the undershift prettily. There had even been matching red felt house slippers left for her, as well as worsted half-hose that she bound under each knee with ribbon so that they would not slip down.

Then, hair decently plaited and covered with a plain gauze veil, Anne was ready to face what the world might throw her way. Taking a deep breath to steady herself, she pushed open the door into the warm solar to rejoin Lady Margaret and Deborah.

Sir Mathew was there now with the others and was waiting patiently, seated beside his wife on a matching gilded chair. Deborah was perched on an oak chest under one of the casements that looked down on the river. All three were serious.

"Welcome to Blessing House, my lady." Sir Mathew had risen and the formality of his tone was backed by the sweeping bow he made to Anne as she entered the room. Ceremonious, he extended her his hand, and as the disconcerted girl took it, a little timidly, he insisted she seat herself where he had been sitting, conducting her to the chair beside his wife.

"While you are under my roof we have decided, with your permission, of course, that we will play a small charade. As far as the household is concerned, you are a cousin of Lady Margaret's, who, in coming to visit us, very sadly fell grievously sick upon the road and must now be kept isolated, waited on only by your woman . . ." He bowed to Deborah. "And your cousin, my wife." He bowed again, more deeply this time, to the seated figure beside Anne. "Meanwhile, arrangements are being made to send you to my lands in the north as quickly as possible. I believe you will be safe there, and sequestered, which is all to the good, for there is work to be done here in London that may take some time."

Mathew had prepared the little speech and was making an effort to explain himself as plainly as he could. However, the very seriousness of his tone released butterflies of anxiety in Anne's stomach. Previously, she'd been focused on the journey to Blessing House, deliberately not contemplating any further ahead than she had to, but now that could not be avoided and she had to become an active partner in her fate again.

Sir Mathew paused for a moment before continuing. "Since we spoke at Windsor, an informant I maintain at court has told me that the letter we seek is held secretly in the Abbey treasure room. It is obtainable with help I believe I can provide. But for now, we must not presume you are safe in London, and so we will pretend that you are . . . other than whom we know you to be." He said it gravely, allowing the words to hang in the air for a moment. "When I know more, we shall speak of these matters. As to the journey north, it's my own captain and crew who will be taking you, and one of my ships too. She brings me the cloth we make each year from our wool up north, and often she's taken out of sight of land, over to France and beyond. You'll not have to do that, I promise. You'll hug the coast the whole way to Whitby, and we'll pick the time and tide."

It was real, all of it. And as Mathew calmly explained his plan, it occurred to Anne that the wheel of fate really was turning with a vengeance now, and she was, through her own choice, strapped to its rim. Going up? Coming down? No one could be sure.

So it was with a sinking heart that Anne allowed herself to be conducted to Aveline's old room, the same one they had shared together before the misery of the other girl's marriage had begun; the same one she'd been locked into, after she'd killed Piers. Of course, Anne was now to be the inhabitant of the box bed—not for her the straw palliasse on the floor—but as she heard the bolt shot home on the outside, she could not stop the fugitive thought that wormed its way into consciousness.

Sir Mathew had, seemingly, picked up her cause unquestioningly, but what if he was not her friend? Was she now a prisoner, and about to be betrayed to the king? The king. With strenuous determination, she'd banished him from her thoughts, but for one strange and delicious moment she contemplated truly being his prisoner—his alone, locked up like the lady in the tower, just for him to find. She looked at the narrow box bed and a momentary picture of him lying there, she, naked, entwined in his arms, was as vivid as if it were real.

But it was a phantom, of course; a romance of the mind. And romance was just fiction, fiction designed to distract and entertain. Real life was what had truly happened in this room: misery, which resulted in betrayal and death. And she'd not been able to prevent any of it. Poor Aveline. Was she looking down at Anne now from wherever her spirit had gone?

Anne slipped to her knees and buried her head in the bolster. "Sister, help me now . . . if you can. For I, too, love and it may be my death."

Chapter Thirty-two

Some days of eating and sleeping followed as Anne and Deborah rested ahead of their next journey. The early January weather was foul. Rain-laden, freezing wind beat around the tower of Blessing House each night and the city air was full of gulls taking shelter from the mountainous seas of the English Channel.

Then a day dawned fine and sharp, with a high, clear sky and completely still air. And, as the morning progressed, a pale sun shone down on the Londoners, emerging blinking from their dark, smoky houses.

Anne woke early, before dawn, into silence—and anxiety crackled down her gut and into her spine. Was this the day? She looked at a new traveling chest that stood between her narrow box bed and Deborah's palliasse, where her foster mother was still asleep.

The chest was hers, given by Sir Mathew, and in it were three sets of new clothes: one good but serviceable woolen gown and two others made from heavy plain velvet, each with sleeves tipped in fur, lined with brocaded damask. There was also a traveling cloak and leather shoes with nailed soles, plus a set of patterns to walk above the slush of the streets below. Things that were much too good for a servant and would never be worn by her inside Blessing House.

Her gut clenched like a fist, she was fully awake, though she didn't want to be. Carefully, she pushed back the covers on her bed and padded naked and barefooted over to the peg on the wall where she'd hung her undershift last night.

Shivering in the chill dark air, she dropped the shift over her head and looked out of the unshuttered arrow slit to see bright, white light obliterate the last of the cold stars. Everywhere the light touched, frost glistened; the day was dawning in a rush of sharp, clear radiance.

Both Margaret and Mathew had slept late after the last night of storms, and now they were talking quietly to one another behind the curtains of their bed. Yseul hurried over and timorously asked if she could get some water to rinse their mouths after the night, and when Sir Mathew agreed, she passed the water bowl through the still-closed curtains, listened to them swill their mouths, and then waited patiently for one of them to speak to her.

"Is it fine, Yseul?" Sir Mathew was careful to be kind, though Yseul made him impatient; he'd never liked nervous girls.

"Yes, Sir Mathew. Fine, bright and quiet."

He appeared between the curtains, decently swathed in a long gown, partly patterned on the old-fashioned houppelandes he favored. "Fetch water for your mistress. We must hurry today."

Though she looked like a frightened child, Yseul was no fool, and as she lugged cans of water back up to the solar she wondered again about the odd relationship between Lady Margaret and her cousin. Over the last few days she'd been permitted to bring food to the door of the little chamber where the mistress's cousin was confined with her woman, and it seemed to her that the beautiful girl she'd glimpsed through a crack in the door was very far from ill. Yet Lady Margaret spent a great deal of time there, cooped up in that tiny space, seemingly unafraid of catching whatever it was her cousin had.

The members of the household were avid for gossip about the two strangers, and Corpus, of course, was spreading the rumor that Lady Margaret's cousin was pregnant and had been sent away from the court, shortly to be banished to a nunnery to bear the baby in disgrace before donning the habit of a sister. Others scoffed at the suggestion—including Maître Gilles, who cuffed Corpus heartily for his foul tongue—yet it did seem strange that no one from the household except Yseul, who'd only lately joined them, had been permitted a glimpse of the girl in Aveline's room.

Aveline's room. That itself was a cause for comment. Why would Sir Mathew allow any person to lodge in that cursed space? It was enough to send chills down the spine of any good Christian . . .

Oblivious to the servants' gossip, Mathew was now dressed for the day and speaking quietly to Anne, while Deborah went to find something to break the nighttime fast. "Today's fine weather seems like to set, and there is a good tide this afternoon. I've sent for my captain, but there is something I should like to discuss with you first."

Mathew swallowed nervously; never had the stakes for his house been so high, and not for the first time he searched his conscience about the wisdom of the gamble he was taking. His relationship with the king was of prime importance to him and to his house, and to take Anne's cause as his own might well be seen as treachery if the truth of her birth was confirmed. Yet there was another possibility also; and that was the gamble. If Mathew could control the timing of Anne's presentation to the king in her new guise, with incontrovertible proof, Edward might be brought to see great advantage in marrying her to one of his *own* chief supporters—someone he could trust—and at one stroke, neutralize the risk of her existence, while delivering a powerful support to his throne if his wife did not bear him a son. In such a case, Mathew might be very well rewarded—if he managed to stay ahead of the developing game.

"For this time, Lady Margaret and I think that we must continue the fiction of your being a servant; you will be more anonymous as you travel. I have a proposal to put to you. Jane Shore is the daughter of an old friend of mine, Master Lambert, the mercer."

Anne nodded. "Yes, I remember him." How could she forget? It was John Lambert who had investigated Aveline's murder of Piers.

"I have not told him your history, but I have asked for his help, in secret. He has agreed that his daughter, Jane, should visit York, where her husband, Master Shore, is currently on business with the Merchant Adventurers, and, of course, she will need to take serving women with her. You and Mistress Deborah. You will meet her at Southampton."

Anne closed her eyes, remembering the strange feeling she'd had when she'd waited on Jane Shore at Aveline and Piers's banquet. She was a girl not much older than Anne herself, and there had been such a feeling of connection, and the vision of a long journey, to be taken together . . . "And the letter, do you have it?"

Mathew frowned. "Not yet, but I have a contact, a monk at the Abbey. He was a serf, born in my father's house, and because he was bright, my father gave him freedom, and helped him enter the monastery to study. He's well thought of, but getting into the treasure house of the Abbey, where the king's papers are kept, is not easy. Still . . ." He brightened. "Just possibly, we have another way. By coincidence I have just donated a new chalice and mazer to the high altar, and this Sunday, Lady Margaret and I will see it used for the first time. I have asked the prior to show me where it will lie between use." He rubbed his hands. "For, of course, it will be housed in the treasure house!" His happy laugh was interrupted by a heavy knock at the door.

"Come," Mathew called, and as the door opened, Anne was astonished to see an enormously tall and broad man ducking through the door. He was even taller than the king. This blond, gray-eyed giant was young, for his skin was still fresh, but the strength of his face gave him presence beyond his age.

"Anne, this is Captain Mollnar. He will take you north today in my cog, the *Lady Margaret,* with Mistress Shore. My son-in-law, Giles Raby, will meet you at Whitby—it's all arranged. Please pack your things as quickly as you can."

Anne curtsied and cast her eyes to the rushes as a good servant should as Mathew hurried away with his surprised captain. Leif Mollnar had never carried women as cargo before.

There was hardly time for Anne and Deborah to dress as warmly as they could before Margaret escorted them both down to the water gate, where Sir Mathew's town barge strained at its moorings on the fast river. Anne quickly curtsied to the Cuttifers and thanked them before she and her box were bodily placed into the handsome boat that bobbed so impatiently at the river stairs of Blessing House.

Leif Mollnar shook his head in perplexity as he covertly glanced at his passengers. The younger one was pretty, that was something, though it was hard to see her face, shadowed as it was in the hood of her cloak. Women worried him. His serviceable cog lying at Southampton Water wasn't equipped for them; how could it be? It was a working vessel with only one tiny cabin—his—under the poop. His men would not like three women on board. All seamen were superstitious, he among them, and women were bad luck, especially bleeding women. They brought storms, and this voyage would be difficult enough. It was winter and yet they had orders from Sir Mathew to sail through the night to save time, rather than put into port each evening as was normal.

Still, Leif lifted the substantial purse he'd been given by Sir Mathew and pondered the case. By the weight of the coin, this was far more than the usual payment for a routine voyage. And he remembered the urgency in Sir Mathew's voice when his master had thrust it into his hands this morning. "Be careful of the three of them, Leif, very careful." Bad luck or no, these women were important to his master.

There was something afoot here, something secret. It would be an interesting journey this time.

Chapter Thirty-three

The king was angry with the queen, and Doctor Moss was furious with Jehanne—both for the same reason. Neither had known that Anne had left the court.

Edward found out by accident. He'd attended the queen's dressing the night before the court removed from Windsor to London, and Rose, with seeming innocence—but a sly glance in the king's direction—had curtsied to the queen and asked if Anne were to be replaced, for if she were, Rose had a sister. The queen, concentrating on the set of her veil, had waved her hand impatiently and frowned. She had other things to think of, such as why this pregnancy was progressing so fast, making all her gowns so unbecomingly tight.

The king appeared to take no interest in what was said, but afterward he strode into William Hastings's chamber, very angry.

William had concerns of his own: his wife was insisting on meeting him in London after the Christmas Court. He smiled ruefully; he had little real excuse to put her off. There was only so much "duty to the king" she was prepared to swallow. As to Anne, he knew she'd gone, and, of course, after the queen's approval, he'd been forced to agree merely as formality. He hadn't told the king because he didn't want Edward distracted from the task at hand. It would take all their efforts to wage the careful, false war they would need to make shortly in the north.

"My leave should have been sought." Edward's nostrils were dangerously pinched.

William swallowed a sigh; he knew that tone. "Your Majesty, there was no time to consult you; the queen dismissed the girl because her mother is dying and she left within the hour. Surely it was not Christian of me to deny permission? She will rejoin the court very shortly."

The king snorted. "That's not the point. She is *my* subject, this is *my* Christmas Court. No one leaves without my permission!"

William changed tack. "I could mention it to the queen, of course, but then, might it not seem strange to her that you are so interested in the fate of one of her maids?"

Edward turned away grumpily, slapping his Russian leather boots with his riding whip. William was right. Any comment about Anne would make the queen even more suspicious. As her pregnancy progressed, she was becoming more and more paranoid about her looks. She was watching him like a hawk, and that was not easy to live with. He'd have to wait until the court was back at Westminster. The king frowned as he thought of the girl, but there was a strange ache too. So far, of the many women he'd wanted, of the many he'd had—though, technically, not this girl yet—she was the first one he'd cherished. She was brave, born with a will like his. And she seemed to want nothing from him. If so, she was the first— in many ways.

The quick flash of such a cynical thought made him laugh to himself. Whatever it was about Anne that so intrigued him would be most enjoyable to investigate.

He looked down on the cold world outside the walls of the castle. Very well, he would be patient, but when she came again to court, well then, there would be a reckoning and William would need to have a care if the king had been lied to!

Meanwhile, Doctor Moss had also heard from Rose that Anne had left court. Rose had a spiteful streak that he put down to a possible Scorpio and Mercury conjunction with Gemini squared to Capricorn—perversity and secrecy allied to a coldness of the humors and a fondness for gossip—but he'd found it useful in the past.

He paid Rose for information about the queen so that he would seem all-knowing when asked to prescribe for her. But now the doctor was uneasy as well as angry. Like the king, he instinctively felt that something was being hidden from him. He said so to Jehanne.

"This was needless, Dame Jehanne, and would have been much better managed by me, for the king is now very angry since he was not told the girl had left. I did not say I would *not* help her, only that I wished time to think on it, to consider the best way to present the case so that neither the king nor the queen was disadvantaged in this matter. I was quite ready to speak to the queen and would have told you so, except that I have been so busy."

"But Doctor Moss, it was urgent that she leave, as you well know."

The doctor grunted. The old woman did not lie well. "So Anne's mother was truly like to die?" He was suspicious—and scornful.

That made Jehanne angry. "Yes, Doctor. The poor woman may already be dead." It was said stoutly. There! The glove had been thrown down.

Moss looked at her sharply, the stubborn face, the mouth clamped shut. He turned to go as Jehanne and her girls went back to packing the coffers for the journey from Windsor tomorrow. At the door he looked back.

"It would not be wise, Jehanne, if the king found that Anne's mother should, perhaps, linger on, thus keeping the girl from the court."

Oh, yes, he'd make sure that Jehanne was kept under pressure until he got Anne back for the king, let there be no doubt in the old woman on that score. It was vital that Anne continue to think of him as her friend, and that he be instrumental in convincing her to become Edward's leman. She'd do well, he thought, very well for them both, if he played his cards right—and he would not give up that opportunity without a bloody fight.

Jehanne's heart hammered in her chest. The doctor's cool tone had a cutting edge to it. He would be a bad enemy, Jehanne knew that, if—*when*—Anne failed to return.

• • •

Anne vomited into a leather bucket in the one tiny, stuffy cabin of the *Lady Margaret,* Leif Mollnar's own. Much against her wishes, he'd insisted that the three women stay belowdecks soon after they'd left port.

Leaving the port at Southampton, after Jane Shore had met them at the dock, and setting out into the sea roads on the crisp midday had been a wonderful experience. Cold, sharp air, seabirds calling, the sails humming and slapping as they took the wind, and then a sight that land people never saw, the rocking, limitless horizon and promise of unknown lands beyond it. But the fair day had turned once they were out of the port and the seas were becoming increasingly mountainous as the wind rose.

The crew began to mutter as the good weather changed, so Leif had sent the women down to his cabin, out of sight. Now the wooden walls of the little ship bucked and tipped around them as the small, thick glass window slid beneath the water and they tried to share the one, tiny box bed.

The ship was very short from stem to stern and rode the waves as heavily as an overladen, pregnant packhorse. Her broad beam and the heavy keel meant she didn't pitch from side to side so much as she bucked up and down, but the unfamiliar movement made all the women in the tiny cabin vomit until they expected to see their hearts and eyes expelled along with all their dinners.

Leif Mollnar made sure that his ship was tightly set to weather the storm, but he wanted a report on how his valuable passengers were faring, so he caught the eye of his mate Simon the Breton and shouted above the roar of the waves, "Simon! See how the women are faring. They'll need help in this blow." Both men could feel the boat flexing under the weight of the running seas, but neither was especially worried—she was a stout ship, the *Lady Margaret,* and they'd seen dirtier weather many times before. Besides, the strong wind blowing from the south was still pushing them at a good pace northward.

Reluctantly, Simon made his way toward the cabin along the deck, scooping up two buckets of seawater and a brush that was used for scrubbing in calmer weather. Then, timing the moment, he wrenched open the cabin door so that the pitch of the boat carried him into the cabin, his buckets balanced so that not one drop was spilled.

Anne roused herself from the half-hallucinations brought on by dehydration and tried to help Simon wash the cabin down, but she was thrown from wall to wall as she attempted to stand on shaking legs. At last, however, the cabin was restored to order with everything that had been flying loose lashed down. Anne felt better, and while her clothes were damp with seawater where she'd tried to sponge the vomit off, at least the smell had lessened.

She'd also given fresh water to Jane and Deborah, and both now lay quiet on the bed together. It had been easy for Anne to like Jane, who had greeted her like an old friend on the dock, and now, out of kindness, she'd managed to help her companion remove her expensive traveling dress. It would be much easier later to clean linen of vomit than Flanders velvet. Deborah, too, was looking a little better now.

Soon the boat was tossing less in calmer seas, but the little cabin was disgustingly stuffy. Deborah insisted that Anne go up on deck. As a young woman, Deborah had traveled by sea once as far as the Wash, on her way to Norwich, and knew that to see the waves, rather than just feel their effect, helped conquer the seasickness.

Jane had dropped into an uneasy sleep, but Anne was troubled to leave them both. Deborah would have none of it.

"Come now, we've been mewed up for too long. Clean air will do you much good. We'll be fine here. Most of all, I want sleep." She yawned deeply, and Anne relented. Furling her heavy cloak around her, Anne stumbled out of the cabin, onto the deck with a welcome feeling of release. It was close to dark, and away to the west, over the land, the sun was going down in a cloud of bloody glory. Out to sea, the first stars shone, piercing the darkness of the east like small, sharp fragments of crystal. Unseen in her dark cloak, she climbed the ladderlike stairs to the poop, beginning to pace her body to the roll of the ship. At the cog's wheel, Leif Mollnar was snuffling the wind like a dog.

"Captain?" She knew he would not want her on his bridge, but out in the open in sight of the pitching sea, her head had begun to clear. It was exhilarating to be up so high, rushing over the wild, wide water as the boat talked to the sea like a living thing.

Leif didn't hear her at first—the wind saw to that. So she approached closer and tapped him gently on the shoulder. "Captain?"

He leaped in shock and for a moment almost lost the wheel at the sight of this pale-faced figure wrapped in darkness. Wild thoughts of water spirits resolved themselves into the form and face of the younger of the serving girls, and then he frowned. He'd given strict orders that the women, all the women, were to stay below. Now here was this girl standing on his poop deck as if she had the right to it, smiling and asking him about the stars and how he steered by them at night. She sounded so interested in all that he was doing that he told her, grudgingly, how he found his way. Before long he was even offering to show her the astrolabe he kept in his cabin, and the unforced way she asked him questions almost made him believe she wanted to learn.

And he saw that she was indeed very pretty, now that the wind had whipped life back into her face, but then his promise to the crew returned to him and he asked her to go back below. Anne understood, but before she left, asked if Deborah and Jane might have a little time in the air when they woke, since she herself was feeling so much better.

Leif had been around women in ports since he was ten, but never did he remember a girl looking up at him so candidly, so trustingly as this one did right now. Breath tightened in his throat and he had the strangest urge to reach out his hand and touch her gently on the mouth. He could even drop his head and kiss her if he was quick and she did not move. But then he remembered where they were. Such things court disaster; the sea was always jealous. And the girl had asked him something that was very hard to grant.

"Go back below. We'll see closer to port." Uncertainty made the words sound harsher than he'd wanted, and embarrassed for being so open and friendly, Anne dropped her head. Truly men were puzzling creatures. She had almost been sure that the captain liked her, and now he looked at her as if she were an errant member of his crew who needed flogging.

Out of habit she bobbed a wobbly curtsy to him and left him to his task. Then one quick look back, and her heart lurched. With eyes half closed against the salt wind, in the darkness, all she saw was a tall blond man, muffled to the eyes in his waxed sea cloak. From his height, he could have been Edward, should have been Edward—if only the fate had been kinder. She yearned to shout aloud the name of the man she loved, for maybe, in his palace far away, he would hear it on the wind from the sea and think of her.

Leif Mollnar watched regretfully as Anne swayed away across the deck to the ladder and the last light went from the sky. Yes, this was a troubling voyage; shifting wool fleece and made-cloth was easier than a cargo of women . . .

At the end of the next day, Leif Mollnar kept his promise to Anne for, as the *Lady Margaret* made her way into Whitby's deep harbor, the captain asked the women—all three—up to the deck to see them come into port. As a seaman he'd always liked Whitby; it was a neat, small town with stout, well-made houses cluttering the hillsides around the serviceable stone wharf, while above, on the great black cliff, Saint Hilda's gray abbey perched.

Whitby was a fishing port, and the reek of fish guts seemed to seep out of the town buildings even in winter. All seamen knew rotting fish and kelp was a healthful smell, though those who did not come from the north always found that first whiff from the docks an assault. Anne and her companions were no different. Hardly had they got down the slippery plank to the shore and taken their first breath on land than the smell hit them.

Poor Jane Shore blanched and turned a waxy green. She was used to the stink of London but this was different, and for the first time in her healthy life she felt as if she were going to faint. Deborah was similarly affected but managed to support the girl, their putative "mistress," as she stood wavering on the wharf. Perhaps Anne was hardier, for she managed to half carry first Jane, and then Deborah, over to the bench under the eaves of a waterfront inn, the Robin Arms. Leif barked orders over his shoulder to get the women's gear off the cog as he strode over to see what could be done for Jane. He was anxious because Sir Mathew had instructed him to look after the daughter of his friend and fellow mercer with special care. The captain was concerned, too, about his charges sitting here in this disreputable quarter of the town, where women from the stews came to work the ships that docked from London.

"Come now, ladies, this is not fitting. I shall take you up to the abbey and there you can rest while I find Sir Mathew's men. They're to take you on the next part of the journey."

One by one, he helped the women to their wavering legs and sent the ship's boy to find a wagon that could take them up the long, slow hill winding through the town toward the abbey. Though it was still early, the little seaport was full of life, and Anne found herself looking with interest at the houses huddled against each other, mostly made from local gray stone, though there were half-timbered buildings too, of oak and lime-washed mud plaster. The people looked strong—brown faces from the sea, white teeth, dark hair—and though they were small in comparison to the better-fed, taller southerners, they moved with energy and laughed readily.

In the end, a wagon could not be found to transport the women up the cliff, only a handcart for their baggage and two donkeys. Leif cursed the ship's boy roundly in Breton French. These women were important cargo and this was the best he could do? The pragmatic youngster shrugged stolidly and bore the stream of insults, even the ones about his parentage; it was hardly his fault if there were not enough donkeys to go around. He'd done the best he could and they all had good legs, didn't they? Of course, Leif would not permit Jane Shore to walk, but he found it odd that the oldest woman tried to insist that Anne ride the other animal, which she'd declined.

Finally, they'd set off, him leading Jane's donkey and Anne leading Deborah's, with the boy hauling the handcart. Leif's conscience was troubled, however, for he could have, should have, delegated this task to Simon; there was much he must see to in making sure the contents of the *Margaret*'s holds were properly brought ashore. But the lure of spending more time with this appealing girl had won over duty, and he was surprised by the lift in his heart when she smiled at him and asked him questions. Too soon for him, the little party arrived at the gates of the abbey, and it was with real regret that Leif Mollnar handed his three charges to the subprior.

An odd thing happened as the captain turned to go. Anne had lingered a moment after saying good-bye, and as he looked back at her, it seemed to him that the girl was rimmed with light from the sun climbing out of the sea, and gilded all over like an icon. For a moment he was dazzled—then she waved to him out of the heart of the light and disappeared! As his eyes adjusted he saw she must have slipped through the door of the abbey as it closed behind her, but still he shivered in the pale winter light, for it was an uncanny moment, and for the rest of that morning he could not shake the feeling of awe. It was as though he'd glimpsed Frey, one of the old ones, so glorious had she seemed.

In London, Mathew Cuttifer was on his knees before Christ's Mother, and as She gazed down at him from the walls of his chapel, a strange sensation prickled his spine. Had her eyes just moved? Perhaps she was trying to tell him something, something important? Mathew upbraided himself—he was presumptuous. If God's Mother wished to speak to him, he would know it without any doubt. He refocused his attention. Another Ave would help him hear her better . . . But try as he did, his attention wandered.

Had the cog made the journey to Whitby safely? It would take a good day, in fair weather, to travel from there to his house at Burning Norton and God, and his Mother, knew January in the Wold was rarely fair. Without conscious thought, his eyes lingered on the face of the Virgin as she gazed out at him across time, calm, serene. He sighed. No, there were no answers for him today. Reluctantly, and slowly, he levered himself to his feet, and turning to go, he saw that his wife had been sitting quietly in the body of the chapel on the benches reserved for the women servants, waiting for him to finish praying.

"May I speak with you, husband?" Immediately he heard the strain in her voice and saw it plainly written on her controlled, white face. "The court has returned, Mathew . . . and the king has sent for you."

Chapter Thirty-four

At court on that chilly afternoon, Mathew was taken to a small presence chamber that looked out toward the west doors of the abbey. He had only a moment to reflect that tomorrow would see the Mass held in which his cup would be first used—the chalice that was his passport to the treasure room—before Edward and William Hastings arrived.

Mathew bowed deeply to the king, who merely grunted as he settled himself into a chair of state. William took up his place silently beside the king and beckoned Mathew forward; the remote and frozen look on Edward's face frightened the merchant profoundly.

"Sir Mathew, have you been disloyal?" The king's harsh voice so startled Mathew that he must have looked innocent. However, Edward didn't allow him to answer. "The merchants of London. I hear they will not grant me the aid I seek and this displeases me greatly! Greatly!" The king was pacing now, too fired with anger to sit in his chair. "Never before, Sir Mathew, has the Crown compromised itself so much to raise money, money that I must have in times like these! What have you said to them?"

Mathew smothered a sigh of relief. "But Your Majesty, I have good news. I do not know where you have heard—"

"What good news?"

Mathew swept off his hat and again bowed low. "Sire, if you will grant an extension of the needle monopoly and—"

"And? What is this *and*? We only spoke of needles at Windsor."

"—a royal charter to the city of London that extends the freedoms of the lord mayor on behalf of the city only slightly." Mathew gulped, he knew as soon as his colleagues had proposed it that Edward would not be pleased about any extension of the liberties of the city, and the face of the king said as much. "Then, your loyal subjects, the merchants of London, will be pleased and grateful to make a loan to the royal treasury of fifteen thousand pounds to pursue your . . . campaign." He'd nearly said "war in the north." "War" was a bad word, a bad omen; speak it, and you gave the thought—and the fear—power.

The silence was intense when he finished speaking.

"An extension to the freedoms of the city?" the king finally asked. At least he was not shouting.

Mathew dared to raise his eyes to that implacable face. "A small one, sire. Merely the right to hold a cloth fair each autumn on the first Sunday after the Feast of Saint Crispin and Saint Jude—and to pay no tax on it."

"No tax! Insolence! How do they expect the court to function if they will not help me pay for it?"

Mathew returned his gaze to the ground. The king was annoyed but he was not enraged. He must have been expecting something of the kind; the London merchants understood the king was short of cash but that he would have no wish to summon Parliament to claim financial aid for running his army. People from the shires were conservative and had had quite enough of war; they'd not be generous.

William Hastings interrupted the king quietly. "May I speak, sire?"

The king nodded assent, grumpily. "Sir Mathew, when will the loan be gathered in from the merchants?" Hastings asked.

"We are preparing a contract now, sire—"

The king bellowed, "Contract? Contract! I said nothing of any contract. Moneylending is forbidden in the Bible, Mathew. Have a care!"

Sir Mathew shuffled from foot to foot and looked stubborn, though his heart was racing.

William continued smoothly. "Bring me the draft as soon as it is prepared and I will show it to the king. There are no guarantees, however, that His Majesty will be prepared to do more than offer his word as to repayment."

Mathew had the sense to bow and say nothing. More and more he and his fellow men of business were reluctant to deal with the debt-ridden court unless some form of surety was offered—and, of course, that was often land that, when forfeited for bad debt, made its new owners men of substance.

William signaled that the audience was over. Mathew bowed deeply and began a long and careful departure backward out of the presence chamber. But before he reached the door, the king called out, "Wait. The serving girl you sent to me. Chamberlain, what was her name?"

William, with a completely blank face, replied, "I believe it was Anne, my liege."

"Anne. Yes. My wife was expecting she would be here at court when we returned from Windsor and she is most displeased by her continuing absence from duty. She was once your servant—do you have news of her? You will understand, this is a most serious blot on her record of service at our court."

Mathew bowed even lower to hide his face from his king. "Sire, as it happens, my wife did mention something to me recently. I believe we've heard from one of our servants who knows the family that the girl's mother continues very ill. Close to death, I think my wife said." He sent a quick prayer to the Virgin asking forgiveness for the lie.

The king scowled. William, however, was pleased. He wanted the king to concentrate on the coming campaign. With luck, in three days they would be gone from London before the girl returned to distract him. "Thank you, Sir Mathew. The king will be graciously pleased to receive more information when you have it."

Mathew bowed lower still and this time managed to back himself through the carved doors before the king could challenge him again.

Inside the presence chamber, the king stalked to the window and looked down toward the cold gray bulk of the Abbey church.

"Sire, I did not know that your wife was displeased by the girl's continuing absence. I must make sure to set Her Majesty's mind at ease on the matter." William's wicked sense of humor would cause him big trouble one day, but he couldn't resist the jibe.

Reluctantly, the king snorted with laughter. "No such thing, William, no such thing—and you know it." As he laughed the pressure in his head seemed to ease, as did the odd feeling of tightness in his belly.

He'd been the one to fret and complain when he had returned to court—with a sense of suppressed excitement at the thought of seeing Anne again, he had to confess that—and had found her not there. Which was the worse for the bedchamber servants when he'd found out that none of them knew when she would return. And, unlike his normal behavior, there was no one currently at court who took his fancy instead. All he could see was Anne looking up at him defiantly, snatching her hands out of his and running away from him after the Christmas play. Christ's bowels! Was it so much to ask that he be able to have a moment with the girl before they went to war?

William saw the glower return and the king's fists clench as he gazed, unseeing, at the Abbey. Distraction, that was the need now; something else to think about instead of this one insignificant girl.

Fortunately, that distraction presented itself, for when the king stalked out of the presence chamber on his way to the mews to see how his French peregrine had survived the journey from Windsor, a palace messenger rushed toward him. The man was accompanied by a soldier draped in a heavy riding cloak and wearing bloodied spurs, spattered with mud and wearing the white boar badge of Edward's youngest brother, Richard, Duke of Gloucester, who, young as he was, held the north for the House of York. The exhausted rider dropped to one knee in front of the king and held up a sealed packet of documents. "Sire, this is urgent. My duke said I must place it in your hands only."

Edward quickly grasped the packet and gestured to William that he should give the man a reward. William sighed and hauled an angel out of the pocket slung from his belt; the king was always doing this. Edward then hurried away to his own quarters, telling William to make sure that the man was fed and given a bed to collapse into.

When the messenger had been taken down to the kitchens, William hurried to find the king and was relieved to see Edward looking close to cheerful as he scanned the single sheet of the letter Richard had sent. The soldier had done his work well. He'd left Richard's stronghold of York little more than three days ago, and hard cold weather of this last few days had made his journey quicker than normal for the ground was frozen hard.

The contents of the letter had merited quick passage, for Richard had news that the earl was massing his affinity at Warwick Castle not to fight a war, but to celebrate a marriage—that of their brother George, Duke of Clarence, to Warwick's daughter Isabelle. After the celebrations, the large group of wedding guests could be turned to another purpose—a march on London, perhaps, to remove Edward from the throne. William wondered at Edward's cheerfulness.

"So, Warwick is making his move, at last."

"Yes. And so is my stupid brother George. We must move, too, now, very fast. No time for the army. It's best clothes into the saddlebags, and ride tonight with a small party."

William was bemused. "Fine clothes, my lord?"

"Why yes, if we are to be guests at the wedding we must on no account look shabby! Come, I need to speak to the queen."

The rest of that day passed in secretive bustle as a small party of trusted men—his riding company—prepared to leave with the king. The plan was an audacious one. They would ride hard for the north and meet Richard, also with a small group, near Warwick Castle. Once inside the castle as surprise wedding guests—who could hardly be turned away—they would kidnap George and bring him back to London. Simple.

William groaned. It was not that he did not believe the king would pull it off; it was the risk of it, walking directly into the lion's den. But he comforted himself with the knowledge that surprise would be on their side and Warwick was not nearly so cool in a crisis as the king.

Edward might just do it, and anyway, what did they have to lose? A kingdom?

Chapter Thirty-five

The party of men from Burning Norton, including Giles Raby, Sir Mathew's son-in-law, had arrived at Saint Hilda's Abbey. Two men would escort Jane to York where she would meet her husband, Master Shore, while Giles and three more of his followers would take Anne and Deborah back to Sir Mathew's lands near Rievaulx Abbey in the Wold.

The wait for Giles Raby had been longer than expected because bad weather had set in. The blizzard was so great that snow had even fallen in Whitby, unusual this close to the sea. So when Giles and his men knocked on the abbey's door they were half-frozen, and even the tough little, shaggy ponies ridden by most of the party needed time to recover before they could begin the journey back.

During the freezing ride across the high fells to Whitby, Giles had become more and more annoyed by the fool's errand he'd been sent on as he battled the ice-filled winds. It had all sounded so un-likely when he and his wife, Alicia, Sir Mathew's daughter from his first marriage, had received word they were to make house room for a lady and her servant for the rest of the winter. And at Mathew's express instruction, they were to tell their neighbors nothing about this guest. Giles had learned to accept Mathew's de-manding ways but the meddling in his decisions where Burning Norton was concerned were the hardest to stomach. Summer had not been good this year and their stock of food for winter would be severely stretched by even two extra mouths. They might be driven to slaughter one of the precious breeding cows they'd been keeping in the byre for spring, as the meat they'd salted at the autumn kill had not been so plentiful as last year.

Unlike the rest of the warlike Rabys, Giles had the instincts of a farmer, not a fighter—and a miser at that. He and Sir Mathew tolerated one another. The older man saw that the younger was more careful with his lands than even he would have been, and was forced to grant grudging approval of Giles's management of Burning Norton. The younger man was full of new ideas for livestock improvement, and in the five years he'd had the run of the ever-expanding property, he'd managed to breed larger sheep that yielded more of the precious fleece than when a hired reeve had run the manor. It was said that Giles had even managed to persuade the notoriously closemouthed Cistercians at Rievaulx to part with some of their secrets on sheep management, and Burning Norton prospered as a result.

For all that, or perhaps because of it, Giles had few of the knightly graces of his clan and deeply disapproved of women gadding about, least of all in the winter countryside. So it was a grumpy man who sat waiting in the conversation room of the abbey at Whitby. All he wanted was rest and then to be away from this cursed and smelly little town before the weather closed in again. Then Anne was ushered into the freezing room, and most of his surliness melted away when the girl looked up at him and smiled.

Now Giles was one of those rare men who had made a marriage for good and sensible reasons—Alicia had a large dowry and the prospect of land, he was a younger son—and then found that he loved his wife. No one had ever called Alicia beautiful since she favored her father, but this girl was that and more. And the more was interesting.

She entered quietly, dressed in simple dark blue velvet. But he saw that the sleeves were richly tipped with marten fur and there was a delicate filigree chain around her neck. Her hair was covered by a low cap and a fine white veil so that he had no way of seeing what color it was, but the clear eyes that looked at him so honestly were the color of new oak leaves, with glints of blue, and finely shaped.

"Sir Giles, my name is Anne and I am forever in your debt for this cold ride. Sir Mathew has been more than good to me, but you have had much the worst of the strange turn of events that brings me here to you."

She was almost humble and that cast Giles into confusion. He was unused to court women or court manners—Alicia said they stayed too much on the farm and he had forgotten his ancestry—but the grace and simplicity of this girl might have made even the most seasoned courtier tongue-tied. He hastened over to raise her and was surprised to feel the roughness of her hands; this girl was no exotic bloom unused to hard work. And while that was odd in a lady, he liked her for it.

"Lady, my house—that is, Sir Mathew's house—is proud and happy that you will honor us with your company until spring. We get few enough visitors in winter so Alicia, my wife, will be very pleased to have a companion in the solar." He spoke the word "solar" with cautious pride. It had been shockingly expensive and he'd just had it built at one end of the first-floor hall. It was two stories higher than the animals in the winter byre beneath the dwelling quarters, and since it was placed a little way over to one side at the end of the hall, that had the benefit of greatly lessening the smell from the animals. Now he was glad he'd spent the extra money, so that the stink would not shame them in front of their guests.

Anne was grateful that Giles had asked her no questions and she was thankful for his tact. She had no answers but evasions of the truth, and she hated that.

"Now where is this woman of yours? I brought a pack animal but I may need to hire another if you have very many things . . ." As if prescient, there was a knock at the door and a moment later Deborah entered in a neat, dark dress and white coif as befitted her new station as attendant to Anne.

Deborah waiting on her had not been of Anne's choosing. It was something her foster mother had insisted on as part of the remaking of Anne's identity. Deborah knew that change for Anne was impossible to avoid. Better to embrace, rather than fight, fate; Anne would never be a servant again—the scrying bowl had shown that much at least—but friends had a role now in helping her become what she should be.

With Jane Shore's willing help, Deborah had insisted that Anne dress in the new clothes that Sir Mathew had supplied. Every morning of the three days they spent waiting for Giles to arrive, Deborah attended her erstwhile "daughter" as Anne had formerly waited on Lady Margaret.

Jane, however, had not asked questions about Anne's obvious change in status because she had been sworn to secrecy by her father and Sir Mathew, and being a good-hearted girl with a sense of adventure, she was happy to enjoy the remaking of Anne into the image of a woman of the court. But it was she who had seen that Anne's greatest strength and distinction, apart from her beauty, was the kindness and simplicity of her manner. There could be no greater ornament to a lady for it said she was her own person—rare in someone so young.

Jane burned to know more, longed to ask questions, but then, when she caught Anne gazing wistfully out to the cold gray sea, something stopped her. Events as strange as these did not happen without good reason, and if her father was concerned in it, and had not told her, would not tell her, there was good reason for a wise person to stay silent and remain in ignorance.

The interview in the abbey between Sir Giles and Anne was short and now the time had come for Jane to go her way to York and for Anne and Deborah to begin the cold ride to Burning Norton. As Anne stood in the lee of the abbey door she was swept by a physical rush of sadness. She and Jane had become close over these last few days and as the two embraced for one last time Jane pressed a present into Anne's hands. It was a brooch to hold a cloak in place, a large smoky green-blue topaz surrounded by pearls. Anne had seen Jane wear it and had admired its beauty, but it was very valuable.

"It's much too fine, I cannot take it. Besides, I have nothing to give you."

"It's the same color as your eyes, nearly, and when I think of you, I shall see it, this brooch, going with you wherever you travel. Whatever the road."

There was a bond between them, each girl felt it. It was as if a feather brushed them and then flew away, the sense of it was so light, but . . . yes, there was a bond.

Giles was impatient to be off and shuffled from foot to foot as Anne waved until her friend was out of sight, heading south to York. Their road was to be a different one; they were away to the west. And so the small party mounted the shaggy, rested ponies, with the exception of Giles on his destrier, and turned their heads for Burning Norton. The animals picked up their hooves daintily on the good road, which lasted less than the distance of an arrow shot once they were away from the abbey, but their heads were high, ears twitching, for they knew that each step they took brought them nearer their own stable.

The weather held for them; there was even a high thin blue in the sky as Anne and Deborah settled themselves to the short, busy gait of their ponies. It was long since any of these rough-haired brown ponies had seen a currycomb, but the bite of the wind made each of the women wish for similar covering. Giles and his men were well dressed for the moors. The knight wore a black cloak lined with wolf fur and his men had sturdy leggings and thick homespun plaid swagged around them. Each one, too, had a bonnet covering his long wild hair.

These men were kind enough in contrast to their looks, though, offering to share bannock bread and salted sheep's cheese from their skin bags. They sang as they rode, high, yearning songs in a language Anne had never heard before. And if she did not understand the words, she understood the feeling: loss of love, loss of home. The keening sound struck to her heart, for it was Edward's face she saw when they sang, and her throat closed when she thought of all that was unsaid between them which now might never be given voice at all.

In London, Sir Mathew paced up and down his workroom. Recently, whenever he drank the rich wines of Burgundy, his gullet burned all through the night and last night had been such a one. He was tired and out of sorts and worried too.

The Sunday last, he'd finally been present at High Mass in the Abbey Church to see his new chalice used for the first time. But anxiety had clouded the pleasure when he'd been given a private tour of the treasure house where it would rest between uses. He'd been shown the new handsome casket that would contain his cup and the mazer, but, now, at last, he knew the resting place of the letter that might prove the truth of Anne's birth.

The treasure of the Abbey was kept in the Chapel of the Pyx, which was part of a long, stone-vaulted undercroft beneath the monks' dormitory, and the prior of the Abbey Church had been delighted to show Mathew the huge store of silver and gold plate, manuscripts, missals, and jewels that were kept there. Gold, Mathew's gold, opened all doors it seemed; such a simple solution to the problem, in the end.

The Chapel of the Pyx was also where the state regalia was kept—the crown of Saint Stephen, the orb, and Curtana the sword of mercy—and the pyx itself containing the standard gold and silver coins of the realm. Each year, with great ceremony, the "trial of the Pyx" was conducted in which the coinage was taken out and weighed and tested to ensure that none had "clipped" the coins in the intervening year and thus debased their value.

There was also the famous door lined with human skin that led from the chapel out into the chapter house of the brothers. The prior had pointed it out with great pride; it served as a warning to all who thought of stealing the treasure. Mathew had felt every word the venerable prior had spoken about thieves as he pointed to the door with its dusty, shredded covering, but Mathew also glimpsed an oak box in one of the niches formed by the vaulting, on which the words "Henricius VI" had been hammered with gold-topped nails. It was new work, for the wood was still light-colored in contrast to the black oakwood of the ancient coffers around it. Beside it was another, even lighter in hue, with "Edwardus IV" similarly displayed on its lid.

Feigning great interest in the prior's words, the merchant had asked questions about all that they saw: "And so, Reverend

Prior, everything in the treasure house has been given to the Abbey?"

"Yes, Sir Mathew, you have joined an honorable host. Many great men of England—yourself now included—have glorified this holy house with gifts. There has been a church here in this place for at least seven hundred years, since the reign of Ethelbert, Saxon King of Kent, and the coming of the blessed Augustine—and it pleases God that our abbey remains a light to the ungodly. You have added to that light."

Mathew had bowed humbly but he could not suppress the surge of pride that swelled his heart. It had nearly distracted him from the business at hand: the oak chest with Henry VI's name upon it. "Yet, Prior, I see many locked chests around us here. They must truly contain objects of even greater value."

"Why yes, Sir Mathew, in some cases. They are the most important of the state papers from a particular reign that are entrusted to us for safekeeping. Some are very ancient . . ." He pointed to a couple of almost black boxes. "These are from the reign of the blessed founder of our Cathedral Church, the holy Saint Edward; and this is from his successor, and the invader of this realm, the bastard William of Normandy."

"Ah, so the newer chests I see here?" Mathew had waved in the general direction of the lighter-colored chests in the shadows.

"Papers from the reign of our current King, Edward, and his predecessor, Henry VI."

The prior had hesitated a moment before saying the last name. A sad expression had shadowed his face as he crossed himself quickly. Silently, the two men contemplated the chest, their thoughts with that poor man; it seemed a small object to contain the sum of one long reign, ended so ignominiously.

Mathew continued to pace his workroom, silently reliving what he'd seen in the dimly lit little chapel. He'd been delighted to see that the chest with Henry's name on it was not locked, but he knew it would be difficult to gain access to it again with enough time to sort through its contents. The only way in was through the chapter house vestibule, a busy place in the life of the Abbey at almost any time of the day. It needed thought, deep thought.

Day—the time of day—that was the key! The vestibule would always see comings and goings during the day, but what about night, after compline?

Of course, he had a ready-made accomplice within the Abbey, but would the monk be sufficiently resourceful? And would he be connected with Mathew's operation in London if the loss of valuable documents was discovered?

He would have to think on this, long and hard.

Chapter Thirty-six

Anne's first sight of Burning Norton was not encouraging. Somehow she'd thought it would be large and imposing like Blessing House, so the undistinguished huddle of gray buildings surrounded by the slimy brackish waters of a ditch pretending to be a moat was disappointing. But she was hungry and stiff and very, very cold, and any shelter from the howling night was welcome, especially since there was a warm flicker of yellow light in several of the small upper windows.

The unshod hooves of the moorland ponies made a busy clatter as they rattled across the drawbridge toward the protection the inner court offered from the bitter wind outside. Young and strong as she was, Anne had suffered from the rigors of this journey over the high moor. It was hard to unlock her frozen hands from the reins, harder still to slip down from the pony's back.

But there were welcome hands to receive her and a woman's clear voice raised over the chaos. "Welcome, Mistress Anne. My husband's house is yours."

Anne found herself looking up into Sir Mathew's face under a housewife's wimple. It took a moment to understand that this was his daughter, and Giles's wife, Alicia. She tried to make her rigid body drop into a curtsy, but the kind eyes looking down into hers smiled and would not let her try. "Come now. The hall is warm and snug and so is the solar. And there is food waiting after your journey."

Alicia took her new guest out of the torch-flickering darkness of the inner court and up exterior stone stairs into an upper room, the first-floor hall of Burning Norton. As they walked into the hall around the sturdy wooden screen that protected the entrance from the wind, Anne saw they were in an unexpectedly large space for what was just a fortified farmhouse, and there was an impressive fireplace in one wall, adorned with a huge hooded mantelpiece. The roof vault was supported by carved timber beams picked out in red, blue, and green and they made a brave sight. At the far end from where the party entered was another flight of stone stairs leading up to the solar door halfway up the height of the wall. Giles smiled proudly as he saw Anne glance toward it. "Yes, mistress, there is the solar I spoke of. I had it built across the end of the hall and it makes us a fine set of private apartments, as handsome as the solar in Blessing House, as you shall see. Come now, up these last stairs . . ."

Once reached, the solar was indeed a pretty room. There were well-burnished wall sconces with wax candles in them, a luxury to welcome their guests, and a set of arras in brilliant colors to enliven the stone walls. The wooden floor with its bright, new, honey-brown oak planks was covered by the unexpected luxury of two beautiful rugs from the Levant. The fire, lit to welcome them, smelled of heather and as its warmth began to penetrate their nearly sodden clothes, Deborah breathed a deep and happy sigh, exchanging a quick glance with Anne. It felt like sanctuary to be here.

But there was more to see. Proudly Giles threw open yet another door and they saw an inner chamber. It was a private bedroom for himself and Alicia, luxurious though not large. Their curtained bed was on a small dais standing in front of an oriel window that was impressive for the large number of its clear glass panes. They could hear the voice of the wind in the dark moors outside, but here inside the room was quiet, snug, and smelled delicious. Anne sighed deeply. At last, she began to feel safe. Surely no one would find them in this remote, hospitable place?

"I will take your clothes to be dried in the kitchen. Then there is food to be served in the hall. No doubt your woman will assist you to dress, but I should be delighted to help also."

Alicia smiled kindly at her guest and Anne felt tears in her eyes.

"You are kind," Anne said as Deborah began to strip her of the sodden wool of the dress she had worn during the journey. "But Deb— My woman is soaked through as well. Here, Deborah, warm yourself. Mistress Alicia will help me."

If Alicia showed no surprise at this thought for the welfare of a servant, it was because she was a practical woman. London ways were not the ways of the north and she, too, had members of her household who were more like family than servants.

Fingers and bodies warmed quickly in that small room beside the solar. And soon Anne and Deborah had peeled off their wet clothes, dried themselves on the linen provided by Alicia, and dropped clean garments over their heads. Chilled flesh came back to life as Deborah rubbed Anne's hands briskly and insisted on lacing the back of the plainest of the velvet gowns from Anne's small traveling coffer. Sadly, the rich cloth was creased even though it had been carefully folded in the packing; still, it would shake out as it was worn, and in the dim light of the hall below, who would see?

Down in the hall, Giles warmed his back by the fire. He was content to be home, though he would speak to Alicia later about the needless expense of the wax tapers he saw everywhere. Sometimes his wife puzzled him. Certainly Anne was something of a mystery and Sir Mathew considered her important, but they had no knowledge of her exact status. Why waste money until they were certain all this show would have some beneficial result?

Still, his slight annoyance cleared away like morning mist when he saw the women descend from the solar. Anne glowed like a dark red jewel as she walked toward the fire, the flickering light touching the delicate shape of her face and the sinuous curves of her body under the scarlet dress. A murmur behind him grew as his assembled household saw her face properly for the first time.

Anne was dressed so simply and yet looked so fine, so cleanly drawn, that Alicia seemed lumpen by her side—until she smiled at him and Giles remembered why he liked her so much. His wife understood he would be dazzled by Anne and, unlike most wives, was not jealous. There was no point; was a woman jealous of the sun?

Anne was not part of their lives, never would be, she was just passing through and they both understood that. There was no need to worry about his faithfulness to her; he knew that she knew that too. But he was a man and he could look.

Gazing almost vacantly at Anne, he barely heard Alicia clear her throat, and then again, more noisily. With a start, he remembered his duty and picked up Anne's right hand, placed it over his own, and escorted her to the place of honor at the board that had been laid across the top of the hall facing its length.

Below them the household of some twenty men and women watched in silence, avid for any detail of the moment that would be endlessly discussed in the kitchen, the dairy, the smithy, and the sheepfolds. Little enough happened in midwinter at Burning Norton, God knew, and now there was this lady, this mysterious lady to talk about. As beautiful as the statue of the Virgin in the Abbey of Rievaulx—more, for this one was real flesh and blood where the Virgin was ivory and gold, and only a statue, after all.

The grace was said and almost before the last "amen" there was a noisy scramble as the household seated itself and the food began to arrive from behind the screens at the entrance door.

Anne smiled privately to herself for a moment. How odd it was that she was sitting here a guest at the high table and below her were the servants of this house. So recently she would have been one of them, down there, gazing up at the master's table. She shivered. The high could so easily be brought low, and the low high, that life seemed mad. Did not God ordain each of their places? Why had he chosen her for this confusing shift in circumstances? She caught Deborah's eye as she sat below the high board with the other servants. Perhaps it was time to look into the scrying bowl again; time to ask what the future might hold.

Questions of the future were very much on Mathew Cuttifer's mind as, away south in London, he finally held an unrolled sheet of vellum in his hands. It had cost him as much as the cup with which he'd endowed the Abbey, but perhaps it would be money well spent. Though the hazard was still very great before a return could be expected. That was the merchant in him thinking. It had been dangerous, expensive, and secret work for Brother Nicholas at the Abbey. He had had to buy his way past the brother who held the key to the Chapel of Pyx at much risk of being exposed and asked very inconvenient questions indeed. Then something else touched Mathew's soul as he looked on the clear black writing before him. Unusually, the letter was written in English, not the Latin or French he would have expected. Whatever the language, its meaning was very clear:

To our dear brother of Somerset, greeting. Inasmuch as it has pleased almighty God to endow our person with the realm and governance of this Kingdom of England, and the governance of all the souls that dwell here within its boundaries, it is our intent always to have the welfare and sustenance of such souls closest to our heart. And in this matter, give heed to this our intent as set forth in this Deed.

In that you hold from our hands all of the lands of the county of Somerset as our liegeman, it is our wish that lands within the Parish of Porlock in the county of Somerset be set aside and dowered in perpetuity to Lady Alyce de Bohun and her get, who are most close to our heart, as is our following wish.

Item. That the village of Wincanton the Less, together with its farmlands, formerly the property of the monks at Appleforth, be transferred to the estate of the said lady for her sole use and enjoyment, and that of her descendants.

Item. That the right to mill flour for the village of Wincanton the Less, together with the mill known as Cobby's Mill, also formerly the property of the monks at Appleforth in the said village, be transferred to the estate of the said lady for her exclusive use & profit.

Item. That the dues payable from the fair held each year the last Wednesday before Michael's Mass in the town of Taunton be given and bequeathed to the estate of the said lady in perpetuity.

Item. That the fortified manor known as Herrard Great Hall together with its lands, fishponds, waters, and all its rights, goods, chattels, and livestock whatsoever, heretofore the property of the Crown, be given and bequeathed to the estate of the said lady and to be hers and the heirs of her body and all in perpetuity.

Let all be done in accordance with our wishes and with greatest dispatch.

Henricius Sixtus. By the Grace of God, Sovereign . . . etc.

And there was a second piece of vellum, attached to the first. It contained few words but these were explosive. Again, they were written in English.

We, Henry, the Sixth to bear that name, hereby acknowledge and declare that the child presently carried by the Lady Alyce de Bohun is of our get. The child that shall be born will therefore be our natural child and as such will ever be close to our heart. It is further our wish and intention that the said child and its mother, the said Lady Alyce de Bohun, shall be dowered with the property hereby separately noted for their good sustenance and that of their heirs and descendants in perpetuity.

Given under our hand, signed and sealed this day of the seventeenth of August 1450 anno domini at the Palace of Westminster.

It all fitted. The scrolls—and the other evidence that Jehanne and Deborah possessed—could prove that Anne was Alyce de Bohun's daughter, and by deduction, they could prove when and how she had been born. She was entitled to the property mentioned in the letter, and, something else, she was entitled to be acknowledged as King Henry VI's natural daughter.

Mathew knew that he held a document only a desperate man would have written. Henry must have thought that in acknowledging his bastard child, and providing for her, he was protecting her mother. But the queen had found out, and in signing that letter, he had, unwittingly, signed Alyce's death warrant.

Now, finally, the time had come to choose, to really choose his course. His intuition had told him from the time he had last met Anne at Windsor that she was a trump card to be played most carefully, but a trump card nonetheless. The question now was, when should the move be made? Every day was vital since events were moving fast, if the intelligence he had from his paid informers at

Westminster was true. He'd heard the king had disappeared with his "riding court" a day or so back—gone hunting, so it was said. But Mathew was aware, as few else were, of the wedding preparations at Warwick Castle. If Edward arrived too late . . . what would Anne's worth be then?

Chapter Thirty-seven

Four days had passed since Edward had received the mud-spattered messenger at Westminster, and though he and his "riding court" had traveled with remarkable speed, common sense told them they'd be too late to stop the wedding of Clarence and Isabelle of Warwick.

Now the king and his youngest brother, the dark, intense, Richard, Duke of Gloucester, sat on their blown and muddied horses gazing down on Warwick Castle in the first uncertain light of a frozen day. The building was deserted but for a few men patrolling the battlements. Edward looked at Richard, puzzled.

"Well? Where are they all?"

Richard frowned. His agents had said a thousand of Warwick's affinity had been billeted in the town nearby, but the lack of obvious comings and goings to the castle, even at this early hour, made him uneasy. "I was reliably informed, Edward. George is in there, I promise you."

Edward urged his horse forward a pace or two, looking across at the gray bulk of the building. He flicked a glance at William and Richard, breaking into a smile. "Very well, dear friends. Let's set this up proud—in we go!"

He flung his cloak back, dropping the hood off his head in the same fluid movement. In the scant, creeping light he was magnificent, with a coat of light, well-burnished riding mail under a velvet particolored tunic of blue and gold quartered with the leopards of

England and the lilies of France. A circlet of gold kept his long hair away from his face and one hand rested lightly on the pommel of the sword at his side. Even William, used to the king's physical presence, sucked in a breath of cold air. Edward looked like a king out of the past, a mythic figure. The chamberlain's skin prickled—he could feel the energy that radiated from this man spreading around the small party on that bleak hillside with greater warmth than the sun struggling up out of the east. As one, the twenty or so tired men gathered their horses around the king and cantered easily down toward the gate of Warwick Castle, new vigor in each one of them.

Sim the Fletcher was not a very clever man, but he was the first of the sentries above the great gate to believe what his eyes were telling him. There beneath them was the Lord Chamberlain of England bellowing for admittance to Warwick Castle and with him was the king—and Gloucester, his young brother!

Sim hurried to tell his sergeant, and the sergeant, confirming the extraordinary news with a terrible sinking feeling in his gut, hurried toward the castle's hall where Warwick's people were waiting for the earl before going to Mass in the family chapel.

The sergeant need not have bothered. Warwick had heard the news. He sauntered in, smiling confidently, holding up one velvet-gloved hand for silence. "Raise the gate. Admit our dearest friend, the king."

Warwick had not survived at court for as long as he had without understanding the need to play a role—and play it well. No one who was unaware of the situation between Warwick, Edward, and the Duke of Clarence would have seen anything but a loyal servant of the king delighted and honored by Edward's unexpected presence.

And that was the tableau that Edward saw as he and his small, dazzlingly dressed party swept in to the hall: Warwick on his knees, head bowed, surrounded by a mass of men and women wearing his colors but all similarly humble in the presence of the king. Edward laughed out loud—a joyful, ringing sound—and strode, beaming, to Warwick, reaching down one hand to raise him.

"Enough, Earl Warwick, enough. Such humility from you and yours is never necessary—we are old friends, after all."

For a moment the king and the earl locked glances before Warwick smiled glitteringly and sprang to his feet. "My liege, will you join me and mine for a Mass?"

"With pleasure, with great pleasure, Earl Warwick. Let us seek the blessing of your Savior and mine, together."

It was as if no hard words had ever been spoken, from the courtesy the king and Warwick showed each other during the Mass and afterward, breaking their morning fast together in the hall.

The castle kitchen had flung together a magnificent meal for their unexpected guests, for it was only a day from the Red Letter Feast of the Conversion of Saint Paul, thus there was plentiful food in the castle. As course followed course—boar pastries; pike and eels in aspic; gull, quail, and plover eggs preserved in salt and spices; hot fricassees of fresh venison, and pears preserved in honey and cinnamon—the earl and the king spoke of almost everything but Clarence, who was absent from the hall. As were Warwick's eldest daughter, Isabelle, and his wife, the countess.

There was much chat about the doings of the court at Christmas and the strange misunderstanding surrounding Warwick's departure. The confusion was blamed by both men on the Countess of Warwick's unexpected illness, forcing the earl's speedy return to his own lands. Then Warwick lightly asked the king what had earned them the pleasure of this visit.

"Why, I was hunting with my brother on some of his lands hereabouts"—Richard had no lands near Warwick Castle and they both knew it—"and thought that we should discuss, you and I, the tourney we have planned for the Feast of Saint Valentine."

Ah, yes, the tourney. Twelve knights to be led by the king, twelve by the earl—and a scant few weeks away.

"And as I understand it, my brother Clarence is currently your guest. Since he has not been at court this little time past, and I wish him to ride with my party . . ." It was said so silkily, so courteously, that none but Warwick heard the edge in those words. ". . . I thought we should speak, George and I, about the contest to come."

The earl smiled, though when he laughed the sound was harsh. "Alas, my liege, I have news to concern you a little. Your brother is not well. I dislike being a messenger of bad tidings but . . . there it is."

The king allowed his face to register concern. "My unfortunate brother—what is this illness? What do the doctors say?"

Warwick looked uneasy. "Little at this early time, though they are confident in his recovery, of course. He sweats, and has fever alternately, though it is not the sweating sickness. I have given him my own chambers and, of course, he must stay here until he is well again. My wife, and Isabelle, have nursed him devotedly."

The king smiled broadly. "How fortunate that Lady Warwick has recovered her own health so quickly. And Isabelle—this is kind and selfless of them both. You have risked your family to secure George . . . to secure his life. That will not be forgotten."

Warwick's smile was frozen to his face as he and the king locked glance to glance once more. The moment was broken by William. "Lord Warwick, I am sure that our liege would be pleased to visit the Duke of Clarence. Sire"—he turned to Edward—"if you have eaten enough to ward off the northern chill this cold morning, perhaps . . . ?"

The king sprang up, hauling Warwick to his feet. "Let us visit Clarence together. There is little time before we must be on our way again."

Warwick's people scrambled up from the benches as the king swept by with his host, and due note was made of the grim expressions of the king's party—and of the men who accompanied the earl.

Nothing was said as they strode toward Warwick's private quarters. It took only a few minutes to mount the stairs to the iron-bound door that guarded the entrance to his sleeping room. Warwick thrust it open and the cold winter light showed Clarence lying in his bed propped up on bolsters, a scarlet flush high on his cheeks.

Isabelle and her mother, the Countess of Warwick, nearly fainted when they looked up from tending George to find the king framed in the doorway. "So, brother, Lord Warwick spoke true. What ails you?" For a moment the king's face softened. George was infuriating, jealous, and impetuous, but they'd been friends as children.

"Nothing, brother. Now that you are here." George coughed as he said the last of the words, so the irony lost its impact. It made the king smile though. George had always had a ready wit.

"I'd thought to talk tourney with you, brother, but I can see you're otherwise occupied." He flashed a quick glance at Isabelle, standing beside her mother. She was a good-looking, disturbingly well endowed girl for a fourteen-year-old, and seeing her again, Edward could understand his brother's lust. The ghost of a smile crossed the king's face. How useful it must seem to George to have a potential wife who was both bedworthy *and* an heiress. But it would never happen—not while he was king.

"Earl Warwick, we have all trespassed on your hospitality for too long. Especially George. Come, brother, I shall take you back with me to court, and you can recover in your own home."

Edward knew that surprise was his only weapon, that and the bluff that Richard had five hundred men waiting for the king to return from his "hunting expedition" just over the hill outside the town; a fact he'd casually slipped into conversation with the earl at the feast.

However, it was the sheer strength of Edward's will that got them out of Warwick Castle, for there was instant turmoil as the king shouted orders for his brother to be dressed. Warwick could do nothing but pretend to assist. To oppose Edward would have meant an open breach—and a fight, probably to the death, with the king's men he supposed to be surrounding his castle. It had galled Warwick to cancel the wedding feast when the duke was ill and now it galled him even more that Edward was riding out of his castle with his daughter's bridegroom safely tucked into the earl's own luxurious litter, borrowed on a promise of return shortly. He knew it would be some time before he saw either again.

Clarence could be wily when he chose, once he absorbed the way the wind was blowing. It was one matter to oppose his brother's will from a distance, another again to take him on at close quarters. So he allowed himself to be bundled into the litter with one long glance at Isabelle. He and Warwick shared a look. "I shall be well for the tourney, my Lord Warwick, never fear. And we shall be glad of your presence at court when that day dawns, shall we not, brother?"

Edward looked down at Clarence with a bleak smile. "Do not fret, brother. The tourney, when it comes, shall be like no other. And without my Lord Warwick, what point would it have?"

George sank back into the luxury of the padded brocade interior of the litter, biting his nails, as the king flicked its curtains closed.

William, Richard, and Edward rode out into that late morning with stoic faces, swords held loosely at their sides. They did not look back at Warwick standing beside his countess in the inner ward of the castle, but as they clattered over the drawbridge each sneaked a glance at the other, every moment expecting an arrow to thud home between their shoulder blades.

But none came, and as they left the castle behind them, the small troop instinctively broke into three parts: the king with his brother Richard at the front with a few men, the greatest mass of soldiers around the litter, and a handful dropping back with Hastings to guard the rear. It would be slow progress across Warwick's lands and the king was worried that the earl might gather himself and come after them with a larger force when he'd had some time to plan and think matters through.

What they needed was support, and Edward couldn't understand why Richard seemed so relaxed about the situation. Especially since the youngster insisted, after they'd been traveling for less than an hour, that they rest. It was then they heard the distant thunder of hooves: riders, a mass of them, approaching fast!

Edward shouted orders: "Ring the litter! Ring the litter!" And in the time it took to draw swords, the twenty men in the king's party had forced their horses into a circle knee to knee around the hapless Clarence. The king's expression was grim, so was Hastings's—only Gloucester seemed relaxed.

There was good cause for his calm: the troop of five hundred men that appeared out of the darkening afternoon was wearing the white boar, Gloucester's emblem. "Well, brother, think you we have enough men now to hunt properly?"

Edward smiled as he clapped Richard on the shoulder delightedly. "Aye, brother, just enough. Let's ride, see if we can flush any foxes from their dens."

And as they picked up pace, Edward's thoughts flashed to Anne. His triumph now would be perfect if she were waiting for him back at Westminster. And by God, he'd relish both tourneys to come. And in their private combat, she was the sweetest prize of all.

Chapter Thirty-eight

January passed slowly at Burning Norton. Anne found the rhythm of the house monotonous after the bustle and intrigue of the court, but there was comfort, too, in this simpler world, for it had no hidden meanings.

For the few visitors who braved the winter weather and arrived at the farm, Alicia and Giles kept up the fiction that Anne was a cousin of Lady Margaret's, wintering over at Burning Norton before continuing her journey farther north in the spring. Thus, gradually, the feeling of fear and urgency ebbed away and Anne learned not to expect that each new day would bring news from London.

Being a kind woman, Alicia did her best not to pry into the mystery of her guest's past, yet at night she and Giles spoke in low voices of what Mathew's motives must be in sending the two women to hide on their farm when Anne so clearly had such a heavy burden of unspoken fear to carry.

But the short unvarying days moved on, and January gave way to February while Anne found she could keep thought and fear at bay with the work of her hands. One particular afternoon in the first week of the new month she had set to and carded, teased, and spun so much wool into fine thread, that Alicia was astonished.

"Truly, lady, you're the best worker I've ever had, but there's no need, you've done much more than enough."

Anne laughed. "It's so long since I've spun. I fear you are being kind."

Alicia eyed the skeins of fine woolen thread and the waiting pile of uncarded fleece with a shake of her head. "Well, at least we should give you something else to do; work that seems endless is bad for the soul. If the weather is fine tomorrow we shall go up on the moors. Perhaps we can gather goose-wort from the beck. They yield a good dark red when boiled long and slow with ashes, and we can weave you material for a red kirtle from all that you've spun."

A sudden commotion from the inner ward outside broke through their quiet conversation. "Visitors? Now, who . . ." Alicia and her guests hurried to take off their rough, sacking work aprons as men's voices were heard. Giles was bringing someone up the stairs.

A gust of cold air found its way around the screens as the entrance door was thrust open, and a moment later Giles appeared accompanied by several men muffled to the eyes in their black cloaks. "Alicia . . . we have guests."

There are moments in a life that are remembered like pictures, like tableaux. For Anne, the sight of a stranger unwinding his cloak to reveal the particolored blue and gold tunic emblazoned with leopards and lilies was one such moment, for she knew, deep in her core, that her life would change in this instant.

"Mistress Anne?" The man had a deep, slow voice and he looked at the three women in front of him for only a moment before he confidently stepped forward and addressed Anne directly.

"My master, the king, has commanded that I escort you to Westminster. We are instructed to leave immediately."

There was nothing Anne could say; fear and agonizing joy clamored equally. Alicia spoke for her.

"You've had a long ride, sir, and you will need warmth and food. Let me take you to the kitchen where we have both. Mistress Anne must have a little time to gather her things and make her good-byes."

Getting over her shock at not only seeing a king's messenger and his men in her hall, but hearing this extraordinary news, Alicia hurried forward to sweep the men away, buying a little time for the girl to think. For weeks she'd longed to ask questions of Anne, but now the time for explanations was gone. She had her own family and household to protect, not just her mysterious guest.

Meanwhile, Deborah said nothing, but quietly seated herself beside the fire, twirling a spindle and winding the thread with hypnotic rhythm. Anne whirled around to confront her.

"Deborah, did you see this?"

"I've been given nothing, though I've tried to see often enough since we've been here." Deborah's tone was grim.

Anne could not trust herself to speak as pictures, unasked, crowded her own mind: frightened faces, drawn swords, blood—and the sound of crying, so real it might have been from a man, or a woman, standing there beside her. She was back in the battlefield of her dream, back in the dream of Edward.

She shivered. The Feast of Saint Valentine loomed and she was going back to London, to the king, and a battle of another kind.

London was a buzzing hive and the palace in a rushing bustle as the small party of soldiers escorting Anne and Deborah arrived close to vespers. The women were hurried into the palace by one of the lesser-used gates near the river and, once inside the warren of buildings, taken to a small, sparsely furnished suite of rooms. A silent servant deposited wooden buckets of hot water together with linen towels as the captain of the escort pointed to a large wooden coffer and nodded to Anne.

"For you, Lady." He left, and both women heard the key turn in the lock.

There was an exquisite dress carefully folded inside the coffer, and as Deborah shook out the tissue-of-gold bodice, the lustrous black velvet skirt sewn all over with pearls, a small vellum packet sealed with plain red wax fell to the floor. Breaking the seal, Anne found a simple message: "Hurry, I dream of you." It was signed with one word, "Edward."

Anne looked at Deborah in confusion.

"He doesn't know?" Deborah grimaced, but agreed that this was a lover's note, not that of a vengeful king.

Anne laughed shakily. There was irony in the beautiful dress, the longing behind his words; all the way on their freezing journey south she had been tossed between passion and dread. Longing to see the king, dread of what he would say to her. Now, as the hairs stood up on the nape of her neck, she forced herself to think what this clandestine meeting would mean. He meant them to be lovers—the game was over. Or perhaps it was beginning in earnest.

Very well. He had unwittingly provided her with the clothes and it would not take long to transform her into the semblance of a king's daughter . . .

Both women heard the key turn once more, then the door was thrown open by Doctor Moss. At last, a friend! Anne smiled a relieved welcome.

"Doctor Moss! How good it is to see you." For a moment the man looked uncomfortable, yet he bowed gracefully, and smiled charmingly.

"I should like the opportunity to speak with you a little later, Mistress Anne, but you are expected and we must hurry."

Moss swung a black velvet cloak around Anne's shoulders, adjusting the hood so that it covered nearly all her face, then stood back and bowed for her to accompany him, waving Deborah back into the room. When Anne went to protest Moss shook his head. "No. This is a meeting for you alone."

Again that note of discomfort. He would not meet her eye, and fear contracted Anne's gut as if she had been punched in the belly. Suddenly she understood: Moss had his own game running and was not to be trusted. Wit alone would save Deborah and herself; and so she said not another word as she matched her pace to his.

Very quickly Anne saw that they were avoiding the most populated parts of the vast building of Westminster. In the distance she could hear music and shouting; somewhere there was a feast and, for a moment, nostalgia swept over her. They'd all be there, she supposed, Jehanne, Evelyn, even Rose. She shook her head impatiently, grimacing. Things had reached a pretty pass, indeed, if she was nostalgic for Rose!

Soon they arrived at the top of a flight of stairs in an ancient, little-used part of the palace. Before them was an oak door that Doctor Moss knocked at once, then twice, then once again. The door opened and there stood Edward, tall and magnificent, dressed in tawny velvet and glittering with jewels. He stood back, unspeaking, his eyes roaming Anne's face and body for one long moment, the expression on his face unreadable.

"Leave us, Moss." His voice filled the girl's head like the sound of the sea. She didn't even notice the doctor close the door as he left.

"The cloak, Anne. Take it off." The king's tone was strange, constrained, but somehow she found the strength to stand straighter, to look at him directly, though her heart was running faster than a hind at the hunt. Silently she undid the silk cord at her neck and dropped the garment from her shoulders. The king's breath exhaled in one long, slow sigh.

The silence stretched between them as he ambled toward the braziers that stood on each side of a magnificent bed made up with high soft pillows and a purple velvet coverlet. Holding out his hands to warm them, he spoke with his back turned to her.

"Why did you run away from me, Anne?"

It was hard not to look at the bed when she answered him. "Sire, it was clear I could not stay."

She closed her eyes—she could not help herself; and saw the pictures. She and he, together, naked . . .

He turned to look at her. "Have you thought of me since last we met?"

She almost smiled.

"I have tried not to, sire."

Casually, he sauntered toward her.

"And why is that?"

She *was* smiling now, but it was very hard.

"You know why."

He was closer to her now—if she chose to, she could touch him.

"I dreamed of you. All night. All day."

That was like a knife in her side. "Then, sire, I am so sorry for you. Truly sorry."

The exchange between them was measured, deliberate—volley and countervolley—and both of them knew it was a prologue. But to what?

"Anne, do you remember the wager we made?"

Close. Closer yet.

"Yes." She offered nothing more.

His voice was low. "The Feast of Saint Valentine. You made me a promise."

"Sire, it was your wager, not mine."

"But you agreed. The tourney is close, so close, and tonight, I think . . . I will test your resolve."

Like fire, like pain, he obliterated the tiny space between them instantly, and in one burning moment, one trembling breath, he pulled her in to his body and, gods help her, Anne responded, kissing him so deeply, matching him moment for aching moment until—her body locked rigid.

"No."

There was a tiny sound: a faint and delicate hiss as a brazier exhaled and the coals burned sudden red. They were apart now. He had his hands on her shoulders as he looked into her eyes.

"How can you be so disloyal to your king?"

"I am disloyal to another king. To my father."

"Your father? I thought you had no father?"

A cold finger touched Anne's heart. There was a moment of choice and she could have stayed silent, but . . . she'd gone too far now. Out of fear? Out of pride? There was complete silence for a moment, then she sighed.

"No, Edward. My father is alive." She used his name deliberately.

He said nothing for one long moment, then a wary smile touched his lips. "Who is your father, Anne?" He said it very softly.

"Henry VI. The king that was." She was looking at him straight, unsmiling, unblinking. After being fatherless for so long she would not lie about her descent now.

There was silence. And then he smiled at her again, yet it was bleak, so bleak. "And so, Henry V is your grandsire, yes?"

Anne nodded—just one nod.

The meaning of that nod was a charged current between them.

Another frozen moment and then the king began to laugh. And laugh and laugh. Great gusts that rang around the room. But then he stopped quickly and seized her face between both his hands, turning it to the light of the windows and the fires. First one side, then the other, looking at her as if to learn each feature for all time. Her hands flew to his but though she was physically strong, she was not stronger than he, and they were both breathing hard—with anger now, not passion.

"I see nothing here that tells me who you might be." He was very controlled. "Unless you are a traitor."

"Traitor? No. I want nothing from you, but there is proof. Letters. Everything I have said is true, and if I am harmed, or any of my people, those letters will be given to someone who is not your enemy now but will be should you deal with me unkindly."

He dropped his hands as she played her bluff, utter certainly in her words. But now Anne saw Edward's real power for the first time. His face was very cold, eyes of black jet looked down on her indifferently.

"Be careful, lady, be very careful. I know how to deal with plots against my throne. Moss!"

A moment and Moss was inside the door with them.

"Moss, you played me a trick. This woman is a traitor. Secure her."

The king stamped out of the open door past the stunned Doctor Moss, his face shut and fierce but very pale. Buying time to gather his wits, Moss bowed to Anne and stood back, indicating she should precede him out of the door.

Without acknowledging Moss's presence, Anne swept up the black cloak and tossed it to him, her gesture plain: she would not hide her face this time.

Moss tasted fear in his mouth, like acid, as he led Anne back to her rooms. He'd returned Anne to the king, but in this he had, unwittingly, overreached himself. But how?!

When Anne disappeared from court, Moss, being suspicious, had become convinced she'd used Mathew Cuttifer's help to hide from the king, with Jehanne's active assistance. Careful bribes within Blessing House had told him what he needed. Mathew Cut-tifer had clandestinely sent his wife's previously unknown "cousin" and her woman to his lands in the north; and the cousin's description matched Anne's. This was explosive information.

Yet events were moving fast at court, including the queen's pregnancy. Elizabeth was close to five months and her condition was swiftly becoming complicated, just as it had been with the last child. As the queen sickened, she cast around to blame someone, anyone, for her fear and discomfort. Moss was the logical candidate. He bought time by deflecting the queen's ire onto Jehanne, but knew he needed help to manage this pregnancy and secure his place. Specifically, he had to have Anne's knowledge of simples and painkillers at his service, so her importance to him doubled. He played his card. He let Edward know that Mathew Cuttifer was helping Anne to remain in hiding.

The king, refusing to believe Anne had been taken willingly out of his life, was enraged. He'd summoned Mathew and threatened him: produce Anne quickly and his life, and commercial interests, would be spared. Fail in this, and every particle of his trade, every monopoly he controlled, would be utterly destroyed by the servants of the Crown, on precise instructions from their king. He'd stopped short of carrying out his threats because he still needed the merchant's support against the uprising he feared—and Mathew was the key to keeping the London guilds on his side—but his sword hovered over Blessing House, and all under that roof knew it.

Poor Mathew. Clarence was outwardly returned to favor and court gossip said that fragile harmony was now restored between the king and Warwick. What could he do? Though Anne had not seen them, he had the letters that proved her identity, but so far as he knew, no one else, certainly not the king, knew of their existence, and how could he reveal them now? This was a terrifying game, but he had allowed it to begin.

And Moss, meanwhile, had no idea how high the stakes had risen. Several times he tried to speak to Anne as they hurried through the darkened palace together, but she refused to respond, though, from time to time when he addressed her, she glanced at him silently. Her look, compounded of contempt, anger, and yes, pity, unsettled him profoundly, as did the king's last words.

Traitor? How could Anne be a traitor unless she'd refused to go to bed with Edward and the king had taken it savagely amiss. Something, Moss knew, that was much unlike Edward's usual attitude where women were concerned. Normally, he shrugged and moved on to the next willing girl.

It was late now and the palace was shutting down, preparing for the night. As he and Anne climbed the last set of stairs leading to the rooms she'd been assigned, he heard a girl's voice call out, "Anne! Anne, is that you?" And before he could prevent it, he watched helplessly as Anne turned and then ran toward Evelyn, her closest friend from among the queen's servitors.

It was hard to know who was the most shocked. Anne clung to the other girl for a moment wordlessly, but then she collected herself, stood back and smiled warmly.

"Evelyn. Don't be fearful. See, I'm back." But the other girl just stared at her, speechless, eyes huge in her white face. Anne laughed shortly. "No, I'm not a ghost . . . Evelyn, for my sake, say something!"

Evelyn flicked a glance at Doctor Moss as he reached out to take Anne's arm, but before she could reply, Anne turned on him, all the suppressed terror she had experienced in the last few days distilling into white rage. "How dare you." It was barely a whisper, but the raw power behind her words hit them both like a blow and Anne's shadow suddenly seemed immense on the walls behind them—flickering, threatening to engulf them both. Evelyn covered her eyes with a sob as Moss dropped his hand, shaken.

"I thought you were dead." Evelyn finally managed to gasp the sentence out. "You disappeared—and there were rumors . . . and the queen became so ill. Then, Dame Jehanne . . ." She dropped her hands, looked up at Anne, suddenly without the words to say it.

Fear congealed in Anne's chest, a massive icy lump. "Where is she, where is Dame Jehanne?"

But it was Doctor Moss who answered. "She has been accused of cursing the queen's child. She is in the Tower."

"Cursing the queen's child? Sorcery? I do not understand. Where has this evil rumor come from? Tell me, Moss." In no sense was her tone threatening and yet when Anne turned her eyes toward Doctor Moss, he felt fear. The flat confidence with which she spoke now hinted at a power he thought she could not possibly possess. It was a warning: be careful how you deal with me.

Evelyn spoke, words flooding out on a tide of tears. "The queen, the queen has been sick. For after we came back from Windsor, the baby seemed not to be well in her womb, and Doctor Moss said . . . he said someone might have cursed the child. Suspicion fell on Dame Jehanne." Evelyn looked fearfully at Doctor Moss. "And you were not there; no one could calm the queen without your simples. Oh, Anne, it's been so frightening. For a while it seemed we, Dorcas, Rose, Lily, and I—we would all be sent to the Tower as well. But then the king came home . . . and he does not think ill of us—yet. I do not serve the queen anymore though. The chamberlain has put us all in different places in the palace. I'm in the laundry. And glad of it!"

Anne turned to Moss. "Doctor Moss, I have a question for you. How did the king know where to look for me?"

He looked down; he could not face her eyes. For the space of two heartbeats, Anne gazed at him calmly then turned to her friend. "Evelyn, there is much I must say to Doctor Moss and you should go . . . Do not speak of seeing me to anyone. Do you understand?"

It was said kindly but the other girl's terrified look said all that was needed; she scooped her skirts up in one hand, but before she scuttled into the darkness she kissed Anne's hands. "I am your friend, Anne. And Jehanne's." One last frightened look at the doctor standing impassive in the shadows, and Evelyn was gone.

In the silence that followed, Moss found himself sweating as Anne gazed at him steadily. Finally, she spoke. "Doctor Moss, I believe you must make good what you have done."

The man found himself staring into the eyes of the girl and a slow shiver worked its way down his spine. Those eyes were pitiless.

Chapter Thirty-nine

It was a long night at the palace and a busy one for Doctor Moss. His interview with Anne—there was no other word to describe it—had been hard for him to bear. She had called him to account for his treachery in a way he had not experienced since the monks beat him as a boy.

He'd been perversely glad she'd realized what he'd done, of how he'd had the power to twist her life to his design, but after enduring her eyes for the last hour, he was crushed by equal parts of fear and self-loathing.

Unlike most men, he had a detached interest in why people did as they did and generally understood himself very well, but during Anne's brief time at court, this girl had come to mean something to him—and that something threatened his carefully won place beside the king, even though he tried to deny it to himself. In the beginning, of course, he'd thought to please Edward by arranging to bring Anne to the palace. But then, as he'd seen her fall in love with the king, the green worm of envy had begun to grow in his gut. As he had allowed himself to know Anne better, he'd become increasingly angry about the corrosive tension between his self-interest in serving the king, and his desire for this girl himself. After all, where was it ordained that one man should be given everything and others, of greater natural ability, nothing?

Yes, he'd been prepared, during his slow ascension to this present that shimmered with promise, to subsume all his needs in those of the king, because graceful, amusing subservience had taken him a long way, a very long way, and could take him further, while he remained useful. Women had been extraneous nuisances during his urgent rise, a passing means of slaking lust, nothing more, so he'd connived to bring Anne back to the court for the king—and his own advantage. But giving Anne to the king, as he'd promised, and waiting obediently outside the room in which he presumed that Edward was making love to the girl, had done violence to his own long-shriveled ability to love. It had been anguish straining to hear, through the stone walls, if the girl was giving herself to Edward. Yet the shocking moment when the king had called her traitor, and the contempt in her eyes when she understood Moss himself had betrayed her, had been even worse: they were salt in the wounds of a lash.

Unknowingly, Moss had raised the stakes to dizzying heights. He saw that now, for Anne had told him who she was. And Moss knew then that what he had begun could consume them all unless Anne escaped.

Then Anne told him what must be done . . .

It was very late, and the new abbot of Westminster Abbey, Doctor John Millington, was not best pleased to be roused in the dead part of this cold winter's night when his lay servant said that a court functionary, a Doctor Moss, was refusing to be turned away without seeing him.

Coals were still burning in the fireplace of the Jerusalem Chamber but the rest of his lodgings were stone cold, so the abbot instructed the remains of the fire be built up again as he contemplated this unexpected visitor. He had met Doctor Moss at court, knew he was high in favor with the queen and trusted by the king, and it was for these reasons he had consented to see him. But nothing in his previous experience prepared him for what was to come.

Wearily Moss rubbed his eyes, buying time as he gathered strength for what must be done. Then:

"Lord Abbot, do you believe in destiny?"

Millington concealed his surprise. "We are all in the hands of

God, Doctor Moss. Only He knows where our paths must go. But yes, I believe there is a road each must walk."

Moss got up and stood warming himself by the fire as he considered what he needed to say. "Well then, I believe it is destiny that brings me here tonight, for I now know things that are a painful burden to carry, and why should that be so? I am an insignificant man, but I am here to ask sanctuary for a daughter of the former king."

John Millington thought he had misheard. "You said a daughter?"

The doctor nodded and only the desperation in the man's eyes convinced the abbot to hear him out; even so, it was many hours before John Millington ceased grilling Doctor Moss about the facts of Anne's case. Indeed, when he was told about the letters stolen from the Abbey treasure house, he'd insisted that they go down into the undercroft together. Of course, no physical evidence of the letters remained and there was no way of telling if the great chests had been disturbed, but still, Doctor Moss had so plainly placed his own life in danger by this visit and was so convinced, and convincing, of the facts of the girl's case that the abbot agreed the woman might claim sanctuary in the abbey while the matter was sifted. There was also the question of Doctor Moss himself and what he would do once Edward found out about his part in the unfolding events.

Just before dawn, Anne and Deborah slipped out of the palace with Doctor Moss and hurried on foot toward the great dark bulk of the Abbey Church. The abbot had arranged for Anne to be housed in his own lodgings rather than the guesthouse of the Abbey. Discretion was something that could be offered for a time, though monks gossiped just like other men, and it would not be long before word began to circulate about the mysterious, nameless lady who had fled from the king's wrath into sanctuary at the Abbey.

John Millington, if he were honest with himself, was burning with curiosity to meet the woman who claimed to be the daughter of Henry VI. However, he had politics to think of. He could not have refused sanctuary—Moss had known that—but the king would surely watch to see how it was administered and on that might very well depend the future financial health of his abbey and its brothers' well-being.

So the abbot was reserved on meeting the girl who was brought to him in the Jerusalem Chamber and did his best not to let her beauty sway him. He saw a girl, richly dressed, with a fine body and fierce eyes.

Anne, from her curtsy, looked up to see a worldly man in his late thirties, balding and well padded with flesh, but whose glance was disconcertingly direct as he asked her to explain why she believed she could call herself the daughter of a king.

In telling the story once more, if she had ever doubted the gravity of her situation, it was brought home once again.

The abbot was reflective. He was not naïve or foolish. If what this girl said was true he housed, under his roof, a potentially potent source of social unrest—were the story to get out. He looked calmly at the lovely face in front of him.

If the story were to get out . . .

He needed to talk to the king, but in the meantime, the sanctuary of the Abbey of Saint Edward the Confessor King was Anne's by right.

Chapter Forty

The queen had had a restless and uncomfortable night and her new body servants were feeling the effects. In this new pregnancy Elizabeth was between five and six months gone but the child had just quickened, in itself incontrovertible proof of sorcery: she should have felt the baby move long ago.

This morning, too, as an added source of annoyance and fear, Doctor Moss could not be found, and everyone in her rooms suffered while he was hunted for.

As Elizabeth lay in her bed, clutching a crucifix to her distended belly, self-pity curdled into rage. Never had she felt more frightened; she had lost the king's affections, she was certain of that. He was distant with her, barely troubled to come to her bed these last weeks since his return from the north, using the pregnancy as an excuse! Now as her women coaxed her into a new dress of mulberry-colored velvet—her own color and becoming to her skin—she made up her mind to speak frankly to Edward. She would be careful, but surely it was best to lance the boil that was growing out of her uneasiness and his detachment, before it did some lasting damage to their marriage. She would talk to William Hastings; he would know how best to deal with Edward. Besides, all this must be so bad for the baby, Edward must see that.

· · ·

To his courtiers, Edward also seemed in a rare foul mood as he busied himself with plans for the tourney. In two days' time he would lead twelve knights against the Earl of Warwick to break lances in honor of his love for Elizabeth, who would preside as the Queen of Love. Now, in his quarters, William brought him word that Anne was gone, escaped—and Doctor Moss with her.

Edward forced all expression from his face and gave orders for William to find her; she was a traitor and would have a traitor's end. Males were beheaded of course, if not hung and quartered; she, as a woman, would be burned. William had never seen the king so angry and was stunned to hear Anne called a traitor. But as he turned to obey, a herald asked permission to admit a brother from the Abbey who had private letters from the abbot for the king— urgent private letters.

Some instinct made Edward stop William from leaving while he nodded absently at the brother, who backed out of his presence after delivering the packet of vellum into the king's own hands. Ripping through the scarlet seal on the outside, the king found two documents. One closed and also sealed, the other a sheet of vellum merely folded. The folded document was a letter from the abbot, briefly telling him that Anne had sought sanctuary, as had Doctor Moss. It also said there were matters that must be discussed between the king and himself of the utmost gravity and importance for the safety of the kingdom.

The other letter, sealed, was from Anne to the king. In it she told Edward of the decision she had taken to seek sanctuary, because she did not trust him. The tone was simple and direct and she offered no excuse or explanation. It was a letter from one prince to another. In it she addressed him as "Edward by the Grace of God, King of England" and signed herself "Anne de Bohun, by the Grace of God, daughter of Henry VI, former king of England." She reminded him that proof of who she was existed and would be produced for him, and also bound him to treat Mathew, Lady Margaret, and Jehanne well on his oath as a Christian king, while she prayed for guidance as to what God wanted her to do next.

It was a masterly letter. There were no demands, only statements about the duty of a king to treat all the people God had given into his care with equal mercy. She had called his bluff.

Wordlessly, the king handed the letters to William, who flushed red and then white when he read the contents.

"You must speak to her, William. If she will not leave the sanctuary . . . well, something must be arranged." William locked glances with his master; there was no mistaking his tone. She would obey the king or the sanctuary would be breached. William, cynic that he was, crossed himself quickly. This would be blasphemy.

Anne was trying to sink herself in silent prayer when the abbot's servant, Brother Walter, announced she had a visitor. Closing the little Book of Hours she had been lent by the abbot, she got up from the prie-dieu in the Jerusalem Chamber and stood waiting quietly for William Hastings. Snow was falling thickly beyond the casements of the abbot's beautiful reception room and the glass in the windows was cold to the touch, though the low-ceilinged chamber was cozy from the fire.

William had not seen Anne for some weeks now, since the Christmas revels in fact, and marveled that six weeks could make such a difference in a person's life. When he'd last noticed her, she'd been a servant that the king had a fancy for. Now she stood before him composed and elegant, finely dressed in discreet dark blue velvet, the daughter of a king.

"Lord William, you are well, I trust?" Even her voice had changed. How could a girl of seventeen sound so decided and speak to him with such implied authority? Rattled, he swept off his hat and bowed deeply to cover his discomfort.

"I am, mistress. Very well." She sat as if it were the most natural thing in the world—again he was taken aback. He was the chamberlain of England, he took precedence over nearly everyone at court except members of the blood family—and the bishops, of course. Normally people waited for him to sit. Was that a slightly mischievous glint he saw in her eye as she waved him to a chair slightly lower than her own?

"Do you come from the king?" She sounded calm, one hand

smoothing the nap of her dress so that the rich fabric caught lights from the fire in its lustrous depths.

Her directness left him no escape. "Yes, mistress. I do. I have this for you."

He had to get up if he was to hand her the letter, she showed no sign of rising to take it from him. "I shall read it presently. Hot wine, Lord William? The abbot keeps a good cellar here; sanctuary is pleasant in this Abbey . . ."

"Thank you. I should appreciate that—the day is cold."

Anne picked up a little bell and rang it, but before the last clear notes had finished, Walter hurried in. He was only too delighted to help serve this beautiful and mysterious lady for the abbot.

"Brother Walter, please fetch hot wine for the Lord Chamberlain. And ask Deborah to attend me here." A meditative silence followed the man's exit that Anne made no attempt to fill as she stared into the flames.

William saw that he would have to be the one to speak. "Lady, no good will come of opposing the king."

"No good, Lord William? How can that be, if the will of the king is contrary to God's law?"

The chamberlain was so astonished by her calm, he forgot to be angry at her words. "Anne, the king wishes you no harm, but he must protect his kingdom from any more upset. You must see that. This is his duty, to his people. He is the Lord's anointed king."

Now she turned on him fiercely. "And what about my father? Was he not anointed too?"

That silenced the man for a moment; there was no answer he could offer that would expunge the fact that she was right. He tried another tack. "Lady, will you not read the king's letter?"

Walter returned with a wooden platter. On it was food and a large tankard filled up with wine that steamed and smelled of cloves and cinnamon bark from the far-distant spice islands.

She thought for a moment, looking at him meditatively. Then nodded. "Very well. It shall be as you wish."

He rose and handed the letter to her, and as he ate and drank, she broke the red wafer sealing it and smoothed out the single sheet on her lap. William half closed his eyes; the picture she made in her dark dress with her white hands touching the cream vellum was very appealing. Skin like that, smooth, clean, and white, was rare. It would feel very pleasing under his hand. Perhaps when the king was tired of this girl he could . . . He shook his head to clear it. This was no ordinary woman to tumble anymore. This body, these eyes, that mouth—they were all a distraction from the danger she represented. The sooner she was found a loyal husband, or a nunnery, the safer they'd all be.

The king's letter was brief, tense, and distant. "Madam, your decision to take sanctuary was ill-advised. You will not help your cause, for soon you must leave the safety of the Abbey, and where will you go then? If you see sense, you shall be offered one more chance. On receipt of the letters confirming your identity, an honorable marriage will be arranged for you with a man of property; the Cuttifers shall live at peace and Jehanne will be permitted to retire to her family's holdings. All this provided you agree to sign a contract that bars you from speaking of any blood connection you might have had with the former king during the whole of your lifetime, including in the confessional.

"If you fail to agree with the terms by the day of the Saint Valentine's tourney, then you will never be offered such consideration again, and you and yours will be confirmed and detained as traitors. Once out of sanctuary, you will be banished from the kingdom and never permitted to return. And you will be responsible for the deaths of your friends, for they will assuredly be burned." It was signed "Edward R."

It took all Anne's self-control to show nothing on her face as she read the king's words. He had ignored much of what she had said in her letter to him, and the spare clarity of his tone, the unsentimental phrases, reinforced the strength of the adversary she had taken on. Carefully, she folded the letter and stood up, allowing William a moment to scramble to his feet before she said, "Please tell the king I shall think on his words. However, you may tell him that marriage is not part of my plans at this time."

William's heart squeezed in his chest. Her tone was polite, distant, but firm. The implication was there: Edward could wait as long as he liked but she did not intend to fall in with his plans for her future.

As a soldier, William knew how important it was never to show a weak face to the enemy—to be ruthless was more important than to be right. This girl had an iron core. She didn't get it from her father, but her grandfather had had it, knew how to use it.

And where Mathew and Margaret were concerned, and Jehanne, well, it was clear she was daring Edward to act against them. There was no obedience in this girl, none at all.

Chapter Forty-one

Two days before the tourney and Elizabeth Wydeville was restless and annoyed with everything. Green was the color of love and since she was to be the Queen of Love above the lists on Saint Valentine's Day, she'd had an elaborate dress made in heavy green velvet. However, the weight of the skirt and train made it difficult to walk. It was also a very expensive dress, even by her standards, because she'd had thirteen great emeralds sewn onto the bodice in honor of her husband and the twelve who would fight with him in the affray. And this was a problem. Lately the king had grown tedious about the matter of her household expenses—something he never had before—and she was in despair, taking this as yet another example of his waning affection.

So it was a welcome distraction from her worries when her new senior body attendant, Marceline—a timid, colorless woman in her thirties—hurried in to the robing room with most intriguing news. There was a mysterious, beautiful lady in sanctuary at the Abbey—and Doctor Moss was with her. It was said that the lady was hiding from the wrath of the king, and so was Doctor Moss. The source of this information was impeccable. Marceline had it from her own brother, Walter, who waited on the abbot.

The queen scowled, and Marceline gulped. Perhaps she'd been overeager to share the information she'd been given.

"Doctor Moss had better look to his future. It is not only the wrath of the king he should fear. What is the name of this lady?" The queen's tone was frigid.

Poor, timid Marceline shuddered. "The lady's name is Anne, Your Majesty."

"Anne?" The queen was very still for a moment. It was a common name, of course, but it had resonance. Oh, yes, it had resonance.

The king and William Hastings were poring over a set of rutters, maps of sea-trading routes, in Edward's tiny private room when, to the surprise of both men, the queen was announced. The queen never visited her husband in his private quarters unless invited.

Edward signaled that William should take the rutters and leave. They would revisit them later when both had more leisure to explore the intriguing idea of a sea passage to India that went west rather than east. He settled his face into an approximate mask of welcome.

Elizabeth glided into the king's little office with a glittering smile on her face. He knew that look and it made him impatient— it meant she was angry but biding her time, waiting for the moment she could play her hand to the maximum advantage.

"Well, madam, this is an honor for your husband." He mustered the courtesy to bow deeply, and sweep her into his own carved chair.

"Well, husband, I've had an idea."

He knew that tone as well, it was sweet as honey and there was much display of fine white teeth as she smiled—she'd escaped the fate of many women with more than one child and kept her teeth thus far. That tone meant significant trouble.

"Husband, I wish to go to the Abbey to contemplate the Holy Girdle of the Mother of God, so that I may ask the blessing and protection of Mary for our baby. How fortunate I was that the good brothers let me gaze upon it when our daughter was being born. It gave me such strength. I wish us to thank them together . . . the people would enjoy the sight of us united, at prayer . . ."

"A worthy thought, Elizabeth." He had learned not to oppose her ideas at first discussion; she sulked too long. "When would you like to go to the Abbey?"

"Why, now, this morning. William told me last night that today would be easy for you. I hope you don't mind, but I've let the ,new abbot know to expect us shortly." She smiled up at him shyly, the picture of a gentle, obedient wife.

It was only rarely in his life that Edward had experienced events spiraling out of his control. Normally he took the forward stance, others followed, but now he hesitated and that was enough for the queen.

"William, call the servants! The king is coming with me to pray at the Abbey."

It seemed he was, for his wife whirled him out of his private rooms surrounded by a small train of courtiers, and very soon he was walking beside her through Westminster Hall and out across the abbey garth. He could have turned back, could have made an excuse about unfinished business, but there was a terrible drag in his belly toward the Abbey and the abbot's lodgings. Truthfully, he burned to see Anne again, and if the queen were to be the means . . . He shrugged, curiously fatalistic. Elizabeth had thrown the dice. Did she know? She never gambled unless she thought she could win, but his history said he had excellent luck at games of chance.

Brother Walter was all atwitter in the Abbot's lodgings. He had heard that the queen and king were praying together in the Lady Chapel before the reliquary that contained the Girdle of the Holy Virgin—and that shortly his master, John Millington, would be entertaining the royal couple in the Jerusalem Chamber. This posed Walter and his master a problem, for Anne was in sanctuary because of the king. The question had become, how should this awkward and unexpected series of events be handled?

Anne solved the problem for both men. She would withdraw to her sleeping quarters—a spartan little monk's cell up under the eaves of the abbot's lodging—and wait out the visit. There was no need for John Millington to fear the embarrassment of her presence. And no one had to prompt Doctor Moss to make himself scarce.

So now, as the brief, bright morning wore away, the queen and her husband had arrived with their suite and were sipping mulled

Burgundy wine and eating sweetmeats in the abbot's finest room, as discreet chatter from their party created a pleasant hum. Elizabeth was at her captivating best—dignified but warmly affectionate to her husband, charming to the abbot—while the king sank further and further into silence as he stood by the fire beside his wife's chair.

He could sense Anne in this room. There was a piece of embroidery on a gate-legged table that must be hers, and try as he might to stop, his eyes wandered far too often to the door that led into the abbot's private quarters.

"Lord Abbot, we hear you have a guest in sanctuary. A beautiful and mysterious lady. Who can she be? Do we know her? Perhaps she would like to join us for a beaker of this excellent wine." The queen was light, flirtatious, smiling radiantly around the room as if to say, well, new, here is a new game for us all to play!

The abbot was deeply uncomfortable. Sanctuary was a holy right available for all Christians. To speak as the queen was doing—as if implying that his sheltering a penitent within his Abbey was equivalent to housing a charming house guest—was to trivialize the sanctity of what was offered. And Anne was here to escape the king himself. Edward saw the abbot's discomfort and saved him the need to reply.

"It is Doctor Millington's business, my dear, to whom he grants sanctuary. And now I fear I must return to my work. If you wish to pray more, I shall leave this suite of gentlemen to escort you back to the palace, when you are ready."

It was seen by all in that room, including the queen, that the king's patience was finally exhausted with the little charade that was taking place. Without another glance at Elizabeth, Edward strode from the chamber, quickly followed by William Hastings, leaving the queen to bite her lips in frustration at her husband's sudden, graceless exit. As usual, he'd made a tactical retreat—a sensitive feint during combat but aggravating within the field of marriage. She would question him later, back at the palace.

But the king did not go back to his rooms at the palace. He walked quickly across the abbot's private yard and through the cloisters, startling the brothers, then strode down the stairs and along the dark tunnel of the undercroft. These were the earliest parts of the

Abbey, hundreds of years old, and they housed the Chapel of the Pyx, the door of which was hastily opened for him by the cellarer he'd found in the cloisters. Dismissing the monk, Edward turned to William with a simple instruction: "Bring Anne to me."

William generally knew better than to question his master in such a mood—he'd rarely seen him so angry—but he was unwise enough to try to express an opinion. "Sire, if the queen is still in the abbot's lodgings . . ."

Edward looked piercingly at his chamberlain. "I'll wait."

In the hour that followed, his anger dwindled and his impatience grew and grew until he was pacing the low-vaulted chamber like an animal that had not been fed. Finally the door of the chamber was eased open by the abbot himself and behind him was the cloaked and veiled figure of a woman.

The abbot was very nervous and it took all his skill as a courtier to hide his fear from the king. "Sire, the lady you have asked to see has agreed to this meeting. I shall remain present as God's vicar of this place."

The king shot him a fierce glance. "No, Master Abbot, you shall not. The business this lady and I have will remain between us, and God."

For all his graceful ways, the abbot was not without courage, and he was the ruler of this place, not the king, because he was the pope's direct representative and, in theory, answered to the pope alone. He spoke up bravely. "Lady Anne, you have heard the king. However, you are in my care. What is your wish?"

"I will speak to the king alone. He will not harm me."

The abbot had gone as far as prudence, and his conscience, had said he must. Silently, he bowed to them both, sketched a cross between them, and then left.

For a moment neither the king nor Anne said or did anything, but then, in three swift strides Edward had covered the flags between them, ripped the veil from her face, and pulled her to him so savagely the breath was crushed from her chest. He plunged his mouth down on hers and from that moment the world dissolved.

Anne had the strength to fight much, but not this. Her rage and fear were gone.

She tried to step back but he would not let her. He pulled her over to one of the long stone benches that lined the treasure house walls, clearing a place for them to sit, oblivious to the fate of the golden plates and chalices as they rolled out of the way. He pulled her to him harder, urgent hands hunting under her cloak, running down her back, her hips, as they stood body to body.

"Anne, Anne—it doesn't have to be like this. We are not enemies. Let me help you. Oh, sweet Jesus . . ." He groaned with mingled elation and despair as she stood there trembling. Anne closed her eyes as he kissed her throat, as his hands moved over her breasts and the curve between waist and hip. She'd said nothing because she had nothing to say—no words could frame the confusion, the love, the *ache* she felt for this man.

He knew it, of course. With shaking fingers he undid the clasp of her cloak and spread the rich fabric out behind her over the bench. Inexorably he lifted her, laid her down as his fingers found the lacings of her gown. This was a man skilled with arrow strings, with the jesses of a hawk; he made short work of what he found. She did not stop him. In the strange world she inhabited, the world bounded by the smell of his skin, the feel of his velvet cotehardie, his mouth on hers, she knew that what was happening was inevitable. She fully welcomed him, all confusion gone. It was a drug to them both, this relationship, and after the turmoil of the last weeks, she just wanted this moment, wanted him.

And so she, the daughter of a king, and he, the son of a duke, helped each other take the clothes from their bodies in the cold still air of the treasure house of the Abbey. Soon she lay on the black velvet with no covering but her long hair and she blushed as his eyes roamed over her body. But that body was a gift—a gift between equals—and she would not be ashamed. She smiled into his eyes proudly. "There is much to say between you and me . . . but not now," she said and reached her arms up to him trustingly.

He was dazzled—but he'd wanted this moment, too, and now that it had come, wild joy ran through him, for it seemed he might have won and he wanted to savor each second.

Carefully, he laid his full length along Anne's naked body and kissed and kissed her mouth, gathering her closer, closer, as one hand roamed her breasts, her belly, down to the cleft between her legs. She was breathing faster now, as was he, and soon, so soon, they were belly to belly as he slipped his fingers between her legs. She whimpered and he hushed her as his fingers went deeper, deeper, feeling the resistance of her hymen. The urge to follow his fingers was very strong, but delaying made his pleasure deeper and more exquisite because he knew that now, this time, she would not leave him.

Gently, he pulled Anne beneath him and she gasped as she felt him push inside her body for the first time. But he held her fast for that moment and somehow controlled himself enough to move with a steady, gradually mounting rhythm, until he felt her hymen tear—she cried out into his mouth—and then there was the rushing shock for them both as he entered her completely.

Now it was much harder for him to control himself because she felt so hot, so soft. Harder and harder, deeper and deeper—he was almost battering her now—and she was lying underneath him writhing with each stroke. He took both her buttocks in his hands and pulled her hips up to meet him as he plunged down, again and again, until she found that she had locked her legs around his lower back and was meeting him, thrust for thrust. Now she began to understand why she had ached for him, as a feeling she had never experienced before concentrated itself between her thighs, and it made her want to faint and scream and . . .

Harder he was slamming into her, slicker and faster went his fingers—for her there was pain and bliss and more bliss and more pain and . . .

He roared, and she screamed from shock and searing, sweet bliss; and for one wild moment they looked deep into each other's eyes, and then all was black.

He thought she had died, that he'd killed her, but then he felt her rib cage move and a wave of tenderness such as he'd never experienced before swept Edward, pierced him to the heart. There were tears in his eyes as he held her to him fiercely, kissed her closed lids softly, and murmured, "I love you. God help us both but this is true . . ."

• • •

When the king and Anne appeared before the abbot as he was on his knees praying in the Lady Chapel, all he could see in the flickering light of the votive candles was that the lady was pale and looked shaken. The king, too, looked different. As if a layer had been stripped away from his face, revealing a softness not normally seen. He conducted Anne into the abbot's presence as ceremoniously as if she'd been at a court audience, bowing to her deeply before he left without another word.

Anne looked up at the altar with its fine icon of the Holy Mother with her child and asked to be left alone to pray. The abbot could hardly insist on hearing what the king had said to her but his face must have given something away since she laughed kindly for a moment.

"Master Abbot, leave me to my prayers. We shall speak a little later. There is much to say, and do, now . . ."

Chapter Forty-two

The daughter of Henry VI had lived the last forty-eight hours in a daze—and she'd spent most of it on her knees apparently praying.

In truth, it had been a way to avoid people and win some time to think after the king's visit. But now, on the evening before the Saint Valentine's tourney, the fog had lifted and Anne knew what needed to be done, the choices that had to be made, and she was praying in earnest—to the Sword Mother and to Mary—the images blending into one woman's face, their voices, one voice. Hers. Her own internal chant of joy.

When did the goddess's voice end and her own begin? To be who she was, and yet to hear, like a beating drum in her brain, "I love him, he loves me, I love him, he loves me," took her to the edge of exhilaration and despair . . . yet, strangely, after all the guilt she had previously felt, none of that mattered now.

She felt no shame for what they'd done for she'd made Edward a gift out of love, freely, and it was magnificent to love so completely. Perhaps she never would again. Now there was the future, and politics to be thought of; she had become a player in a remarkable game of chess. Deborah had taught her how to play the game, in the forest, and she would use that training with Edward, for she had responsibility to protect the friends who had given her so much.

Edward, too, had experienced complete disorientation over the last two days that had driven William Hastings to distraction, for there was much still to be decided on, not least how to deal with Warwick and his affinity during the tournament. He'd tried to get the king to talk about what had happened with Anne, but for once Edward was completely silent—the experience in the Chapel of the Pyx had changed something in the king.

Normally, as William knew, Edward consumed a woman as if she were something delicious, then moved on, driven by the sensual pleasure of the hunt, the hunger to win. Sex had always been about his body and his pleasure. Elizabeth had worked that out very early, and because she was extremely skilled, clever, and beautiful, she'd kept the king's lust alive for nearly three years, a record for Edward. But Hastings knew that Anne had led the king to another aspect of himself, a quality he'd not suspected. With deep surprise Edward had experienced a spiritual bond between himself and a woman for the first time.

Edward was haunted by what had happened at the Abbey. He was frightened to call it love, though he'd said the word to Anne, but he wanted to protect and care for her. That was agonizing. Would he be strong enough, hard enough, to do what was needed for his kingdom if it meant putting her out of his life? Already William had preached the benefits of a carefully arranged marriage for Anne, or perhaps a nunnery—whether she wanted to be a nun or not. Edward smiled briefly at the thought of "Sister" Anne.

His mind teeming, Edward tried to give proper attention as his worried chamberlain walked him through the procedures for the five days of the tournament to come, focusing on dealing with Warwick and his brother George, until William unwittingly overstepped the mark. He was talking of the queen's entrance to the tournament as the Queen of Love and commented that there were some spectacularly pretty young women at court this winter season. He'd personally picked two of them to wait on the queen, sure they'd distract the king from his present cares.

Edward rounded on Hastings. What did William think he was, a child to be bought off from sulking by a sweetmeat? The king allowed himself to flame into incandescent rage, an awesome sight because it was so rare.

William understood the anger was not meant for him, but

there was no reasoning with the king at such a time. He waited quietly for the explosion to die away and then, when Edward fell silent, asked to be excused. He was needed to see that all was well with the flood of guests arriving at the palace ahead of the great banquet of welcome tonight.

Staring down on to the river beneath his windows, Edward waved assent, barely noticing when Hastings went. The short winter's day was nearly gone and the wind was cutting off the water when he opened one of his casements. It was less than two hours before he would be expected to join Elizabeth in the great hall and take part in the festivities that had been planned, but he'd never felt less like celebrating in his life. All he could see, and hear, was Anne; he just wanted the world to go away so that they could be together, so that he could hold her again. He'd never felt so alone, so uncertain.

He surrendered to the feeling. Snatching up a beaver-lined cloak, he left his private rooms by the way known to very few: a door he'd had installed in new oak paneling, which led to a passage ingeniously contrived in the thickness of the outer wall of the palace. He would give himself one more taste of freedom.

On her knees on the hard, smooth tiles in the Lady Chapel, Anne had finally faced what she'd tried so hard to avoid. She'd found some peace, for, in the end, there wasn't a choice; her only fear was that courage would leach away when the time came. All she wanted was to sink back into that time, two short days ago, when the king's arms were around her and his every touch had been like food to the starving.

She closed her eyes, tried to pray, but found herself chanting his name, softly, softly. "Edward, Edward, Edward . . ." Was it hallucination that made her feel his hands on her again, sense his smell?

No. Those hands were real—he was here! In her surprise she nearly fell as she jumped to her feet, but he was there to catch her, gathering her to his chest, holding her, stroking her back gently as if she were one of his hunting dogs in need of reassurance. She stood quietly in a warm daze, and then lifted her face to be kissed by him as if it were the most natural thing in the world.

How he loved the taste of her mouth, and how much it stirred him to stand there, holding her body to his. But it was nearly time for compline; the brothers would flood into the church and she and he must not be discovered.

"Come with me . . ." His knowledge of the Abbey was their savior again as they hurried down one of the dimly lit side aisles of the church, searching for the entrance to the cloister. It was very dark with only the occasional torch flaring uncertainly in its sconce to light their way, but Edward was like a boy again, playing a game of hide-and-seek with his brothers. He lifted a torch from the wall and, holding Anne tightly by one hand, felt along the cloister until he found what he was looking for.

In a corner, concealed unless you knew where to look for it, there was an elaborate metal grille with a ring handle on one side. Giving Anne the torch to hold, he wrenched the ring around with all his strength, the hinges of the grille protesting as he forced it to open; they gave to the irresistible force, and Edward was able to push the little door inward. Once they were inside, the torch light spilled down a flight of unexpectedly noble steps that disappeared down into darkness.

"This is where we used to come, Richard and George and I, when our parents were at court and we were bored . . ." He held the torch above their heads as they descended the stairs.

Anne could see they were in a large, windowless vaulted room. Around them were niches built into the wall in which stone coffins lay and in front of them, raised on an ornamented stone bier, lay another, larger marble coffin with two carved effigies on top of it: a crusader knight, from his armor, lying beside his lady.

"Look at their hands . . ." Edward said softly.

At first Anne did not see what he meant but he held the torch closer and then tears filled her eyes. Two hundred years ago this husband and wife had gone into eternity together, holding hands. And as she looked more closely, she could see their heads were turned toward one another; all those stone eyes had seen for two hundred summers, two hundred winters, was the loving face of the other lying so close.

He was standing quietly beside her, his arm around her waist.

"I wanted you to see them. I didn't understand what they meant to each other until you came into my life." Helplessly they turned to one another and he held her tight as she sobbed. Tears were slipping down his face as well—he had not cried since the death of his father . . .

Edward knew they only had a stolen hour together and that they were no closer to solving what needed to be done. He loved her and he wanted to trust her as well, but years of double-dealing still held him back. She must truly be the one to decide on her own future but, for them both, England must come first. There was no other way.

Swiftly, tenderly, he picked her up and sat her on the edge of the crusader's tomb as she twined her arms around his neck. Gently he kissed her, little soft kisses, all over her face, her eyes. She held him tighter, let him take her mouth, feeling her heart beat faster. He shivered, pulling her as close as he could, but neither of them felt the cold air of the crypt as he stood between her legs, only her long skirt separating them.

"Ah, Jesu, how I want you . . ." he whispered in her ear, his breath so warm. She closed her eyes as he kissed her throat. It was her turn now to be bold because this was such a precious moment, and she might never have another. She let him feel that she was drawing up the velvet skirt of her gown—soon her thighs and belly were naked against him.

His breath was coming shorter and shorter. "Take me inside you, my love." She fumbled as she tried to find the points for his hose and the codpiece, but each touch made him want her more, made him harder. Eventually she found the way into his clothes and quite timidly slipped her fingers inside. He guided her until they closed around him—he sobbed with sheer pleasure. "I'll help you."

But she needed no help to take him in—just a little wriggle as he pushed between her legs and she felt him enter her fully. She gasped as he began to rock back and forth, back and forth, each time pulling her toward him closer and tighter. She could feel him inside her, higher and higher in her belly. She wanted him, wanted him as she felt the hot itch between her legs build up as it had the first time, and build and build as he dug his nails into her buttocks and she tried to ride his rhythm. In the delicious heat between them she felt the shaft rubbing against the outside of her cleft with each stroke, and unconsciously she helped him do it by opening her thighs wider. The feeling was wilder and wilder, wilder and hotter and . . . she could not help crying out into his chest.

"Hush, my darling. Shhh. The brothers will hear," he whispered directly into her ear, and unaccountably that made her giggle, setting him off laughing in turn. And it was true that the brothers at compline heard something, but then the building was so old, it was no wonder strange sounds were heard from time to time . . .

The great hall of Westminster was brilliantly lit, filled with the court in its finest, most expensive clothes as they waited for the king and queen to appear. But the glittering array was unaware of the drama then taking place in the rooms of the queen.

Elizabeth was distraught; she was dressed and waiting for the summons from Edward, but none came. More than an hour's mark had burned through on the largest time-candle and still he had not appeared. William had sent a message that the king was delayed and would be with her shortly, but the queen knew he was lying. She'd sent Marceline to ask questions of the king's dressers; no one knew where he was. But she did. Her eyes darkened dangerously, tears dried abruptly, as she thought on it—he'd gone to the Abbey!

The baby lurched in her belly. The fear and anger she felt must have touched the child, another cause for her to feel so wretched. But Elizabeth was not queen for nothing; if she'd learned anything from the last three years it was how to put on the mask of imperturbability, so now she breathed deeply and closed her eyes. At all costs the court must not see her vulnerable or cowed. It was then she decided to change her headdress—she would have her hair rebraided into a corona and wear her light crown. Let the court see her as Edward's queen and lawful wife, no matter what rumors began to fly about the king's unexplained absence.

Edward knew he was very late as he bounded up the concealed stairs that led to his apartments, but since he had lived for years fenced around by protocol and crowds of hangers-on, this last hour spent alone with Anne was very precious to him, worth all he might have to deal with now. As he cautiously pushed the door open onto his empty bedchamber he could hear William's voice beyond the closed door. He sounded angry and afraid as he berated someone for failing to find the king.

Edward strode over to the door and wrenched it open. The relief on William's face when he saw the king was almost painful to see. Beckoning his chamberlain, and a dresser, Edward hurriedly closed the door on all the curious faces. His servant quickly proffered an array of clothing for the king to choose from. Black and gold. He would be the Leopard King. Wasting no time, he ripped his current clothes off unassisted, though not without regret, for there was still a scent of Anne about them.

"I should let you know the queen is said to be displeased." William used his most neutral voice as he helped Edward on with the garter below his left knee.

The king grunted in reply; he would not be drawn. His servant was attempting to curl his hair with hot tongs, and he waved him away impatiently. "There, William, all arrayed. No harm done." Edward flashed a glance like a rapier at his oldest friend.

"No, sire. I'm sure you're right." If only he was, thought William.

Not for the first time William regretted the king's marriage. This was a rare prince, a great bird of prey unlikely to be mewed by one woman alone. If he'd married royalty, had made a polite marriage formed for contractual and national purposes, his life would have been much easier. A well-schooled young princess could have been molded to understand why Edward needed his diversions, she would have expected as much and, perhaps, not been troubled by it. Elizabeth was too old to be trained, and without the benefit of a royal upbringing expected too much from her husband. And the kingdom would suffer for that in time. William sighed. They'd be in for a wild ride tonight.

But Elizabeth surprised William again. When he and the king hurried in to her apartments, he was forced to admire the will that sustained her.

She received her husband arrayed gloriously in tissue of gold—a happy contrast to his own severe black and gold—with her butter-colored hair braided high to support the glittering crown. She looked anything but the betrayed wife, greeting Edward with a happy laugh as the last rings were slipped onto her fingers and new slippers of embroidered white velvet were placed on her feet. "Husband, I fear I must make you wait a few moments. Time quite escaped me as I was being dressed. I am a laggard!" It was said with a musical laugh and the lightest of emphasis.

Edward bowed and stood waiting patiently, silent, refusing to be drawn into her little game. Elizabeth understood immediately and gave him another big happy smile. "There, ready now."

Rising gracefully, she extended her hand to the king, who bowed deeply again as he took it and placed it over his own. Then, stately as two bishops, the king and queen processed down to the great hall into the heaving, buzzing mass of courtiers who had grown hungrier and hungrier and more and more curious.

Over in the abbot's lodgings, Anne heard the cry of the trumpets, the noise of the courtiers greeting the king and queen as they arrived at dinner. For a moment, she stopped at her task, closing her eyes, an agonized expression on her face. Then, breathing deeply, she opened her eyes, staring sightlessly at the vellum in front of her. It had only lately arrived from Mathew Cuttifer and it was necessary she decide how, and when, to show it to the king. Now she bent back to the task of writing her own letter that must accompany the proof of her birth.

"Are you well, Lady Anne?" Abbot John was concerned, his guest was so pale.

"Quite well, thank you, Reverend Abbot. Quite well . . ."

Doctor Moss, quietly reading an illuminated missal in his corner by the fire, glanced quickly at Anne, wondering at the distant tone in her voice. He had lost weight in these last few days and a concentrated look of misery had settled on his face. He and Anne had barely spoken during their time in the Abbey because he, too, had spent much of his time in prayer at the direction of the abbot to whom he had confessed everything, including the reason he had brought Anne to court. It had been a long time since he'd prayed with anything like sincerity: it had been a hard and humbling experience. He hardly dared look at the girl now; to do so reopened the wound again, the wound of his betrayal. John Millington had given him severe penance for his actions, penance he was grimly observing. He'd agreed to go on pilgrimage to the shrine of Saint James of Compostela when he was out of sanctuary, and then, after that, to serve the poor of any city he found himself a part of for the next five years. It would not be easy, but perhaps it would give him peace.

For Anne there was no peace, and no sleep. Painfully, slowly, she had added the last few sentences to the letter she'd been composing earlier in the abbot's parlor. Each word had been the tolling of a distant bell, the tocsin perhaps, the bell that warned of danger. And then, there was nothing more to write and so she signed what she had written with only one word, "Anne." She, too, was a prince, it was her right. Later, open-eyed, she lay on the hard little bed of her cell, Deborah breathing peacefully beside her, and listened to the sounds of distant revelry from the palace. She could see him so clearly at the high table—and the queen, and William Hastings. And she was not there; perhaps would never, ever, be there again.

Chapter Forty-three

It was the Feast of Saint Valentine and from first light the tournament grounds had been pulsing like an anthill as Londoners in their thousands tried to buy tickets for the tourney.

The king had picked out a ground at West Smithfield, and for three weeks before today, builders, carpenters, painters, and tent-makers had all been busy at William's direction. Gaudily painted galleries for spectators lined all sides of the three-hundred-foot long lists, and pavilions for the combatants were erected outside the double palisade that surrounded them. The stand built to hold the queen, her ladies, honored noncombatant knights, and particularly favored courtiers was three stories high and very finely decorated with gilded allegorical figures of all kinds. It was surmounted by an enormous flagstaff, which today bore the king's personal standard, cracking bravely in the sharp wind above their heads.

A second stand, close by but lower than the queen's, was for the lord mayor and his aldermen. This caused a lot of gossip; the king was favoring merchants again, with judges and lesser magnates also included. Today, William was to oversee the Lists—a special honor—and would conduct proceedings from a specially built raised tribune in front of the queen's gallery.

Edward's pavilion was the largest of the many put up over the last few days. It had as many rooms as a small castle, though it was all on one level, and was made of wood and canvas painted to look like masonry. It was surrounded by a "forest" of half-sized trees potted in great tubs, all in very early spring leaf as they'd been coddled in a warmed forcing house.

It was hard to believe this was a temporary construction designed to last only five days.

The king was resting before the lists in his own magnificent room on a carved and gilded bed of state. He'd been able to avoid the queen's bed last night and this morning, and a conversation about his most recent absence, by declaring that if he were to fight well for her honor, he must spend his time surrounded by his companions praying for victory. Still, it had been very late last night when he and his chosen twelve, including George—who was extremely drunk and had to be brought in a litter—had arrived at the tent city erected around the lists. And true to his word, the king had insisted that his group of knights attend him at a Mass in a specially consecrated tent-church and stay with him to pray for strength and guidance in the tourney to come.

Edward was not a particularly religious man. He wore his faith comfortably and could most often square the very pragmatic decisions he made as king—which were often not very Christian—with the knowledge that God had chosen him for the task. It was difficult to rule and yet abide by all the commandments in the Bible. Besides, there must be some special rules for kings, who needed to have the good of so many, and not the few, at the heart of what they did. However, he did go to confession from time to time, and last night, fleetingly, he'd thought of confessing the truth about Anne.

Even though he saw himself as a modern man, a certain dread assailed him when he thought about Anne's strange history. Her life was like something out of troubadours' songs: a lost princess loved by a king. No, he had not confessed last night, but he promised himself now that once the tournament was over, he would solve the conundrum of her destiny.

Suddenly there was the bray of many trumpets and the boom of great drums.

It was mid-morning and the queen had arrived at her stand. Edward grimaced. It was time: time to become the warrior-king again. Time to face what must be faced. Elizabeth, meanwhile, was waving and being cheered. They didn't like her much because of her greedy family, but she was beautiful and she was pregnant. If she was good enough for Edward, she was good enough for them.

Elizabeth was also pleased, because she'd solved the problem of the heavy green gown by deciding she would have eight maidens to bear up the train, none lower than the daughter of an earl. Even the king's sister, Margaret of York, had been commanded to be one of the bearers, which William Hastings had had to negotiate at first light this morning, and which had caused uproar in the Lady's rooms—Margaret was no lover of the queen. However, in the event, Margaret had been forced to agree, because she could not reach her brother in time to plead her cause, and she could not withdraw without his permission. So it had given Elizabeth great satisfaction to hear the voluble surprise of the crowd when they saw who her chief servant was.

Now the queen and the Lady Margaret of England sat together beside the Countess of Warwick and William's own wife, Catherine, who was down from their northern lands for this occasion and even more pregnant than the queen, as if they were all the very best of friends. To the adoring eyes of the crowd they looked like goddesses, or fairy folk, graciously visiting London for a reason best known to themselves.

The ladies of the court were very knowledgeable about the rules of combat in the lists and keenly looked forward to the contest. Money was surreptitiously changing hands behind the queen's back as favorites were backed to win. Elizabeth, no less experienced, was torn between excitement, pride, and fear.

This first day of the contest was to be jousting between invited pairs of champions from each side, followed tomorrow by combat on foot. Then each succeeding day would see different weapons used—pole-axes and spears, bows and maces—and there was even to be wrestling. On the final day, there would be an all-out mêlée between both sides.

Each night there would be prizes awarded at a feast, and an entertainment for the court. Finally, the queen herself would bestow the prize, as Queen of Love, to the most gallant knight of the whole tournament, as judged by the ladies in her Court of Love.

The crowd was becoming restive as William took his seat on the tribune and raised his baton of honor. Immediately, trumpets sounded and a loud crash was heard at the door of the lists. A moment later a great voice announced that, in honor of Saint Valentine, an unknown knight and his companions asked entrance to the lists. Solemnly, William dropped his hand and the doors slowly opened.

A collective sigh escaped the crowd. There, all alone on a white horse, wearing black armor and bearing a shield lacquered black, was a huge knight. The horse was trapped out with silvered leather harness and black velvet hangings, a horn of pearl strapped to his head. Then in a puff of smoke, as if by magic, the knight was suddenly surrounded by twelve knights all in white armor, riding black horses and carrying white shields. A further puff of red smoke and a dwarf appeared in a green doublet and hose, mounted on a donkey with red leather bridle and saddle.

The crowd applauded wildly as the dwarf led the unknown knights out into the lists to the sound of music until the party was grouped in a semicircle in front of the queen. The music ceased as the dwarf spoke in a surprisingly loud voice.

He addressed himself to William: "Lord Judge of this fierce contest, I am sent by this unknown knight"—the black knight bowed to William who bowed in return—"to crave your favor. He is under a vow of silence and may not speak until he has accomplished, with his companions, a great service to the Queen of Love and her fair companions. He brings twelve champions to fight in their honor but he asks that he may be the first to tilt against any gallant opponent who may come against him." The crowd screamed, they knew it was the king dressed in black and for him to fight first was a graceful compliment to them all.

The dwarf had hardly finished his speech when trumpets sounded at the gate of the lists again. This time the doors opened and a lone knight entered first, arrayed entirely in gold armor, who was led into the arena by twelve girls wearing green kirtles with snowdrops in their hair. Each girl was attached to the great destrier by a long green ribbon and as they came forward, they danced in and out scattering jonquils for the horse to trample on.

The golden knight bowed to the queen and William, and announced that he was the champion sent to defend the honor of Saint Valentine on his feast day. He would fight the black knight, and his companions would aid him in the contests to come. Another trumpet blast and twelve knights in silver armor rode at full tilt through the gates to surround him, white ostrich plumes tossing.

It was a very pretty spectacle and pleased Elizabeth greatly, especially when the "unknown" black knight leaped off his destrier in front of her stand and, kneeling in the sand of the lists, begged a token from her as her special champion. This was the queen's moment and she savored it. Slowly she stood and, when she saw she had the attention of the whole crowd, prised the largest of the emeralds from its specially made clasp on her gown and threw it down in a graceful arc to the man kneeling below her. "There, sir knight, a token of my love, which is still green, as the Queen of Love, for all champions of strength and goodness. May you fight well for the honor of Saint Valentine."

The knight jumped to his feet, held the stone up to the low morning sun so that it flashed green fire for everyone in the crowd to see, and then sprang back onto his white horse and swept out of the lists, following his companions to await the signal for the joust.

William breathed a small private sigh of relief; so far, all was well. The queen looked radiant and pleased and his little bit of ceremonial mummery had gone over well with the crowd. But, of course, the real danger was about to begin. William dropped his baton to signal the first joust.

He watched with pride and fear as the black knight entered the arena supported by eight pages on horseback, again dressed in white. The great emerald, given him by the queen, was now mounted on his helm, where it glittered and flashed as he bent his head from side to side, acknowledging the roar from the crowd. Two squires handed him up the jousting lance with its blunted end as Edward caressed the neck of his destrier, Mallon. He knew the heart of this horse, his love of battle, he could feel it in every fiber of the animal as the stallion fidgeted from hoof to hoof under the heavy cloth trapping that swept the ground.

More trumpets and the Golden Knight, Warwick, entered the

lists surrounded by six squires and pages. In his gilded battle helm he was strangely idollike, yet his frivolous crest of nodding feathers and streaming ribbons seemed playful. Edward didn't underestimate the earl, however; there was nothing playful in the way he fought.

Now the two men were ready at each end of the tilt as William held his baton high. The king had the advantage, for the climbing sun was in his opponent's eyes. The chamberlain waited for utter silence and then dropped his arm—the trumpets blared and the horses began to lumber forward faster and faster each side of the wooden tilt. Closer and closer, sand from hooves flying higher and higher, Edward braced in his saddle, legs rigid in the stirrups as he dropped his head and aimed the lance to the right of Warwick's body: impact!

Warwick's lance caught him a glancing blow on the vamplate for no score, but Edward had struck his opponent high just beneath and beside the shoulder and splintered his lance well and truly. Two points! The crowd roared for their champion, the "unknown knight," as both men cantered to the end of the lists to receive fresh lances.

Again they turned to face each other, the sun against Edward this time. Mallon was champing foam on the bit and pulling on the reins, nerved for another pass. Edward could have dropped the reins if he chose, confident the animal would hold its line.

Warwick's horse was no less worthy, and this time without the sun in his eyes, Warwick did better when the two men met in the center, planting his lance squarely just below Edward's chin for one point. Edward lost a point as his lance went badly awry, skidding off the top of Warwick's shoulder piece. The score was even as the two cantered on down the lists, each carrying the smart from two shuddering blows.

At the final course the crowd was utterly still as they watched each knight given his lance. The queen sat rigid, as did the Countess of Warwick, the nails of each biting into their palms.

As if dreaming, Elizabeth saw William's arm fall, the baton glinting, flashing in the sun, saw the horses spring away. She watched the hooves thud, felt the sand fly, heard the roar of the crowd, as distant as the sound of the sea, and then . . . a crash and suddenly the golden knight was arcing through the air, his horse screaming as it hit the ground.

The two women sat in shock as the ladies around them leaped to their feet, screaming too, but in delight. The black knight sat on his white horse like a statue just beneath the stand and was showered with snowdrops and jonquils from the court, as squires ran on to the field to help the Earl of Warwick up. At present he lay in a helpless mass of armor as men tried to catch his destrier, who had gone careering around the arena, to the great delight of the crowd.

The queen turned to the countess. "Come, lady, there is your husband. Unhorsed by this unknown knight, but he lives." Elizabeth did not dislike the countess but she could not help the note of triumph in her voice. Her husband had won yet again, and both he and she were safe. His kingdom was safe. Unconsciously, she rubbed her belly. Perhaps tonight she could ensure the king's presence in her bed . . .

Suddenly, the trumpets sounded again as if someone else were demanding entrance to the lists. This was irregular, the rules said the field had to be cleared of current contestants before more combatants could be admitted.

All eyes swung to the gates as they opened slowly and a strange sight presented itself to the crowd. A veiled woman, simply dressed in black velvet, was riding a gray donkey. Leading the donkey was a man in the long purple robes of a doctor. Gravely he led the donkey toward the tribune where William sat as judge of the tourney and a buzz of speculation ran like flame through the crowd. Doctor Moss walked the donkey past the unknown knight to a point just in front of William and the queen's stand. Bowing low to Elizabeth, he asked, in a loud voice, if he might be permitted to address the judge of the tourney, to ask a favor on behalf of the veiled lady.

The crowd was delighted; this was another bit of intriguing byplay and they strained hard to hear what was said. William nodded for Doctor Moss to approach and asked the lady's name. "Sir, I cannot tell you that, except to say she has lately been in sanctuary at the abbey and now craves your aid, and the aid of the queen."

His words could only be heard by the people in the two stands closest to the tribune where William sat, but the tension that seemed to flow from the still, black figure had the crowd hushing itself in an effort to try to catch even some of what was said.

William looked helplessly at the queen, who sat frozen and uncertain, giving him no sign. He cast a glance at Edward, who had eased his destrier closer to the lady on the donkey, though he had not pushed up the visor on his helm. He, too, was silent.

William called out strongly, "Sir, how may we aid this lady?"

Moss looked across at the veiled figure and she handed him a sealed packet. He took it from her to William, who bowed as he received it. "Sir, my mistress asks that you read the letter aloud, if you will."

The chamberlain cast another desperate glance at Edward and, after a moment, the armored head nodded. He was to read the letter. Helpless up in her stand, the queen was white, biting her lips with fear and anger. She knew, she knew who the woman was below her. Anne! Her erstwhile body servant.

In perfect silence William opened the packet and began to read. " 'Gracious queen, lady of the unknown knight, I, your unhappy servant, ask aid and sustenance for me and mine. Lately I was in sanctuary but now I must ask your help to leave my safe haven, and this kingdom, never to return.' "

The king's horse was suddenly restive as a strong hand convulsed on the reins; on her donkey, Anne sat proudly but, unseen, the sweat ran down her sides and it was hard, so hard, to breathe.

" 'I may not say my name but it is an honorable one and my only crime was to have been born . . . ' " There was an aaaah of sympathy around the crowd. "Once your knight made me a promise that if I came to him on this day I might have whatever I asked for. My request is this: that those who are my friends are made free from fear for having taken my part, and henceforth live beneath his protection. Your champion laid down one condition only and I freely say, here, in this place, that I have broken it, and thus in truth have forfeited the right to ask his mercy. But still, on his honor as a knight, he may feel I am owed this service so that I may leave this kingdom in peace.' "

It was done. There was no going back now—for Anne, or the king.

The queen was thinking fast and her voice was clear with a certain icy ring to it as she addressed the unknown knight before her: "Sir knight, it seems you owe service to this lady. I give you leave to speak so that you may answer."

The knight was silent for a moment and then, unexpectedly, he laughed. "Gentle queen, I do indeed owe knight's service to this lady. She shall have my protection and so will her friends. I shall bind myself to see that they remain free and prosperous from this moment. And since their freedom has been so dearly bought by this lady's sacrifice, your honor as her queen will not be less than mine. She shall leave free, and unmolested."

There was an edge to his tone and it was heard by every breathless member of the court. The queen's mouth snapped shut and she did not trust herself to say more. She'd heard the despair in his voice, under the fair, measured words; it made her gorge rise with fear. Love had never been part of the equation with Edward's lemans before.

The king bowed to his wife, then to the lady on the donkey, signaling that Anne should precede him out of the lists, led by Doctor Moss.

Was it only one small moment before Anne bowed to the king in return? So little time in which to feel that all the old life was gone. And the new one—the mystery—beginning.

Outside the lists, they did not speak, but Doctor Moss was seen by Warwick's squire as he handed the "unknown" knight three letters before he and the lady rode away.

For a long time, the "unknown" knight watched them go, but Anne did not look back, and he made no move to follow them.

Later, he rode against three other knights of Warwick's party, and nearly killed them all.

Chapter Forty-four

It took Anne three days to ride to Dover after the tourney. She was very cold and weary as they arrived in the town at the end of a bone-shaking ride. A storm had just closed over the little port, drenching them all, and adding to Anne's misery. But word had preceded them and they were to lodge in the guest quarters at the Benedictine monastery there, with a special room and its own parlor set aside for her and Deborah. Doctor Moss, too, had been given his own quarters on orders of the king.

Anne no longer cared if she ate or where she slept. She had done what was needed in London; assessed what was possible, understood she could not win against Edward the king, maybe did not want to win, because Edward the man was her lover; all that remained to her was honorable defeat. But the daughter of a king would not leave without that one last gesture at the tourney; you will not acknowledge me, that I understand, but you owe me and mine honorable treatment.

Her reward had been one last meal in the hall of Blessing House with Sir Mathew, Lady Margaret, Deborah, and Jehanne, who had been released from the Tower by the king's order. Well fed by Maître Gilles, she had left Blessing House for the last time—it would have been too agonizing to sleep another night under their roof, reminding her of all she had lost.

Now soaked, shivering, and achingly lonely, she huddled over the fire in their monastery quarters as Deborah stripped the sodden clothes off Anne and encouraged her into the warmed bed. The strain of the last weeks had finally gripped the girl's healthy body—she was flushed and a dry cough hurt her chest. Listlessly she did as she was asked but that night alternate chills and fever shook her. She was so cold her teeth chattered, and Deborah, in the same bed, tried to keep her warm with extra clothes and her own body. Then Anne burned with fever, throwing the clothes off, stumbling around in the dark naked, and muttering of betrayal.

By morning she was very ill and Deborah was frightened. She had few herbs with her except some willow bark and dried feverfew—that was little enough to dose Anne with. She was so worried she even asked Doctor Moss to see Anne—she had some respect for his skill though he had no great opinion of hers—and they took it in turns to get Anne to swallow the fever teas Deborah made and apply an embrocation Doctor Moss brewed from ingredients he found in the monastery's infirmary.

For three days as the last storm of winter howled around the little town, Anne lay in a state between sleep and waking, tossing, crying out with bad dreams, and mumbling snatches of strange visions.

Deborah and Doctor Moss almost came to blows on how best to treat her. He wanted to seal all sources of the potentially poisonous air and build up the fire to make Anne sweat the sickness out, while Deborah believed they needed to let the sea wind sweep noxious vapors from the room. It was their low-voiced arguing that Anne heard first as she came back to true consciousness, it made her laugh, though the laugh was closer to a wheeze she was so weak.

For the first time, Anne truly saw where they were: a little dark room with a groined stone ceiling. There was pared horn in the small-paned window and a massive fireplace covering one entire corner of the small space. She was in a large box bed wadded firmly with fresh straw, lying between clean, coarse unbleached sheets, but as she tried to raise her head to see more, the effort was too much and she closed her eyes as everything suddenly swam and she spiraled into the dark again.

The next day was again closer to dreams than reality but she allowed herself to be washed by Deborah—again against Doctor Moss's vehement protests—and her sweaty hair freshened with a soothing rosemary wash that Deborah blotted dry with linen warmed at the fire.

With the gradual return of health came awareness and with it the need to plan for the future. When she'd left London, she'd asked nothing for herself, but Mathew Cuttifer had arranged that Leif Mollnar would meet her at Dover with the *Lady Margaret*.

Optimism gradually returned as Anne took stock of her situation. A year or more ago she'd lived day to day, no real thought of the future in her head, equipped with nothing but her wits, the education she'd been given by Deborah, and the beginnings of skills at doctoring.

She was a woman now and knew herself to be the daughter of a king but she was no fine lady and for that she was grateful. She was not afraid to earn her living. She and Deborah could use what they knew of physic to treat the sick, she could make cosmetics, too, and if they were desperate, she could work as a seamstress. Mathew Cuttifer had supplied her with a letter to his factor in Brugge insisting there was safe haven at his trading place in that city for as long as they needed or wanted it.

Also she had her clothes. They were valuable and she could sell some to raise money if they had to, though being young and loving clothes as she did, that caused a pang. Similarly it would take much for her to part with the topaz brooch given to her by Jane Shore or the little filigree cross that Lady Margaret had given her, but for the moment she would not have to. Mathew had given her a good purse of coins so their case was not hopeless. She and Deborah would have the means to survive, to start again. Now all that was required was her full recovery and passage with Leif across to France.

Her musings in the chair by the fire were interrupted by Deborah, who ran suddenly into the room. "Quickly, cover yourself."

Anne was astonished by this whirl of activity as the shawl she was wearing over the fine silk sleeping shift was whipped from her shoulders and a velvet cloak flung over her. Deborah hauled her to her feet while simultaneously trying to brush her hair out.

"Deborah—ow! Stop that! What has possessed you to—" Her words dried in her mouth as she heard the sound of booted feet and spurs on stone outside the door of her room.

She knew those steps—knew the man who made them. She clutched the cloak around her and sat down suddenly again. Her legs would not hold her up.

The footsteps stopped. There was a moment, a knock, and then a man's voice: "Anne?"

The door was pushed open and there stood the king in a mud-spattered riding cloak; it had been a hard, fast ride from London. Wordlessly, Anne looked up at Deborah. The other woman patted her hand then slipped from the room.

"Sire . . ." Anne started to rise from her chair, wanted to stand, as his equal, but her legs had no strength. In a moment he was beside her, holding both of her hands in a painful grip, intense eyes locked with hers. He knelt beside her chair like a supplicant.

"My darling, my sweet Anne . . ." It was hard for him to speak. "I could not come before the tourney was over—and I thought I would never see you again. But then I was told you were dying . . ." He shook his head, blinking tears away. For a man who spoke very little about his feelings and was wary of those who did, the heartbroken note in his voice brought tears to her own eyes. "You understand—please tell me you understand. I had to let you go. You left me no other choice."

Yes, she understood, she understood everything.

"I read the letters from . . . the former king, your father. Sir Mathew himself told me they are copies, witnessed by Doctor Millington at the Abbey. He keeps the originals for surety, somewhere."

There was the ghost of a smile from both of them then.

Shakily, she extracted her hands and, at last able to stand, walked toward the fire and looked into its depths with her back to him.

"I wish, I deeply, deeply, deeply wish, that things could be different. That you had the power, the magic, to make the world go away." It was the last childlike thing she would ever say and she sounded so forlorn he was beside her in one stride, wrapping his arms around her, rocking her gently, holding her tight. She turned in his embrace and, burying her head, allowed herself to sob for all that was lost to her: him, the person she truly was, her life at his court, their future—which could not exist.

The agony he felt was a physical pain. She would leave his kingdom, he knew it. Not for her the safety of a marriage he could arrange that would keep her near him at least.

This was her way of telling him that it remained her choice to go. He sighed.

"No. I have no magic. But things of this earth I can accomplish. See, I have something for you . . ."

"I don't want anything from you, Edward." She meant it. Pride was all she had left to sustain her.

He kissed her again, so gently, with such longing. "Let me restore what was once given."

He had a leather bag strapped to his belt and when he opened it she saw he had two scrolls, tied with red ribbon and sealed. "Open them, please."

The first scroll was a title deed. There, word for word, were the phrases that had been in her father's first letter: "To our dear brother of Somerset . . . lands of the county of Somerset . . . dowered in perpetuity . . . to be hers and the heirs of her body and all in perpetuity . . ." But there were two differences from the original: she was the person named, not her mother, as the owner of these lands and farms and fishponds and mills, and the name of the king at the end of the document was Edward's, not Henry's.

Anne looked up at Edward. "But breaking sanctuary means I may not live in England."

Edward moved a tendril of hair away from her eyes. "Yes, but the income will be sent to you. I'll let Mathew Cuttifer know, it shall be done through him. Your estates will be excellently managed, that I promise you. And these lands will always belong to your children." He said it so sadly. She would have children, but not with him.

She unfurled the second scroll as tears slipped down his face, and hers. It was a grant of arms to Anne in her own right. She would be Baroness Wincanton, Lady Anne de Bohun and her crest was made up of the Angevin leopards rampant above two drops of blood. "The blood is for you, and for me, for that is what we have given—hearts' blood," Edward whispered.

And there was one last thing. It was a ring, a great square ruby that had been engraved with her arms and the initials of their names, A and E, entwined above the leopards. Kissing the palm of her left hand, he then turned it over and slid the jewel onto her middle finger. "A ruby because you are above price and this is the stone of constancy." For one last time he looked into her eyes then, once, only once, he kissed her.

Helplessly they clung together, body to body, but neither cried now; the feeling of loss was too achingly great to find expression. Then he left her, more alone than she had ever felt in her life, listening to the shouts in the yard of the monastery as the party of men and horses left.

And later that night, as she and Deborah were being rowed out to the waiting cog at anchor in the harbor, she smelled the sea and remembered her vision of loss and parting. She shivered. And prayed. *Sword Mother, let the dreams not be true . . . Let him be safe.*

One last time, Anne lifted her eyes from the dark water. One last time, she looked back at the homeland she'd lost as the light of the wavering torches touched her face. Only the sound of the waves, the seabirds calling; nothing else was left.

But Anne was wrong, for as she turned away from the shore, the vision came to Deborah, unbidden. Anne carried the king's child in her belly.

This was not an end. This was a beginning.

THE
EXILED

The romance and intrigue begun
in *The Innocent* continue in
the second volume of the Anne trilogy.

Turn the page to read the first chapter

Chapter One

"Enough. Rest now. You must be stiff."

The girl kneeling in front of the casement window stretched and sighed, easing her clenched muscles. It was true she was stiff, and cold also, from holding the pose. The charcoal braziers had burned out long ago and the room was frigid.

"We have worked well today, you and I." The painter, oblivious to the temperature and happy to chat as he ground pigment in his mortar—it would yield rich scarlet when bound with boiled linseed oil and powdered gum arabica—spoke truthfully, for the girl had knelt uncomplainingly for several hours. That was unusual among his clients, and he was grateful.

Satisfied, finally, with the consistency of the bloody paint he'd now mixed in an oyster shell, he took some to the tip of his brush and smiled apologetically.

"If you are ready, I must use this light, mistress; perhaps a little more padding for the knees?" He smiled encouragingly as she knelt again, but then frowned as he leaned toward his canvas, lost once more in catching that annoyingly elusive highlight on one small fold of the velvet that was giving him trouble, such trouble . . .

Sound traveled well in that still, icy dusk. The shouts of children playing on the frozen canal outside the painter's narrow house bounced off the walls inside the studio when, finally, the man put his brush down and stood back from the picture.

He flicked a glance toward his sitter, obediently kneeling still. She was rimmed by the last of the light outside his casement and he could barely see her face, for the red sky in the west was darkening; soon the oil lamps, the tallow dips, and the candles would be lit against shadows all over his city.

"That is all for today, mistress. The light is gone."

Gratefully, Anne de Bohun sat back on her heels, allowing her body to slump, as she flexed stiffened fingers one by one.

"Maestro? May I look?"

"Not yet, mistress. Bad luck to look on it unfinished. Perhaps tomorrow."

She understood his reluctance perfectly. It would be hard letting something out into the world, even when it was finished, if you'd brought it into being. Very well, she could wait a little longer.

Without fuss, Anne picked up a winter cloak and draped it around her shoulders. Best to cover the garnet-red velvet of the dress she was wearing, for it was the most valuable thing she owned and there were strangers on the streets this winter. She did not want to invite robbery—or worse.

"Lotta! Bring light!" The painter's voice was shockingly loud as he yelled for his servant, not even bothering to open the door and call down the stairs. She would hear him.

As they waited, Hans Memlinc, the German painter, watched Anne covertly while he cleaned his brushes—those ivory hands with their long, capable fingers pinning her cloak together, smoothing the folds of the stiffened veiling surmounting the embroidered cap that hid her hair. He'd never seen her hair. He was sad about that.

Anne de Bohun was a mystery. His paintings cost a great deal of money, but she'd not balked at the price when they'd struck the contract. Yet, if gossip was correct, she was not, herself, personally wealthy, even if her guardian, Mathew Cuttifer, the English merchant, was. Perhaps he had paid.

There was a timid little thump at the door. Suppressing irritation, Memlinc leaned over and flicked the iron latch up. The door swung into the room, revealing the anxious face of his servant, Lotta. She was holding a branch of lit candles in one hand, a small, sputtering oil lamp in the other. She was very young and flustered, and her anxiety to please her master made her clumsy. She dripped oil from the lamp onto her kirtle as she curtsied to her master and his guest.

"Set the candles down, girl. Not there!" Lotta had hurried to comply, putting the branched lights down on the first available surface, his worktable cluttered with mortars for grinding pigment and pots full of brushes. "How many times? No! Put the candles in front of the mirror; it will double the light."

Anne took pity on the harried child. It had been only so little time since she, too, had been a servant. "There, Lotta, give me the lamp for your master. And please let Ivan know I am ready to go home."

Gratefully, Lotta scuttled out of the studio, and Anne glanced at the painter as he dropped a fine muslin cloth over the face of his work. The material was held away from the surface by a delicate wire prop. Delicate things pleased them both. They smiled at each other.

"Thank you, Maestro. Today was a good day. I shall look forward to our final session together tomorrow." Such a subtle stress on the word "final," but the painter heard her, heard what she meant, and surprised himself by nodding. Yes, they would finish tomorrow.

Anne reached up and carefully placed the little terra-cotta lamp on a shelf above his worktable, where the uncertain light spilled down to the painter's best advantage, then began fastening iron-shod wooden pattens over her soft shoes.

"Until tomorrow, then."

She was grateful that tomorrow would bring completion, for it had been a lengthy process, sitting for the painter, and she was impatient to have the picture home.

Hans Memlinc had no idea how important his work was to Anne. It was only paint, canvas, and the skill of his hands, but this picture was Anne's private, tangible symbol of hope, hope for her future, and her future success in this city, and as such was worth every one of the carefully hoarded gold angels she would pay.

Anne's pattens clicked on the painter's tiled floor as she left his studio smiling happily. Belated conscience struck him and he called after her, "I've kept you late, mistress. You must be careful going home. There are too many mercenaries in town this winter. Wild and silly, most of them, but no one is safe after the curfew bell."

She laughed. "I'm not worried. The Watch'll have chained the streets by now. Soldiers all drink too much anyway. I can outrun them, Maestro!" He heard her giggle as she clattered happily down his staircase and he found himself grinning.

Anne was still smiling as Ivan, her guardian's Magyar manservant, closed the front door of the painter's house behind them. He'd been waiting in Master Memlinc's warm kitchen, quite happy to while away another winter's day chaffing little, shy Lotta and flirting with Eva, the cook-housekeeper. She was substantial, Eva, with an abundance of good flesh packed tightly into a pretty skin. He liked that. She liked him. They had been pleasant times.

"The picture will be finished tomorrow, Ivan, so no more happy days with Eva." Spooked by Anne's prescience, the man nearly dropped his flambeau. He crossed himself quickly, but she saw it.

"What's this, Ivan? A prayer? Who for? Eva?"

Her laughter was so unforced, so clear in the dark, sharp air that Ivan was ashamed. She was not a witch, this girl, just clever— for a woman. Cautiously he smiled, and held the light higher.

Anne pulled on her one winter indulgence—fleece-lined mittens—as she breathed deeply of the wood-smoke air. A few minutes' brisk walk beside the frozen canal and she would reach her guardian's new house with its warehouse near the Kruispoort—one of the nine fortified gates of the city of Brugge—but Ivan would have his hand on the hilt of a short stabbing sword the whole way.

It was a good feeling, if she was honest, that he was her protector, for the town was filled with outlanders this winter: mostly mercenaries in the service of the Duke of Burgundy who roamed the streets waiting for the end of winter and the certainty of the coming spring campaigns. The Lowlands were still restless and their new duke had much to do to secure his duchy, let alone deal with the French. Mercenaries are only ever half tame, everyone knew that, and winter made them dangerous: too much time on their hands and too much blood from rich food and good beer.

Ivan understood. As a very young man he, too, had been dangerous—still was, in a more controlled way—which was why he'd been hired by Sir Mathew Cuttifer, Anne's patron and guardian, to help protect his interests in this city. Anne fell into that category for reasons Ivan was not paid to understand.

Brugge, this Venice of the North, was booming and there were rich pickings to be had, and not just for English merchants with interests outside Britain, like Sir Mathew. Young, landless men are always attracted to wealth, and many here had more ambition than a short lifetime's service as one of the Duke of Burgundy's paid fighters.

And it was hard to be poor in such a place, hard not to be envious of other people's good fortune—if you had none yourself—for wool, spices, and jewels arrived daily in barges down the Zwijn from the coast. More wealth to add to that already stuffed in behind the sturdy walls of this dynamic city—and Sir Mathew and his friends, the English Merchant Adventurers, commanded much of it.

Thus it was Ivan's job to see that his master, and his master's ward, Lady Anne de Bohun, lived in peace, the peace he could help give them in dangerous times when so many coveted Sir Mathew's rich possessions, this girl included. He took the office seriously as a matter of professional pride.

Anne was a realist, too, for all the joking with Meinheer Memlinc. It was the darkest time of the year and she was grateful to have this short, powerfully squat man pacing at her side, alert as a hunting dog.

Cold air breathed up from the ice of the canal as she walked. Anne shivered, though she and Ivan were moving briskly, her pattens clicking on the cobbles, he pacing beside her in good leather boots, matching his stride to hers.

Around them, houses crowded thick and tight, and warm light bloomed from some proud windows, though much of the town was dark. It was the wealthy who kept lights burning on into the night: the merchants, nobles, and priests who thronged around the new Duke of Burgundy as his court formed, eager for advancement.

Sensible people went to bed even before the curfew bell, however, for heat and light were expensive in winter and it was easier, and cheaper, to stay warm under the covers. You didn't need light in bed.

Nearly there now, nearly there. Anne could see Mathew's house on the other side of the frozen canal just past the bridge. It was well lit for her homecoming and that was good: her toes were burning, tingling with the cold, pattens or no pattens to keep them out of the muck.

"Mistress?"

Ivan had slowed his pace and spoke softly.

"Hold the light, lady."

He was always calm in a crisis, Ivan, for he'd survived far too many bloody turns to get excited, but even he, now, was tense, because ahead of them, blocking the narrow bridge across the canal that led to Sir Mathew's house, was a compact group of silent men. Faint light from the stars caught the movement as they silently drew swords.

"Behind me. Drop the light when I tell you." Ivan breathed the words and Anne slid quietly into his shadow.

"Now!"

The flambeau's light hissed out into the dirty, banked snow at the lane's edge, but as it died, the flame showed Anne another three men behind them.

"Ivan, behind us. Three more!"

"The canal. Jump when I yell." It was the only choice and so, as he sprang toward the men on the bridge screaming, "A moi, Sainte George!" Anne kicked off her pattens, scooped up her skirts, and ran to the edge of the canal.

Too late to think, too late to judge the drop from bank to ice, she half fell, half dropped down, and though she rolled as soon as she hit the hard surface, to cushion the jolt, she knew she'd soon feel the shock in her muscles—if she survived.

Above her there were shouts from the bridge as Ivan fought his way into the midst of the attackers. The men had seen her drop and someone was yelling, "Get the girl, get the girl!" but Anne still had an advantage of seconds, though she was encumbered by long skirts.

Breathing raggedly, heart jolting, she scrabbled to her feet and blessed the lessons of moving over the ice that Ivan had made her practice this winter—one foot, next foot, striving for balance. Then fear turned to panicked acid in her throat: she had to cross the fragile, new ice in the center of the canal if she was to reach Sir Mathew's frozen water gate ahead of her attackers. On the bridge, Ivan was fighting with the fury of his berserk ancestors, but he could not, single-handedly, hold them all away from her. She must do it, must move on.

With a yell, two men dropped down off the center of the bridge, but the freeze was only two days old and the ice was not as thick as it soon would be. Their yells changed to screams as they fell through into the frigid black waters of the Zwijn.

Anne saw the cracks in the ice shoot out from the hole they'd made as she slid on toward the farther side of the canal, but she was far enough away from them, and so much lighter, that the ice held together under her soft shoes. Breathing hard, she reached the other bank and scrambled toward Sir Mathew's water gate—it was frozen shut but it was close, closer. Perhaps she could climb it.

Now she was yelling, too, "Help us, help us!" as lights flared in houses above the canal. No one liked another's dispute, especially if it was just a fight among drunken mercenaries, but they had heard her calling out and a woman's voice stirred the conscience—a little.

Blessedly, torchlight suddenly shone down and willing hands reached out to haul her up—Sir Mathew's steward, Maxim, and two of the stable boys. "Help Ivan! There, the bridge." She could hardly gasp the words as her arms were wrenched above her head, but then they had her onto the roadway and Maxim was hurrying her inside, into the warm hall, while he shouted for more men.

It was over very soon. Maxim and Sir Mathew's servants rushed the bridge where Ivan was viciously defending the honor of his master's house. Two assailants, lethally slashed, were groaning at his feet and one man was dead, his blood a black steaming puddle in the snow. Of the two who had jumped from the bridge, one was lying on the cracked ice half drowned and gasping, while his companion hadn't surfaced. The other men, the followers, had disappeared.

Now Anne stood in front of the expensive new fireplace in Sir Mathew's hallhouse under a painted panel of Saint George destroying the dragon; it was an apt expression of her life: she must slay the dragon of fear here, tonight. Holding out her hands to the flames, she swallowed hard, trying to control her breathing, trying to banish the burning vomit in her throat.

It was a shock. All she had been warned about was true. And if this was more than it seemed—a kidnap for ransom—then she had enemies and it was time to face these facts, time to think her way through her situation very carefully.

"Mistress? Are you harmed?" It was her foster mother's anguished voice Anne heard now and she turned slowly, giving herself enough time to gather a smile to her face.

"Not at all, Deborah. As you see. Where's Edward?" She must not give in to the fear; must not. Shakily she forced herself to breathe slowly and deeply as she tried to unfasten her cloak with suddenly useless fingers.

Deborah answered the unasked question. "He's fine. Just fine. Here. Let me." Deborah hurried to help, gently detaching the cloak from Anne's shoulders and unpinning the crushed and distorted headdress. "He's asleep, bless him. We've got his cradle near the fire in the kitchen. He fed well again tonight—I'm very pleased with the new nurse; she's a fine strong girl, abundant milk."

Routine. Reassuring, safe routine. All was well—Deborah could always do that for her. Anne summoned another smile and carefully smoothed the folds of her expensive red dress. She grimaced. It would never be the same. The hem was dragged and dirty and there were dark wet patches where she'd fallen on her knees; it would have to be carefully dried and brushed if the fabric was not to be completely ruined. Hans Memlinc would see her in another dress tomorrow.

"I shall see how my nephew fares." She needed to see the baby, needed to hold him. Deborah smiled at her, touched her hand gently. "Yes, it's nice and cozy in the kitchen. I'll see to warming the solar."

Anne was calmer now, soothed as always by Deborah's care of her. Tremulously the girl smiled in return and would have leaned against her foster mother for strength, except that Maxim or one of the other servants might see the moment of weakness and be curious.

She was too new to Brugge, too new to the role she'd been given—that of Mathew Cuttifer's ward—to be anything but careful; too much was at stake. She and Deborah must always retain the appearance of servant and mistress in front of the household, yet both women found the constant role-playing a strain, especially now. They'd get used to it, they had to. For the moment, it was their only safety for they had nowhere else to go.

Anne sighed, then consciously relaxing her rigid shoulders, folded her hands at her waist, and stepped down the wooden staircase to the kitchens without fuss, breathing deeply as the peace of being home and safe clothed her softly as a cloak.

The kitchen was always busy in a large household, especially now as it was close to suppertime, but as Anne appeared, all work stopped. She was well liked, their master's ward.

"Lady, are you harmed?" The Flemish cook, Maître Flaireau, hurried forward. "Please, please, sit here by the warmth."

Anne nodded brightly in return for the relieved smiles from Ralph, the filthy scullion; Henri, the spit boy; and Herve, the Maître's meat man. She allowed herself to be led to the ingle seat beside the largest of the cooking fires. She must not let them know how strange she still felt or let them see how hard it was to keep her tightly clasped hands from shaking. She had one aim now.

"Is Edward . . . where is he?" As Maître Flaireau pressed her to sit. "There, mistress, do you see?"

They had moved his cradle into the shadows, out of the light of the cooking fires into a warm corner of the cheerful tiled room. And he slept on, oblivious to all the bustle around him in the busy kitchen.

Anne yearned to pick him up, to kiss him awake, to hug him tightly to her breasts—the breasts that had never fed this child, but she restrained herself. Time for that later, when she was alone again with Deborah, the baby safely in the little annex of her solar.

"Wine! Hot wine for our mistress. Herve, hurry now!" Anne smiled slightly at the courtesy title "Mistress." Lady Margaret

Cuttifer, Mathew's wife, was mistress in this house, even though she was so rarely here.

Four months since Edward's birth, four months of lies. She sipped the hot, rich wine; they'd spiced it with honey and nutmeg and beaten an egg yolk into it for strength. She was tired now, and aching. Leaning into the ingle seat, she closed her eyes, just closed them and . . .

"Sssh! Herve, move quietly!" The cook hissed at his assistant as he pantomimed creeping silently around the girl, who seemed to have fallen into a deep sleep. Chastened, Herve took care to sharpen the wicked boning knife as quietly as he could. He would be mortified to wake her, poor lady.

But Anne was not asleep. She smelled the blood again; it was animal blood from the carcass Herve was butchering, but it was enough, she was back there. . . .

His birth, Edward's birth. Four months ago and a long, long way from Brugge. A tiny, suffocatingly hot room in the convent she'd been sent to by Sir Mathew to await the labor well away from prying eyes, away from gossip.

Blood. Blood everywhere. On the straw-stuffed mattress, the whitewashed wall beside the bed, all over her. But he'd been born, alive and strong. Deborah had taken him from her belly and given him to a woman who'd been hired to suckle him, immediately, not even wiping the wax and the blood off his little body.

It was best this way, said Deborah, best that Anne never suckled him for if she did, to give him to another would be unbearable. It would be easier with time. These words were muttered as a prayer by her foster mother as she bound Anne's breasts with bruised arnica and mallow to help with the pain when her milk let down, the milk that would not be given to her child.

And now she and the Cuttifers called the baby her sister's son. Her dear dead "sister," Aveline.

Anne frowned in the strange half sleep as the light from the fire flickered on her face, her eyelids. Aveline . . . her name was a breath, not even a sound. For Aveline was indeed dead, and she, too, had borne a child named Edward. Yet she was never a sister of Anne's, although, in the end, in that other life lived as the Cuttifers' servant in London, Anne had loved her like one.

Aveline, who'd served in the Cuttifer household as Lady Margaret's maid; Aveline, raped and made pregnant by Piers, Mathew Cuttifer's only son; Aveline, who'd endured a forced and dreadful marriage to Piers Cuttifer, finally killing both her repellent husband, then herself, and leaving her own child an orphan to be raised by his grandparents Sir Mathew and Lady Margaret.

The tears were genuine when Anne spoke of the sadness of Aveline's life and death, and perhaps it was easier to believe, for others, that Anne's baby was Aveline's son for he was not much like his "aunt;" his skin was olive and he had speedwell-blue eyes, his father's eyes in truth, where her own were some strange amalgam of green and blue. Jewels, he'd called them, sea topaz, kingfisher bright.

Anne remembered too well every word they'd spoken, every moment they'd ever had together. But it was useless to dream. Dreaming would not bring Edward's father to Brugge and she had her own way to make in life without him—an aching, lonely thought.

But then Anne's courage rose a little as she dismissed the image of her lover's face. She had much, so much, to be thankful for in comparison to many others. She'd been left a small estate in Somerset, gifted to her mother, Alyce de Bohun, and that provided a small income faithfully accounted to her each quarter day. She had good, warm clothes, a house to live in—even if it was not hers—and a small number of jewels, if all else failed her: a topaz brooch, a great ruby ring (a precious keepsake given her by Edward's father), and the little pearl-and-garnet cross presented to her by the Cuttifers when she'd left their house for the Court of Edward IV and his queen, Elizabeth Wydeville.

Anne shifted uneasily in her chair, frowning as, unbidden, the images came; pictures from that time as Elizabeth Wydeville's body servant when dread and joy were her constant companions.

For it was at court she'd fallen in love with Edward the King, and it was at court she'd found out who she really was: the natural daughter of the old king, Henry VI. Thus the man she loved, adulterously, had usurped her father's throne.

That knowledge had brought fear, and sudden clarity. Yes, Anne was illegitimate, but she was the illegitimate daughter of a king. Sighing, almost groaning, Anne shook her head. It hurt, it still hurt like a deep, deep burn, the choice she'd made: self-exile to Brugge rather than remain in England. For if she'd stayed, she'd have to have chosen a side, eventually, as the old king's daughter.

A terrible choice, for how could she support her father's natural enemy, the man who'd taken his throne, driven him into hiding, even if she loved him?

But then, she'd not known she was pregnant when she'd sailed from Dover into exile. Perhaps Edward might have wanted her to stay if she could have told him, even with the risk to his throne. He'd had only daughters with Elizabeth Wydeville, the queen—but she, Anne, had a son. England desperately needed a male heir if Edward was to consolidate his reign. Perhaps he'd have forgiven Anne her ancestry for the sake of their child—this combination of York and Lancaster.

Forgive her? Better she should think of forgiving him! He was her father's usurper! And how could she allow herself to contemplate, for even one moment, allowing her own child to be engulfed by the vicious game of English politics just because she loved his father still?

Anne's eyes snapped open with the turmoil of her anguished thoughts and she sat up. England was in her past forever, and life must continue if she, little Edward, and Deborah were to find a real home for themselves, a place not dependent on the kindness of others. There was a lesson in this attack—she must plan, seriously, for their future. If she did not, others would do it for her. Perhaps after she had eaten, clarity of thought might return and the tide of emotion recede. For now, though, she was tired, very tired, and her knees ached, for the ice on the canal had been hard and jagged as thorns in places.

"Thank you, Maître." Courteously she sipped a little more of the wine he had prepared for her. "Delicious. I shall enjoy this with supper."

Gently, Anne kissed the sleeping baby in his cradle, tucking one small hand under the velvet counterpane. How much she yearned to pick him up, but his sleep was so peaceful, it would not be kind.

"Please call me when he wakes, Maître Flaireau."

"Of course, lady. This so dear baby delights us all, but truly, his heart is in his aunt's keeping." The cook bowed gallantly, understanding how much Anne loved the little boy. Fear touched her heart for a moment. Perhaps he knew, perhaps they all knew that he was truly her son.

She must be careful, and go on being careful, if they were all to survive.

Tonight was the tolling of a bell: a tocsin, a warning. From her brief time in Brugge, Anne had begun to believe that she could make a new life for herself here—and for little Edward. The Cuttifers had been very kind in their support, but she was a guest in their house; she would not, could not, allow herself to live on their goodwill forever. She had a choice. She must find a way to make her own living independently or . . . marry.

But if she was to have a husband, let him be one of her own choosing, not someone who came at the point of a sword.

Anne shivered as she stopped near the top of the stairs outside her solar; dark images from the attack forced themselves behind her eyes. Breathing faster, she let the pictures come, trying to understand. Perhaps a calculating young bravo had been watching her—the ward of a powerful, wealthy man—and decided to improve his fortune. She wouldn't be the first.

But was there another explanation?

Had someone paid to have her killed? Someone eager to remove her from the board of European politics? Someone who knew about her—her relationship with Edward, King of England—and, perhaps, also, knew about her son?

Anne's hand shook as she pushed open the door into her own private solar—yet another kindness from the Cuttifers. The pretty room was softly lit by a hanging brass candelabrum whose six fat wax candles burned clear and bright, a very great extravagance, but one she was happy to pay for from her own modest means; the smell of burning tallow made her sick.

She entered the solar with gratitude; it was peaceful and beautiful, a well of calm in a mad world. The room faced the canal at the front of the house, and the windows were so extravagantly large that they took up the entire width of the central gable. Thus her room was never dark during the day, no matter how sullen the skies might be; and sometimes, on the night of a full moon, Anne slept with her shutters drawn back and the casements flung open, a practice opposed by Deborah. It was common knowledge that the moonlight had power to strike the unwary. It was unhealthy to lie within that treacherous silver glimmer, breathing night air—in itself, profoundly harmful—for bad dreams and bad luck came from Luna's light, especially for women at the time of their monthly flow.

Anne had kissed Deborah softly on the brow when the older woman first voiced her fears—kissed her, but ignored her. The moon was her friend. It had been on a moon-flooded night that her son had been conceived and for that she would always welcome the brightest nights.

On this dark evening, Deborah had had a fire lit so the room was warm and cozy, though a wind was rising off the canal now, moaning around her casements and rattling the fastenings with spectral fingers. Despite the warmth, Anne shivered. How close had she just come to other cold hands tonight? Without Ivan she might have been a prisoner now in a very different room, among rapacious strangers. Or she might be a corpse.

Wearily, Anne slumped down onto the chair set ready for her by the fire as a quiet voice called her. "Mistress, may I come in? I have water for you."

"Yes, Jenna. You are welcome." It was not like Anne to allow others to sense when she was tired or frightened, she'd learned that in the last few years, but tonight, shock brought her defenses down.

The other girl, open faced, a silvery blonde, entered the room silently carrying a brass bowl and a ewer filled with hot water from the kitchen.

"Would you like me to help you with the gown, lady?" Anne shook her head.

"No. Deborah will be here very soon, I expect. But I do need to clean my hands, Jenna."

Anne inspected her palms, and then her nails, dispassionately. She had grazed the heels of her hands when she'd dropped down onto the icy canal and broken several nails as she'd been hauled up the brick wall on the other side. Ordinarily she was proud of her hands, and now that she did not have to work with them, as once she'd had to, they were soft and white, the calluses at the base of each finger nearly gone. The broken nails would need trimming and cleaning, though—best to soak them first.

Jenna was a sensible girl. It was one of the reasons Deborah, as Lady Margaret's recently appointed housekeeper in Brugge, had given her a post in this house, so she didn't wince or fuss when she saw the blood on Anne's hands; she poured warm water in a steady, gentle stream, not even commenting as it turned rose-red.

"I'll get some more water for you, mistress."

"Yes, do that, Jenna. There's a large cauldron on the fire in the kitchen; it should be hot by now." Deborah had entered the room unseen as Jenna opened a casement and threw the dirty water into the canal, then paused for a moment to tidy the room as the older woman bustled forward.

"Here, mistress. Let me dry your hands. I've brought some fresh woundwort salve; it will help the healing."

Without protest, Anne let Deborah lift each of her hands and gently dry them on the linen towel she'd spread across her lap.

"Where is Ivan, Deborah?"

Deborah coughed to hide the chuckle that had risen unbidden. Fear did that to her sometimes. "I left him down in the kitchen, throwing back good Gruuthuse beer and boasting. He has a slash through his sleeve on one arm, but that's all. Luck of the Devil—or protected by him." Deborah did not approve of Ivan; he distracted the women of the house too much.

The older woman's astringent tone roused Anne from exhaustion. She was grateful to Ivan and it was important to voice that. "He did his job, and he did it well. When I am changed I shall thank him." Deborah kept silent, though she was hurt by Anne's sharp tone.

Anne felt the knife of guilt, but for now, in front of Jenna, she must play the role of their master's ward.

"Jenna, will you get the water, please, while Deborah helps me off with this heavy thing?" The door of the solar opened, and then closed quietly. Jenna had left.

Anne rose out of the chair, allowing her foster mother to unlace the back of the red dress. She closed her eyes for a moment. All she could hear was the crackle of the flames and the buffeting wind outside her curtains. What she would not give to lie down on her bed and fall into a long, dark sleep.

"Mistress? The rose-pink or the blue?" How hard it was to open her eyes. "The blue kirtle, I think. And the French linen shift, if you please. I hate feeling wool next to my skin."

So tired, so tired, it was hard to talk.

"Would you still like your body washed before I dress you, lady?"

Deborah's tone was formal and correct. It made Anne grin, a blessed lightening of her spirit.

"Yes, Deborah. As you used to do when I was little," and she smiled warmly, fondly at the older woman. "It will be nice to be clean again." There was a genuine smile in return, and suddenly the women felt like friends again. Close and loving friends.